Chocolate Cream Pie Murder

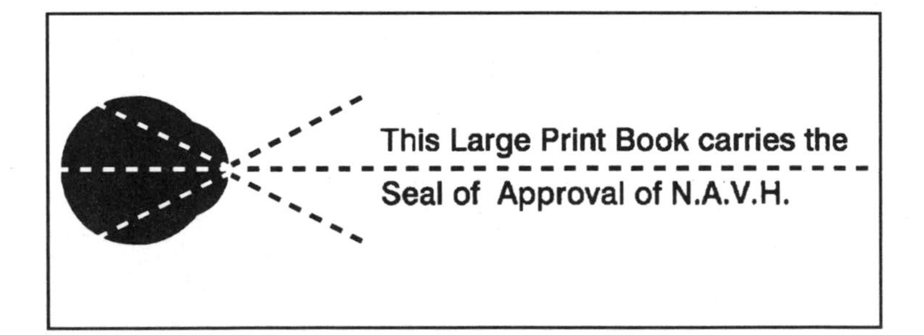
This Large Print Book carries the
Seal of Approval of N.A.V.H.

A HANNAH SWENSEN MYSTERY WITH RECIPES

CHOCOLATE CREAM PIE MURDER

JOANNE FLUKE

THORNDIKE PRESS
A part of Gale, a Cengage Company

Farmington Hills, Mich • San Francisco • New York • Waterville, Maine
Meriden, Conn • Mason, Ohio • Chicago

A Hannah Swenson Mystery with Recipes.
Thorndike Press, a part of Gale, a Cengage Company.

Thorndike Press® Large Print Mystery.
The text of this Large Print edition is unabridged.
Other aspects of the book may vary from the original edition.
Set in 16 pt. Plantin.

**LIBRARY OF CONGRESS CIP DATA ON FILE.
CATALOGUING IN PUBLICATION FOR THIS BOOK
IS AVAILABLE FROM THE LIBRARY OF CONGRESS**

ISBN-13: 978-1-4328-6204-6 (hardcover)

Published in 2019 by arrangement with Kensington Books, an imprint of Kensington Publishing Corp.

Printed in the United States of America
1 2 3 4 5 6 7 23 22 21 20 19

This book is for Karen Auerbach.
Team Swensen misses you!

ACKNOWLEDGMENTS:

Many thanks to my extended family for putting up with me during the writing of this book.
You all deserve second pieces of Chocolate Cream Pie.
A big hug to Trudi Nash for her ability to read through a recipe and immediately know exactly how it's going to taste, and marrying a man who doesn't seem to mind all the time we spend on food talk.
Thank you to my friends and neighbors: Mel & Kurt, Lyn & Bill, Gina, Dee Appleton, Jay, Richard Jordan, Laura Levine, the real Nancy and Heiti, Dan, Mark & Mandy at Faux Library, Daryl and her staff at Groves Accountancy, Gene and Ron at SDSA, and everyone at Homestreet Bank.
Hugs to my Minnesota friends: Lois & Neal, Bev & Jim, Val, Ruthann, Lowell, Dorothy & Sister Sue, and Mary & Jim.

A big hug to my brilliant editor, John Scognamiglio, who never loses patience with me. I'm still trying to figure out exactly how he does that.

Thanks to Karen Auerbach, who shepherded *Raspberry Danish Murder* and *Christmas Cake Murder* through the publicity maze.

And thanks to all the other wonderful folks at Kensington Publishing who keep Hannah sleuthing and baking yummy goodies.

Thank you to Robin, who manages to keep from tearing her hair out when I ask stupid questions about production.

Big hugs for Meg Ruley and the staff at the Jane Rotrosen Agency for their constant support and their sage advice. And thanks for being there every time I call.

Thanks to Hiro Kimura for his scrumptious cover art. It's just not fair that your Chocolate Cream Pie is prettier than mine!

Thank you to Lou Malcangi at Kensington for designing all of Hannah's gorgeous book covers. They're always just wonderful.

Thanks to John at ***Placed4Success*** for Hannah's movie and TV placements, his presence on Hannah's social media platform, the countless hours he spends

helping me, and for believing that it's what
a son should do.
***(If you meet John, please don't
tell him that not all sons work as hard
as he does.)***
Thanks to Rudy for managing my website
at **wwwJoanneFluke.com** and for giving
support to Hannah's social media.
And thanks to Annie for helping with social
media and everything else.
Big thanks to Kathy Allen for the final
testing of Hannah's recipes and coming up
with her own recipes like the Frozen
Sugared Grapes!
And thanks to Kathy's friends and family
for taste testing.
A big hug to JQ for helping Hannah and
me for so many years.
Hugs to Beth for her gorgeous embroidery.
Thank you to food stylist, friend, and
media guide Lois Brown for her expertise
with the launch parties at Poisoned Pen
and the TV baking segments at KPNX
in Phoenix.
Hugs to the Double D's and everyone else
on Team Swensen.
Thank you to Dr. Rahhal, Dr. and Cathy
Line, Dr. Levy, Dr. Koslowski, and Drs.
Ashley and Lee for answering my
book-related medical and dental questions.

Big hugs to all the Hannah fans who share their family recipes, post on my Facebook page, **Joanne Fluke Author,** and read the Hannah books.

You've been asking for this book and here it is!

Chapter One

It was a cold Sunday morning in February when Hannah Swensen left the warmth of her condo and drove to Lake Eden, Minnesota. A frown crossed her face as she traveled down Main Street and passed The Cookie Jar, her bakery and coffee shop. It had snowed during the night, and they would have to shovel the sidewalk before they could open for business in the morning.

Hannah gunned the engine a bit as she began to drive up the steep hill that led to Holy Cross Redeemer Lutheran Church. The church sat at the very top and it overlooked the town below. Hannah pulled into the parking lot and came very close to groaning as she realized that her entire family was standing at the bottom of the church steps, waiting for her to arrive. Perhaps their intent was to allay her anxiety about what she planned to do, but it didn't work and

Hannah was sorely tempted to turn around and put things off for another week. Of course she didn't do that. Hannah was not a quitter. Somehow she had to gather her resolve and carry on with as much grace and dignity as she could muster.

The first person to arrive at her distinctive cookie truck was Hannah's youngest sister, Michelle. Hannah resisted the urge to tell Michelle that she ought to be wearing boots and plastered a welcoming smile on her face. "Michelle," she said, by way of a greeting. "Get in the backseat. It's cold out there."

"I'm okay. I just wanted to be the first to talk to you, Hannah. Are you completely sure that you want to do this?"

Hannah shook her head. "Of course I don't *want* to, but I don't really have a choice. It's only right, Michelle."

"But you *don't* have to do it, not really," Michelle argued, sliding onto the backseat and shutting the door behind her. "Word gets around and everyone's probably heard what really happened by now."

"That's doubtful, Michelle. Nobody in our family has said anything to contradict our cover story for Ross's absence. And I know that Norman and Mike haven't mentioned it to anyone. You haven't heard any gossip about it, have you?"

"No," Michelle admitted.

"And you know the whole town would be buzzing about it if anyone knew."

"Well . . . yes, but we can figure out another way of telling them. You don't have to put yourself through the pain of getting up in front of the whole congregation and talking about it."

"Yes, I do. They deserve an explanation. And they also deserve an apology from me for lying to them."

The front door opened and Hannah's mother, Delores, picked up the heavy cookie platter that was nestled on the passenger seat and got in. "I heard what you just told Michelle and you're wrong, Hannah. No one here expects you to apologize. What happened is no fault of yours."

The other back door of Hannah's cookie truck opened and Hannah's middle sister, Andrea Swensen Todd, got in. "And nobody here wants to see you upset. If you think we owe anyone an apology, let *me* do it. I can get up there and tell them what happened."

"Thanks, but no. It's nice of you to offer, Andrea, but this is something I have to do myself."

"I understand, dear," Delores said, "but I wish you'd told me your plans earlier. We could have gone shopping for something more appropriate for you to wear."

Hannah glanced down at her blue pantsuit. "A lot of women wear pantsuits to church, especially in the winter. What's wrong with mine?"

"Nothing's wrong . . . exactly," Delores explained. "It's just that the color washes you out. At least you're here early and we have time to fix your makeup. A darker color lipstick would do wonders, and you need some blusher on your cheeks."

Andrea opened her purse and glanced inside. "Mascara and eye shadow couldn't hurt. I've got something that would bring out the color of Hannah's eyes."

"And I can do something with her hair," Michelle offered.

"Hold it right there!" Hannah told them. "My appearance doesn't matter that much. What really matters is what I'm going to say. I've worn this same outfit to church at least a dozen times and you've never criticized my appearance before."

"Today is different," Delores pointed out. "Grandma Knudson told me that you asked to stand in the front of the church right after Reverend Bob makes his announcements. Everybody's going to see . . ." Delores stopped speaking and a panicked expression crossed her face. "You're not planning to wear your winter boots, are you?"

Hannah had the urge to laugh. She had never, in her whole life, walked down the aisle of their church wearing winter boots. She came very close to saying that, but she realized that the root of her mother's concern was anxiety about how the congregation would receive what Hannah had to tell them.

"Relax, Mother," Hannah told her. "I brought dress shoes with me and I'll change in the cloakroom as soon as we get inside."

Delores nodded, but she still looked worried. "Your dress shoes aren't brown, are they?"

"No, Mother. I know how you feel about wearing brown shoes with blue. These are the black shoes we bought at the Tri-County Mall last year."

"Oh, good!" Delores drew a relieved breath and glanced at the jeweled watch her husband, Doc Knight, had given her. "Then let's go, girls. It'll take us a while to get Hannah ready."

Hannah wisely kept her silence as she walked to the church with her family. Once the cookies she'd brought for the social hour after the church service had been delivered to the kitchen next to the basement meeting room, Hannah suffered her family's attempt to make her into what Delores deemed *church appropriate.*

"It's time," Delores declared, glancing at her watch again. "Follow me, girls."

As they walked down the center aisle single file, Hannah spotted her former boyfriend, Norman Rhodes. Norman was sitting on one side of his mother, and Carrie's second husband, Earl Flensburg, was sitting on her other side. Norman smiled at Hannah as she passed by and he held his thumb and finger together in an *okay* sign.

Hannah swallowed the lump that was beginning to form in her throat and reminded herself that she knew almost everyone here. The Holy Redeemer congregation consisted of friends, neighbors, and customers who came into The Cookie Jar. They would appreciate her apology and no one would be angry with her . . . she hoped.

She was beginning to feel slightly more confident when she noticed the other local man she'd dated, Mike Kingston. He was sitting with Michelle's boyfriend, Lonnie Murphy, and both of them smiled and gave her friendly nods. Mike was the head detective at the Winnetka County Sheriff's Department and he was training Lonnie to be his partner. Both men usually worked on

Sundays, but they must have traded days with a pair of other deputies so that they could come to hear Hannah's apology.

Doc Knight saw them coming up the aisle and he stepped out of the pew so that they could file in. Hannah went first so that she would be on the end and it would be easier for her to get out and walk up the side aisle to the front of the church when it was time.

"Are you all right?" Michelle asked her as they sat down.

It took Hannah a moment to find her voice. "Yes, I'm all right."

"But you're so pale that the blusher on your cheeks is standing out in circles." Michelle reached for the hymnal in the rack and flipped to the page that was listed in the church bulletin.

"Is something wrong?" Andrea asked in a whisper.

"Everything's fine," Hannah told her, pretending to be engrossed in reading the verse of the familiar hymn they were preparing to sing.

The organist, who had been playing softly while people filed into the church, increased the volume and segued into the verse of the hymn. This precluded any further conversation, and Hannah was grateful.

If there had been a ten-question quiz

about the sermon that Reverend Bob delivered, Hannah would have flunked it. She was too busy worrying about what she wanted to say to pay attention. There were times during the sermon that Hanah wished Reverend Bob would hurry so that she could get up, apologize, and go back home. At other times, she found herself wishing that the sermon would go on forever and she'd never have to walk to the front of the church and speak.

When Reverend Bob finished, stepped down from the pulpit, and went into the room at the side of the nave to hang up his vestments, the butterflies of anxiety in Hannah's stomach awoke and began to churn in a rising cloud that made her feel weak-kneed and slightly dizzy. She concentrated on breathing evenly until Reverend Bob reappeared in the black suit he wore once the sermon was over.

The announcements Reverend Bob made were short and sweet. There was a request for donations of canned food from the Bible Church for their homeless shelter in the church basement, an announcement of the nuptials scheduled on Valentine's Day, a reminder that the lost and found box in the church office was overflowing with forgotten mittens, gloves, and caps, a notice of a time change in Grandma Knudson's Bible study group, and two notifications of baptisms to be held after church services in the coming month.

"And now we have a special request from Hannah Swensen," Reverend Bob told them. "She'd like to say a few words to you before the social hour."

Hannah stood up and slid out of the pew. She walked up the aisle at the side of the church on legs that shook slightly to join Reverend Bob. She cleared her throat and then she began to speak.

"Almost everyone in the congregation today attended my wedding to Ross Barton in November. Most of you were also at the Lake Eden Inn for the reception."

There were nods from almost everyone in attendance and Hannah went on. "I asked to speak to you today because I need to apologize. I think you all know that Ross is gone, and my family and I told you that he was on location for a new special that he was doing for KCOW Television. That is *not* true. I'm sorry to say that we lied to you and we owe you an apology for that."

"If Ross isn't out on location for a special, where *is* he?" Howie Levine asked.

Hannah wasn't surprised by the question. Howie was a lawyer and he always asked probing questions. "Ross is in Wisconsin."

"Is he filming something there?" Hal McDermott, co-owner of Hal and Rose's Café, asked.

"No. I'll tell you why he's there, but first let me tell you what happened on the day Ross left Lake Eden."

Haltingly at first, and then with more assurance, Hannah described what had happened on the day Ross left. The words were painful at first, but it became easier until all the facts had been given.

"Did Ross leave you a note?" Irma York, the wife of Lake Eden's barber, asked.

"No, there was nothing. His car was still there, his billfold was on top of the dresser, where he always left it when he came home from work, and he'd even left his driver's license and credit cards. It was almost as if he'd packed up his clothes and . . . and vanished."

"You must have been very worried," Reverend Bob said sympathetically.

"Not at first. I was upset that he hadn't called me to say he was leaving, but I thought that he had been rushed for time and he'd call me that night. Then, when I didn't hear from him that night or the next day, I got worried."

"Of course you did!" Grandma Knudson,

Reverend Bob's grandmother and the unofficial matriarch of the church, said with a nod.

"After three days," Hannah continued, "I was afraid that something was very wrong and I asked Mike and Norman to help me look for Ross."

Mike stood up to address the congregation. "It took us weeks of searching, but two of my detectives finally found Ross. Right after I verified his identity, Norman and I went to Hannah's condo to tell her." He turned around to face Hannah. "Go on, Hannah."

"Yes," Hannah said, gathering herself for the most difficult part of her apology. "When I came home that night, Mike and Norman were waiting for me. Both of them looked very serious and I knew right away that something was wrong. That's when Mike said that they'd found Ross, and . . ." Hannah stopped speaking and drew a deep, steadying breath. "Mike told me that Ross had gone back to his wife."

"His *wife*?" Grandma Knudson looked completely shocked. "But *you're* his wife, Hannah! We were all right here when *you* married Ross!"

There was a chorus of startled exclamations from the congregation. Hannah waited until everyone was quiet again and then she continued. "Ross was already married when he married me. And that means my marriage to him wasn't legal."

"You poor dear!" Grandma Knudson got up from her place of honor in the first pew and rushed up to put her arm around Hannah. Then she motioned to her grandson. "Give me your handkerchief, Bob."

Once the handkerchief was handed over, Grandma Knudson passed it to Hannah. "What are you going to do about this, Hannah?"

"I . . . I don't know," Hannah admitted truthfully. "I just wanted to tell all of you about this today because my family and I lied to you and we needed to set the record straight."

"Hannah could sue Ross for bigamy," Howie pointed out. "And since bigamy is a crime, Ross could be prosecuted. Do you want to press charges, Hannah?"

"I'm not sure. All I really know is that I never want to see him again." There was a murmuring of sympathy from the congregation as Hannah dabbed at her eyes with the borrowed handkerchief. "I know all of you thought I was married. I thought I was married, too, but . . . but I wasn't. And since you gave me wedding presents under false pretenses, I'd like to return them to you."

"Ridiculous!" Grandma Knudson snorted, patting Hannah's shoulder. And then she turned to face the worshippers. "You don't want your wedding gifts back, do you?"

"I don't!" Becky Summers was the first to respond. "Keep the silver platter, Hannah. Consider it an early birthday present."

"The same for me!" Norman's mother chimed in. "You keep the crystal pitcher, Hannah."

Several other members of the congregation spoke up, all of them expressing the same wishes, and then Grandma Knudson held up her hand for silence. "If anyone here wants a wedding gift back, contact me and I'll make sure you get it. And in the meantime, I think we've kept Hannah up here long enough." She turned to Hannah. "I know you brought something for our social hour, Hannah. I saw Michelle run down the stairs with a big platter. What wonderful baked goods did you bring today?"

Hannah felt a great weight slip off her shoulders. It was over. She'd come and accomplished what she'd set out to do. Now she could relax and spend a little time with the people she knew and loved.

"I brought Valentine Whippersnapper Cookies," she told them. "They're a new cookie recipe from my sister Andrea. Since we're about ready to start baking for Valentine's Day at The Cookie Jar, Andrea and I really want your opinion. Please try a cookie and tell us what you think of them."

Grandma Knudson turned to the congregation. "I'll lead you downstairs so you can start in on those cookies. And then I'm coming back up here for a private word with Hannah." She took Hannah's arm, led her to the front pew, and motioned to her to sit down. "I'll be right back," she said. "Just sit here and relax for a few moments."

Hannah watched as the church emptied out with Grandma Knudson leading the way. Then she closed her eyes for a moment and relished the fact that the tension was leaving her body. She felt good, better than she had for a long time. Perhaps Reverend Bob was right and confession was good for the soul.

Hannah turned around when she heard the sound of footsteps. Grandma Knudson was coming back. "Thank you," she said, as Grandma Knudson sat down next to her.

"You're welcome. I heard some very interesting things down there, Hannah. I'm really glad I got those fancy new hearing aids."

"I didn't know you had hearing aids!"

"Neither does anyone else except Bob, and I swore him to secrecy. I've changed my opinion about a lot of people in this town. Why, the things I've heard could fill a gossip column!"

"But you wouldn't . . ."

"Of course not!" Grandma Knudson said emphatically. "But I may not tell anyone about my hearing aids for a while. It's a lot of fun for me."

Hannah gave a little laugh. It felt wonderful to laugh and she was grateful to Grandma Knudson for giving her the opportunity.

"Seriously, Hannah," Grandma Knudson began, "you haven't heard from Ross since Mike and his boys located him, have you?"

Hannah shook her head. "No, not a word."

"All right then. If Ross calls you, tell him that if he knows what's good for him, he'd better never show his face in Lake Eden again. I heard Earl say he wanted to run Ross down with the county snowplow, and Bud Hauge asked Mike and Lonnie to give him five minutes alone with Ross if they picked him up. And Hal McDermott claimed he was going to leave out Rose's heaviest frying pan so he could bash in Ross's head."

Hannah was shocked. "But do you think

they'd actually do it?"

Grandma Knudson shrugged. "If I were Ross, I wouldn't chance it. And I can tell you one thing for sure. If Ross comes back and winds up dead, you're going to have a whole town full of suspects!"

Valentine Whippersnapper Cookies

DO NOT preheat your oven yet. This dough needs to chill before baking.

1 cup pecans ***(buy the bits and pieces of pecan — they're cheaper than pecan halves)***
1/2 cup cherry jam ***(I used Smucker's)***
1 box ***(approximately 18 ounces)*** Cherry Chip cake mix, the kind that makes a 9-inch by 13-inch cake ***(I used Betty Crocker)***
1 large egg, beaten ***(just whip it up in a glass with a fork)***
1/4 cup cherry liqueur ***(I used cherry herring — substitute cherry juice if you'd rather***)
1 teaspoon vanilla extract
1/2 teaspoon cherry extract ***(substitute vanilla extract if you don't have cherry)***
2 cups Original Cool Whip, thawed ***(measure this — a tub of Cool Whip contains a little over 3 cups and that's too much!)***

1/2 cup powdered ***(confectioners')*** sugar ***(you don't have to sift it unless it's old and has big lumps)***

Small jar of maraschino cherries, drained and cut in half vertically ***(optional for decorating your cookies)***

Hannah's 1st Note: If you live in an area where Betty Crocker Cherry Chip cake mix is difficult to find, you can use white cake mix with a half-cup of white chocolate or vanilla chips chopped up in it. (Just put the chips in the food processor with a steel blade and process them until they're in small pieces.)

Use a food processor with the steel blade to chop the pecans into small pieces. ***(If you used white cake mix, you can chop up the white chocolate chips with the pecans.)***

Transfer the contents of the food processor to a small bowl.

Put the cherry jam in the food processor. ***(You don't need to wash it out — you'll be adding the cherry jam to the pecans anyway.)***

Process with the steel blade until the jam is smooth.

Add the jam to the pecans in the smaller

bowl on the counter.

Pour HALF of the dry cake mix into a large mixing bowl.

Add your beaten egg to the large mixing bowl and stir it in.

Add the contents of the small bowl to your large mixing bowl and mix them in with a rubber spatula.

Rinse out the smaller bowl, dry it with a paper towel, and pour in the cherry liqueur.

Add the vanilla extract and the cherry extract.

Stir to combine contents of the smaller bowl thoroughly.

Measure the Cool Whip and add it to the smaller bowl.

Stir gently with a rubber spatula until everything in the smaller bowl is combined. Be very careful not to stir too vigorously. You don't want to stir all the air out of the Cool Whip.

Add the contents of the small bowl to the large mixing bowl with the cake mix.

STIR VERY CAREFULLY with the rubber spatula. Stir ONLY until everything is combined. Be very careful not to over-stir.

Sprinkle in the rest of the cake mix and gently fold everything together with the rubber spatula. Again, keep as much air in the batter as possible. Air is what will make your cookies soft and give them a melt-in-your-mouth quality.

Cover the bowl with plastic wrap and chill the cookie dough for at least 1 hour in the refrigerator. It's a little too sticky to form into balls without chilling it first.

When your cookie dough has chilled and you're ready to bake, preheat your oven to 350 degrees F. and make sure the rack is in the middle position. DO NOT take your chilled cookie dough out of the refrigerator until after your oven has reached the proper temperature.

While your oven is preheating, prepare your cookie sheets by spraying them with Pam or another nonstick baking spray, or lining them with parchment paper.

Place the powdered sugar in a small, shallow bowl. You will be dropping cookie dough into this bowl to form dough balls and coating the balls with the powdered sugar.

When your oven is ready, take your dough out of the refrigerator. Using a teaspoon from your silverware drawer, drop the dough by rounded teaspoonful into the bowl with the powdered sugar. Roll the dough around with your fingers to form powdered sugar-coated cookie dough balls.

Hannah's 2nd Note: Work with only one cookie dough ball at a time. If you drop more than one in the bowl of powdered sugar, they'll stick together. Also, make only as many cookie dough balls as you can bake at one time. Cover the remaining dough and return it to the refrigerator until you're ready to bake more.

Place the coated cookie dough balls on your prepared cookie sheets, no more than 12 cookies to a standard-size sheet.

Hannah's 3rd Note: If you coat your fingers with powdered sugar first and then try to form the cookie dough into balls, it's a lot easier to accomplish.

If you decide you want to decorate your cookies, press half of a maraschino cherry, rounded side up, on top of each cookie before you bake them. Alternatively, you can decorate them with candy hearts or any other Valentine candy. For Valentine's Day, Andrea uses the little hearts with sayings printed on them or the red gelatin hearts with sugar on the top.

Bake your Valentine Whippersnapper Cookies at 350 degrees F. for 10 minutes. Let them cool on the cookie sheet for 2 minutes and then move them to a wire rack to cool completely. ***(This is a lot easier if you line your cookie sheets with parchment paper — then you don't need to lift the cookies one by one. All you have to do is grab one end of the parchment paper and pull it, cookies and all, onto the wire rack.)***

Once the cookies are completely cool, store them between sheets of waxed paper in a cool, dry place. ***(Your refrigerator is***

cool, but it's definitely not dry!)

Yield: 3 to 4 dozen soft, delicious cookies that taste a bit like macaroons but are much easier to eat.

Chapter Two

More parishioners stayed for the social hour than anyone expected. Most of them wanted to reassure Hannah that they weren't angry she'd misled them about Ross's absence. There were also plenty of favorable compliments about the Valentine Whippersnapper Cookies that Hannah had brought. Andrea, who was sitting next to Hannah at one of the long tables, looked delighted to take credit for creating the recipe.

Hannah smiled as Del Woodley, the head of DelRay Manufacturing, came up to greet her. "Hi, Del. How's everything with you?"

"Good." Del gave a quick nod. "Benton and I listened to what you had to say, Hannah, and I just want to tell you that if Ross ever shows his lying face in Lake Eden again, Benton and I want you to call us. We'll be glad to take care of that lowlife for you!"

There was a determined expression on

Del's face, and Hannah gave a little shiver. It was clear that he was serious. Del had a reputation for being tough in his business dealings, and Hannah had no doubt that he could also be tough when it came to something personal.

"Thank you, Del," she said, trying to think of some way to accept his sentiment without actually accepting what she thought he was proposing. "It makes me feel better just to know that I can count on you and Benton."

"Don't forget that we'll be there if you need us."

"I won't forget," Hannah promised.

The next people to arrive at Hannah's table were Lisa and Herb Beeseman. Lisa was Hannah's business partner at The Cookie Jar, and Herb was Lake Eden's marshal in charge of local security and parking enforcement.

"Lisa!" Hannah was surprised to see her. "I thought this was your week at St. Jude's."

"It is," Herb explained, "but when Lisa found out that you planned to address the congregation here, we decided to go Lutheran two weeks in a row and Catholic for the next two weeks."

Hannah smiled at her partner. Since Lisa's family was Catholic and Herb's family was Lutheran, Lisa and Herb had worked out a plan even before they were married. The whole family would spend one Sunday at Lisa's church, St. Jude, and the next week at Herb's church. Since Herb's mother, Marge, had married Lisa's father, Jack, this worked out well for both families.

Herb cleared his throat and leaned close to give Hannah a piece of paper. "Here's my cell number, Hannah. Call me if Ross ever bothers you again and I'll take care of him for you."

"And I'll help!" Lisa said with a frown. "Herb and I talked about it last night and I'm already on the lookout for him at The Cookie Jar."

"Thank you," Hannah said, tucking the number in her purse, "but I really doubt he'll come back to Lake Eden again. He must know that there's nothing for him here."

Lisa did not look convinced. "Maybe, but it never hurts to be prepared. Herb and I worked out a plan. If he sees Ross, he's going to stop him for some trumped-up traffic violation and give you time to make yourself scarce."

Once Lisa and Herb had left, Lisa's Aunt Nancy bustled up to the table. She was wearing the lovely engagement ring that Heiti had given her at Christmas. "Hello,

Hannah," she said. "I thought your speech went very well. I watched everyone's reaction, and there isn't a single person here who's not completely on your side. Ross is a rat and he doesn't deserve a wonderful person like you."

"Thank you." Hannah could tell that Aunt Nancy had rehearsed what she planned to say because she'd blurted it out rapid-fire. "Lisa told me that you're working on a new cookie recipe for me."

"That's right. I'm going to bake them again tonight and I'll bring some in tomorrow morning. They'll be perfect for Valentine's Day."

"Hannah, I need a private moment with you please."

Hannah turned to the man who had come up behind Aunt Nancy. There was no mistaking the authoritarian voice or the imposing figure of Mayor Bascomb.

"Yes, Mayor Bascomb?" she greeted him once Aunt Nancy had hurried off.

"You have no need to worry about Ross coming back to Lake Eden. He won't get more than a block inside the city limits before he's ticketed and arrested."

"Ticketed for what?" Hannah asked him.

"We'll start with a parking ticket and go on to failure to stop at a stop sign. And if he goes past Jordan High, we'll nail him for speeding through a school zone." Mayor Bascomb looked proud of himself for citing all these violations. "We don't want liars like Ross Barton in our midst. I've ordered Marshal Beeseman to pick him up if he comes back. That'll give you plenty of time to take cover."

Take cover? Hannah almost asked, but she quickly thought better of the idea. It was quite obvious that Mayor Bascomb had been watching late-night war movies again.

"Thank you, Mayor Bascomb," Hannah said instead. "I appreciate your efforts on my behalf."

The mayor looked pleased as he walked away, and Andrea nudged Hannah. "I heard that," she said in a barely audible voice. "I'm proud of you, Hannah. You handled him perfectly. And just for your information, Bill planned a little surprise for Ross, too."

Good heavens! Does everyone in town think I need protection? Hannah thought, but instead of asking that question, she substituted another. "What surprise did Bill plan?"

"He went out to the courthouse and got a warrant for Ross's arrest for bigamy."

"Good heavens!" Hannah exclaimed,

thoroughly shocked.

"That's right. Bill and Mike talked to Howie Levine and he drew up the paperwork for them."

"But . . . I wasn't legally married to Ross."

"I know, but all they need is intent. Bill got a copy of the marriage certificate that you and Ross signed from the county records office. It's true that you're not legally married, but the intent to defraud was there. And that's why the judge signed off on the warrant."

"Did you know about this?" Hannah asked Michelle, who was sitting on the other side of her.

"No. I figured they'd do something like that, but I didn't know it had actually happened. Ross did do something illegal, you know."

"I know."

"And you were hurt by it!" Andrea pointed out. "It can't have been easy to give that speech in front of the congregation. And you wouldn't have had to do that if Ross hadn't been such a louse."

Hannah couldn't argue with that. Ross *had* been a louse. He'd put her through the charade of a wedding when he was married to someone else.

Grandma Knudson came up to the table

and put her arms around Hannah. "We love you, Hannah. Everyone here loves you and we want the best for you. You believe that, don't you?"

It took Hannah a moment to find her voice past the lump in her throat. "Yes, I do believe that."

Grandma Knudson gave her another little hug. "You've been through a lot, Hannah, and we all want to help you through this."

"Please tell everyone that I appreciate that," Hannah managed to say. And then her eyes filled with tears and she knew she had to leave. "I have to go, Grandma Knudson."

"I understand. I'll tell everyone that you're grateful for their support." Grandma Knudson waited for Hannah to push back her chair and get to her feet. "I'll walk you to the stairs, Hannah."

Hannah gave everyone the best smile she could muster, and walked to the door with Grandma Knudson. When Grandma Knudson pulled open the door to the stairs, Hannah gave her a tremulous smile and headed up the steps to the cloakroom. Once there, blinking back tears, she put on her parka and boots. Then she opened the outside door to the church and hurried across the parking lot to her cookie truck.

The snow was beginning to fall as she drove back to her condo, but Hannah barely noticed. And once she got home, she scooped up Moishe, no easy task with her twenty-three-pound feline, and carried him to the bedroom. She placed Moishe on a pillow, waited until he had made a nest for himself, and then she changed into sweatpants and a warm turtleneck sweater.

"It's naptime, Moishe," she said, stretching out on the bed to pet him.

Her eyes filled with tears and she blinked them away. It was nice to know that everyone in Lake Eden wanted the best for her and wished her well, but that didn't help one iota when it came to fixing her shattered dreams or mending her broken heart.

Moishe seemed to know that something was wrong and he reached out with his paw, claws retracted, and patted her cheek. Then he snuggled closer and Hannah, comforted at last, fell asleep.

Snow came down in big, icy flakes that fell faster and faster to cover the drifts that already existed in an irregular, lumpy blanket of white. Children who were out playing in Lake Eden backyards, released for good behavior in Sunday school and church, began to form snowballs to throw at their friends.

The weathermen on local radio and television had not predicted this sudden winter storm. It had blown in seemingly out of nowhere. In the space of a few short minutes, the wind had reached gale force and mothers, glancing out kitchen windows as they made preparations to start the family supper, realized that some of their young offspring were holding on to the arms of their older siblings and trying to trudge through the snow to the back door.

Parents rushed outside to herd their children into warm houses and to dry wet, snow-covered clothing. Soup was heated, and soon the children, dressed in warm bathrobes and slippers, were sipping hot soup from mugs at kitchen tables.

Even though it was only mid-afternoon, the sky began to darken as the snowfall intensified. The readings on outdoor thermometers dropped lower, and levers on thermostats all over town were raised to higher temperatures. Windows rattled like a cadence played on snare drums, and television sets and radios were tuned to weather reports.

The hillocks in backyards turned into snowbanks that shot up faster than a preteen with a growth spurt while local weathermen compared this winter storm to the blizzard of ought-nine. Hearing that news, farm wives donned parkas and went out to make sure the ropes from the house to the barn were intact while their husbands and hired hands rounded up livestock and led them into the barn. And while all this was happening, Hannah was sleeping, exhausted and depressed from her morning ordeal.

Once Hannah woke up, after a two-hour nap, she barely recognized the landscape outside her bedroom window. Everything, as far as she could see, was covered with an unending sheet of snow. The familiar scene she saw every day was completely transformed into a pillow of white. She could no longer see where the planter between the buildings began and ended. And to her surprise, she could barely see the building only a bit over several dozen feet away from hers. Her view was obscured by blowing snow, and the icy flakes were still falling, swirling in dizzying patterns outside the double-paned glass.

"It's snowing, Moishe," Hannah said to the cat who was sleeping next to her. "It's a winter storm and it looks like a bad one."

Moishe yawned widely and gave a little quiver as he roused himself. Then he got to his feet, reluctantly she thought, and yawned again.

Hannah glanced at the clock on her bed table, blinked several times, and then read the time again. She had to wake up and get ready to meet her whole family for dinner at the Lake Eden Inn. When Delores and Doc had married, they'd decided to make Sunday family night. Thankfully, as far as everyone was concerned, Delores was no longer cooking their family dinners. Hannah's mother only knew how to make three entrées and, for years, Hannah and her sisters had suffered through Hawaiian Pot Roast, EZ Lasagna, or reheated baked chicken purchased from the Lake Eden Red Owl Grocery store.

"Come on, Moishe." Hannah sat up on the edge of the bed and grabbed her warm, fleece-lined slippers. "We'd better check the weather report."

Hannah got to her feet and walked down the carpeted hallway to the living room with Moishe following behind her. The interior of the condo was chilly, and she turned up the thermostat a couple of degrees and switched on the gas log fireplace before she sat down in her favorite spot on one of the reclining couches that her family had given her for a wedding present. The television control was on the coffee table in front of her, and Hannah grabbed it to switch on the giant flat-screen television.

Even though it was time for the Sunday afternoon movie, Rayne Phillips, the KCOW Television weatherman, was on the screen. The words SEVERE STORM WARNING flashed across the bottom of the screen, and the map of Minnesota displayed on the screen was covered with bands of yellow, orange, and red. The bright red color was centered over the Lake Eden area, and Hannah turned up the volume so that she could hear what Rayne had to say.

". . . inches before morning." Hannah caught the tail end of Rayne's sentence. "You'd better hope your pantries are full, folks, because there's no relief in sight until mid-afternoon on Wednesday. At that point, we may have as much as three feet of snow on the ground."

Hannah shivered even though the living room was warming up nicely. Three feet of snow was a lot, especially if the winds continued to blow and even larger snowdrifts were formed. If Rayne's prediction was accurate and the storm continued until Wednesday, she could forget about going in to work in the morning. It would be futile to bake when she'd have no customers to eat her cookies.

"And now we have Chuck Wilson and Dee Dee Hughes standing by in the newsroom with winter weather tips, some travel advisories from the Minnesota Highway Patrol, and a list of school closures for Monday morning."

Hannah watched as Chuck Wilson, the chisel-faced anchor, began to talk about the storm. One glance at the weather map behind him and Hannah could see that the storm was already rolling in with the speed of a freight train.

"Currently, the winds are from the north with a velocity of thirty miles an hour and occasional gusts up to sixty miles an hour. Wind speeds are expected to increase to gale force over the course of the night, and the Minnesota Highway Patrol is advising drivers to seek shelter immediately." Chuck stepped a bit closer to the camera and flashed his perfect smile. "I can tell you folks out there that everyone here at KCOW Television plans on hunkering down right here for the night so that we can bring you the latest news."

Dee Dee Hughes, the anorexic blond anchor, walked onscreen to take her place behind the news desk next to Chuck. Both of them had a sheaf of papers that Hannah knew, for a fact, they'd never read and wouldn't use during the newscast. Betty Jackson, who had moved from a temporary position to a permanent job at the television station, had told Hannah that the newsroom gave them the same sheaf of papers every day. There was nothing written on the papers and they were simply a prop. Betty also said that both Dee Dee and Chuck used the TelePrompTer during their newscast, and that neither of them had ever noticed that the papers were blank.

As Dee Dee began to read the news alert on the TelePrompTer, Hannah reached for the remote control. She turned up the volume on the television to override the noise outside her living room windows and closed her eyes again. She began to doze off, but caught the words "worst storm of the century," followed a few seconds later by a long list of school closures. Jordan High in Lake Eden was among them, and that meant Michelle wouldn't have to teach English and drama at their local high school in the morning.

Hannah didn't bother to turn up the volume again, even though the drum roll of icy snow pelting against her windows was increasing in both speed and volume. A list of winter storm precautions appeared in a scrawl at the bottom of the screen, and the words MOTORISTS ARE ADVISED TO RETURN TO A PLACE OF SAFETY appeared in bold black type. DRIVE ONLY IN CASE OF EMERGENCY scrolled across the screen, followed by several other common cautions for driving on local roads and highways in hazardous conditions.

The camera switched to Chuck and he quickly put down the glass he was holding. Idly, Hannah wondered if it really was the ginger ale that it appeared to be. Then she reached for the phone, picked it up, and punched in her mother's number.

Delores answered on the first ring. "Hannah! Where are you?"

"I'm here at home," Hannah answered, wondering why her mother sounded panic-stricken. "Are you and Doc all right, Mother?"

"We're fine, dear. We were worried about you. I tried to reach you three times on your cell phone and it kept saying that your phone was out of service."

Hannah gave a little groan. "Sorry, Mother. That's my fault. I forgot to recharge it when I got home from church."

"Well, go plug it in right now while you still have electricity. I'll wait."

Hannah grabbed her cell phone, which

was on the table by her house phone, and plugged it into the charger cable. "Okay, Mother. It's charging right now."

"Good. They're saying this storm is going to turn into a blizzard, Hannah."

"I know. I was watching KCOW and that's why I called you. Have you heard from Michelle and Lonnie?"

"Yes, dear. They're here right now. I told them to stay here until the storm's over and not try to drive out to your condo. Doc just got home from the hospital and he says the roads are close to impassable already."

"That's the reason I called. Did Michelle and Lonnie agree to stay with you and not try to drive out here?"

"Of course they agreed, dear. Both Doc and I were very firm with them. We're all going down to the Red Velvet Lounge for dinner, and then we'll come back up here and enjoy the garden." There was a pause and Hannah heard her mother sigh. "I wish you could join us, but I don't want you to drive in weather like this, Hannah."

"I wouldn't dream of it, Mother. I'm fine here."

"But aren't you lonely?"

Hannah glanced down at the cat who'd just nestled down in her lap. "I'm not lonely with Moishe here. He's sitting in my lap and purring right now."

"Oh, good. I'll let you go then, dear. Will you promise to call me if there's any problem?"

Hannah couldn't imagine any problem that would necessitate a call to her mother, but she knew better than to argue. "Of course I will, Mother."

"And call if you're lonely. It doesn't matter what time it is. I'll be here for you, Hannah."

To Hannah's surprise, tears came to her eyes. Her mother was being uncharacteristically empathetic. "Thank you, Mother."

Once they'd said their goodbyes and Hannah had replaced her phone in the cradle, she reached for a tissue and wiped her eyes. But the moment after she'd dried her eyes, she felt them well up with tears again. She hadn't felt at all lonely until her mother had mentioned it. And now, even holding her sleeping cat, she began to wish that she was with her mother and Doc and Michelle and Lonnie, enjoying good conversation and good food at the Red Velvet Lounge in their condo building.

Hannah imagined the evening they'd have together. After dinner, they'd go back up to Delores and Doc's penthouse and sit in the climate-controlled garden under the dome that would protect them from the elements. Hannah's mother would open a bottle of Perrier Jouet, her favorite champagne, and they'd watch the snow swirl outside. Now that Hannah thought about it, she missed her family dreadfully.

"Nonsense!" Hannah said aloud, startling the cat in her lap. She gave him a scratch under his chin and a rub behind his ears, and soon Moishe was asleep again. The attention had soothed Moishe, comforted him and assured him that everything was okay. And knowing that made Hannah wish she had someone beside her to comfort her.

There was only one cure for feeling lonely and abandoned, and Hannah knew exactly what it was. She would bake. She always felt better when she baked. She'd try out the new cake recipe that Lisa's Aunt Nancy had given her. If it worked well for her, it would be a great addition to their Valentine catering menu.

The recipe was in the bottom of her purse, neatly folded with Hannah's inscription "TO TRY." She read through the ingredients and began to smile. She had everything she needed to bake Aunt Nancy's Ultimate Strawberry Bundt Cake.

Hannah headed to the kitchen with a smile on her face. The day that Aunt Nancy had given her the recipe, she'd picked up a strawberry cake mix at Florence's Red Owl Grocery. She had sour cream in her refrigerator and she'd even stopped at Lake Eden Municipal Liquor to buy a bottle of strawberry liqueur. Instant vanilla pudding was no problem. She always had that on hand in case she wanted to make her Fake Orange Julius. And there was a jar of strawberry jam in the refrigerator.

Quickly, Hannah assembled the ingredients and prepared her Bundt pan. Since Aunt Nancy's recipe said to use something called Pan Coat to brush on the inside of the Bundt pan instead of greasing and flouring it, Hannah followed the second recipe Aunt Nancy had gotten from her friend Judy to mix up the Pan Coat. She brushed it all over the inside of the Bundt pan, set the oven to preheat at the proper temperature, pulled out her electric stand mixer, and began to mix up the cake.

In less than fifteen minutes, Hannah's cake was ready to bake and once she'd slipped it into her oven, she flicked off the overhead lights in the kitchen and went back to the living room to find something to watch on her flat-screen television set.

Pan Coat

This recipe is from Judith Baer and it works like a dream!

1/2 cup flour ***(just scoop it out and level it off with a knife)***
1/2 cup vegetable oil
1/2 cup Crisco

Place the three ingredients, in the order given, in a bowl.

Judy's 1st Note: This recipe is simple: Today, I made some more Pan Coat and put the flour in the bowl first, the oil next, and then the Crisco. I use the same half cup measure for all of them, and I do not wash it until I have all three ingredients in the bowl. If you do this in order, the Crisco will easily slide out of the measuring cup.

Whip the ingredients together until the mixture is thick and creamy. ***(This is easier with an electric mixer.)***

Brush Pan Coat all over the inside of your baking pan.

Yield: Enough Pan Coat to coat the inside

of several baking pans.

Judy's 2nd Note: If you have Pan Coat left over, place it in a jar, cover the jar with a square of wax paper, and screw on the lid. It will keep in your pantry or cupboard without refrigeration until you are ready to use it again.

The ingredients will separate, but all you have to do is mix them together again.

Aunt Nancy's Note: Judy got this recipe when she took a cake decorating class. She uses it when she bakes wedding cakes and gingerbread houses for Christmas.

Hannah's Note: Pan Coat will work on any pan that needs to be greased and floured. (And it's a lot easier than greasing it first, dumping in some flour, and then standing over the kitchen wastebasket trying to get the flour on every inside surface.)

Ultimate Strawberry Bundt Cake

Preheat oven to 350 degrees F., rack in the middle position.

4 large eggs
1/2 cup vegetable oil
1/2 cup strawberry liqueur ***(I used Drillaud Strawberry Liqueur)***
8-ounce ***(by weight)*** tub of sour cream ***(I used Knudson)***
1 Tablespoon strawberry jam
box of Strawberry Cake Mix, the kind that makes a 9-inch by 13-inch cake or a 2-layer cake ***(I used Pillsbury)***
5.1-ounce package of DRY instant vanilla pudding and pie filling ***(I used Jell-O)***
12-ounce ***(by weight)*** bag of white chocolate or vanilla baking chips ***(11-ounce package will do, too — I used Nestlé)***

Prepare your cake pan. You'll need a Bundt pan that has been sprayed with Pam or another nonstick cooking spray and then floured. To flour a pan, put some flour in the bottom, hold it over your kitchen waste-basket, and tap the pan to move the flour all over the inside of the pan. Continue this until all the inside surfaces of the pan, including the sides of the crater in the center, have been covered with a light coating of flour. Alternatively, you can coat the inside of the Bundt pan with Pam Baking Spray, which is a nonstick cooking spray with flour already in it or use Pan Coat.

Crack the eggs into the bowl of an electric mixer. Mix them up on LOW speed until they're a uniform color.

Pour in the half-cup of vegetable oil and mix it in with the eggs on LOW speed.

Add the half-cup of strawberry liqueur. Mix it in at LOW speed.

Scoop out the container of sour cream and put it into a small bowl. Add the Tablespoon of strawberry jam and stir it in.

Add the sour cream and strawberry jam mixture to your mixer bowl. Mix that in on LOW speed.

When everything is well combined, open the box of dry cake mix and sprinkle it on top of the liquid ingredients in the bowl of the mixer. Mix that in on LOW speed.

Open the package of instant vanilla pudding and pie filling and sprinkle in the contents. Mix it in on LOW speed.

Shut off the mixer, scrape down the sides of the bowl, remove it from the mixer, and set it on the counter.

If you have a food processor, put in the steel blade and pour in the white chocolate or vanilla baking chips. Process in an on-and-off motion to chop them in smaller pieces. ***(You can also do this with a knife on a cutting board if you don't have a food processor.)***

Sprinkle the white chocolate or vanilla baking chips in your bowl and stir them in by hand with a rubber spatula.

Hannah's 1st Note: If you don't want to use strawberry liqueur in this recipe, use whole milk or water with a little strawberry jam mixed in for flavoring.

Hannah's 2nd Note: The reason the white chips in this recipe are chopped in smaller pieces is that regular-size chips are larger and heavier, and they tend to sink down to the bottom of your

Bundt pan.

Use the rubber spatula to transfer the cake batter to the prepared Bundt pan.

Smooth the top of your cake with the spatula and put it into the center of your preheated oven.

Bake your Ultimate Strawberry Bundt Cake at 350 degrees F. for 55 minutes.

Before you take your cake out of the oven, test it for doneness by inserting a cake tester, thin wooden skewer, or long toothpick. Insert it midway between outside edges of the pan and the metal protrusion that makes the crater in the center of the pan.

If the tester comes out clean, your cake is done. If there is still unbaked batter clinging to the tester, shut the oven door and bake your cake for 5 minutes longer.

Take your cake out of the oven and set it on a cold stove burner or a wire rack. Let it cool in the pan for 20 minutes and then pull the sides of the cake away from the pan with the tips of your impeccably clean fingers.

Don't forget to do the same for the sides of the crater in the middle.

Tip the Bundt pan upside down on a platter and drop it gently on a folded towel on the kitchen counter. Do this until the cake falls out of the pan and rests on the platter.

Cover your Ultimate Strawberry Bundt Cake loosely with foil and refrigerate it for at least 1 hour. Overnight is even better.

Frost your cake with Cool Whip Strawberry Frosting. ***(Recipe and instructions follow.)***

Yield: At least 10 pieces of sweet and tasty strawberry cake. Serve with tall glasses of ice-cold milk or cups of strong coffee.

COOL WHIP STRAWBERRY FROSTING

This recipe is made in the microwave.

1 heaping cup ***(6 to 7 ounces by weight)*** of white chocolate or vanilla baking chips ***(I used Nestlé chips)***
8-ounce ***(by weight)*** tub of FROZEN Cool Whip ***(Do not thaw! Leave in the freezer.)***
1/2 teaspoon strawberry extract

2 drops red food coloring, the liquid type

Hannah's 1st Note: Make sure you use the Original Cool Whip, not the sugar free or the real whipped cream.

Hannah's 2nd Note: If you use the gel food coloring, the color will be brighter and you may need less than 2 drops.

Start by chopping your white chocolate or vanilla baking chips into smaller pieces or placing the chips in a food processor with the steel blade and processing in an on-and-off motion to chop the chips into smaller pieces.

Get the Cool Whip out of your freezer and scoop it out. Place it in a microwave-safe bowl. ***(I used a quart Pyrex measuring cup.)***

Add the white chocolate or vanilla baking chips to the bowl.

Microwave the bowl on HIGH for 1 minute and then let it sit in the microwave for an additional minute.

Take the bowl out of the microwave and stir to see if the chips are melted. If they're not, heat them in 30-second intervals with 30-second standing times on HIGH in the microwave until you succeed in melting the chips and stirring the mixture smooth.

Put the microwave-safe bowl on a towel on your kitchen counter and add the 1/2 teaspoon strawberry extract.

Add the 2 drops of red food coloring to your microwave-safe bowl.

Stir the mixture to combine everything.

Look at the color of your frosting. If it's a nice pink, you're done. If the color is too light, add more food coloring and stir it in until your frosting is the desired color.

Let the bowl sit on the countertop for 15 minutes to thicken the frosting.

When the time is up, give the bowl a stir and remove your cake from the refrigerator. Frost your Ultimate Strawberry Bundt Cake with the frosting and don't forget the sides of the crater in the middle. You don't need to frost all the way down to the bottom of the crater. That's almost impossible. Just frost an inch or so down the sides of the crater.

Hannah's 3rd Note: You can decorate the top of your cake with fresh strawberries cut in half, cut side down, if you wish. If you are baking this cake for Valentine's Day, you can decorate the top of your cake with the little pastel-colored hearts that have sayings on them.

Return your cake to the refrigerator for at least 30 minutes before cutting it and serving it to your guests.

Hannah's 4th Note: You can also use this frosting on cookies. Simply frost and let your cookies sit on wax paper on the kitchen counter until the frosting has set and is dry to the touch.

Yield: This frosting will frost a Bundt Cake, a batch of cookies, a 9-inch by 13-inch cake, or a round two-tier layer cake.

Chapter Three

It didn't take very long for Hannah's cake to fill the condo with a mouthwatering aroma. Hannah smiled as she realized that her mood had improved dramatically. The storm, which was now officially categorized as a blizzard, continued to rage outside, but Hannah knew that she was in no danger. She had plenty of food in the pantry, her electricity would not fail for more than a few seconds, thanks to the generator in the garage that served all four units in her building, and her cable television would continue to operate. When her condo complex was built, all the utilities had been run underground. It had been one of the selling points that Al Percy, their local real-estate agent, had mentioned when he'd shown Hannah and Delores the condo.

Rayne Phillips, Dee Dee Hughes, and Chuck Wilson were still warning viewers about the "blizzard of the century." Hannah picked up the remote control and switched to one of the movie channels included in her cable package. The channel was running a romance movie, and that was the last thing she needed to see. Her romance, along with her marriage to Ross, had turned to ashes.

A sigh escaped, unbidden, from Hannah's throat. If things had turned out differently, she would be sitting here on the comfortable leather couch with her loving husband. Then a blizzard would be just another adventure, a welcome excuse to stay home and be with each other.

The memories of her time with Ross began to surface. She'd made him hot chocolate the way he loved it, with a scoop of marshmallow fluff sprinkled with cinnamon on top. They had cuddled up together in this very spot, sipping from their mugs and laughing at the marshmallow mustaches that both of them had worn as they drank.

Hannah roused herself from the happy memory. Thinking about the good times would only make her wish that things could be different. It was time to face reality. Things couldn't be different, not anymore. The situation was not salvageable. Ross had abandoned her and gone back to his wife. Memories of their romance had no place in her life. She had loved him with all her heart, but now that she knew the truth, her love had turned to a darker emotion. Ross had betrayed her. He'd lied and played her for a fool. She had to harden her heart against him.

Hannah's living room window rattled with each gust of wind, and all she could see was a sheet of shifting, swirling white outside. Normally, she could see Marguerite and Clara Hollenbeck's living room window from hers, but the visibility was down to only inches outside. The escalating storm suited Hannah's mood perfectly. Her very soul felt icy cold. Ross was out of her life forever and she couldn't let herself miss him.

The questions that plagued her sleepless nights emerged with the howling of the wind. Had there been warning signs that she should have spotted? Should she have insisted on a longer engagement so that she could find out more about Ross's life during the time they'd been apart? Was she a fool for missing him so dreadfully, even now?

There was a knock, a very loud knock that successfully competed with the howling wind. Hannah moved Moishe to another cushion, sprang to her feet, and rushed across the room to the door. "Who is it?" she asked, shouting to compete with the cacophony of the storm.

"It's Norman! I've got Cuddles with me! Let us in, Hannah! Another couple minutes out here and she's going to turn into a cat-sicle!"

Hannah opened the door to a snow-covered figure carrying a snow-covered cat carrier. She helped Norman in, took his parka the moment he shrugged it off his shoulders, and dodged the orange-and-white blur that jumped off the couch with a thud and raced to see his favorite kitty friend.

"Ready?" Norman asked, preparing to pull up the grate on the cat carrier to let his pet out of confinement.

"Rrowww!" Moishe replied, and both Hannah and Norman laughed.

"That says it all!" Hannah remarked. "Go ahead, Norman."

Norman pulled up the grate, Cuddles shot out like a rocket, and the kitty-derby down the carpeted hallway to the bedroom was on with Moishe in the lead and Cuddles chasing him.

"Feet up!" Hannah said, hurrying to the couch with Norman following suit. Once there, both Hannah and Norman tucked their feet under them and waited a scant second before they heard the sound of the two cats racing back into the living room.

Both Hannah and Norman knew that the derby consisted of three laps, from the bedroom out to the living room and back again. They counted them off, one by one, and after the third lap Hannah asked, "Are they through?"

"I'm not sure," Norman replied. "Cuddles still has that crazed look in her eyes. She might be getting ready for one more lap."

"If she is, Moishe will go for it. He's panting, but he'll chase her if she . . . oops!" Hannah drew her feet up quickly. "Feet up, Norman! They're off and running!"

Norman laughed and lifted his feet as the two cats ran past him. Then he turned to Hannah with a puzzled expression. "What smells so good?"

"Ultimate Strawberry Bundt Cake. If it's good, we're going to bake it for Valentine's Day."

"If it tastes as good as it smells, it'll be great."

There was the sound of a timer ringing and Hannah got up from the couch. "I have to test the cake," she told him. "If it's done, I'll take it out of the oven. I'll be right back."

"With cake?"

"Not quite yet. It has to cool for twenty minutes in the Bundt pan before I can put it on a plate."

"That long?"

Hannah smiled. "That long. Patience is a virtue, Norman."

"Patients are what I have in my dental chair every day," Norman corrected her.

Hannah was saved from attempting to come up with a clever reply when her stove timer began to beep again. "That's my second warning," she told him. "If I don't shut that off, it'll beep steadily until I do."

Norman sighed. "Then I guess I'll have to practice the other kind of patience."

Hannah chuckled all the way to the kitchen. She loved Norman's ability to come up with the perfect rejoinder in a lot less time than it took for most people.

Once she'd shut off the timer, Hannah tested the cake, decided that it was done, and set it on a cold stove top burner. Then she reset the time for twenty minutes, the length of time it would take it to cool, and went back to the kitchen doorway.

"I've got Chicken in Cabernet Sauce in the Crock-Pot," she told Norman. "I put it up this morning before I left for church and it should be almost ready by now. I was going to freeze it because I planned to go out to dinner with the family tonight, but we can eat it tonight. It'll take me a few minutes to thicken the broth, but would you like some when that's done?"

"You betcha!"

Norman's answer came immediately in Minnesota vernacular, and Hannah smiled. Despite Norman's years in dental school and the time he'd spent practicing at a large clinic in Seattle, he was still a Minnesotan at heart.

The aroma that escaped when Hannah lifted the lid on her slow cooker was enticing and her mouth began to water in anticipation. She heard the sound of footsteps behind her and she turned to smile at Norman.

"That really smells good, Hannah," Norman said, crossing the kitchen floor to look at the contents of the Crock-Pot. "There's a whole meal in there! It must have been a lot of work to make it."

Hannah shook her head. "It wasn't, not really. The slow cooker does most of the work while you're doing something else. All you have to do is remember to turn it on before you leave the house. You could do this, Norman. And then you'd have a hot meal waiting for you when you got home. It's so simple, even Mike could do it and he never cooks for himself."

"I don't think he ever does," Norman said, and then he began to smile. "And speaking of Mike, I'm surprised he's not here yet."

"So am I," Hannah admitted. "Just give him a little time, Norman. He'll probably show up just after I set the table."

"You're right," Norman agreed, acknowledging Mike's uncanny knack for arriving at Hannah's doorstep right before she was planning to serve dinner.

Just then there was a loud thump on Hannah's door, and they exchanged amused glances.

"That's probably him now," Norman said, heading for the door. "I'll let him in."

Hannah finished adjusting the seasonings and thickening the broth. Then she clamped the lid on the Crock-Pot and went to greet Mike. But it wasn't just Mike. When she emerged from the kitchen, she saw that Norman was taking parkas from Michelle, Lonnie, *and* Mike.

"How did you get through all this snow?" she asked Mike, draping their snow-covered parkas over several chairs.

"Carrie and Earl stopped by Mother's place," Michelle explained. "Earl wanted to make sure that Doc had made it home from the hospital. And when Earl saw us, he offered to lead us here in his snowplow."

Hannah began to frown. "Didn't you invite them in?"

"Of course we did," Mike reassured her, "but they said they had to move on. Carrie managed to get through to Edna Fergusson at the farm and Earl promised to plow her driveway."

"I wish you'd told them to wait until I could give them a thermos of hot coffee."

Lonnie shook his head. "They've got plenty. Carrie brought three thermoses, and your mother gave her another one filled with hot chocolate."

"Carrie was having the time of her life in that snowplow," Mike told Hannah. "She said that Earl let her drive and only took over when she dumped a load of snow on Mayor Bascomb's sidewalk by mistake."

"Are you sure it was by mistake?" Norman asked.

"That's what they said," Michelle reported.

Hannah and Norman exchanged amused glances. Both of them knew about Earl's current feud with Mayor Bascomb, and Carrie had never been fond of the mayor's wife, Stephanie.

"Something smells really good," Mike commented.

Hannah suspected that he was changing the subject, but she responded anyway. "It's Chicken in Cabernet Sauce in the slow cooker."

"And that's not all," Michelle said. "I smell something with strawberries."

Hannah gave her youngest sister an approving nod. "Your nose is correct. I just took an Ultimate Strawberry Bundt Cake out of the oven."

"What kind of frosting are you using on it?" Michelle wanted to know.

"I thought I'd try a Cool Whip White Chocolate Frosting with strawberry extract and a couple of drops of red food coloring to make it pink. Then we can call it Cool Whip Strawberry Frosting. And I think I'll decorate the top with strawberries."

"Fresh strawberries?" Norman asked her.

"No, Florence doesn't carry them this time of year. We'll have to make do with frozen strawberries."

"That's okay," Mike said quickly. "I like frozen strawberries."

Since Mike liked everything that could be classified as food, Hannah wasn't surprised. "I'll have to wait for the cake to cool before I can frost it," she explained. "And the Chicken in Cabernet Sauce needs at least another twenty minutes in the Crock-Pot.

Would you like an appetizer while we wait? I've got cheese and crackers."

"And I'll make Mike's Busy Day Pâté," Michelle offered. "Mother gave us some groceries to bring with us. She was afraid you'd run out of food before the blizzard was over."

Hannah avoided meeting Michelle's or Norman's eyes for fear she'd burst out laughing. With Mike as a member of their little blizzard survival group, running out of food was a distinct possibility. Instead of replying, she beckoned to Michelle and both sisters went into the kitchen.

"Sorry about barging in on you like this," Michelle said once the men headed for the leather couches and began to talk.

"That's okay." Hannah went to the refrigerator to get out the cheese. "Actually, I'm glad to have company."

"But it was nice being alone with Norman, wasn't it?"

"Of course it was, but I'm a marri . . ." Hannah stopped herself from saying the words *married woman.* She knew she wasn't married, at least not legally, but she still thought of herself that way. "Never mind."

"That's okay," Michelle said, giving Hannah a little hug. "I know what you were going to say. It'll probably take a while to get back to thinking of yourself as single."

"Hannah?" Mike called out from the living room.

"Yes, Mike?"

"If you're not too busy in there, could you come in here a minute? I have something important to tell you."

"I'll be right there," Hannah said, but instead of heading for the kitchen doorway, she turned to give Michelle a questioning look.

"I don't know," Michelle said with a shrug. "Mike didn't mention anything important to me."

"How about Lonnie?"

"Nothing. The only thing we talked about was the storm, and then Mother called and wanted us to come to the penthouse."

"Then I guess I'd better go in to see what Mike wants," Hannah said with a sigh. "I just hope it's not more news about Ross. I've talked about him enough today."

Chapter Four

"Sit down, Hannah," Mike instructed, gesturing toward the couch. "Mayor Bascomb called me and he wanted me to get in touch with you immediately. He said he tried to call you, but he couldn't get through. That's one of the reasons I asked Earl to lead us out here."

Hannah drew a sigh of relief. At least Mike's important news didn't involve Ross! "What did the mayor want, Mike?"

"He said he got a call from the head of programming at KCOW-TV this morning."

"On a Sunday?"

Mike nodded. "Yes. He said it was important and then he asked me if I could contact you. That's one of the reasons I came out here with Michelle and Lonnie."

"What did Mayor Bascomb want?"

"He wants you to host a series of interviews to be filmed at The Cookie Jar."

"That sounds interesting."

"It is and that's not all. KCOW is going to rerun the movies that are set in Minnesota at a Minnesota Movie Festival. And the festival will be held right here in Lake Eden. The mayor wants to know if you'll agree to host those interviews or whether you'd rather not do it. He also asked me to remind you that having KCOW-TV's movie festival here would do wonders for the businesses in Lake Eden."

Hannah began to smile. "Of course I'll do it. It should be fun."

Mike held up his hand. "Don't jump in quite yet, Hannah. I'm supposed to tell you that KCOW-TV is running a marathon of the movies right before the festival, and they're going to ask their viewers to call in and say which movie they liked best."

"Oh." Hannah felt her anxiety begin to grow. "Are they going to run *Crisis in Cherrywood*?"

"Yes, they are. And they're going to invite all the movie producers, including Ross. They got his number and called him this morning."

"And . . . what did he say?" Hannah asked, giving a little gulp of dismay.

"Ross wasn't there. His wife answered the phone and they left a message for Ross to contact them."

Hannah swallowed again, this time with difficulty. "Do you think Ross will actually come here to Lake Eden to be interviewed?"

"Your guess is as good as mine, Hannah."

Hannah did her best to stay calm. "What if Ross comes here for the interview?"

Mike shrugged. "If Ross shows up here, it won't be pretty. I heard some people at church talking about what they'd like to do to him. Nobody in Lake Eden likes him now. As a matter of fact, some people actively hate him for what he did to you."

"I know, but do you think anyone would actually do anything to . . . to *hurt Ross*?"

"It's a distinct possibility."

"What do you think they'd do?" Hannah held her breath, waiting for Mike's answer.

"They might fight with him, punch him a couple of times for hurting you."

"But would they actually . . . kill Ross?"

Mike thought about that for a moment. "Maybe, but I doubt that it would go that far."

Hannah drew a relieved breath. "That's what I thought. Do you think someone should warn Ross that he might get hurt if he comes back here?"

"Yes." Mike gave her an assessing look. "Do you want his home number so that you can warn him?"

"No! I meant what I told you the last time we talked about Ross. I never want to speak to him again!"

"Then who do you want to do it?"

"I . . . I'm not sure. All I know is that I don't want to do it."

"How about me? Do you want me to warn him?"

Hannah gave a little nod. "Yes. That would be best, Mike. And it might be best to do it in an official capacity and not as my friend. That way your warning would carry more weight."

"I agree. I'll call him from the sheriff's station as soon as this storm stops."

Hannah was so grateful, she felt like throwing her arms around him and giving him a big hug. "Thank you, Mike," she said instead. "It's not really Ross that I'm worried about. It's just that I'd hate one of my friends here to get in trouble for fighting with Ross . . . or even worse."

"I understand." Mike glanced over at Lonnie and Norman to see if they were listening. Then he turned back to Hannah. "You still love Ross, don't you."

It was more of a statement than a question, and Hannah knew she had to be honest. "It's hard to stop loving someone, even when you know it's impossible. I still love

Ross and I wish that things could be different, but I know I can't ever be with him again."

Mike reached over to pat her shoulder. "I know what it's like to love someone and wish that things were different. I still feel that way about my wife. It's been three years and every now and then, I wake up in the morning and turn over to hug her. And then I realize that she isn't here anymore."

Hannah felt the urge to hug him again, but patted his hand instead. "I'm so sorry, Mike. I guess you never quite get over something like that."

"You'll never forget it, but you have to put it behind you, Hannah. I have. There's a future out there for both of us."

"You're right, but I'm not sure how to put it behind me."

"I can't be sure that my way will work for you, but I'll tell you what works for me. I keep busy, I have my work, and I have my friends. Try keeping busy at work and enjoy your friends. Don't dwell on it and keep actively involved in your life. You can get over this, Hannah. You're a strong woman and I know you can."

"Hey, guys . . ." Lonnie broke into their conversation. "What's so serious?"

"We're talking about Ross and how he

might be coming back to Lake Eden," Mike replied.

"What?!" Norman looked completely shocked.

Hannah turned to Mike. "If you don't mind, you can tell them about it while I help Michelle in the kitchen."

Mike patted her shoulder again. "Go ahead. You probably need a break. And besides, I'm getting really hungry."

Hannah laughed and got up from the couch. She heard Mike start to tell Lonnie and Norman what Mayor Bascomb had told him, and she escaped to the kitchen.

"What did Mike want?" Michelle asked when Hannah came through the kitchen doorway.

Hannah knew she needed a few moments to compose herself before she told Michelle the news. "Let's get dinner all ready to go and we'll have a cup of coffee while I tell you about it. Do we have anything for a salad?"

"Yes, and it's in the refrigerator. You had a big package of fresh baby spinach and some cooked bacon. I just whipped up a sweetened cream dressing and put it in the bottom of your salad bowl. Then I washed the spinach and put it on top of the dressing. I gave the bacon a little more time in the microwave to crisp it up, crumbled it over the top, and sprinkled on some chopped red onion. We can mix it up at the table and fill individual salad bowls."

"Sounds wonderful. You must have been busy."

"Not really. I still had time to make an appetizer and it's almost ready to come out of the oven."

Hannah was amazed. Michelle had wasted no time completing their meal. "I thought you were going to make Mike's pâté."

"I did, but I made something else, too."

"What?"

"French Baked Brie With Bread Knots."

"I had Brie in my refrigerator?"

"No, Mother had it in her refrigerator and I brought one of the small wheels of Brie with me."

Hannah began to grin. "Don't tell me you raided Mother's refrigerator!"

"Not exactly. Doc told me to take anything we'd need, that Georgina offered to keep the Red Velvet Lounge open for everyone in the building and the chef agreed to stay, too. Everyone will be eating down there until the storm is over. I found one of Mother's big grocery bags and filled it with all the stuff I thought we might want, and that's what I was carrying when I came in."

"I lucked out with the Ultimate Strawberry Bundt Cake. I had everything I needed in the . . ." Hannah stopped speaking as she realized that her cake was no longer on the cooling rack. "Where is it? I should put it in the refrigerator."

"It's in there already. I knew you'd want to frost it and it had to chill first. We'll let it sit in there until we're through eating and then we'll take in the coffee while we frost it."

"Perfect!" Hannah complimented her sister. "You thought of everything, Michelle."

"Not quite. I was so busy gathering up groceries, I forgot to bring along the pajamas that Mother said she'd let me borrow."

"That's okay. You can borrow a pair of mine. They'll be too big, but they'll do as long as you don't wake up in the middle of the night and go out to the kitchen to make yourself a snack."

Michelle looked puzzled. "What would be wrong with that?"

"It'll take two hands to make a sandwich and if you don't hold on to my pajama bottoms, they'll fall right off on the floor!"

Spinach Salad with Bacon and Sweet Cream Dressing

12-ounce bag baby spinach
1/2 pound regular sliced bacon ***(Don't use thick-sliced bacon because it doesn't crumble as well.)***
1/2 cup chopped red onion

Wash the baby spinach under cold water and remove the stems. (You can just pinch them off.)

Remove the spinach leaves to a strainer or colander to drip dry.

Fry the bacon slices until they are crispy.

Let the bacon cool on a bed of paper towels to absorb the grease. When they cook enough to handle, crumble them in a small bowl.

(Recipe for Sweet Cream Dressing follows this recipe.)

Hannah's Note: You can use a prepared dressing if you don't feel like making it from scratch, but it's very simple if you want to make Michelle's Sweet Cream Dressing. Any already

prepared sweet dressing will work. Aunt Nancy says she sometimes uses honey mustard dressing, which is readily available in most grocery stores.

Pour the dressing you've made or chosen in the bottom of a large salad bowl.

Pat the baby spinach dry with paper towels and place it on top of the dressing in the salad bowl.

Scatter the bacon crumbles over the top of the spinach.

Scatter the chopped red onion over the bacon.

Place the salad bowl in the refrigerator. There's no need to cover it if you plan to serve it in an hour or so. If you've made the salad earlier than that, cover it loosely with foil. If you cover it right away, the bacon won't be crunchy any longer.

When it's time to serve, simply mix the salad at the table and either leave it in the bowl so that the guests can serve themselves with salad tongs, or place each serving in salad bowls in the kitchen.

SWEET CREAM DRESSING

2 Tablespoons raspberry vinegar ***(or red wine vinegar)***

1 Tablespoon white Karo syrup ***(you can substitute honey for the white Karo syrup)***

1 teaspoon stone ground mustard

1/8 teaspoon salt

1/4 teaspoon freshly ground black pepper

1/2 cup whipping cream

Put the 2 Tablespoons of raspberry vinegar in a small bowl.

Use a whisk to whisk in 1 Tablespoon of white Karo syrup ***(or honey)***.

Whisk until the white Karo syrup has been incorporated with the vinegar.

Add 1 teaspoon of stone ground mustard and whisk it in.

Whisk in the salt and the ground black pepper.

Pour in the heavy cream and continue to whisk until your dressing is smooth and creamy.

Yield: 1/2 cup of sweet and creamy dressing that is especially good on spinach salads.

French Baked Brie with Bread Knots

Preheat oven to 375 degrees F., rack in the middle position.

2 small rounds ***(each approximately 4 inches in diameter)*** of ripe Brie ***(I used President soft ripened Brie)***
4 teaspoons Herbs Provencal
1 roll of refrigerated unbaked French bread ***(I used Pillsbury in the blue foil package)***
2 ounces ***(1/2 stick)*** salted butter

Prepare two 9-inch pie pans by spraying them with Pam or another nonstick cooking spray, or covering the bottoms with a round of parchment paper cut to fit and then sprayed with nonstick baking spray.

Unwrap the Brie and use a sharp knife dipped in water to cut/peel off the top rind. ***(This is easier if you use a knife with a long, flat blade and keep rinsing it off in water.)***

When the top rinds have been removed, sprinkle the top of each Brie with 1 teaspoon of Herbs Provencal.

Place your herbed Brie rounds in the center of the prepared pie pans, herbed side up.

Open the can of unbaked French bread and use a sharp knife to cut it into pieces that you can shape into 1-inch balls.

Roll the pieces into balls and place them on a piece of wax paper on the counter.

Place the salted butter in a shallow, microwave-safe bowl.

Heat the butter on HIGH in the microwave for 20 seconds to melt it. If the butter isn't completely melted, heat it in additional 20-second intervals until it is.

The bowl may be hot, so use pot holders to remove it from the microwave and place it on a folded towel next to the pie pans with the herbed Brie rounds.

Using tongs, dip each bread dough ball into the melted butter and place the balls around the bases of the Brie rounds. ***(It's okay if they touch each other.)*** Work until the Brie rounds are ringed with circles of bread dough balls.

Sprinkle the remaining 2 teaspoons of Herbs Provencal over the tops of the bread dough balls.

Bake your Brie at 375 degrees F. for 20 to 25 minutes or until the bread dough balls have turned a nice golden brown.

Let your French Baked Brie With Bread Knots cool in the pans for 5 minutes. Then remove them using a large flat metal spatula and place them on a serving platter.

Yield: 2 delicious appetizers that will serve 8 to 10 guests.

CHICKEN IN CABERNET SAUCE

Made in a 4-quart slow cooker — must cook 7 hours or longer.

1 bottle good cabernet or burgundy ***(both are full-bodied red wines)***
1/2 pound thick-sliced bacon ***(see Hannah's 1st Note below)***
3 stalks celery, chopped into 1/2-inch slices
1 large sweet onion peeled and cut into quarter-inch slices ***(I used Vidalia)***
10 boneless, skinless chicken thighs
1/2 teaspoon coarse ground black pepper
3 shallots, peeled and quartered
20 small fresh carrot nuggets
12-ounce package frozen pearl onions
1 pound fresh white mushrooms
2 minced garlic cloves ***(see Hannah's Substitution List below)***
2 cups chicken broth
3 Tablespoons tomato paste ***(I used Hunt's)***
5 fresh thyme sprigs ***(see Hannah's Substitution List below)***
5 fresh rosemary sprigs, chopped ***(see Hannah's Substitution List below)***
3 fresh basil leaves ***(see Hannah's Substitution List below)***
2 packages chicken gravy mix (the kind that makes 1 cup gravy per package)

4 Tablespoons ***(2 ounces, 1/2 stick)*** salted butter

Hannah's Substitution List: There are shortcuts you can take, even to this simple recipe, to reduce the preparation time. I've tried all of these and they work.

For the half-pound of thick bacon, you can use a half-cup of cooked chopped bacon *(I used Hormel)* . Just be careful to buy REAL bacon, not the bacon bits that are made of non-meat products.

For the pound of fresh white mushrooms, you can use 4 four-ounce cans of button mushrooms, but you must drain them before adding them to the crock.

For the minced garlic cloves, you can use a teaspoon of jarred minced garlic.

For the spices, rather than buying fresh thyme sprigs, fresh rosemary sprigs, and fresh basil leaves, you can use 1 teaspoon of powered thyme, 1/2 teaspoon of powdered rosemary, and 1

teaspoon of dried basil leaves.

Spray the inside of the crock of your slow cooker with Pam or another nonstick cooking spray. ***(This will make it easier for you to wash later.)***

Measure the contents of your bottle of cabernet by pouring it into a measuring cup. You are going to reduce the wine to half of its present volume.

Pour the wine into a saucepan and place it on the stovetop. Heat the wine on MEDIUM HIGH until it reaches a boil.

Turn the heat down to MEDIUM, making sure that the wine still maintains a gentle boil.

Set your timer for 15 minutes. It should take the wine approximately that long to reduce by half.

Place the uncooked bacon on a cutting board and dice it with a knife.

Place the diced, uncooked bacon in a microwave-safe bowl.

Heat the bacon on HIGH for 2 minutes. Leave it in the microwave and let it sit for 2 minutes.

Check the bacon to see if it's cooked through. The bacon fat should be liquid and the diced bacon should look like bacon bits.

If your bacon needs more cooking, heat it in the microwave on HIGH for increments of 1 minute, followed by another minute of standing time. Do this until the bacon is crisp and the fat has liquefied.

Use a slotted spoon to take out the bacon and place it in a small bowl on the counter. You will add it to your Crock-Pot later.

Hannah's 1st Note: If you like to fry your breakfast eggs in bacon fat, pour the fat in a container with a cover and place it in the refrigerator. If you don't care to save it, pour it into a disposable cup and place it in the garbage.

When 15 minutes have passed, pour the contents of your saucepan into the same measuring cup you used earlier. If it is reduced by half of its original volume, it's ready. If not, pour it back into the saucepan and continue to gently boil it until it is.

Place the celery slices in the bottom of your crock.

Lay the sweet onion slices over the celery.

Arrange the chicken thighs on top of the onion slices.

Sprinkle HALF of the black pepper over the chicken.

Arrange the shallots on top of the peppered chicken.

Place the carrot nuggets on top of the shallots.

Sprinkle on the contents of the frozen pearl onion package.

If the white mushrooms are large, cut them in half and arrange them on top of the pearl onions.

Sprinkle on the minced garlic.

Remember the bacon bits you cooked?

Sprinkle them over the minced garlic.

Sprinkle the rest of the black pepper over the top of the bacon bits.

Add the 2 cups of chicken broth to the reduced wine in your saucepan.

Stir in the 3 Tablespoons of tomato paste.

If you are using fresh herbs, tie the thyme sprigs, rosemary sprigs, and basil leaves in a square of cheesecloth. You will want to remove them from the finished dish before you serve it. Alternatively, you can put everything into a tea ball, affix the lid, and remove that when your meal is ready to eat.

Hannah's 2nd Note: If you are using powdered thyme, powdered rosemary, and dried basil leaves, simply sprinkle them all into the saucepan and stir them in.

Sprinkle in ONE packet of gravy mix and stir it in.

Pour the contents of the saucepan over the ingredients in your crock.

Cut the cold butter into several pieces and arrange them on top of your crock.

Put the lid on your Crock-Pot, plug it in, and turn it on LOW heat. Your Chicken in Cabernet Sauce will be ready in 7 hours, but it will hold for several more hours if your guests are late.

Check the progress of your meal 20 minutes before you're ready to serve. If the sauce that had formed is too thin, add the second packet of gravy mix, stir it in, and put on the lid again. Then turn the Crock-Pot on HIGH and let it cook for an additional 20 minutes.

Hannah's 3rd Note: If you invite Mike for dinner, be sure to put Slap Ya Mama hot sauce on the table for him.

Yield: A delectable dinner for 5 to 6 guests. It can serve 8 if you also offer a green salad and hot, crusty bread.

Chapter Five

When Hannah woke up the next morning, she felt oddly content. It was nice to have Michelle and the guys in the condo. She'd been anticipating being by herself for three or four days and although the prospect certainly didn't frighten her, it was nice to have company when you knew you were snowed in and couldn't get out because of the weather.

She flicked on the light, glanced at the alarm clock, and realized that it was almost seven in the morning. She'd slept for a lot longer than she usually did, especially on Sunday nights. It was great knowing that she didn't have to go to work in the morning, and the prospect of relaxing all day on a Monday with people she liked was wonderfully appealing.

Her neck was unusually stiff and Hannah rubbed it. Then she glanced at the other side of her bed and realized that Moishe had given Cuddles his pillow and he'd stolen hers in the middle of the night. She thought fleetingly of telling him he was bad for taking her pillow, but the two cats looked so angelic sprawled out on their matching pillows, she just didn't have the heart to complain.

Hannah was just pulling on her slippers when she realized that there was a delicious scent in the air. It took her a moment to identify it, but when she did, she began to smile. Peaches. And the scent of peaches was probably what had awakened her in the first place.

"Michelle must be baking something with peaches," she said to the sleeping cats. "I'm going to take a quick shower, get dressed, and go see what Michelle has in the oven."

Moishe opened one eye when he heard her voice. He gave a soft, rather kittenish mew and began to stretch. Again, Hannah was amazed at how long her pet was when he stretched. He was lying on her pillow lengthwise and even though it was a king-size pillow, his head extended over one side and his back legs extended over the other side. He stretched for several seconds and then he sat up and reached out with one paw to rouse Cuddles.

Cuddles opened her eyes, stretched in a

smaller version of Moishe's stretch, and sat up. Then both cats swiveled their heads to watch Hannah as she headed for the master bathroom to take her morning shower.

When Hannah came back into her bedroom, ten minutes later, the cats had deserted her and there was a new scent in the air, the scent of coffee brewing. This caused her to make short work of dressing and within five additional minutes, she was heading toward the kitchen for her morning wake-up cup of the beverage that her father had always called *Swedish Plasma.*

She could hear the shower running as she passed the guest bathroom and Hannah knew that at least one of the men was awake. A few steps later, quietly tiptoeing past the two occupied sleeping bags in the living room, she entered the kitchen.

Just as she'd expected, Moishe and Cuddles were parked in front of their food bowls. Their heads were down, almost buried in whatever Michelle had fed them with their Kitty Kibble, and they didn't even look up to see who had come in.

Hannah began to smile. As usual, Michelle had accomplished all of the chores that Hannah would have had to do if Hannah were alone. Her youngest sister simply pitched in and didn't even expect any thanks for doing it.

Michelle was on the other side of the kitchen, removing something from the oven. It smelled so delicious that it made Hannah's mouth begin to water. She stood there watching as her youngest sister carried a baking sheet with the aromatic treat to a wire rack she'd placed on the counter, and then Michelle went back to the oven for a second baking sheet.

"Good morning, Michelle," Hannah said once Michelle's precious cargo had been stowed on the wire racks. "Whatever that is, it smells absolutely wonderful!"

"Good morning, Hannah. I baked Peach Scones. It's a new recipe and it seemed like the perfect time to try it."

"If the scent is any indication, it's a great recipe."

"I hope so." Michelle turned and hurried to the coffeepot. "Sit down, Hannah, and I'll bring you a cup of coffee. And before you think to ask me, the scones have to cool for five to ten minutes."

"I vote for five," Hannah told her, pulling out a chair at her kitchen table and sitting down in her favorite spot. "I don't think I can wait any longer than that."

"Neither could Heiti. Aunt Nancy said that she made them for breakfast one morning and he almost burned his mouth by tasting them too soon."

"Too bad we don't have a little table outside. They'd cool faster out there."

"And if they didn't blow away in the wind gusts we're having this morning, they'd be covered with snow in no time flat."

"It's bad outside?"

"The worst I've ever seen." Michelle set Hannah's coffee mug in front of her and went back to fill hers. Then she sat down in an adjacent chair and sighed. "Just look out the window."

Hannah turned to look and began to frown. "The snow's still coming down in sheets. I can't even see the building next door and it's only a few feet away."

"I know. After we have some breakfast, I want to see if KCOW-TV is still on the air. They should have the latest news on the blizzard."

"I'll turn it on after we eat." Hannah opened the refrigerator and looked inside. "What shall we have with the scones? The guys will probably want a bigger breakfast."

"That depends on what you have in your refrigerator."

"I have some breakfast sausages and several cartons of eggs. And I think there's a package of shredded cheddar in there."

Michelle thought about that for a moment and then she nodded. "I think there's one on the second shelf, right next to the sliced ham."

"Great! Then we could cook the sausages and have scrambled eggs with cheese. And if we wanted to, we could cut up the cooked sausages and add them to the eggs when we scramble them. We could even throw in some chopped onions and add those right before we add the cheese."

Michelle looked a bit concerned. "That sounds good, but we'll need more than one big frying pan. There are five of us at breakfast and all of the men will be hungry."

"That's true, especially Mike. Why don't we make a baked dish in the oven with all of those ingredients?"

"I like that idea, but what shall we make?"

"I'm not sure, but preheat the oven to three hundred and fifty degrees. That's a standard temperature. If we need a hotter oven, we'll simply increase the temperature."

"Will we need both ovens?"

"No, just the top one. We'll use a nine-and-a-half by eleven inch cake pan. That should hold enough for all five of us."

Michelle hurried to the oven and set it to preheat. Then she came back to the table.

"Do you want to taste the scones now?"

"Yes! Are they cool enough?"

"I think so." Michelle went over to pick up a scone and when she turned around, she was smiling. "They're just right."

"Great!" Hannah began to frown as the doorbell rang. "Wait a minute, Michelle. Someone's at the door."

When she got to the door and pulled it open, Hannah gave a welcoming smile. "Marguerite!" she greeted her next-door neighbor. "Come in before you get cold."

Marguerite stepped into Hannah's living room and began to smile as the two cats rushed out of the kitchen to greet her. "Hello, Moishe. Hello, dear Cuddles." Then she looked up at Hannah. "How wonderful! I think Cuddles remembers me!"

"I'm sure she does. Come have a cup of coffee with Michelle and me."

Once Marguerite had been seated at Hannah's kitchen table with Cuddles in her lap and a cup of coffee in front of her, they began to discuss the situation with the weather.

"Do you and Clara have enough food to last through the blizzard?" Hannah asked her.

"Oh, yes. We went to the Red Owl right after class on Friday night and shopped for the week."

"You and Clara are taking a class?" Michelle asked.

"Yes. It's so much fun! It gets us out in the community with the other senior citizens in the Encore program."

Hannah was puzzled. "Where is this? And what's the Encore program?"

"It's an offering of free classes for senior citizens at the community college. The variety to choose from is amazing. Clara is taking a painting class and she doesn't appreciate this weather one bit! If it doesn't clear up soon, she won't be able to complete her assignment before the next class."

"She doesn't usually paint outside, does she?" Michelle drew the obvious conclusion.

"No, she paints inside. But her assignment this week is to go outside at various hours of the day and night to take cell phone photos of an object that casts a shadow. They have to use the same object every time and Clara's already done the morning and afternoon hours. She was going to start on the evening hours yesterday, but the weather didn't cooperate."

"I thought it was a painting class," Hannah said.

"It is. Clara says it's to teach the students

the difference the time of day and night make. And also the difference in color between the shadows cast by the sun and shadows cast by the moon."

"And now, with the blizzard, Clara can't go outside to do it," Michelle concluded.

"That's right. The moon's not casting any shadows that Clara could photograph with all this blowing snow," Hannah added. "Which object did Clara choose?"

"That big lone pine tree at the edge of the woods. You know the one, don't you?"

"Yes," Hannah answered. "It's a majestic tree and I just wish we could see it from our building."

"So do I." Marguerite gave a little sigh. "Then Clara wouldn't have to go out at night and wade through the snow. I just hope they shovel the path that goes around the complex after this storm stops."

"I'm sure they will," Hannah reassured her. "Tell us about your class, Marguerite. What subject are you studying?"

"I have a poetry class. We're working on writing poetry and the professor is teaching us about word choice. We bring in the poems we've written during the week and he reads them in class. Everyone discusses them and suggests ways that we can improve them."

"I'd love to read some of your poems," Hannah said.

Marguerite began to smile. "That's good because I wrote one for you. Our last class was about how to capture the essence of meaning with an elegance of words. Our professor said that if we can find the best word to describe what we mean, we won't have to use two or three adjectives to convey it."

Hannah was impressed. Marguerite's professor sounded like a very good teacher.

"Here." Marguerite pulled a folded sheet of paper from her pocket and handed it to Hannah. "After I heard your speech in church yesterday, I went straight home and wrote this. Its message is that one small bit of time can completely change a person's life."

Hannah unfolded the paper and read what Marguerite had written.

It only takes a moment
A baby's first cry
A lover's lie
A kiss goodbye
And a dream's dying sigh.
It only takes a moment.

"Oh, my!" Hannah said, handing the

paper to Michelle. "It's wonderful, Marguerite! Are you taking this one to class?"

"Yes, I think it's what our professor was talking about."

Hannah nodded. "So do I."

"It's really very good, Marguerite," Michelle commented.

Marguerite looked pleased at their praise. "I'm so glad you like it. I hate to drink coffee and run, but Clara's waiting for me. It's my turn to make breakfast this morning."

Michelle jumped up and wrapped four scones in a piece of foil. "Take these home with you. They're Peach Scones and I just made them this morning."

"Thank you!" Marguerite stood up and accepted the package with a smile.

"Would you and Clara like to join us for dinner this evening?" Hannah asked as she walked Marguerite to the door.

"I would, but Clara can't. Her allergies are worse and I don't think she can handle being in a place with two cats, even if she doubles up on her allergy pills."

"You're right, of course. We understand. Would it work if I send one of the guys over with a plate of dinner for Clara so that you can come over here and see Cuddles again?"

"That would be perfect!" Marguerite was clearly delighted with Hannah's suggestion.

"What time is dinner?"

"We'll eat dinner at seven, but we'll have wine and appetizers at six," Hannah told her. "Please join us for those, too."

"I'd love to." Marguerite waited until Hannah had opened the door and then she reached out to give her a little hug. "Thank you for being my friend, Hannah."

"And thank you for being mine," Hannah said, watching as Marguerite walked across the bridge between the two buildings, entered the second-floor condo she shared with Clara, and closed the door behind her.

"I thought of something," Michelle said, as Hannah came back to the kitchen.

"What?"

"I've been thinking about how to make the baked egg dish and I checked to see if you had any other ingredients we could add."

Hannah was curious. "What did you find?"

"Sliced ham, Pepper Jack cheese, mustard, red onions, and sliced black olives."

"Those are all good ingredients."

"Yes, and we can make Country Egg Bake."

"I've never heard of that before!"

Michelle laughed. "That's because I just made it up, but I'm sure it'll work."

"I'll trust you on that. The recipes you make up always work."

"Thanks, but no, they don't."

"Really? Name one recipe you just made up that didn't work."

"That's easy. It's tuna hotdish."

"But . . . that's so easy. It's just a casserole with tuna and cream of mushroom soup! Why didn't our tuna hotdish work?"

"Because I started putting it together and I didn't have any cream of mushroom soup."

Hannah shrugged. "You could have used any cream soup. I've used cream of celery, cream of chicken, and even cream of asparagus."

"I know that, but I didn't have any of those, either."

"So what did you do?"

Michelle gave a little laugh. "I used cream of tomato. And the tuna hotdish was so bad, we had to call out for pizza."

PEACH SCONES

Preheat oven to 425 degrees F., rack in the middle position.

3 cups all-purpose flour ***(pack it down in the cup when you measure it)***
1/2 cup brown sugar ***(pack it down in the cup when you measure it)***
2 teaspoons cream of tartar ***(important)***
1 teaspoon baking powder
1 teaspoon baking soda
2 teaspoons cinnamon
1/2 teaspoon salt
1/2 cup salted butter ***(1 stick, 4 ounces, 1/4 pound)***

2 large eggs, beaten ***(just whip them up in a glass with a fork)***
3/4 cup sour cream ***(or peach yogurt)***
3/4 cup peach jam ***(I used Smucker's)***
1/2 cup whipping cream

Use a medium-size mixing bowl to combine the flour, brown sugar, cream of tartar, baking powder, baking soda, cinnamon, and salt. Stir them all up together. Cut in the salted butter just as you would for piecrust dough.

Hannah's Note: If you have a food

processor, you can use it for the first step. Cut the half-cup COLD salted butter into 8 chunks. Layer them with the dry ingredients in the bowl of the food processor. Process with the steel blade in an on-and-off motion until the mixture has the texture of coarse cornmeal. Transfer the mixture to a medium-sized mixing bowl.

Stir in the beaten eggs, sour cream, and peach jam, and then mix everything up together.

Add the whipping cream and stir until everything is combined.

Drop the scones by soup spoonful on to two cookie sheets sprayed with Pam or another nonstick baking spray. Alternatively, you can line your baking sheets with parchment paper. Divide your dough so that there are 9 scones for each cookie sheet.

If you have two ovens, you will bake one sheet in the upper oven and one in the lower oven. If you have only one oven, it will probably have 4 racks inside. Bake your scones on the two middle racks, switching their positions halfway through the baking time.

Once the scones are on the cookie sheets, wet your impeccably clean fingers and shape them into more perfect rounds. Then flatten them with your moistened palms. They will rise during baking, but once you flatten them, they won't be too round on top.

Bake the scones at 425 degrees F. for 10 to 12 minutes, or until they're golden brown on top. ***(Mine took the full 12 minutes.)***

Cool the scones for at least 5 minutes on the cookie sheet and then remove them to a wire rack with a metal spatula. ***(If you used parchment paper, all you have to do is position the cookie sheet next to the wire rack and pull the paper over to the rack.)***

When the scones are cool, you can cut them in half lengthwise and toast them for breakfast.

Yield: Makes 18 delicious scones.

COUNTRY EGG BAKE

Preheat oven to 350 degrees F., rack in the middle position.

4 cups shredded Pepper Jack cheese ***(or Swiss cheese)***
1/3 cup chopped red onions
2 cups chopped ham
4 cups shredded cheddar cheese ***(or mozzarella)***
1 small can sliced black olives, drained
3 cups half-and-half or whipping cream
6 Tablespoons all-purpose flour
1 teaspoon salt
1/2 teaspoon ground black pepper ***(freshly ground is best)***
2 Tablespoons honey mustard (***I used Beaver)***
6 large eggs

Prepare a 9-inch by 13-inch cake pan by spraying it with Pam or another nonstick cooking spray.

Layer half of the shredded Pepper Jack cheese in the bottom of the pan.

Sprinkle half of chopped red onion over the Pepper Jack cheese.

Scatter half of the chopped ham over the onion.

Sprinkle half of the shredded cheddar over the chopped ham.

Distribute the sliced olives on top of the shredded cheddar.

Repeat, using the rest of the cheeses, the chopped red onions, and the chopped ham.

Pour the half-and-half or cream into a bowl. Sprinkle the flour, salt, black pepper, and honey mustard on top of the bowl.

Crack the eggs and mix them into the bowl, beating until you have a smooth texture and all the ingredients are incorporated.

Pour the egg mixture into your prepared pan, distributing it as evenly as possible.

Bake your Country Egg Bake for 50 minutes or until the top is golden brown.

Test for doneness by inserting a knife from your silverware drawer 1 inch from the center of the pan. If it comes out milky, bake for 10 minutes longer and test again. Except for the melted cheese that might stick to the knife blade, the knife should come out clean.

Take the pan out of the oven and place it on a cold stovetop burner or a wire rack on the counter.

Cool for at least 10 minutes before cutting and serving it.

Cut your Country Egg Bake into squares, but do not remove them from the pan. Instead, put the pan on pot holders in the center of the table and let each person serve themselves, or pass you their plates so that you may serve them.

Yield: Serves 8 breakfast guests as long as you also serve muffins, toast, biscuits, or scones.

Chapter Six

Hannah was smiling as she opened the back kitchen door of The Cookie Jar and walked in. The blizzard had raged for two more days, but on the third day, the snow had stopped falling, the winds had ceased to blow. A few hours later, they'd heard the welcome sound of Earl's snowplow coming down the access road that led to the condo complex. Hannah had put on the coffee, Michelle had prepared a plateful of their newest creation, Chocolate Mint Cookies, and Mike and the men had gone out to intercept Earl to invite him in for coffee and cookies.

Mike and Lonnie had been the first ones to leave, and before he'd left, Mike had promised Hannah that he would warn Ross. Hannah, Norman, and Michelle had been ready to follow Mike out, but then the phone had rung and the call had been from Lisa, who'd told them that she'd opened

The Cookie Jar that morning for their customers who lived in town. There weren't many customers since the country roads hadn't yet been plowed and the long farm driveways were still impassable. Lisa said that the school would be closed for another couple of days, so Hannah and Michelle should take an additional day or two off. Since there weren't many customers, Lisa insisted that she was managing just fine with Aunt Nancy and Marge. And since they weren't that busy, they were going to test some Valentine recipes. She'd recommended that Hannah should stay home with Michelle and do the same. Then they could compare notes when Hannah got back to town.

Hannah had felt a bit guilty staying at home when The Cookie Jar was open for business, but Lisa had convinced her. And there were several recipes she wanted to test. But this morning, Hannah's mini-vacation had ended as early as sunrise when she'd glanced out the window to see a beautiful, calm morning outside.

Once she'd unlocked the back door to the kitchen, Hannah stepped inside, slid out of her boots, changed to shoes, and hung up her parka. Then she headed straight for the kitchen coffeepot to make herself a fresh, hot supply of her favorite morning wake-up drink.

A few minutes later, coffee mug in hand, she'd opened the swinging door to the coffee shop. Everything was in place, ready to go, and she was the only occupant in the building. Instead of feeling lonely, Hannah was grateful for this time alone in one of her favorite places. She carried her coffee to her favorite table in the back of the coffee shop and sat there, sipping and waiting for the sun to come up.

It was so quiet in The Cookie Jar, Hannah could hear the clock on the wall behind the counter clicking off the minutes. This was her favorite time of day, the half-light that began to brighten the sky right before the sun peeked over the horizon. Shapes began to appear in the distance, and the shops across the street gained recognizable form. There was nothing else moving. No cars. No lights. It was as if she were the only person awake at this hour in Lake Eden. There was a sense of peace, of feeling comfortable in her own skin, the beginnings of happiness after Hannah's long weeks of feeling abandoned and bereft. She relished in the moment until she heard a knock at the back kitchen door.

Could it be Norman? Or Mike? Or Michelle? Or Delores? Hannah went through the possibilities with lightning speed as she rose to her feet and hurried to the door. The knock came again, just as she reached it, and that was when she realized that the knock was not distinctive and she could not identify it. It was probably an early delivery of baking supplies that Lisa had ordered.

"Coming!" she called out, releasing the deadbolt and turning the doorknob. She pulled the door open and gasped in shock as she recognized the man standing there. Despite the warning Mike had given him, it was Ross! He was back!

"Hannah!" he said, reaching out to her.

Hannah stepped back out of sheer reflex. "Ross. What are *you* doing here?"

"I love you, Hannah. My wife is going to get a divorce and I want to marry you again the minute it's final."

Hannah shivered at the thought. "No!" she said. "Never!"

"But, Hannah . . . I love you. All I need is the money I left in the safe deposit box. I'll give it to my wife and she'll file the papers."

Hannah felt cold all over and it had nothing to do with the freezing temperature outside. "No!" she said again, even louder this time. "You're a liar and a cheat! I wouldn't marry you again even if you were the last man on earth!"

"But I'll make it up to you, I promise. And this wasn't my fault, Hannah. When I left my wife a year ago, she said she was going to divorce me. She was the one who didn't keep her word, not me!"

Hannah just stared at the man she thought she'd loved. Her heart was leaden in her chest and she knew she could never trust him again. "No!" she said again. "Go away and don't come back!"

"Look, Hannah. I'll be perfectly honest with you. I'm in big trouble and I need that money. Just give me the money and the key that was under the money in the safe deposit box and I'll never bother you again."

"I don't carry that key with me."

"All right, fine! Where's the money!?"

Hannah heard a note of desperation in Ross's voice and she did something she never thought she'd be able to do. She faced him squarely and smiled. "It's back in your checking account, along with the money you deposited in my bank account. Write yourself a check, cash it at the bank, and get out of town! There's nothing here for you."

"I can't wait until the bank opens. I'm in danger here. Mike said a lot of people are mad at me and he couldn't be responsible for protecting me. Why do you think I drove all night to get here before anyone else was awake?"

Hannah just stared at him. There was no way she was going to invite him inside to hide until the bank opened. "Mike's right," she said coldly. "I guess you'll just have to be careful. You got yourself into this mess and you'll have to get yourself out. I can't help you. And I don't *want* to help you!"

"I've got to get that money!"

"Fine. You know where it is. Come back as soon as the bank opens and get it. I told you before. It's in your account. I don't want your money. You can't make up for the way you treated me with *any* amount of money!"

A cold, hard expression crossed Ross's face, an expression that Hannah had never seen before. Suddenly, she realized that everyone in town was still asleep and she was alone with a dangerous man.

"Don't play games with me, Hannah! I can hurt you! And believe me, I will!"

Hannah took another step back as Ross moved toward her again. The sky was lightening and she could see the way his eyes had narrowed. He didn't love her despite what he'd said. And she was suddenly afraid.

"What do you want, Hannah? Half the money?"

"No!" Hannah told him, matching his icy tone. "What I want is for you to get out of my life . . . permanently!"

He reached out for her and Hannah leaped back into the warm interior of the kitchen. She slammed the door in his face and turned the deadbolt. And then she somehow made her way to the stool at the work station. Her legs were shaking so violently, they collapsed the moment she reached a stool.

It might have been a matter of moments or much longer than that. Hannah had no way of knowing. She drifted in and out of fear so intense, she might have lost consciousness. Dimly, almost as if it were a dream, she was aware of the front door opening and the sound of footsteps heading toward the kitchen.

"Hannah?"

Lisa! Hannah began to breathe again. She hadn't been aware that she had been holding her breath. She did her best to look up, but she couldn't quite focus on Lisa's face.

"Hannah! Are you all right?"

Lisa's hand was on her shoulder and Hannah forced herself to concentrate. "No," she said in a voice that was still shaking with fear.

"What's wrong? Are you sick?"

"Call Mike." Hannah forced out the words. "Call now! He's back and he's going to kill me!"

She had managed to drink several swallows of water by the time Mike rushed through the door. "Mike," she said in a small voice. "He's back."

"Okay. Just relax, Hannah. Nobody's going to hurt you as long as I'm around. You're safe with me."

"Yes," Hannah said, and she could feel herself begin to relax. "I'm safe now. Sorry, Mike. I just . . . lost it for a minute or two. I'm better now that you're here."

"Good. You should be. I'm armed."

He reached out to give her a little pat on the back and Hannah managed a smile. "Which arm will you use?"

Mike laughed. "You cracked a joke and I can tell that you're better now. You had me scared, Hannah. Your face was so pale, I thought you were going to faint."

"I might have," Hannah admitted. "There was a kind of reddish haze over everything when I got back inside, and I put my head down. I don't know how long it was before Lisa came in the front door."

"You had a panic attack," Mike decided, patting her back again. "I'm assuming you ran into Ross?"

Hannah nodded. "He knocked on the back door and I thought it was a delivery. I opened it without asking who was there. I should have known better."

"Yes, you should have. And I'm having Lonnie install a peephole as soon as he gets to the station." Mike pulled his cell phone out of his pocket and sent a quick text to Lonnie. Then he turned to Lisa. "Do you have any orange juice? She still looks a little rattled."

"That's from the loose screws in my head," Hannah quipped. "I should have known better than to open the door, especially since I didn't recognize the knock."

"True, but we all make mistakes." Mike watched Lisa pour a glass of orange juice and walk over to hand it to Hannah. "Can you hold this glass?" he asked her.

"Yes. I'm not shaking as much now." Hannah grabbed the glass and took a big swallow of orange juice. "I'm feeling better, Mike."

"That's what all the ladies say around me. Drink more, Hannah. You need the sugar."

"It's the first time in my life that anyone's told me I need sugar." Hannah took another swallow. "He said he'd hurt me if I didn't give him the money that was in the safe deposit box."

Mike nodded. "That figures. Where's the money?"

"Back in his bank account. Doug deposited it for me. And I put back the money Ross deposited in my account, too."

"That must have made him mad, especially since the bank won't be open today."

Hannah just stared at Mike in shock. "It *won't*?"

"No."

"Why not? It's not a bank holiday, is it?"

"No, but the wind was so strong, it blew in a couple of windows and there's glass all over the floor and the counters. Doug and Cliff managed to get down there to board up the windows, but there was a lot of damage done. They've been working on it, but they don't expect to open for business again until Monday morning."

Hannah began to frown. "I didn't know anything about the damage and I didn't drive past the bank when I came in to work this morning. I told Ross he'd have to go there today if he wanted to get his money. And now he won't be able to do that! He's going to think that I was lying to him and he's going to be even more furious with me!"

Hannah felt herself begin to shake with

fear again, and she did her best to stop. Even though she knew she was safe now with Mike and Lisa here, she couldn't help thinking about what might happen if she encountered Ross alone.

"You're okay, Hannah," Lisa said, sitting down on the other side of Hannah and giving her a hug. "You're safe with both of us here, and maybe it's a good thing that the bank is closed. Since he can't get his money, Ross won't be back before Monday."

"But how will Ross know that the bank is closed today?" Hannah asked. "He could be standing outside the building right now, waiting for the bank to open."

Mike shook his head. "Doug posted a sign on the door saying the bank won't be open until Monday. Ross will see it and he'll know he can't get his money until then."

"This could turn out to be good for you," Lisa pointed out. "At least you won't have to worry about Ross coming back to Lake Eden until Monday morning."

"Not necessarily," Mike pointed out. "Ross may decide to stay in the area until the bank opens on Monday."

Hannah felt her anxiety begin to rise again. "Then I'm not safe anywhere in Lake Eden!"

Mike put his arm around her. "Yes, you

are. It's the best place you could possibly be. We'll take care of you, Hannah. I promise."

"I just want him gone!" Hannah said, and she felt tears coming to her eyes. "I never thought I'd say this, but I'm afraid of him!"

"You'd be a fool if you weren't afraid," Lisa said.

"That's right." Mike reached into his pocket and drew out his pen and notebook. "Okay, Hannah. I want you to tell me everything that happened from the time you first opened the door and saw Ross. Don't leave anything out. I need to know everything he said and everything that you said until you locked the kitchen door behind you."

"I'll get coffee," Lisa said, hurrying to fetch two cups of Hannah's favorite beverage. She added a generous spoonful of sugar to Hannah's cup and carried the coffee back to the work station.

"Thanks, Lisa," Hannah said, raising the cup to her lips and taking a sip. A startled expression crossed her face as she swallowed. "I don't take sugar!"

"You do today," Lisa insisted. "You're still shaking and it'll help. And I'm willing to bet that you didn't have breakfast before you came in this morning."

"I . . ." Hannah stopped objecting and sighed instead. Lisa was right. She hadn't bothered to eat breakfast. "You're right, Lisa. I didn't fix any breakfast this morning."

"That's what I thought. Drink the coffee," Lisa ordered. "Your blood sugar's probably low. Take a couple of swallows right now and then I'll get you a plate of cookies that you can share with Mike. Tell him everything, Hannah. It doesn't matter how small and insignificant you think it is. I'm going to go out to the coffee shop and get things ready to open in there."

"Concentrate," Mike ordered, once Lisa had left. "Tell me everything you remember, Hannah."

Hannah took another swallow of coffee and a bite of her cookie, and began to recite the events that had happened after she'd heard the knock on the back kitchen door. It took quite a while and she was surprised at all the small things she remembered, even facts like how Ross had been dressed, the boots he'd been wearing, and how his appearance had changed in the weeks that had gone by since he'd left her.

"Very good, Hannah," Mike said, closing his notebook and sliding it back into his pocket.

"I'm back," Lisa announced, coming through the swinging door again. "Aunt Nancy and Marge are here and I'm going to start the baking."

"I'll help," Hannah said, rising from the stool.

"No, just sit there, Hannah," Lisa ordered. "You've been through an emotional morning already and I can handle the baking. Drink coffee, eat cookies, keep me company, and do your best to relax. That's all I need from you right now."

"Lisa's right," Mike told her. "You'll be okay, Hannah. And just to be on the safe side, I'm going to assign a couple of my deputies to stay with you wherever you go. There's no way we're going to take any chances with your safety."

"The minute he hears about this, Herb will offer to help," Lisa told Mike. "Herb can watch the entrances to Lake Eden, and we can make sure Hannah is safe while she's here at The Cookie Jar."

"Thanks, Lisa. And tell Herb thanks, too. My detectives will make sure Hannah is escorted everywhere she goes," Mike promised, and then he turned to Hannah. "You'll have constant protection, Hannah. I'm going to order round-the-clock security for you."

Hannah was about to tell him that she didn't need bodyguards, but before she opened her mouth, she remembered the menacing look on Ross's face when he'd tried to grab her and keep her from going inside. Perhaps she *did* need bodyguards.

Mike looked surprised when Hannah didn't voice her objections to round-the-clock security. "You're not going to argue with me about this?"

"No," Hannah said, and then she gave a long, drawn-out sigh. "I don't like it, but you're right. Ross really scared me when he threatened to hurt me, and I know that I might need protection."

Chapter Seven

"I'm really glad you're here, Lisa," Hannah said once Mike had left. "Where were you when the blizzard hit us?"

"At home with Herb. He'd just gotten off work. He was only home for a half hour or so when it started to snow, and we heard the blizzard warnings on KCOW. We just stayed in the house until the snow stopped blowing. How about you?"

"I was taking a nap at the condo. I slept for most of the afternoon."

"I can understand that. You must have been exhausted after dealing with all the people at church."

"I was. Moishe was sleeping with me and when I woke up, I looked out the window and it was a solid wall of swirling snow."

"You were alone?"

"Yes, except for Moishe. I think the howling of the wind woke me up, either that or the fact that Moishe was restless. He was scared, so I petted him to calm him down, slipped on my robe, and went out into the living room. That's when I looked out the living room window and realized that I couldn't see Clara and Marguerite's condo across the outside landing."

"Did your electricity go off?"

Hannah shook her head. "When they built the condo complex, they ran everything underground. I had cable television for the entire time, too. I was just watching the weather warning on KCOW-TV when Norman knocked on my door with Cuddles."

Lisa looked shocked. "Norman made it all the way out to your place?"

"Yes. He started before the blizzard got really bad, but it took him almost an hour and a half. And it's only a twenty-minute drive."

"Where was Michelle?"

"At Mother and Doc's penthouse with Lonnie. Mother called Michelle on her cell phone, told her that it was too dangerous to drive back to my place, and invited them over to ride out the blizzard."

"But Michelle was with you when I called."

"I know. Earl Flensburg came by with his snowplow and brought Michelle, Lonnie, and Mike out to my place."

"So you had Norman, Cuddles, Mike, Lonnie, and Michelle with you for the whole time?"

Hannah smiled. "Yes, and I was glad for the company. The guys camped out in the living room and Michelle and I cooked and baked a lot. It kept our minds off what was happening outside. I think we came up with some good recipes for Valentine's Day and I brought samples for you." Hannah walked over to the kitchen counter, picked up the box she'd packed that morning, and carried it over to give to Lisa.

Lisa took the box and set it down on the stainless-steel surface. "It's really heavy. You must have baked the entire time!"

Hannah laughed. "Michelle and I had to do something. We were getting a little stir-crazy. The guys tested cookies, pies, and cakes for us and so did Clara and Marguerite Hollenbeck. It was something productive for us to do."

"It sounds like you didn't mind the blizzard at all."

"Not true. I can tell you this, Lisa. I'm really glad it's over and I can get out again! I never thought I was claustrophobic, but I guess I am. I felt anxious knowing that I couldn't get out of the condo if we had an emergency."

"I know what you mean, but at least you had people with you. Herb and I were stuck in the house and the only time we left was to step outside and walk the dogs around the inside of the fence."

"You must have felt terribly confined." Hannah walked to the kitchen coffeepot and poured herself another cup. "What did you and Herb do to pass the time?"

Since Lisa didn't answer immediately, Hannah turned to look at her. That's when she realized that her partner was blushing. "Sorry," she apologized. "I guess I shouldn't have asked that."

"That's okay. I *did* have time to come up with a couple of new recipes we can use for Valentine's Day."

"Great! What are they?"

"One is Pink Grapefruit Cake. The glaze is pink and it's pretty. And another is White Chocolate Brownies. I've got a White Chocolate Fudge Frosting, too, and I thought we could color that pink and put Valentine candies on top of each brownie."

"Good idea! Did you hear the news about the movie festival?"

"Yes. Mayor Bascomb called Herb to see if he knew anyone he could hire for extra security. The mayor said that there were going to be a lot of extra people coming to town for that."

"He's probably right."

Lisa began to look slightly worried. "You don't think Ross will come back for that, do you?"

"I'm almost sure he won't. Once he gets his money, he'll be long gone. Mike told Ross that he couldn't guarantee his safety, and that's probably why Ross drove all night so that he could arrive so early this morning."

"You mean he wanted to get here before anyone in town was awake?"

"Yes. And he wanted to get here while I was alone at The Cookie Jar."

"That's scary," Lisa said, but she was clearly relieved that Hannah didn't think Ross would come back for the movie festival. "I really hope he won't be back here. Herb was pretty hot under the collar about how Ross treated you, and Aunt Nancy said that Heiti felt the same way. Everyone's on your side, Hannah. And they all think that what Ross did to you was horrible."

Hannah frowned slightly. She really didn't want to talk about Ross anymore. It was best to change the subject, so she gestured toward the box. "Take a look at what Michelle and I baked."

Lisa lifted the cover on the large box and

her eyes widened as she saw what was inside. "You two must have baked the entire time!"

"It was something to do and it made us feel better. Between the two of us, we came up with quite a few new recipes."

"What are these cookies?" Lisa pointed to a row of cookies in the middle of the box.

"We're calling them Chocolate Mint Cookies. Grab a cup of coffee and try one. I want to find out what you think of them."

Lisa got up and headed for the coffeepot. In less than a minute, she was back with her coffee.

"Go ahead," Hannah invited. "I already had one when we baked them, but I think I'll have another."

"They smell nice and minty," Lisa remarked, choosing a cookie from the box and taking a bite. "Mmmm!"

"That sounds like you approve."

Lisa nodded and took a sip of coffee. "I love the combination of chocolate and mint. They're wonderful, Hannah!"

"Thank you. Do you think we should offer them on our takeout list of cookies for Valentine's Day?"

"Yes, but only after you let people sample them today. You know everyone who comes in likes to critique our cookies. And not just because they get a free cookie. I think our customers really like it when we ask for their opinion."

"I'll bake more this morning and we can test them out on the customers today. How about your Pink Grapefruit Cake and the White Chocolate Brownies?"

"We can test those, too. I brought in the rest of the Pink Grapefruit Cake and the brownies. You test those and if you like them, I'll bake the cake when I take my lunch break."

"But then you won't get lunch."

"Yes, I will. I can order a hamburger and fries from Rose at the café and run down to get it while the cake is baking. And after I eat, I can bake the brownies."

There was a knock at the back door and Hannah got up from her stool. "It's Mother," she told Lisa. "I'll go let her in."

"Four knocks in rapid succession, polite, but insistent," Lisa said. "I can recognize her knock now, but I still have problems with Norman's knock."

"That's because he changes it deliberately. He likes to try to fool me, but I'm right more often than I'm wrong."

"Oh, good! You're in this morning!" Delores greeted Hannah the moment she opened the door. Then she stepped in, wiped her boots on the rug Hannah kept by the door in the winter, stepped out of her boots and replaced them with slippers, and handed Hannah her parka to hang from a hook just inside the door. "How are you, dear?"

"I'm fine. Lisa and I were just having coffee. Would you like to join us?"

"That would be lovely." Delores followed Hannah to the work station, took a stool next to Lisa, and noticed the box of cookies. "What are these? They look divine!"

"They're Chocolate Mint Cookies," Hannah told her.

"I haven't had these before, have I?"

Hannah shook her head. "No, Michelle and I came up with the recipe and we baked them yesterday, just in time to invite Earl for coffee and cookies before he plowed us out. Try one, Mother. I'd like to know what you think of them."

"You don't have to ask me twice," Delores said with a laugh, reaching for a cookie and taking a bite, "I absolutely love the combination of chocolate and mint. These are fabulous, dear! You're going to serve them here, aren't you?"

"Yes," Lisa answered, reaching for another cookie. "Our customers are going to love them."

Delores turned to Hannah. "What did you think of the mayor's news, Hannah?"

"It's exciting. They're going to do the interviews with the movie people right here at The Cookie Jar. It'll be fun to see some of the movie people again, and they're even going to interview some of the locals who were in *Crisis in Cherrywood.*"

"Will they interview Tracey?" Delores asked.

"I think so. She had a big role in the movie."

"How about you, Hannah?" Lisa wanted to know.

"I doubt it. My part wasn't that big. I'm hoping that Lynne and Tom will fly in for the festival. It would be good to see them again."

"Stephanie Bascomb told me that she's keeping a list of the people who are coming in for the festival," Delores told them. "I'll ask her if Lynne and Tom are on it."

"Thanks, Mother. I really would like to know. I tried calling Lynne last night to ask her if she was coming, but she wasn't home."

"Stephanie's coming over this afternoon for coffee. She invited herself and of course I agreed. You should drop by, Hannah. I'll ask her to bring the list with her."

"I would, but it's our first day back and . . ."

"Go ahead, Hannah," Lisa interrupted the excuse that Hannah was about to give. "Aunt Nancy will be here, and Marge and Dad are coming, too. We can handle things here."

"Wonderful!" Delores said quickly. "Hannah can help me think of something to serve. Stephanie loves appetizers, and I hate to serve crackers and cheese every time she comes for coffee."

Hannah knew when she was beaten and she put on a smile for her mother's benefit. There were usually strings attached to her mother's invitations and she should have expected it. "I'll bring some cookies and if Florence has grapes, I'll make frozen grapes."

"Frozen grapes?" Delores looked puzzled. "I haven't had those before."

"It's a new recipe I've been meaning to try. If Florence has any seedless grapes, I'll make those. And I'll bring some of Aunt Kitty's Jamaican Rum Balls, too."

"Stephanie loves those! I had some left over from Christmas Eve and we had them with champagne."

Delores finished her cookie, drank the last of her coffee, and stood up to go. "I'll see you about three-thirty then, dear. That way we'll be all ready when Stephanie gets there at four."

"Before you go, I need to know whether Stephanie prefers vodka or tequila."

Delores looked confused. "I'm not sure, dear. She did mention that she sometimes drinks vodka tonics in the summer, though."

"Good enough. And we know she likes champagne."

"Oh, yes. Expensive champagne. The last time she came over for coffee, I had to open a second bottle of Perrier Jouet. But you're not planning to bring champagne or vodka, are you, dear?"

"No, but I need them for the grapes. They're marinated in a mixture of Prosecco and tequila, but I'll substitute champagne and vodka."

"Oooh! That sounds lethal!" Delores looked slightly worried. "You may have to drive Stephanie home, dear."

Hannah laughed. "Or I'll leave her with you to sleep it off."

Delores looked properly horrified. "You wouldn't . . . would you, dear?"

"No, I was joking, Mother. Are you going to Granny's Attic this morning?"

"Yes, Carrie's meeting me there and we're going to price some antiques that Luanne found at an estate sale in Browerville. I'm sure they're wonderful. Luanne has a very good eye for a bargain."

Once Delores had left, Lisa turned to Hannah. "Sounds like Luanne is doing very well working for your mother and Carrie. She's managing the store now, isn't she?"

"Yes, and she's also their accountant. She finished her last class right before Christmas."

"Is she thinking about going to work at Stan Kramer's accounting firm?"

"I doubt it. Mother and Carrie gave her a big raise. And she loves going out to auctions and estate sales. If Luanne worked for Stan, she'd be stuck in an office all day."

Lisa glanced up at the clock on the kitchen wall. "If you're planning to go to the Red Owl, maybe you'd better go now. We still have forty-five minutes before we open."

"Good idea." Hannah stood up, carried her coffee mug to the sink, and went to grab her parka. "I'll be back before we open," she promised as she slipped on her boots and went out the door.

It was cold outside and Hannah pulled up the hood of her parka and slipped her hands into the fur-lined gloves that Norman had given her for Christmas. She'd walk to Florence's grocery store. It was only a block away. As she hurried down the alley, passed the back of Claire's dress shop, Beau Monde Fashions, and crossed the street at Third and Main, she was smiling. It was good to be out walking again after three days of confinement in the condo. The air was frosty and it smelled fresh and clean, the sun cast golden sparkles on the snow, and the icicles hanging from the branches of the big pine in the middle of the block glistened like they were made of melted diamonds.

There wasn't a soul on the street. Most of the businesses didn't open until nine, and it was too early for shoppers. Florence's Red Owl Grocery was open though. She always opened early so that she could stock the shelves with the food items that had come in during the night. Her regular supplier had a key to the office in the back, and he stacked the crates and boxes in there. It would have been folly to leave them on the loading dock. Produce would have frozen and turned brown during the winter nights, canned goods would have frozen and broken open, and liquids would have popped their tops and formed a frozen frosting of dish soap, or beer, or soda on the tops of bottles and cans.

The front door of the Red Owl was still locked, but Hannah knocked loudly. Florence appeared at the end of the canned soup and meat aisle and smiled as she saw Hannah standing there.

"Hannah!" Florence greeted her as she unlocked the door. "Come in! Where's your cookie truck?"

"At The Cookie Jar. I walked here."

"Pretty cold, isn't it?"

"It's not so bad now that the winds have died down. Have you unpacked your produce yet, Florence?"

"Just did it. What did you need, Hannah?"

Hannah crossed her fingers even though it was difficult to do in the bulky, fur-lined gloves. "Seedless grapes," she said.

"You're in luck. I just got a shipment of fruit from Venezuela. Do you want red fire grapes? Or green grapes?"

"Both please."

Florence led the way to the produce section and pointed to the grapes. "They look good, don't they?"

"They sure do. I'm so glad you have them, Florence. I need them for a recipe I'm making at The Cookie Jar."

Florence looked puzzled. "I didn't know you could bake with grapes!"

"I don't know if you can, or you can't, but I'm not going to bake with them."

"But you bake so much, Hannah." Florence looked confused. "What kind of recipe is it, then?"

"Frozen Sugared Grapes."

"I didn't know you could freeze grapes!"

"Neither did I until an old friend of mine from college sent me this recipe. She included it in the Christmas card she sent to me."

"And you're going to try them out on your customers at The Cookie Jar?"

"Not exactly. Mother's having Stephanie Bascomb over this afternoon and I promised to bring something interesting to have with their coffee."

"Coffee for Stephanie Bascomb?" Florence began to grin. "Whatever it is, your recipe had better have champagne in it. Stephanie's crazy about champagne. I should know. I order it by the case for her."

"I know and this recipe does call for champagne. It also has vodka."

"That sounds interesting. And it's certainly something that Stephanie would like. She definitely has a sweet tooth, especially when she's enjoying the cocktail hour. Every time I get in a shipment of imported chocolates, I call Stephanie so that she can buy what she wants before I put it on the shelf. Will you bring me a couple of those frozen grapes on your way to your mother's place?

They sound interesting and I want to try them."

"Of course I will. It sounds like they pack a wallop, though. You might be better off if you stick them in the freezer and wait until you get home to try them."

"Really?" Florence looked interested. "How do you make them, Hannah?"

"You marinate the grapes in champagne and vodka for an hour. Then you take them out and roll them in white sugar. You put them on a baking sheet, freeze them for several hours until they're hard, slip them in a freezer bag to save on freezer space, and get them out right before you serve them so that they're still frozen when people eat them."

Florence began to smile. "They'd be great for a New Year's Eve party. You wouldn't have to serve as much liquor. You'd save a ton of money and people could just eat the grapes and celebrate."

Chocolate Mint Cookies

DO NOT preheat oven yet. This dough must chill before baking.

1 and 1/2 cups salted butter ***(3 sticks, 12 ounces, 3/4 pound)***
2 cups cocoa powder ***(unsweetened — I used Hershey's)***
2 cups brown sugar ***(pack it down in the cup when you measure it)***
2 teaspoons baking soda
1 teaspoon salt
1 teaspoon vanilla extract
1 teaspoon mint extract
3 large eggs, beaten ***(just whip them up in a glass with a fork)***
3 cups flour ***(not sifted — pack it down in the cup when you measure it)***
1 cup mini chocolate chips ***(1/2 of an 11 or 12-ounce bag)***

1/2 cup white granulated sugar in a small bowl ***(for later)***
1 large bag Mini York Peppermint Patties ***(for later)***

Hannah's 1st Note: This recipe is easiest if you use an electric mixer, but it

can also be mixed by hand.

Place the 3 sticks of salted butter in a microwave-safe container. ***(I used a quart Pyrex measuring cup with a spout.)***

Heat the butter on HIGH for 1 minute. Let it sit in the microwave for an additional minute and stir it with a heat-resistant spatula to see if it has melted. If it hasn't, heat it on HIGH for another 20 seconds, let it sit for 20 seconds, and stir it again. Repeat in 20-second intervals until your butter is melted.

Pour the melted butter in the bottom of a mixing bowl.

Add the cocoa powder and mix it in.

Mix in the 2 cups of brown sugar. Make sure the brown sugar is completly incorporated.

Hannah's 2nd Note: If your brown sugar has hard lumps in it, remove the lumps, then add more brown sugar until you have a full 2 cups.

Add the baking soda and salt to your mixing bowl. Mix until they are completely combined.

Add the vanilla extract and the mint extract. Mix them in thoroughly.

Feel the sides of the mixing bowl. If the contents are so hot that it might cook the eggs if you add them now, let everything cool to slightly above room temperature.

If you haven't yet beaten the eggs, put them in a glass and whip them up until they are completely blended. ***(I still use a fork from my silverware bowl to do this the way my great-grandmother Elsa used to do.)***

Add the beaten eggs to your mixing bowl. Mix them in thoroughly.

Add the flour to your mixing bowl in half-cup increments, mixing after each addition.

Hannah's 3rd Note: If you're using an electric mixer and you add all the flour at once, it will poof out all over your counter and floor when you turn on the mixer.

Once the flour has been thoroughly incorporated, scrape down the sides of the bowl with a butter spatula and take the bowl out of the mixer.

Set the bowl on your counter and give it another stir.

Add the cup of mini chocolate chips and stir them in by hand. Make sure they're evenly distributed.

Cover your bowl with plastic wrap and place it in the refrigerator for 2 hours. ***(Overnight is fine, too.)***

Once your cookie dough has chilled and you're ready to bake, take the bowl out of the refrigerator.

Preheat the oven to 350 degrees F., rack in the middle position.

While your oven is preheating, prepare your cookie sheets by either spraying them with Pam or another cooking spray or lining them with parchment paper.

Roll the Chocolate Mint Cookie dough into walnut-sized balls with your impeccably clean hands.

Working one dough ball at a time, roll the dough balls in the bowl of white sugar and place the balls on your prepared cookie sheets, 12 to a standard sheet.

Hannah's 4th Note: This dough may be sticky, so roll only enough cookie dough balls for the cookies you plan to bake immediately and return the bowl to the refrigerator.

Flatten the dough balls a bit with a metal spatula ***(or with the heel of your hand if the health board's not around).***

Press one Peppermint Pattie in the center of each cookie.

Bake your cookies at 350 degrees F. for 10 minutes.

Take your cookie sheets out of the oven and cool the cookies on their cookie sheets for 1 to 2 minutes.

When the cookies have cooled for a bit, use a metal spatula to transfer the cookies to metal cooling racks on your counter. If you leave them on the cookie sheets for too long, they may stick and fall apart when you try to transfer them.

Hannah's 5th Note: If you used parchment paper, let the cookies cool on the cookie sheets a bit and then pull the parchment paper, cookies and all, over to the cooling racks. (Don't forget to use oven mitts or pot holders to do this! Metal cookie sheets take longer than 1 or 2 minutes to cool enough to handle with your bare hands.)

Yield: 4 to 5 dozen deliciously minty cookies that everyone who enjoys chocolate-covered mints will love.

Hannah's 6th Note: Chocolate Mint Cookies are a big favorite at The Cookie Jar, especially around the Christmas season. Be sure, however, to serve them with tall glasses of icy cold milk, cups of strong coffee, or mugs of hot chocolate.

FROZEN SUGARED GRAPES

1 bunch green seedless grapes
1 bunch red seedless grapes
1 cup Prosecco or champagne
1 cup tequila or vodka
1/2 cup white ***(granulated)*** sugar ***(variable — you may need to add additional sugar)***

Hannah's 1st Note: You can make several batches of both kinds of grapes with this recipe, as many as you need for your party. Just save the marinating liquid for the next batch. It will work for up to 4 batches without losing its *oomph.* And yes, *oomph* is a culinary term!

Choose a bunch of green seedless grapes that has grapes that are plump and fresh. You can make this recipe with 2 bunches of green seedless grapes or 1 bunch of green and 1 bunch of red seedless grapes, or 2 bunches of red seedless grapes.

Prepare your freezing pans by making sure the pan size you choose has sides that will keep the grapes from rolling off and that it will fit in your freezer. ***(Don't laugh — the first time I made these, I used a baking sheet with sides that were too wide to fit in***

my freezer at the condo!)

Remove the grapes from their stems and wash them under cold, running water. (This is easier to do if you use a colander or a large strainer.)

Pat the grapes dry with paper towels.

Fill a large, shallow bowl with 1 cup of Prosecco or champagne and 1 cup of tequila or vodka. Mix them together with a whisk.

Leave the liquor mixture and the grapes on the kitchen counter at room temperature.

Hannah's 2nd Note: If you have too many grapes in your bowl and the liquor mixture doesn't cover them, simply add additional amounts of each liquid to completely cover the grapes.

Hannah's 3rd Note: I used champagne and vodka when I made these grapes for Stephanie Bascomb and Mother.

Let the grapes marinate in the liquor mixture for 1 hour. ***(Longer is okay but don't let the liquor evaporate.)***

Once the grapes have marinated in the liquor mixture for at least 1 hour, fill a shallow bowl with white ***(granulated)*** sugar and roll the grapes in the bowl, one by one.

Hannah's 4th Note: If you're making several batches of grapes, you may need to add more white granulated sugar to your bowl. If the sugar gets sticky and doesn't adhere to the grapes any longer or sticks to them in clumps, just dump out the sugar, rinse and thoroughly dry the bowl, and put in fresh sugar.

As you roll the grapes in the white sugar, place them on the pan you've chosen with a small space separating them from touching each other.

Once the pan is full of sugared grapes, place it in your freezer in a nice flat space and let the grapes freeze overnight.

In the morning, get out a freezer bag, pluck the frozen grapes off the freezing sheet, and place them in the bag. Seal the bag, place it back in the freezer, and proceed marinating and freezing more grapes if you've chosen to make more than 2 bunches.

Serve these grapes frozen. They're very refreshing on a hot, summer day and a great addition to a barbecue or a pool party.

Hannah's 5th Note: Be careful with these grapes! They taste delicious, but if you've marinated them for a long time, they can pack a real wallop!

Chapter Eight

Of course Stephanie Bascomb had loved the grapes. And Hannah had assumed the duty of driving her home after Stephanie had consumed a second bottle of Perrier Jouet. Unfortunately, Hannah still didn't know whether Lynne and Tom were coming to Lake Eden for the Minnesota Movie Festival because they hadn't yet called Mayor Bascomb to reply to the invitation.

"Did you find out if Lynne and Tom are coming?" Michelle asked, greeting Hannah as she came in the back door of The Cookie Jar.

"No. Their names weren't on Stephanie's list, but that doesn't necessarily mean that they're not coming. I'll try calling Lynne again tonight to see if I can reach her."

"Good. I'd like to see her again." Michelle hurried toward the oven as the stove timer rang. "I'd better get the cakes out before they get too dry."

"What are you baking?"

"Lisa's Pink Grapefruit Cake. She told me that it was one of Lois Brown's recipes and she mixed up the batter before they got busy in the coffee shop. I volunteered to bake her cakes and glaze them for her."

"Lisa mentioned she'd made Pink Grapefruit Cake during the blizzard. I wonder where she found pink grapefruit at this time of year. I meant to ask her this morning, but I forgot."

"The same thing occurred to me and I asked her." Michelle removed the cakes from the oven, set them on the baker's rack, and turned back to Hannah. "Someone sent Lisa and Herb a package of pink grapefruit from Florida a couple of days before the blizzard hit us. Lisa and Herb had pink grapefruit for breakfast twice, but Lisa realized that they wouldn't be able to eat all of them before they spoiled. Rather than taking that chance, she zested them, juiced them, and froze the zest and the juice."

"That makes sense," Hannah said. "Lisa's very thrifty. Was she thinking about the recipe she had for the Pink Grapefruit Cake?"

"Yes, and that's why she did it. And now we don't have to worry about finding pink grapefruit for Valentine's Day. Lisa says she's got enough ingredients for at least two dozen Pink Grapefruit Cakes and Pink Grapefruit Glaze in her freezer."

"Hannah?" Lisa stuck her head in the kitchen. "There's a phone call for you. It's Lynne Larchmont."

Hannah hurried to the phone and she was smiling as she picked it up. "Lynne! Are you coming here for the film festival?"

"I'm here already," Lynne replied, with a laugh that made Hannah smile. "We flew in last night and we're staying at the Lake Eden Inn. I called to see if you'd like to join me for dinner tonight."

"I'd love to!" Hannah answered quickly. "What time? And where are we going?"

"Seven o'clock right here in Sally's dining room. Unless, of course, there's another blizzard. That's all anyone can talk about around here. Everybody says we're just lucky that we didn't fly in a week earlier or we would have been stuck in the middle of it."

"The Lake Eden Inn is a great place to be stuck," Hannah said with a laugh. "Sally's got huge freezers full of food, and they have their own generator at the inn. When Dick and Sally moved here and opened the inn, Dick told Sally that the weather could be brutal way out there by Eden Lake and they'd better be prepared for anything."

"Tell Lynne hello for me," Lisa said as Hannah prepared to leave The Cookie Jar and drive out to the Lake Eden Inn. "And take this cake for Sally. I want her to taste it."

"Stay out as late as you like," Michelle told her, walking Hannah out to her cookie truck. "I'll feed Moishe when I get home, and Lonnie's coming over tonight to watch a movie with me."

"Lonnie has the night off?"

"Yes, Mike said that he didn't need him tonight."

"Since I'm going out tonight, I'm surprised Mike didn't assign him to my bodyguard detail."

"He did, but when he told Mike that you were going out to the Lake Eden Inn for dinner with Lynne, Mike said not to worry, that you'd be fine."

Hannah was a bit puzzled as she started her truck and drove off. Why had Mike changed his mind about the bodyguards? He'd been worried about her safety this morning, but tonight he'd told Lonnie that she'd be fine all by herself. She didn't understand, but being without a chaperone was fine with her. Mike must assume, or perhaps he knew, that Ross had left Lake Eden and wouldn't be back tonight.

The sky was beginning to darken as Hannah turned onto the road that led around Eden Lake. She switched on her headlights and gave silent thanks to Earl Flensburg for plowing the county road. Since no one else was on the road, it didn't take long for her to get to the turnoff for the Lake Eden Inn. This narrow road had also been plowed and Hannah suspected that Dick Laughlin had been out with his truck, which was equipped as a snowplow, to clear the road.

She was about to turn to go to the parking lot when she saw a large sign stuck on top of a snowbank. It read, HANNAH PARK IN DELIVERY SPOT IN BACK. Hannah laughed. It was obvious that Sally and Dick knew that she was meeting Lynne for dinner and they hadn't wanted her to walk all the way to the restaurant from their parking lot.

Hannah did as she was told and parked in the delivery spot by the delivery door. Then she picked up the Pink Grapefruit Cake that Lisa had asked her to bring and carried it to the door. She was about to press the buzzer when the door opened.

"Hi, Hannah," Sally greeted her. "I saw you stop to read the sign and I figured you'd be at the door about now. Come in. Now that it's getting dark, it's turning colder."

Hannah gave a little shiver. "You're right," she agreed as she followed Sally into the warmth of the hallway. "The wind picked up and it has a real bite to it."

"I reserved a curtained booth for you and Lynne, and I'll join you two for dessert if you don't mind."

"Not at all!" Hannah assured her. "It's always a pleasure to have dessert and coffee with you. And speaking of dessert . . ." she handed the Pink Grapefruit Cake to Sally. "Lisa sent this for you. It's a Pink Grapefruit Cake with Pink Grapefruit Glaze and we're thinking of using it for Valentine catering."

"Well, it's certainly pretty enough," Sally said, opening the box to peek inside. "I don't think I've ever had a grapefruit cake before. I've had lemon cake and orange cake, but never grapefruit. It makes me wonder if you could make a pink grapefruit meringue pie."

Hannah thought about that for a moment before she answered. "Why not?" she decided. "The juice is certainly flavorful enough, and it would be a little like Key Lime Pie or Lemon Meringue Pie. I'll have to get some pink grapefruit juice from Lisa and try it. Someone sent Lisa and Herb a box of pink grapefruit from Florida for their anniversary and Lisa zested the rind, juiced the pink grapefruit, and froze it."

Sally smiled. "Lisa's got a good head on her shoulders. And if this cake tastes as delicious as it smells, she's also one heck of a good baker!"

Sally led the way to the curtained booth on the end of the raised platform that contained the row of private booths. She opened the curtain and announced, "Here's Hannah. I'm going to go get her a hot lemonade to warm her up. It's getting really cold out there. Would you like one, too, Lynne?"

"Yes, please," Lynne answered quickly. "Dick makes the best hot lemonade in the world!"

"That's because he puts really good rum in it," Sally explained. "I'll be right back, girls, and I'll send Dot over to get your dinner order."

"You look good, Hannah," Lynne told her as soon as Hannah had taken off her parka and slid into the booth. "After what Sally told me about you and Ross, I expected you to be a pale shadow of your former self."

Hannah laughed. "Not quite. It's difficult to fade into a shadow when you're as mad as a wet hen."

"I'm sorry we didn't come to the wedding," Lynne apologized. "We didn't get your invitation until we got back from Europe and by then it was too late. Did you get my wedding present?"

"Yes, it's beautiful. Thank you, Lynne. I've never had a beautiful teapot and tea cozy like that before. There's just one thing . . . would you like it back since I wasn't really married in the first place?"

"No! Of course not!" Lynne looked shocked at the suggestion. "You thought you were getting married and that's all that counts! I wish we'd had a chance to talk before you got engaged to Ross. I would have told you what a louse he is! That man broke my heart, and it sounds like he broke yours, too."

Hannah gave a little nod. "It felt that way at first. There were times when I actually had trouble breathing, I was so upset. I just couldn't believe he'd left me without a word. And when that feeling left, I began to wonder what I'd done wrong to make him want to go away."

"I heard that," Sally said, pulling back the curtain and placing mugs of hot lemonade in front of them. "You did absolutely nothing wrong, Hannah. He deserves all the blame. If you'd told me that you felt that way, I would have come into The Cookie Jar to shake some sense into you!"

"I believe it," Hannah said with a little laugh. "It's okay, Sally. And I feel much better now that I told Ross to get out of my sight and stay out of my life."

Sally looked completely shocked. "You *saw* Ross again?!"

"Yes, this morning. I got in to work early and he knocked on the back door of The Cookie Jar."

"You let him inside?" Lynne asked her.

Hannah shook her head. "No, I stepped out. He said he needed the money he'd left in the safe deposit box and I told him it wasn't there anymore, that I'd deposited it in his checking account. I returned all the money he gave me."

"You're a good person, Hannah," Lynne told her. "I don't think I would have returned his money. I would have kept it to make up for all the pain and grief he caused."

Sally began to frown. "Why did Ross need the money? Do you know?"

"All I know is what he *said.* I don't know if it's the truth, but he told me he needed to give it to his wife so that she could pay for a divorce."

"Good heavens!" Sally looked completely

shocked. "That man has colossal nerve! He wanted you to pay for his divorce with the money he gave to *you*?"

"Yes. And then he said that he still loved me and he wanted to marry me again just as soon as he was free."

Both Lynne and Sally groaned, and Lynne reached out to take Hannah's arm. "You didn't fall for that, did you, Hannah?"

"Of course not!"

"Did he go to the bank to get the money?" Lynne asked.

"No. I didn't know anything about it at the time, but the bank was closed and it won't reopen until Monday morning. They had a lot of damage from the blizzard and they have cleanup and repair work to do."

"Oh boy!" Lynne gave a little gasp. "Ross must have been furious when he found out. Did he come back to confront you?"

Hannah shook her head. "No. Mike was there by that time and if Ross came back, he didn't come inside."

"He probably saw Mike's cruiser and decided that flight was the better option," Sally offered her opinion. "Have you heard from him again, Hannah?"

"No, and I hope I don't. He was really nasty and I was actually afraid that he might hurt me."

"That's a possibility," Lynne told her. "He wasn't exactly gentle with me when he stormed out of our apartment. I had bruises for weeks from where he grabbed me."

Hannah drew a deep breath. "In that case, I'm glad Mike decided to detail some bodyguards for me."

Sally looked puzzled. "But you're here alone tonight," she pointed out. "Where's your bodyguard?"

"Right here," the voice came from outside the booth.

Sally reached out to pull back the curtain. "Norman?"

"Hi, Sally." Norman turned to Lynne and Hannah. "I'm detailed to Hannah tonight. Do you mind if I sit down?"

"Not at all!" Lynne said quickly. "Please join us for dinner, Norman. It's good to see you again."

"It's good to see you, too, but I didn't mean to intrude. I just wanted Hannah to know that I'm here and I'll take her back to the condo."

"But I drove and I don't want to leave my cookie truck here."

"You won't have to. Lonnie and Michelle rode out here with me. They're going to have dinner and then they're going to drive your truck back to the condo. Lonnie's going to stay there with Michelle because Mike doesn't want to take any chances that Ross might show up there."

"That makes sense," Sally said. "From what Hannah's told us, Ross could be dangerous."

"That's what Mike thinks, too." Norman turned back to Lynne. "Thank you for the invitation, Lynne, but I'm going to join Michelle and Lonnie for dinner. I'll come back here to have dessert with you and Hannah if that's okay."

"That's just fine!" Lynne told him. "Sally's going to join us for dessert too, and she's got something new for us to try . . . right, Sally?"

"Right, and it's a surprise so I'm not going to tell you what it is."

Norman smiled and slid out of the booth. "I'll be thinking about your dessert all through my dinner, Sally. Can you give us just a little hint about what it is?"

"It's a cake," Sally said, also sliding out of the booth. "And it was inspired by Hannah's Bundt cakes. Wait for me, Norman. I'll walk you to Lonnie and Michelle's table." She turned back to Lynne and Hannah. "Bye, girls. I'd better leave now because you'll be hungry soon and I want you to try my new appetizers."

"I love your appetizers!" Hannah said quickly. "What are they tonight, Sally?"

"Rusty's Cheese and Garlic Stuffed Mushrooms. Rusty was one of Dick's friends in college, and he used to make these every time they watched football on television."

"I love stuffed mushrooms!" Lynne said, taking another sip of her lemonade. "How long do we have to wait, Sally?"

"No more than fifteen minutes. And in the meantime, I'll have Dot bring you tonight's menu. We have quite a few specials. Would you two like wine with dinner?"

"I would," Lynne said.

Hannah smiled. "So would I. I don't have to worry about drinking, now that I'm going to be riding with Norman."

"And I don't have to worry about drinking because all I have to do is take the elevator upstairs," Lynne added.

Sally gave a little wave. "I'll be back with your appetizers."

Once Sally and Norman had left and the curtains were back in place, Hannah turned to Lynne. "I'm sorry I didn't get to see Tom. He came with you, didn't he?"

"He did. But he's gone . . . again."

Uh-oh! Back off! Hannah's mind warned her. Lynne didn't sound happy about the fact that her husband wasn't with her tonight. But Lynne was her friend and this time around, Hannah ignored her mind's warning. "Is there something wrong, Lynne?"

Lynne nodded and a tear slipped down her cheek. And even though Lynne was an actress and Hannah knew that her friend could cry on demand, this tear was no act. "What's wrong? Can you tell me?"

"I . . . just a minute," Lynne said, pointing to the curtain, which was being pulled back by a feminine hand.

"Hi!" Dot, Sally's receptionist, head waitress, and dining room manager, stuck her head inside. "Are you two ready for menus?"

"Yes, we are," Lynne said, smiling the sunniest smile that Hannah had ever seen. Lynne was, indeed, an excellent actress, and Hannah felt almost as if she'd imagined that tear and the quaver of distress in Lynne's voice.

"Good to see you again, Mrs. Larchmont," Dot said, pushing the curtain back and stepping in. "We have several specials tonight and I'll let you read all about them. And please, if you have any questions, just ring for me and I'll be glad to answer them."

"Oh!" Hannah commented as Dot set a small intercom on the table. "That's new!"

"Yes, it is. Sally thought it would be convenient and she was right. Otherwise people in these booths have to wait until the busboy or the waitress comes by to ask questions about the food or request additional service. With this," Dot tapped the intercom, "you just press the red button and I'll answer."

"Very nice," Lynne agreed, "but do you find many people abuse the fact that they can contact you?"

Dot shook her head. "No, not at all. This is Lake Eden. People here are usually very polite and patient. They're not going to buzz me if they don't get a second bread basket right away, or if they want a refill on their iced tea."

"You're lucky," Lynne said with a laugh. "You couldn't use something like this in Los Angeles. People would call for you if they dropped their napkin and didn't feel like picking it up themselves."

Dot laughed. "I'm glad I don't work there. Our customers use the intercom mainly for questions about the items on the menu."

"Actually, I do have a question, and since you're here, I don't have to use the intercom," Lynne told her.

"Okay. What is it?"

"Which white wine would you recommend for us tonight?"

"That may depend on your entrée. What were you thinking of ordering?"

"Hannah?" Lynne asked, turning to her.

"I'll probably have the Cornish game hens. I love the way they do those out here."

"With apricot glaze? Or raspberry glaze?" Dot asked.

"Apricot, please."

"Then white wine would be all right for you tonight?" Lynne asked Hannah.

"Yes, I'd prefer it. The only time I really want red is when I have an entrée with beef."

Lynne smiled. "Good! I prefer white wine with any entrée." She turned to Dot. "Do you have a white wine that's a bit dry and fruity?"

Dot opened the wine list and pointed to a wine. "How about this? Dick says it's excellent with chicken or pork."

"We'll try it, then," Lynne decided. "Thank you, Dot."

When Dot had left and the privacy curtains were closed again, Hannah turned to Lynne. "Would you like to talk about what's happening with Tom?"

Lynne nodded and Hannah could tell that she was close to tearing up again. "It's just that we don't talk anymore. Tom doesn't seem to care what I think or how I feel. We used to be close, but now we're like strangers who barely know each other. He's always gone, Hannah. And his business is more important to him than I am. That's why I wanted to come here early. I was hoping we could work things out."

Hannah was silent, but she squeezed her friend's hand. Sometimes it was best to be silent and let the other person speak.

"Tom gets a phone call and he leaves. He already has a bag packed in the closet and he adds a couple of things and goes to the airport. He doesn't even ask me to take him there like I used to do. He just puts his car in long-term parking and gets on a plane. And sometimes . . ." Lynne stopped speaking and cleared her throat. "He doesn't even tell me where he's going. All he says is that he'll be back in a couple of days, but there have been times when it's a week or longer. He calls me every once in a while, but usually he can't talk long. I know it has something to do with his work, but I'm not entirely sure exactly where he is or what he's doing there."

Hannah sighed. "That must be very difficult for you, especially since you have your own career to think of. I knew that Tom was a successful businessman, but I don't think

I ever knew exactly what he did for a living."

"He's an investment counselor, but on a higher level than most investment counselors. Tom works with big corporations and he brings them investment opportunities. He knows everyone who's on the boards of corporations and he keeps his ears open for any rumors about mergers and takeovers and things like that. When he hears something he thinks is viable, he alerts his corporate clients that there may be an opportunity for them to invest."

"But he also does something with theater and movies, doesn't he?"

"Yes, and he's very good at that. Tom's corporate clients have made a bundle investing in Broadway plays, pilots for television, and independent films. He has a real knack for it. He doesn't get burned very often and every one of his corporate clients knows that. And that means they usually take a chance on anything Tom brings them."

"Here's your wine, ladies," Dot said as she opened the curtain and delivered the white wine that Lynne had chosen. "Shall I pour for you?"

"That would be nice," Lynne said with a smile.

Dot poured a small bit of wine in one

wineglass and handed it to Lynne. "Would you please taste this and see if it's to your liking?"

"Of course." Lynne took a sip and nodded. "That's lovely. Thanks for your recommendation, Dot. It'll be perfect with our entrées."

"And it'll be perfect with Rusty's Cheese and Garlic Stuffed Mushrooms," Sally said, appearing behind Dot and placing a platter on the table between Lynne and Hannah. "They're a little hot, so please let them cool a bit before you taste them."

"How long?" Hannah asked.

"Three minutes or so should do it." Sally smiled at Hannah. "Do you think it's possible for you to wait that long?"

"It'll be hard, but I can do it," Hannah declared, reaching out to touch one of the mushrooms and drawing her finger back quickly. "You're right, Sally. I'll wait."

"It's that or you won't taste anything else for the rest of the night." Sally reached for the wine bucket to fill Lynne's wineglass all the way and pour a glass for Hannah. "Just sip a little wine and keep on talking. It'll distract you."

"How can we be distracted when those mushrooms smell so wonderful?" Lynne asked her.

"I don't know, but I do know that it's a good thing I'm not that hungry," Sally replied. "If I hadn't had lunch earlier, I would have burned my mouth when I took them out of the oven."

Rusty's Cheese and Garlic Stuffed Mushrooms

Preheat oven to 350 degrees F., rack in the middle position.

8 ounces white mushrooms
1/4 cup Panko bread crumbs
1/4 cup grated Parmesan cheese
4 ounces Pepper Jack cheese
1 Tablespoon salted butter
1/2 teaspoon minced garlic
salt, fresh ground pepper, and smoked paprika ***(to taste)***

Prepare a standard-size cookie sheet by spraying it with Pam or another nonstick cooking spray.

Clean the mushrooms with a soft brush or damp paper towel.

Remove and discard the mushroom stems.

Mix the Panko bread crumbs and the grated Parmesan cheese in a medium-size bowl and set it aside on the counter.

Dice the Pepper Jack cheese into 1-inch squares and set them aside in another bowl.

Melt the salted butter in a 9-inch or larger saucepan on the stovetop over MEDIUM heat.

Add the garlic.

Stir everything together and cook until the contents turn a light golden brown. This will take about 2 minutes.

Add the cleaned mushroom caps on top of the garlic and butter with the cavity facing up.

Cook the mushrooms for 2 minutes.

Turn the mushrooms over and sprinkle them with salt and freshly ground black pepper.

Cook the mushrooms for 1 minute.

Remove the mushrooms from the pan while still firm and slightly browned, and place them on your prepared cookie sheet with the cavity facing up.

Insert the Pepper Jack cheese squares into the cavity of each mushroom.

Lift one mushroom at a time with tongs, dip into the Panko mixture, and return them to the cookie sheet with the Pepper Jack center facing upward.

Use a Tablespoon to generously top each mushroom with the remaining Panko and Parmesan mixture, covering the Pepper Jack center. Finish with a sprinkle of smoked paprika.

Place the cookie sheet in the preheated oven.

Bake for 8 to 9 minutes.

Remove the cookie sheet from the oven and let stand on a cold stovetop burner or a wire rack on the counter for several minutes before serving.

Rusty's Note: You can prepare these mushrooms for baking in advance. Simply stop before baking the mushrooms, cover the cookie sheet with plastic wrap, and leave it out on the kitchen counter. Then preheat your oven when your company comes and bake them. If you do this, it will be 15 minutes before you can serve them to

your guests.

Rusty's 2nd Note: As an alternative to Pepper Jack cheese, use your favorite cheeses to stuff the mushrooms. I have tried goat cheese, Dilled Havarti, Smoked Gouda, Cambozola, and Brie with rave reviews.

Hannah's Note: These appetizers are simply yummy. When I tried them, both Norman and Mike raved about them. Michelle and I decided that we're going to double the recipe, get two plastic-covered cookie sheets to get them ready to go in the oven, and take them over to Mother and Doc's penthouse so that the whole family can taste them.

Yield: Enough delicious appetizers to serve 6 people.

CHAPTER NINE

"I'm really sorry that things aren't good with Tom," Hannah said, once Sally and Dot had left. "I can understand why you came here early to try to work things out."

"It didn't exactly turn out the way I planned, though. We can't work on our marriage if Tom is nowhere around."

"That's true. Have you thought about what you'll do if it doesn't work out with Tom?"

Lynne gave a little shrug that was intended to be casual, but Hannah had known Lynne all through college and she could tell that her friend was deeply upset.

"I guess if things don't get better, I'll have to . . ." Lynne stopped speaking and blinked away a tear. "I'll have to give Tom the divorce he wants."

"He's asked you for a divorce?" Hannah tried not to look as surprised as she felt. She hadn't realized that things between

Lynne and Tom were this bad.

"Yes. That was the last thing he said to me before he left this morning. Maybe Tom's right and we should divorce. I just don't know. The only thing I know for sure is that we can't go on this way."

"I'm really sorry, Lynne." Hannah reached out to pat Lynne's hand.

"So am I. It was so good at the beginning. Then we were always together. But now I don't see Tom for weeks at a time. He says it's business, but . . ." Lynne stopped speaking and an expression of fear and pain crossed her face. "I'm not sure that's it."

"Do you think it could be . . ." Hannah paused, wondering how to phrase her question, but she knew that even if she found the perfect words, it wouldn't be easy for Lynne to hear. "Do you think it could be another woman?"

"I don't think so," Lynne replied immediately. "I really don't, Hannah. It's something else, and he won't tell me what."

"Do you think it has anything to do with his business?"

"He told me it doesn't." Lynne drew a deep breath. "The logical conclusion is that Tom found another woman that he cares for more than he cares for me. But . . . I don't think that's it, either."

"Maybe you'll learn more when he comes back," Hannah suggested, hoping that it would be true. "Just hang in there, Lynne, and I'm here if you need me. You don't have to go through this alone. And even if you and Tom divorce, you can always come back here to Lake Eden. Everyone here really likes you."

"Thanks. That means a lot to me, Hannah. Maybe it's time for me to do something different and stop being subsidized by Tom. L.A. is brutal, Hannah. There are a ton of good actresses, and it's depressing to go on hundreds of auditions without getting a good part. I've done a few commercials, but holding a bottle of household cleaner and convincing people that it's better than any other product isn't what I want to do with my life."

"What do you want to do with your life?" Hannah asked her.

"I'm not sure, but I don't have to be an actress. I have fallback positions and I can always earn my own living in another way." Lynne reached for one of the stuffed mushrooms. "Have one, Hannah."

It was clear that Lynne didn't want to talk about her problems any longer and Hannah reached for a mushroom. She popped it into her mouth, chewed, swallowed, and smiled.

"They're really good!"

"They're excellent," Lynne agreed, taking a sip of wine.

"I remember a question that Michelle asked me once," Hannah said as an old memory surfaced. "It was right after I came home from college and decided not to go back. Michelle and I were talking and she said, *If you could do anything you wanted to do, what would it be?* And I told her that I'd like to open a bakery and coffee shop and call it The Cookie Jar."

Lynne looked interested. "How old was Michelle when she asked you that?"

"I think she was sixteen. I know that she was a junior in high school."

"That's a great question."

"I know. If you could do anything you wanted to do, what would it be, Lynne?"

"I'm not completely sure, but I think I might like to teach acting. I finished my degree in theater arts and I do have a teaching certificate, but I'd rather give private lessons to both adults and students. I wonder if there's a market for something like that in Lake Eden."

Hannah began to smile. "There is!" she said quickly. "Mayor Bascomb's sister was giving private acting lessons in her condo."

"Was?" Lynne picked up on the tense that

Hannah had used. "Did she get another position?"

"Not exactly." Hannah gave a little sigh. "She was murdered."

"Good heavens!" Lynne gave a little shudder. "I hope they caught whoever did it."

"Yes," Hannah answered, not mentioning that she had been the one to catch Tori Bascomb's killer.

Just then Dot pushed aside the privacy curtain and delivered their entrées. "I see you liked the stuffed mushrooms," she said, handing the empty plate to her busboy.

"They were delicious," Lynne said as Dot delivered her entrée. Hannah's entrée was next and once she had refilled their wineglasses, Dot told them to enjoy their dinner and left.

Hannah was amazed to discover that she was ravenous and Sally's Cornish game hen was every bit as good as it always was. She especially liked the apricot glaze, but she vowed that the next time she ordered it, she'd try the raspberry glaze.

Lynne seemed to enjoy her entrée too, and Hannah was pleased to see that their discussion about Tom and about Lynne's future plans hadn't affected her friend's appetite. Hannah hoped for the best with Lynne's marriage, but if push came to shove, she hoped that Lynne would move to Lake Eden, where everyone liked her and she could have a fresh start.

Once they'd finished their entrées, Dot cleared their table and delivered after-dinner coffee for them. The two friends sat there talking for a moment and then they heard a summons from outside the booth.

"Knock, knock," a female voice called out, and Sally pushed back the privacy curtain. "Am I interrupting?"

"Not at all," Lynne assured her. "Hannah and I were just talking about Lake Eden. Come in and join us, Sally."

"Me too?" another, deeper voice inquired.

"You too, Norman." Hannah motioned for him to come in and patted the booth beside her.

"Dot's bringing more fresh coffee and our dessert," Sally told them, and then she turned to Lynne. "If Tom is coming back tonight I'll cut a slice of cake for him and you can take it back to the room."

Lynne shook her head. "Thanks, Sally, but I don't expect him. He hasn't called and that usually means he's tied up with business. I think he'll probably decide to stay in Minneapolis overnight."

"Then I'll put a slice in the cooler for him and he can have it tomorrow," Sally decided.

"I wonder where Dot's busboy is with . . ." She stopped and began to smile as the curtain was pulled aside and the busboy came in with a large carafe of coffee, cups, cream and sugar, silverware, and dessert plates.

"Oh, my!" Hannah gasped as Dot arrived with a beautiful cake on a silver platter. "Is that chocolate?"

"Yes," Sally answered. "It's chocolate *and* butterscotch. This is my Ultimate Chocolate Butterscotch Bundt Cake. I got the idea from you, Hannah. I combined my two favorite ultimate cake flavors, the Ultimate Fudgy Chocolate Bundt Cake and the Ultimate Butterscotch Bundt Cake and made them all in one." Sally stopped and looked slightly worried. "I hope you don't mind, Hannah."

"I don't mind at all!" Hannah reassured her. "It looks lovely, Sally. I love how you frosted it with butterscotch icing and drizzled chocolate down from the top."

"That's so my waiters will know exactly what kind of cake it is by simply looking at the frosting. If I'd just used the butterscotch frosting, they might have thought that it was Ultimate Butterscotch Bundt Cake and not Ultimate Chocolate Butterscotch Bundt Cake. This way they can tell the difference between them."

"Makes sense," Norman commented. "It looks absolutely delicious, Sally."

"Hannah's recipes are always delicious," Sally told Lynne as she reached out for the carafe of coffee and poured cups for Norman and herself. Then she topped off Hannah and Lynne's cups and picked up the knife to cut the cake.

"There's something wonderful about a cake in a Bundt pan," Hannah said.

"It's a great design and it makes any cake look special," Lynne agreed.

Hannah began to smile. "Sometimes Andrea uses a Bundt pan for one of her Jell-O molds. She says it's a little harder to get out because the pan is thicker and doesn't warm up as fast as a regular Jell-O mold, but whenever she goes out to a potluck dinner, she puts the Bundt pan in the back of her car with a platter over the top. By the time she drives to wherever she's going, the Jell-O has jiggled its way loose and it's ready to unmold."

Sally laughed. "Andrea's nothing if not resourceful. Most Minnesotans are. One time I made a big platter of Jell-O in a turkey roaster."

"How did that turn out?" Norman asked her.

"It was harder to unmold, but once it was on the platter, it looked great. I used it at one of my Sunday brunches right here in the dining room, and Betty Jackson told me she'd never seen so much Jell-O in one place before."

Sally passed the cream and the sugar, and then she pulled the cake platter toward her. "Let's taste this cake and then you can tell me if you think it should go on the dessert menu."

Hannah watched as Sally sliced the cake and plated it. She thought again of the Minnesota man who'd invented the Bundt pan. Hannah wondered whether his wife had been insulted because he'd told everyone that he'd devised the ridged cake pan because her cake slices were different sizes.

"Ready?" Sally asked after she'd passed them the dessert plates.

"Ready," Hannah said as they all picked up their dessert forks.

For the space of several seconds, no one said a word. They were too busy tasting, swallowing, and cutting off a second bite. It took several more seconds before Lynne put her fork down on her plate and gave Sally a thumbs-up. "Wonderful!" she said, reaching for her coffee cup to take a sip. "It's delicious and it's really rich. And it's great with strong coffee."

"Agreed," Hannah echoed. "It's a wonderful cake and I'm glad we have a lot of coffee, Sally."

Sally nodded and gestured toward the intercom. "And we can always call Dot for more if we run out."

Once they'd finished their slices of Ultimate Chocolate Butterscotch Bundt Cake, Sally removed the silver lid from another dessert platter and uncovered Lisa's Pink Grapefruit Cake. "I hope you saved room for another taste trial."

"I did," Norman said quickly. "That's pretty, Sally. What is it?"

"It's Lois Brown's Pink Grapefruit Cake," Hannah told him. "Lisa mixed it up, Michelle baked it, and I brought it in for Sally to taste."

"I love pink grapefruit, but I don't think I've ever had grapefruit in a cake before," Lynne said.

"Neither have I," Norman agreed. "But if Lisa mixed it up and Michelle baked it, it's bound to be good."

"It's made from a recipe that Aunt Nancy got from her friend Lois Brown," Hannah said, picking up her fork and preparing to taste it.

"Lois Brown gave you the recipe for the

lemon cookies that you serve in The Cookie Jar, didn't she?" Norman asked Hannah.

"Yes, and they're a favorite with the morning crowd. We bake them every Tuesday."

Once everyone tasted Lisa's cake and agreed that it was wonderfully delicious, Hannah realized that her cell phone was ringing. She pulled it out of her purse and said, "This must be important. Not that many people have my cell phone number. Will you all excuse me while I answer it?"

Everyone nodded and Hannah slid out of the booth to step outside the privacy curtain. "Hello?" she said, grateful that she could get reception outside the booth.

"Hannah!"

The voice on the other end of the line was icy cold and Hannah gave a little shiver when she recognized who was calling. "Ross," she said, keeping her voice deliberately low so that no one else could hear.

"Just what are you trying to do to me!?"

Hannah felt herself tense. Ross must have found out that the bank was closed, and it was clear by his tone that he was furious with her.

"What do you mean?" she asked, hoping that he wasn't anywhere near the Lake Eden Inn.

"You knew the bank was closed, but you

tried to send me there anyway! Are you trying to set me up?"

"I . . . no, of course not," Hannah said quickly. "I had no idea that the bank was closed. This was the first day I got back to work after the blizzard and I didn't drive past it on my way to The Cookie Jar."

Ross gave a derisive laugh. "That's a lie! You're trying to get even with me, aren't you, Hannah!"

It was a comment, not a question, and Hannah gulped involuntarily. Ross sounded livid with anger. "No! Really, Ross! I had no idea the bank wasn't open."

Hannah stopped speaking and took a deep breath as she realized that Ross had put her on the defensive. It would be useless to try to convince him that she hadn't lied. And there was no way she owed him an apology for not knowing that the bank was closed. "So what are you going to do?" she asked him.

"Wouldn't you and your boyfriend cop like to know!?" Ross retorted. And then he called her a word that Hannah hoped her nieces would never hear.

You owe him nothing, the rational part of her mind reminded her. *Don't react. He's trying to get you off guard. Don't let him do that to you! Just try to get as much informa-*

tion about his whereabouts as you can so that you can tell Mike.

"Where are you?" Hannah asked, keeping her tone deliberately neutral in a manner that she hoped Ross would interpret as non-threatening.

"I'm very close. I know where you are and who's with you. I told you this morning, I would hurt you, Hannah."

Even though she tried her best to be calm, Hannah felt her knees begin to shake. This was not the man she had thought she'd married. This was a stranger, a cold, calculating stranger.

"You don't scare me, Ross," she said, even though she was beginning to feel terribly frightened. "Why are you calling? What do you want from me?"

"My money. I told you this morning, I need it. Look, Hannah . . ."

Hannah's eyes widened as she heard the change in his voice. Instead of a threatening thug, Ross was now sounding like a reasonable person.

"I'm sorry if I scared you, Cookie. I didn't really mean to. It's just that this is so important to me. I love you. You know that. I've loved you for years and all you have to do is get that money for me and we can be together again. Just do it, Cookie. Do it for me. Remember how good it was when we were together. It was great for me and I love you with all my heart. It was good for you too, wasn't it, honey?"

She had to say yes. She knew she had to. For the first time in her life, Hannah wished that she'd taken acting lessons. Somehow, through sheer force of will, she managed to choke out her assent.

Ross seemed to buy her assurances of love because he said, "That's my girl! You've always been my girl, and you know Doug really well. If you ask him, he'll open the bank for you and give you the cash. And then, once I pay my wife off, we can be happy together. You love me. You know you do. Just think about our honeymoon and how much fun we had. We'll do that again and it'll be even better this time."

Hannah felt slightly sick to her stomach. Ross was obviously crazy if he thought that he could win her over again by claiming he loved her. This wasn't the Ross she'd known in college. This wasn't the Ross she'd married. This was a dangerous stranger, and Hannah wasn't sure what she should do.

You're right, Hannah, her rational mind said. *Ross is crazy, but not about you! The only person he's crazy about is himself and the power he thinks he has over you. Don't be a fool! Pretend to go along with him and find out where he is so that you can tell Mike.*

Hannah gave a little nod, even though there was no one to see it. Mike had called Ross a loose cannon and he was right. Ross was definitely dangerous and he'd do anything, break any law, and even kill to get his money. The wisest course she could take was to think of a way to trick him into telling her where he was so that Mike and his deputies could take him into custody before he hurt her or anyone else in Lake Eden who got in the way of his plans.

"I remember how it was when we were together," she said, forcing out the words and hoping that she sounded sincere. "But do you really love me, Ross?"

"Of course I do!"

The answer came immediately and Hannah took heart. Ross really believed that she had fallen for his assurances of love.

"Where are you, Ross?" she asked again, trying to put honey in her voice instead of vinegar. "It's been a long time. I want to see you."

There was a pause and Hannah knew he wasn't entirely convinced by the sweetness in her tone. Had she laid it on too thick?

"I want to see you, too, Cookie, but it's too dangerous for me to come to Lake

Eden. Mike warned me that he couldn't guarantee my safety."

"I know, but . . ." Hannah paused, thinking fast. "Maybe you could come to our condo. No one would expect you to come there."

There was silence on the other end of the line and Hannah's hopes rose. Would Ross take her bait?

"No," he said at last. "I want to see you too, but I can't take that chance. Just get me the money, Hannah. Call Doug and meet him at the bank tomorrow. He's a friend of yours. He'll give it to you. Tell him you need it for something important. Convince him that it's a matter of life and death. You can convince him and even if you don't, it doesn't matter. You're entitled to take a withdrawal of any amount you wish and he's got to give it to you. I don't care what you say, Hannah. Just get me that money!"

"But what if Doug doesn't want to give me the money?"

"Make him do it. If you really want to be with me again, you'll get it. It's just too bad you opened your big mouth and told everyone that we weren't really married. You have to make up for that by getting me the money."

There was a click and the line went dead.

A moment later, Hannah heard a dial tone. Ross had hung up on her. She took a deep breath, did her best to calm down, and pulled back the curtain to re-enter the booth.

Norman took one look at her, jumped to his feet, and pushed her down to sit in the booth. Then he pushed aside the dessert plates.

"Put your head down, Hannah," he told her. "You look like you're about to faint."

"I'm . . . okay," Hannah said, but she knew she wasn't. There was a high-pitched ringing in her ears, and her peripheral vision was fading into shimmering dots of light. She lowered her head, swallowed again, and did her best to breathe normally. Her heart was pounding so loudly, she could hear it in her ears and it took long moments before she relaxed enough to bring it back to a normal rate.

Everyone in the booth was quiet, and Hannah knew that they were waiting for an explanation. When she felt calm enough to speak, she raised her head and faced them. "It was Ross," she said.

Ultimate Chocolate Butterscotch Bundt Cake

Preheat oven to 350 degrees F., rack in the middle position.

4 large eggs
1/2 cup vegetable oil
1/2 cup chocolate liqueur ***(I used Ghirardelli Chocolate Liqueur)***
8-ounce ***(by weight)*** tub of sour cream ***(I used Knudson)***
box of chocolate cake mix, the kind that makes a 9-inch by 13-inch cake or a 2-layer cake ***(I used Betty Crocker Triple Chocolate Fudge Cake Mix)***
5.9-ounce package of DRY instant chocolate pudding and pie filling ***(I used Jell-O)***
12-ounce ***(by weight)*** bag of butterscotch baking chips ***(11-ounce package will do, too — I used Nestlé)***

Prepare your cake pan. You'll need a Bundt pan that has been sprayed with Pam or another nonstick cooking spray and then floured. To flour a pan, put some flour in the bottom, hold it over your kitchen wastebasket, and tap the pan to move the flour all over the inside of the pan. Continue this until all the inside surfaces of the pan, including the sides of the crater in the center, have been covered with a light coating of flour. Alternatively, you can coat the inside of the Bundt pan with Pam Baking Spray, which is a nonstick cooking spray with flour already in it.

Crack the eggs into the bowl of an electric mixer. Mix them up on LOW speed until they're a uniform color.

Pour in the half-cup of vegetable oil and mix it in with the eggs on LOW speed.

Add the half-cup of chocolate liqueur. Mix it in at LOW speed.

Scoop out the container of sour cream and add it to your mixer bowl. Mix it in on LOW speed.

When everything is well combined, open the box of dry cake mix and sprinkle it on top of the liquid ingredients in the bowl of the mixer. Mix that in on LOW speed.

Open the package of instant chocolate pudding and sprinkle in the contents. Mix it in on LOW speed.

Shut off the mixer, scrape down the sides of the bowl, remove it from the mixer, and set it on the counter.

If you have a food processor, put in the steel blade and pour in the butterscotch baking chips. Process in an on-and-off motion to chop them in smaller pieces. ***(You can also do this with a knife on a cutting board if you don't have a food processor.)***

Sprinkle the butterscotch baking chips in your bowl and stir them in by hand with a rubber spatula.

Hannah's 1st Note: If you don't want to use chocolate liqueur in this recipe, use whole milk or water with a little chocolate sauce mixed in for flavoring.

Hannah's 2nd Note: The reason the butterscotch chips in this recipe are chopped in smaller pieces is that regular-size chips are larger and heavier, and they tend to sink down to the bottom of your Bundt pan.

Use the rubber spatula to transfer the cake batter to the prepared Bundt pan.

Smooth the top of your cake with the spatula and put it into the center of your preheated oven.

Bake your Ultimate Chocolate Butterscotch Bundt Cake at 350 degrees F. for 55 minutes.

Before you take your cake out of the oven, test it for doneness by inserting a cake tester, thin wooden skewer, or long toothpick. Insert it midway between outside edges of the pan and the metal protrusion that makes the crater in the center of the pan.

If the tester comes out clean, your cake is done. If there is still unbaked batter clinging to the tester, shut the oven door and bake your cake for 5 minutes longer.

When your cake tests done, take it out of the oven and set it on a cold stove burner or a wire rack. Let it cool in the pan for 20 minutes and then pull the sides of the cake away from the pan with the tips of your impeccably clean fingers. Don't forget to do the same for the sides of the crater in the middle.

Tip the Bundt pan upside down on a platter and drop it gently on a folded towel on the kitchen counter. Do this until the cake falls out of the pan and rests on the platter.

Cover your Ultimate Chocolate Butterscotch Bundt Cake loosely with foil and refrigerate it for at least 1 hour. Overnight is even better.

Frost your cake with Cool Whip Butterscotch Frosting. ***(Recipe and instructions follow.)***

Yield: At least 10 pieces of fudgy butterscotch cake. Serve with tall glasses of ice cold milk or cups of strong coffee.

Cool Whip Butterscotch Frosting

This recipe is made in the microwave.

1 heaping cup ***(6 to 7 ounces by weight)*** of butterscotch baking chips ***(I used Nestlé)***
8-ounce ***(by weight)*** tub of FROZEN Cool Whip ***(Do not thaw! Leave in the freezer.)***

Hannah's 1st Note: Make sure you use the original Cool Whip, not the sugar free or the real whipped cream.

Start by chopping your butterscotch chips into smaller pieces or placing the chips in a food processor with the steel blade and processing in an on-and-off motion to chop the chips into smaller pieces.

Get the Cool Whip out of your freezer and measure out 1 cup. Place it in a microwave-safe bowl. ***(I used a quart Pyrex measuring cup.)***

Add the butterscotch baking chips to the bowl.

Microwave the bowl on HIGH for 1 minute and then let it sit in the microwave for an additional minute.

Take the bowl out of the microwave, then stir to see if the chips are melted. If they're not, heat them in 30-second intervals with 30-second standing times on HIGH in the microwave until you succeed in melting the chips and stirring the mixture smooth.

Put the microwave-safe bowl on a towel on your kitchen counter.

Let the bowl sit on the countertop for 15 minutes to thicken the icing.

When the time is up, give the bowl a stir and remove your cake from the refrigerator. Frost your Ultimate Chocolate Butterscotch Bundt Cake with the frosting and don't forget the sides of the crater in the middle. You don't need to frost all the way down to the bottom of the crater. That's almost impossible. Just frost an inch or so down the sides of the crater.

Hannah's 2nd Note: You can decorate the top of your cake with chocolate drizzle. The recipe follows.

Return your cake to the refrigerator for at

least 30 minutes before cutting it and serving it to your guests.

Chocolate Drizzle

1 cup semi-sweet chocolate chips ***(half of a 12-ounce bag)***
1 Tablespoon salted butter ***(1/8 stick, half of an ounce)***
1 teaspoon vanilla extract

Hannah's Note: The easy way to measure a half-ounce of salted butter is to divide a stick of butter into 8 pieces and use only one piece. Put the rest back in your refrigerator.

Place the chocolate chips in a microwave-safe bowl. ***(I used a 2-cup Pyrex measuring cup with a pour spout.)***

Add the half-ounce of salted butter on top of the chocolate chips.

Add the vanilla extract on top of the butter.

Heat the contents for 1 minute on HIGH in the microwave.

Let the bowl or cup sit in the microwave for an additional minute.

Remove the bowl from the microwave and

attempt to stir the contents smooth with a heat-resistant spatula.

If you cannot stir the contents smooth, heat the mixture for an additional minute on HIGH in the microwave.

Let the bowl sit in the microwave for another minute.

Take out the bowl and again, try to stir the contents smooth.

Repeat the above steps as many times as it takes to achieve a smooth mixture of chocolate chips, salted butter, and vanilla extract.

When the mixture is smooth, take the Ultimate Chocolate Butterscotch Bundt Cake out of the refrigerator and drizzle the liquid chocolate mixture over the top and down the sides of the cake.

Don't forget to drizzle a bit of the chocolate mixture down the sides of the crater in the center of your cake.

Return the cake to the refrigerator for an additional 30 minutes and then serve it to your guests.

PINK GRAPEFRUIT CAKE

(THIS RECIPE IS FROM LOIS BROWN.)

Preheat oven to 325 degrees F., rack in the middle position.

1/2 cup ***(1 stick, 1/4 pound, 4 ounces)*** salted butter, softened to room temperature

2 cups white ***(granulated)*** sugar

8 ounces light cream cheese ***(Neufchâtel)*** softened to room temperature

3 large eggs

1/2 cup vegetable oil

1/2 cup whole milk

1 Tablespoon grated pink grapefruit ***zest (just use the colored part)***

1 teaspoon vanilla extract

1 teaspoon baking powder

1 teaspoon salt

2 cups all-purpose flour ***(pack it down in the cup when you measure it)***

Hannah's 1st Note: You will be using pink grapefruit zest in the cake recipe and pink grapefruit juice in the glaze recipe. Zest the pink grapefruit first and juice it later, when it's time to make the glaze.

Prepare a Bundt cake pan by spraying it with Pam, or another nonstick cooking spray, and then coating the insides with flour. To do this, sprinkle some flour in the bottom of the Bundt pan, stand over your kitchen wastebasket, and turn the cake pan so that the flour touches the sides and coats them. Don't forget to coat the outside of the crater in the middle of the pan. When you're through preparing your pan, hold it upside down over the wastebasket and shake out the excess flour.

Place the softened butter in the bowl of an electric mixer.

Add the white sugar and the softened cream cheese. Beat everything together until the mixture is light and fluffy.

Mix in the eggs. Beat until they are thoroughly incorporated.

Drizzle in the vegetable oil and continue to beat until the oil has been incorporated.

Add the milk and the pink grapefruit zest. Mix them in thoroughly.

Mix in the vanilla extract, the baking

powder, and the salt. Mix well.

Add the flour in half-cup increments, beating after each addition. The object is to create a smooth, well-mixed cake batter.

Pour the cake batter into the prepared Bundt pan.

Bake at 325 degrees F. for 45 minutes or until the top surface of the cake does not indent when touched with a finger. Be very careful not to overbake this cake.

Let your Pink Grapefruit Cake cool for 15 minutes before taking it out of the pan. To do this, place a platter on top of the Bundt pan and turn the platter and the pan upside down on your kitchen counter. When the cake has cooled enough, it will fall out of the Bundt pan and onto the platter.

When the cake is completely cool, glaze it with Pink Grapefruit Glaze. ***The recipe follows.***

PINK GRAPEFRUIT GLAZE

4 Tablespoons pink grapefruit juice
2 cups powdered ***(confectioners')*** sugar

Using an electric mixer, combine the pink grapefruit juice with the powdered sugar.

Hannah's Note: You can experiment with the amount of juice and the amount of sugar. This glaze is very forgiving. If it's too thick to pour over your cake, add more pink grapefruit juice. If it's too thin to coat the cake when you pour it on the cake, add more powdered sugar and give it a second coat.

Lois's Note: The more glaze, the better!

Chapter Ten

"Okay, Hannah. Try these." Lisa walked over to the work station and set a platter down on the stainless-steel surface. "I baked them last night and I need to know if you want to sell them for Valentine's Day."

"They look great, Lisa," Norman said, reaching for one. "I like the pink frosting."

"It had to be either pink or red," Lisa told him. "And red is a lot harder to do with liquid food coloring. It only takes a few drops of red to make pink if you're adding it to something that's naturally white."

"White chocolate?" Norman guessed, taking one and pushing the platter toward Hannah.

"Yes," Lisa said, and then she turned to Hannah. "Are you still nervous about Ross?"

"I guess so. I just know that I'm not at all hungry and I feel a little queasy. I hope I'm not getting sick."

"It could be anxiety," Lonnie suggested, reaching out to snag a brownie. "What do you call these, Lisa?"

"White Chocolate Brownies."

Hannah knew that Lisa was disappointed when she hadn't reached out for a brownie right away. She didn't want one, far from it, but there was no way she'd disappoint her partner. "Maybe I'm just hungry," she suggested, grabbing a brownie from the platter. "All I had for breakfast this morning was coffee and these look really great, Lisa."

"Thanks!" Lisa was all smiles, and Hannah was glad that she'd made the effort. Now all she had to do was eat the brownie and declare how good it was. She had no doubt that it was wonderful. It looked absolutely delicious. The only problem was that her stomach was roiling and she was having all she could do not to look as sick as she felt.

It's probably just stress, Hannah told herself, but she didn't believe it. The reason her stomach was acting up wasn't important. The important thing was to convince Lisa that she loved her White Chocolate Brownies.

"I love the color of the frosting," Hannah said, staring down at the brownie. *Good for you!* Her rational mind said. *Don't let Lisa know that you're still feeling sick to your stomach.*

"It smells wonderful, and the texture looks perfect," Hannah went on, not listening to her mind's running comments. *Atta girl!* her rational mind complimented her.

Oh, yeah? her suspicious mind argued. *If Lisa's White Chocolate Brownie is that perfect, why don't you take a bite? If you don't, Lisa will know you're just paying her compliments to keep from tasting her brownie.*

Hannah forced herself to open her mouth and take a big bite. She chewed, swallowed, and took a sip of coffee. "Delicious," she declared. "They'll be perfect for Valentine catering, Lisa."

"Oh, good! I was hoping you'd like them," Lisa said with a big smile. "Thanks, Hannah."

"They're going to be a huge hit with our customers. As a matter of fact, I think I'll take another and run next door to give it to Mother. She adores white chocolate."

That said, Hannah rose from her chair, grabbed a brownie, wrapped it in a napkin, and hurried out the door, totally ignoring Lisa's warning about taking her parka. As she hurried across the parking lot to the back door of Granny's Attic, her mother's antique shop, Hannah began to feel slightly better. The cold air was having a bracing effect and her stomach was no longer roiling. Perhaps she'd overdone it on the coffee this morning and that was why she'd felt sick. Or perhaps skipping breakfast hadn't been a good idea and she'd just been hungry, after all.

Several hours later, Hannah stood outside the door to Lake Eden First Mercantile Bank and knocked loudly on the glass. She could see several workmen and the bank president, Doug Greerson, inside. Since one workman was holding a nail gun and the other was using a framing hammer, Hannah assumed that they were probably making too much noise to hear her knock. Since Doug was out in the main part of the bank and not in his office it probably explained why, that despite her repeated telephone calls, Doug hadn't answered the phone.

Hannah stood there, waiting. Although it was cold, the bank had a covered portico and she was out of the wind. This made it fairly comfortable. She didn't bother to knock until the workman with the nail gun put it down and turned to say something to Doug. Then she knocked again, as loudly as she could.

This time, Hannah got results. Doug

looked up, saw Hannah standing under the portico, and walked quickly to the door. He pointed to the sign and Hannah gave a nod. She knew that the bank was closed, but she still had to speak to Doug. She motioned toward him, mouthed the words *I need to talk to you,* and began to smile as Doug held up one finger and hurried back to the counter to pick up his key ring.

"Let's go in my office," Doug said after he'd unlocked the door and let her in. He relocked the front door behind Hannah and led her toward his office in the back.

"Thanks, Doug," Hannah said, following him through the corridor and into his private space.

"Coffee?" Doug asked her, gesturing toward the espresso machine that his wife had given him for Christmas several years ago.

"Thanks. That would be great," Hannah responded, even though her stomach still felt a bit unsettled.

"You drink cappuccino, don't you?"

"Yes. Thank you, Doug." Hannah waited until the coffee machine had finished brewing her coffee and then she reached out for the cup and took a sip. The chocolate that Doug had sprinkled on top of the cappuccino seemed to settle her stomach and Hannah began to feel much better.

"How can I help you, Hannah?" Doug asked, settling in his chair behind his desk with his own cup of coffee.

"I brought you some of Lisa's White Chocolate Brownies." Hannah set the small bakery box on top of Doug's desk and lifted the lid. "They have pink frosting because we're going to use them for Valentine's Day. Have one with your coffee, Doug."

"Thanks. I will." Doug took a brownie, bit into it, and made a sound of approval. "They're really good!" he said once he'd swallowed his first bite. "Now tell me why you needed to see me."

Hannah took another sip of her coffee and drew a deep breath. "Ross asked me to come in and . . ."

"You saw *Ross*?" Doug asked, interrupting her.

"Yes. Don't worry, Doug. Mike knows about it. Ross claimed he needed the money from the safe deposit box so he could ask his wife for a divorce and marry me again. Except, it's not really *again* since we weren't married in the first place."

"Oh, Hannah!" Doug looked thoroughly disgusted. "You didn't fall for that, did you?"

"Good heavens, no! And that's what I told

Ross. I said I wouldn't marry him if he was the last man left on earth!"

Doug nodded. "I'm glad to hear that, Hannah. I didn't think you could possibly be that much of a . . ." He stopped himself and looked slightly embarrassed. "Well . . . you know what I mean."

"I do. And you're right. I'm not that much of a fool. You've heard the old saying, *Fool me once, shame on you. Fool me twice, shame on me!*"

"I certainly have. My mother used to say that." Doug looked thoughtful. "So what do you want me to do, Hannah?"

"I don't know what you *can* do, Doug, since it *is* his money. I just came to you for advice. Ross threatened me when I said I'd put all the money he'd given me back in his checking account and he'd have to go to the bank himself to withdraw it."

"How much money did Ross want to withdraw?"

"A hundred thousand dollars, exactly what was in his safe deposit box."

"The bank won't be open until Monday, Hannah."

"I know that, but Ross wanted me to contact you personally and get the money for him."

"No."

"What?"

"No. Even if I wanted to, and I don't, I couldn't give you that money, Hannah."

"Why not? I put it back in his account."

"I know you did. I helped you make the deposit. But it's not in Ross's checking account any longer."

Hannah was confused. "But . . . it *was* there a week ago! What happened to it?"

"We're a small bank, Hannah. We don't keep that much money on hand in our safe. It's a matter of bank security. If someone wants to withdraw a large sum in cash like Ross does, we have to request the funds and wait for the cash to be delivered by armored truck."

Hannah thought about that for a moment. "I guess that makes sense. So the money is there, but . . . it's not physically here?"

"That's right. We don't take any chances with sums that large. What if someone robbed our bank and broke into our safe? Or there was some kind of natural disaster that destroyed our safe and its contents? If that happened, the physical cash could be lost. It's a lot safer at the central depository. That's a much more secure location."

"Yes, I suppose it is." Hannah was silent for a moment, and then she thought of another question. "How about the money that Ross put into my checking account? I transferred that to Ross's checking account, too. It was seventy thousand dollars. Is that still here?"

"No, we keep enough cash here for normal banking business, but not for withdrawals of large amounts in cash. Does Ross know he can't get his hands on that cash immediately?"

"No. I explained about transferring the money to his checking account, but I didn't realize that the money wasn't here and he'd have to wait for you to get the cash. He was really angry when he found out that the bank wouldn't be open until Monday."

"No doubt." Doug sighed. "Is Ross coming in on Monday to try to withdraw that money?"

"I don't think so. He expects me to do it for him. Mike warned him not to show his face around Lake Eden because people here were really upset about the way Ross treated me. Mike told Ross that if he came back to Lake Eden, he couldn't guarantee his safety."

"But Ross came back anyway."

"Yes, but he came back so early that none of the other businesses were open and most people were still sleeping. He told me he needed the money. That's when I told him that I'd put all that money in his account. And that's when he accused me of trying to get him killed!"

"Did Ross say that his wife was going to kill him if he didn't produce the money?"

Hannah shook her head. "Not exactly. He didn't say who was going to kill him, just that *someone* was."

"Makes sense. I'd guess that Ross is involved in something bigger than a troubled marriage."

"So what do you think I should do?" Hannah clasped her hands together tightly in her lap. She was beginning to feel very afraid and she didn't like that feeling at all!

"I think you'd better watch your back. And I think you'd better tell Mike exactly how you feel."

"I did that. And Mike decided that I needed bodyguards round the clock. Norman's sitting outside in his car right now, waiting for me to come back from talking to you."

"Good. Did Ross sound desperate when he asked you to come to see me and get the money?"

Hannah nodded. "Yes, he called me on my cell phone last night and I could hear it in his voice."

"What do you think he's going to say

when you tell him that I wouldn't give you the money and that he has to come in here to sign a withdrawal slip to request it?"

"I . . . I'm not sure, but I know he's not going to be happy!"

Doug closed his eyes and Hannah knew that he was deep in thought. When he opened them again, he had a slight smile on his face. "Do you mind if I go out to the sheriff's station to see Mike? I have an idea that might work."

"What is it?"

"Bait Ross with something that you don't think he'll go for."

Hannah was surprised at Doug's response. "But what would that be?"

"Suggest that he write a check to his wife. She can deposit it in her account and Lake Eden First Mercantile Bank will honor it immediately."

"Really?"

"Yes, I'll approve it myself."

"But . . . what if he says that he doesn't want to do that?"

"Then give him the alternative."

"What's the alternative?"

Instead of telling her, Doug posed another question. "It's clear to me that Ross is afraid of someone who might harm him, perhaps even kill him unless Ross gives him the money. Do you think that's the case?"

"Yes."

"Then we have to set a trap to get Ross. If the only way he's communicating with you is by phone calls, we'll never get the truth out of him. We'll have to set a trap to get him here in person so that Mike can question him."

"How can we do that?"

"When you suggest that he write a check to his wife and he gives you some sort of excuse for not doing that, tell him that you talked to me about withdrawing the money and that I was perfectly willing to do that."

"But . . . I don't have the money."

"True. Tell Ross that I'll get the money and give it to you, but I need his signature to withdraw an amount that large. Promise him that I'll fill out the withdrawal slip ahead of time and have it all ready for him. Then all he has to do is zip in here, sign it, and leave. Tell him I said I was sorry for the inconvenience, but that it's a banking regulation."

"Is it?" Hannah asked him.

"It will be."

Hannah took a moment to think about Doug's plan. "Do you think that Ross will agree to that?"

"Yes, if it's the only way he can get the

money. I'm almost sure that Ross would rather dash in here on Monday to sign a withdrawal slip, than risk telling whoever he owes that he can't pay his debt."

"You're probably right, Doug. If Mike agrees to your plan, it's certainly worth a try," Hannah decided, finishing her coffee and standing up. "Thanks a lot, Doug. I really appreciate your help. Will you call Mike and tell him what we're planning to do?"

"I'll do better than that. I'll go out to the sheriff's station and talk to Mike personally. If this works and Ross comes in to the bank, we'll figure out what's going on here. And then you can get back to leading a normal life."

White Chocolate Brownies

Preheat oven to 350 degrees F., rack in the middle position.

2 cups all-purpose flour ***(pack it down in the cup when you measure it)***
1/4 cup powdered sugar ***(No need to sift unless it's got big lumps.)***
1/2 teaspoon baking soda
1/2 teaspoon salt
1 cup white ***(granulated)*** sugar
1 cup brown sugar ***(pack it down in the cup when you measure it)***
3/4 cup salted butter ***(1 and 1/2 sticks, 6 ounces)***
6 ounces white baking chocolate squares ***(I used Baker's)***
1 and 1/2 teaspoons vanilla extract
3 large eggs, beaten ***(just whip them up in a glass with a fork)***
2 cups white chocolate chips or vanilla baking chips ***(an 11-ounce bag will do — I used Nestlé)***
1/2 cup finely chopped pecans ***(optional)***

Line a 9-inch by 13-inch cake pan with heavy-duty foil. Spray the foil with Pam or another nonstick cooking spray. Set it aside to wait for its yummy contents.

Place the flour, powdered sugar, baking soda, salt, white sugar, and brown sugar together in the bowl of an electric mixer. Mix on LOW speed until they are thoroughly combined.

Place the stick and a half of salted butter in a microwave-safe bowl. ***(I used a quart Pyrex measuring cup.)***

Break the white chocolate baking squares in pieces and place them on top of the butter.

Heat on HIGH in the microwave for 1 minute and then stir with a heat-resistant rubber spatula. ***(If you don't have one, you really need to buy one. They're not expensive and they're dishwasher safe. You'll use it a lot!)***

If the white chocolate squares are not melted, take the spatula out of the bowl and return the bowl to the microwave. Heat the butter and chocolate mixture for an additional minute.

Let the bowl sit in the microwave for 1 more minute and then take it out and stir it with the heat-resistant spatula again. If you can stir it smooth, let it sit on the counter to cool for at least 5 minutes. If you can't stir it smooth, heat it in increments of 30 seconds, letting it sit in the microwave for 1 minute after each increment, until you can stir it smooth.

Hannah's 1st Note: You can also do this on the stovetop over LOW heat, but make sure to stir it constantly so it won't scorch.

Stir the vanilla extract into the melted butter and white chocolate mixture. Let it continue to cool on the counter.

Add the eggs to your mixer bowl and beat together at MEDIUM speed until they are thoroughly incorporated.

Feel the bowl with the white chocolate and butter mixture. If it's so hot it might scramble the eggs by adding it now, wait a few minutes until it's cool enough to add.

Turn the mixer down to LOW speed and slowly pour the white chocolate, butter, and vanilla extract mixture into the mixer bowl. Mix this until it's combined, but do not over-beat.

Roughly chop the white chocolate chips into smaller pieces. ***(I used my food processor with the steel blade in an on-and-off motion.)***

Take the bowl out of the mixer and fold in the pieces of white chocolate chips by hand. ***(You can use the same heat-resistant spatula that you used earlier.)***

If you choose to use the pecans, stir them in now.

Scoop the batter into your prepared pan. It will be very thick. Use the same rubber spatula to scrape the bowl and get every wonderful bit of tasty batter into the cake pan.

Smooth the batter out with your impeccably clean hands and then press it down evenly with the back of a metal spatula. Make sure the batter gets into the corners of the pan.

Bake your White Chocolate Brownies in your preheated oven at 350 degrees F. for exactly 23 minutes. DO NOT OVERBAKE!

If you do, you'll end up with dry brownies.

When you take your brownies out of the oven, set them on a cold stove burner or a wire rack to cool.

When the White Chocolate Brownies are cool, frost them with White Chocolate Fudge Frosting. ***(Recipe follows.)***

WHITE CHOCOLATE FUDGE FROSTING

This recipe is made in the microwave.

2 Tablespoons ***(1 ounce, 1/4 stick)*** salted butter
2 cups white chocolate chips or vanilla baking chips ***(I used Nestlé)***
1 can ***(14 ounces)*** sweetened condensed milk ***(NOT evaporated milk — I used Eagle Brand)***

Place the butter in the bottom of a microwave-safe bowl. ***(I used a quart Pyrex measuring cup.)***

Place the white chocolate chips on top of the butter.

Pour in the 14-ounce can of sweetened condensed milk.

Heat on HIGH for 1 minute. Then remove from the microwave and stir with a heat-resistant rubber spatula.

Return the bowl to the microwave and heat for another minute.

Let the bowl sit in the microwave for 1

minute and then take it out ***(careful — it may be hot!)*** and set it on the counter. Attempt to stir it smooth with the heat-resistant spatula.

If you can stir the mixture smooth, you're done. If you can't stir it smooth, return the bowl to the microwave and heat on HIGH in 30-second intervals followed by 1 minute standing time, until you can stir it smooth.

To frost your White Chocolate Brownies, simply pour the frosting over the top of your brownies, using the heat-resistant rubber spatula to smooth the frosting into the corners.

Let the frosted brownies cool to room temperature until the frosting is "set". Then cover with a sheet of foil and store them in a cool place.

When you're ready to serve, cut the White Chocolate Brownies into brownie-size pieces. They are rich so serve them with icy cold glasses of milk or cups of strong coffee.

Lisa's Note: We always make these brownies and Double Fudge Brownies for Valentine's Day. We like to decorate

these with maraschino cherries cut in half lengthwise. We cut them BEFORE we make the frosting so that we're ready to push them into the frosting before it "sets".

Chapter Eleven

"Hannah!"

The call came at five o'clock, just as Hannah, Lisa, and Michelle were preparing to mix up the cookie dough for the following day. "Yes, Ross," she answered, motioning to Mike, who was sitting at the work station with them.

"Did you get the money?"

"No," Hannah answered quickly. "The bank doesn't carry that much cash on hand, but Doug said you could write a check to your wife so that she could deposit it and the bank would honor it immediately."

"I can't do that," Ross said, and his words were clipped. "I can't believe you could be that stupid, Hannah!" Ross gave a laugh that was both derisive and humorless. "Did you and Doug really believe that I'd fall for something like that?"

Hannah was so angry, she came very close to losing it and giving Ross a piece of her mind. How dare he call her stupid! She wasn't the stupid one. He was for thinking that she'd fall for his lies again.

And then Mike reached out to squeeze her shoulder and she gave a reluctant nod. She knew she had to go along with Doug and Mike's plan so she repeated one of her great-grandmother Elsa's favorite sayings to herself. *You'll catch more flies with honey than with vinegar.* It took a moment or two, but it worked and that was when she realized that she should react as if she were the injured party, the tearful wronged woman who was still in love with the man she'd thought was her husband, the woman who would do anything to have him back. "But . . . Ross," she did her best to sound upset, which wasn't difficult, and heartbroken, which was. Ross was a rat and she knew she was better off without him.

She took a deep breath and managed to put a little quaver in her voice when she continued. "You told me that you needed to give that money to your wife so that she would get a divorce. And then you said you loved me and when the divorce was final, you'd marry me all over again. Did you mean it, Ross? Or were you . . . lying to me?"

"Of course I meant it, Cookie. I'd never

lie to you. You have to believe that. But I can't write a check to my wife."

"Why not?" Hannah felt Mike's hand pat her back. He obviously approved of the effort she was making.

"Because she doesn't have a checking account. No, Cookie. You have to get that money somehow. Go see Doug again and tell him that it won't work for me to write a check and I need that money now."

He was beginning to sound desperate again and Hannah knew that she had to be careful. "I . . . I could do that, but it won't work. The bank doesn't keep that much cash on hand and Doug has to request the cash. Doug told me that the earliest it could be delivered by armored truck would be right before the bank opened on Monday."

There was a long silence while Hannah held her breath and then Ross sighed.

"All right. Just be there when the bank opens and you can get it for me."

"I'll be at The Cookie Jar on Monday morning," Hannah said quickly, "and I could do that, but there's another little problem."

"What's that?"

Ross sounded suspicious again and Hannah knew she needed to be very careful. "Doug can't release the cash to me unless you sign off on the withdrawal slip."

"Are you sure?"

"That's what he said. And he also said that it wouldn't take more than a minute or two because he'd have the slip all ready for you to sign. And once you sign off, you can call me to tell me to go to the bank. Then you can drive out to our condo, I can pick up the money, and we can meet there."

"Are you sure you can't convince Doug to give you the money without my signature?"

"Well . . . I can meet with him again, but I really don't think he'll go for it. He told me that it was a banking regulation and Doug's a real stickler for protocol like that."

"All right." Ross didn't sound happy and he sighed again. "We'll do it Doug's way."

"Oh, good!" Hannah hoped she sounded absolutely delighted. "Just call me Monday morning right after you go to the bank. Then I can get the money and meet you at our condo. You can meet me there, can't you, Ross?"

"Of course I can, darling. It'll give us a chance to be together again before I take the money to my wife. All I need is the key to that storage unit and the money. That's very, very important to me, Cookie. And remember . . . I love you even more than life itself."

Hannah was trying to decide what she could say to Ross's declaration of love when the line went dead. Ross had disconnected the call. She shut off her phone and turned to Mike. "Did you get it?" she asked, knowing that he'd planned to trace the call.

"Yes, but it won't do us any good. He was in transit."

"You mean on the road, driving?"

"Yes, he's miles away from Lake Eden now."

"Do you know which way he was going?"

Mike nodded. "South, toward Minneapolis. He was just passing through Anoka when he hung up."

Hannah gave a relieved sigh. "At least he's not coming here!"

"No, he's not . . . at least not now. We'd better plan out what to do about Monday morning, Hannah. I'm going home with you for the night, just in case he decides to come back here." Mike turned to Lonnie. "We'll both go home with Hannah. I wouldn't put it past Ross to come to her condo to stay there until Monday morning."

Hannah looked at Mike in surprise. "But why would Ross do that?"

Mike gave a little smile. "Number one, to intimidate you just in case you changed your mind. Number two, your condo complex is isolated." Mike ticked off the point on his fingers. "Number three, he's bound to have a different car by now, and none of the residents will recognize it parked in the visitor's lot. Number four, he could even have changed his appearance, bleached his hair, dressed in clothing he didn't normally wear, things like that. And number five, he might think that you got the money from Doug already and you're keeping it until Monday so that we can set a trap for him."

Hannah's eyes widened in shock and surprise. "But I thought I'd convinced Ross that I still loved him and I wanted to help him get the money so that I could marry him again!"

"Look, Hannah," Mike slipped an arm around her shoulders. "For you, that was an Academy Award performance. But don't forget that Ross knows you pretty well. And he knows that he hurt you deeply and you're not the type of woman to simply sit there and take it. He may suspect that you're trying to trap him. And if he does, he may come to the condo to confront you again and scare you into submission. There's no way we'll leave you alone tonight and take the chance that Ross might come there to hurt you."

Hannah began to feel anxious again. She'd

been so sure that she'd convinced Ross, but perhaps Mike was right to be cautious. "All right, Mike. You're probably wise not to take chances. But . . . what are you going to do if Ross does show up?"

"He's threatened to hurt you, but that's your word against his. It won't stand up in a court of law. And he doesn't have a history of physical abuse toward you, does he?"

"No! Never! That's why I have trouble believing that he'd actually do anything violent."

"We already asked his wife about that. She claims Russ never laid a hand on her all the time they were married."

"Russ?" Hannah asked, catching the name that Mike had used.

"Yes, Russell Burton. That's the name he used with her."

Hannah felt slightly faint. "That's the name he used on the storage locker in Minneapolis! The supervisor thought that the temporary secretary they used when they transferred over to their new computer system simply misread the name!"

Mike nodded. "Ross has probably used a couple of different names in different places."

Hannah closed her eyes and winced as another possibility occurred to her. "Ross used Russell Burton with her and Ross Barton with me and with Lynne. Do you think that he could have more than one wife?"

"It's possible." Mike gave a little shrug. "Criminals often change their names when they go to new locations. For all we know, Ross's real name could be John Jones, or something ordinary like that."

"But don't most people keep their initials? Ross had personalized velveteen lounge suits with the initials *RB* on them. He loved those outfits and he wore them all the time when he was home with me."

"There are a lot of names that begin with those initials, Hannah," Lonnie pointed out. "Ross could have been Robert Barnes, or Ralph Burns. Just look in a big-city phone book and you'll find a bunch of people with the initials *RB.*"

Hannah nodded. "You're probably right, Lonnie. It's just that . . . I've never encountered anyone who went by multiple names before."

"You might have encountered some without knowing it," Mike told her. "Most con men change their names when they travel from place to place. That makes it more difficult for the authorities to track them."

"Yes, I know about things like that, but I never thought that . . ." Hannah stopped and swallowed hard. "I hate to think I got taken in by someone like that. I thought that since I'd known Ross in college and he used the same name then, he was the man I knew from before!"

Mike looked thoughtful. "I think I'd better give Lynne Larchmont a call. I'd like to find out if Ross, or Russ, or whoever he really is ever threatened her."

"Lynne told me that she had bruises from the time he grabbed her," Hannah told him. "I had dinner with her last night."

Mike turned to Lonnie. "You stick with Michelle tonight. I don't want her going out to Hannah's condo alone. Stop at the Corner Tavern or Bertanelli's Pizza and use the department credit card to pick up takeout for dinner." He turned back to Hannah. "Call Lynne and ask her if she's free for dinner tonight. If she is, tell her that both of you have a dinner date tonight courtesy of the chief detective from the Winnetka County Sheriff's Department."

"It's really good to see you again, Mike." Lynne smiled across the table at Mike. "And, Hannah . . . two nights in a row! I'm blessed."

"I'm sorry I didn't get a chance to see your husband, Lynne," Mike told her. "I only met him briefly when you were in town for the movie, but he seemed like a really nice guy."

"He is," Lynne said. "I'm sorry he's gone on business, but something important came up and he had to take care of it."

Right, Hannah thought. *And it must have been more important than your marriage or he wouldn't have left just when you two were trying to work things out.*

"I'm sorry to bring up a subject that might be uncomfortable for you," Mike faced Lynne across the table, "but I really need to know more about your engagement to Ross when you were in college."

Lynne looked slightly surprised, but she nodded. "Okay. What do you want to know?"

"What name was he going by then?"

"Ross Barton. He said his father had shortened his last name. It used to be Bartonovitch, but he didn't think that was American enough."

Mike nodded. "That makes sense, and it was certainly easier to spell when Ross got into school and had to write it on his homework."

Lynne laughed. "That's what Ross told me. He said he was grateful that his father had changed it."

Mike pulled his notebook out of his shirt pocket. "I have just a couple of other questions if that's okay."

"It's okay. What would you like to know?"

"During your relationship with Ross, was he ever violent toward you personally?"

It took Lynne a minute to answer. "Yes, I told Hannah about it last night. It's the reason I called off our engagement. Ross was angry at me over something. Now I don't even remember what it was. And he hit me. Hard."

"How hard?"

"Hard enough to give me a black eye. And then he grabbed me and shook me so hard, I thought that one of my arms was broken."

Hannah could feel the room start to spin around her. Lynne had told her about her bruises the preceding night, but she'd had no idea that Ross had actually done *that*!

"What did you do when Ross attacked you?" Mike asked.

"I hit him with a pot I had on the stove and ran out of the apartment and down the stairs to the street. I was holding my arm and one of my friends saw me outside. She asked me what happened and I said I thought I'd broken my arm and I needed a ride to the hospital."

"And your arm was broken?" Mike asked her.

"No, they took X-rays and found my shoulder was dislocated. They popped it back into place and kept me overnight. They asked me if I wanted to press charges and I said I didn't."

"Why?" Mike asked her.

"Because I wasn't hurt that badly. The black eye would heal and they'd already fixed my dislocated shoulder. And I knew the bruises he'd given me when he grabbed me would fade."

"What happened after that?" Hannah asked, a question she hadn't asked the previous night.

"When I got back to the apartment the next day, Ross was gone, along with all of his things. He'd left a note saying that he was very sorry, but he thought it was best if we didn't see each other again."

Hannah took a deep, steadying breath. "But you did see him again."

"Yes, but it wasn't until years later when I was married to Tom. I didn't know anything about it, but several of Tom's clients had invested in one of Ross's independent films. It turned out to be *Crisis in Cherrywood.*"

"How did you get the lead in the film?" Mike asked.

"Ross called me. He apologized for fighting with me back in college and told me that he didn't blame me for calling off our engagement."

"But you didn't call it off, did you?" Hannah asked her.

"No, Ross did by leaving that note saying that he thought it would be best if we didn't see each other again."

"What else did he say?" Mike asked her.

"He asked me if it was possible for me to let bygones be bygones and audition for the lead in his film."

"And you said yes?" Hannah was amazed that Lynne would even have talked to Ross after what she'd been through.

"Not at first, but I told Tom and he urged me to try out for the film. He said it was important to his clients and it might be a real break for my acting career. He promised me that he'd go with me to Lake Eden and be with me the whole time. And he was."

"Did Tom know why you and Ross broke up?" Hannah asked.

"No, not really. I told him about my black eye, but I downplayed the rest. I said we'd called off our engagement because it just hadn't worked out."

"Hello," Sally said, coming up to their table. "Could I interest you in trying my newest white wine?"

Mike shook his head. "Sorry, Sally. I'm working tonight. Just coffee for me, please."

Sally turned to Hannah and Lynne. "How about it, girls?"

"As long as it's not a sweet wine, I'm game," Lynne answered.

"Me too," Hannah said. "What type of wine is it, Sally?"

"It's a Fumé Blanc made by the Mondavi Winery. And don't let the name put you off. It's true that they're known for their cheaper wines, but this one is top of the line. It has a hint of sweetness, but only a hint. And it's as smooth as one of my Chocolate Cream Pies."

"Chocolate Cream Pie?" Hannah was immediately interested. "I'll be delighted to try your new wine, but please tell me more about your pie. I've never seen that on the menu out here."

"That's because it's never been on the menu before," Sally told her. "I'm trying it out on my customers for the first time tonight. And I knew that just mentioning it would intrigue you, Hannah. Everyone knows you love chocolate."

"So do I," Lynne said quickly. "Chocolate is number one on my list of favorite things."

"Not me, can't stand it," Mike said, and

all three women turned to look at him in shock.

"I'm joking," he told them. "Don't look at me like I have three ears and two heads. I love chocolate and you know it, Sally. I order your chocolate soufflé every time I come out here."

"That's true. And the last time you ate it I think you must have licked out the inside of the soufflé dish. It was so clean, I thought twice about putting it in the dishwasher."

"Forget the entrée," Hannah told her. "I'll just pig out on dessert."

"Not a bad idea," Lynne echoed her sentiments.

Sally gave a little laugh. "It's okay, girls. I'll bring a whole Chocolate Cream Pie to your table right after you order your entrées. And I'll join you for the chocolate fest."

"Then you'd better bring two pies," Mike warned her. "Four chocolate lovers and only one pie doesn't compute."

"Done," Sally promised. "I hope you'll try my new soup tonight. It was Dick's idea and he named it Pub Soup."

"That sounds interesting," Hannah commented. "What's in Pub Soup, Sally?"

"It's a really easy recipe, just cheddar cheese, cream, garlic, and beer. But the flavors meld perfectly and it's delicious."

"And the beer is why it's called Pub Soup?" Lynne guessed.

"That's right."

Mike looked very disappointed. "I'd love to try it, but I'm afraid I've got to pass. I can't have any alcohol when I'm working."

"Not even a quarter cup of beer? I don't think there's even that much in a bowl of soup, Mike."

"Well . . . I guess that would be all right."

"Not only that, the soup is made on the stove in a large pot. If the surface area of the soup pot is large, some of the alcohol evaporates."

"How much?" Hannah asked. She'd often wondered about that when she used alcohol in baking.

"Twenty-two percent of the alcohol is gone in twenty minutes if the soup is heated to one hundred eighty degrees. According to the article I read, it all depends on the surface area of the pan and how long it's cooked or baked."

"You convinced me," Mike said, putting on his famous grin, the grin that was so sexy, it always made Hannah feel slightly out of breath. "And I'm sure you convinced the ladies, too, especially since Lynne is staying here and I'm driving Hannah home. All Hannah has to do tonight is eat your fantastic food, drink your special wine, and get some really good, peaceful sleep."

If only life were that simple, Hannah thought, gazing at Mike as he continued to talk to Lynne. *But life isn't simple. Life is horribly complicated, filled with sorrow and longing for what might have been. I do want Mike to find Ross and lock him up for the pain he caused me. I really do. Ross hurt me emotionally, and now I know that he could hurt me physically, too. But at the same time, I want him to love me again, to hold me in his arms and tell me how much he loves me, only me. And it just about kills me to realize that something I want so badly just isn't going to happen ever again.*

Pub Soup

You can use a Crock-Pot or make this soup on the stove.

3 cans ***(10.5-ounce each)*** condensed cheddar cheese soup ***(I used Campbell's)***
1 can of domestic beer
1/3 cup real bacon bits ***(make your own or buy them at the store — I used Hormel real bacon bits from the store)***
8-ounce package of shredded sharp cheddar cheese
1 teaspoon jarred fresh garlic ***(or 1 clove, peeled and crushed)***
1 teaspoon coarsely ground black pepper ***(or 1 teaspoon seasoned pepper — I used Lawry's Seasoned Pepper)***

3 Tablespoons sour cream to float on top of the soup bowls
3 Tablespoons real bacon bits to sprinkle on top of sour cream to garnish
1 Tablespoon finely chopped fresh parsley to sprinkle on the bacon bits to garnish

If you are using a slow cooker to make this soup, spray the inside of the crock with Pam or another nonstick cooking spray. If you are using a large saucepan and making the soup on the stovetop, there's no need to spray the inside.

Open the soup cans and empty them in the crock or the saucepan.

Hannah's 1st Note: Save one soup can to use as a measuring cup. Don't bother to wash it out because all it contained was the same soup that's already in your Crock-Pot or saucepan.

Open the can or bottle of beer and fill the empty soup can. Pour it into the crock or the saucepan.

Add the third-cup of bacon bits to the crock or the saucepan.

Add the shredded sharp cheddar cheese to the crock or the saucepan.

Add the teaspoon of jarred garlic.

Add the teaspoon of coarsely ground black pepper.

Stir or whisk the contents of the crock or the saucepan until all the ingredients are thoroughly combined and the cold soup is smooth.

Turn the slow cooker on LOW and walk away. Since you worked so hard, you can finish the can or bottle of beer if you like.

Heat the Pub Soup for approximately 2 hours in the Crock-Pot or until the soup is piping hot.

If you're using a saucepan for your soup, turn the burner on MEDIUM and heat your soup, stirring every minute or so. This will keep your Pub Soup from sticking to the bottom of the saucepan. Heat until the soup is piping hot.

Once your soup is the proper temperature, stir it again to check for thickness. It should be approximately as thick as cream of mushroom soup or potato soup.

If your soup is too thick, add a little heavy cream to thin it slightly. If your soup is too thin, add a little more shredded cheddar cheese and check for thickness again once the cheese has melted and you've stirred the crock or the saucepan again.

Ladle the Pub Soup into soup bowls or

large mugs, spoon a dollop of sour cream in the middle of the bowl, sprinkle the top of the sour cream with bacon bits, add the finely chopped parsley on top of the bacon bits, and serve.

Hannah's 2nd Note: When I eat this delicious soup, I always stir the garnishes in before I take my first spoonful.

Sally's Note: At the Lake Eden Inn, we always serve bowls of Pub Soup with warm French rolls and soft salted butter, or a warm baguette with soft, salted butter. When Dick serves it at the bar, he teams it up with assorted salted crackers in a napkin-lined basket.

Hannah's 3rd Note: Be sure to tell your guests that it's perfectly acceptable to dunk their bread in the soup if they're so inclined.

Chapter Twelve

She was terribly off-balance and everything around her was fading into little dots of color, very like a pointillist painting. The bright noon sky was taking on a reddish glow, and her legs were shaking as she gripped the branch above her and hung on for dear life. If she fainted now, she'd crash to the ground and break into little pieces like a china doll falling from a high shelf.

"I can't do any more," she told him. "I don't feel good, Ross."

"You have to do more. You promised you'd get a bushel for me. I need them, Hannah. I have to give them to Doug so he'll give me the money."

"But . . . I think I'm going to faint."

"Don't you dare!"

His voice was hard and Hannah's knees began to buckle. There was a weakness in her legs that she couldn't seem to control.

"I can't, Ross. I want to help you, but I can't!"

"When we got married, you promised to love and obey. Now obey and pick some more! You don't have a whole bushel and I need this bushel full to the brim!"

She reached up and plucked another apricot from the branch above her head. Just one apricot, but it was large, and juicy, and it looked delicious. Even though she knew she should drop it into the bushel basket, she was so hungry and thirsty she brought it to her mouth and took a huge bite.

"What are you doing? Are you crazy? You're ruining my life! Get another apricot, Hannah. Pick another one right now! I need at least another dozen, maybe more."

"I . . . I can't," she said, tears forming in her eyes. How could she cry when she was so thirsty? It was impossible, but tears were rolling down her cheeks. And then she was sobbing as she reached up to get another apricot and place it in the bushel basket.

"Hurry! We don't have much time!" he ordered. "Faster! Pick faster! How can you pick so slowly when I love you a bushel and a peck."

And that was when Ross started to sing an old song that her great-grandmother used to sing to her. *I love you a bushel and a peck, a bushel and a peck and a hug around the neck. A hug around the neck and a barrel and a heap. A barrel and a heap and I'm talking in my sleep. About you, about you.*

"Great-grandma Elsa used to sing that to me," she told him.

"I know. She taught it to me."

"But . . . how could she have taught it to you? She died when I was only six years old!"

"That's probably true, but she's here right now. Say hello to your great-grandmother, Hannah."

Hannah looked down at Ross, who was standing by the trunk of the tree. And her great-grandmother was standing right next to him!

"Gigi!" Hannah used her nickname for her great-grandmother. "How did you get here?"

"He came to get me. Be very careful, Hannah. Don't believe a word he says. He's a liar and a con man."

"Hush!" Ross shouted, pushing Hannah's great-grandmother to the ground. "Go back where you came from!"

"No!" Hannah screamed. "Stay with me, Gigi! I need you! Please stay with me!"

Ross waved his hand and Hannah's great-grandmother disappeared. Then he turned to give her an icy cold smile. "She's gone and that's your punishment, Hannah. Now you'll never see her again and it's all because you didn't fill the bushel basket with apricots. If you want me to change my mind, you'd better pick more now. And hurry!"

"But . . . I can't pick any more apricots! There aren't any more," she said, staring up at the bare, fruitless branches above her. "I picked them all, Ross."

"No, you didn't. There were more on that tree and I know it. What did you do? Eat them?"

"No! Just that one, Ross. I only ate one. And it was because I was so thirsty."

"That one apricot would have convinced him to give me the money. You killed me, Hannah! It's all your fault! You killed me and all you care about is yourself!"

She could feel herself slipping, beginning to fall as his words shot arrows through her mind. He hated her now and there was nothing she could do to convince him to love her again. It was too late. She'd missed the boat and now she was missing the ladder, falling down to the bed and grabbing the pillow to try to break her fall.

She might have screamed then. She wasn't sure. But she must have made a sound because Moishe gave a startled yowl, scrambled to his feet, and raced to the foot of the bed as if the demons of hell were chasing him.

"Wha . . . ?" Hannah half-formed a question as she sat up and tried to catch her breath. And then she got out of bed and hurried to the bathroom because she suddenly felt so thirsty, she could barely stand it. Perhaps she shouldn't have had Sally's freshly baked salted pretzel appetizer at the Lake Eden Inn last night. She'd dipped Sally's delicious pretzels in Kalamata olive aioli and that had been salty, too. She'd consumed more salt than she usually did, and that must be why she was so thirsty this morning.

But was it morning? Hannah came out of the bathroom clutching a half-empty glass of water. It was still dark outside the window, but that told her nothing about the time of day. It was February in Minnesota and daylight didn't come until after seven in the morning. It could be six-thirty and that meant she was late to work. Or it could be ten or eleven-thirty at night.

There was only one way to find out what time it was and Hannah checked her alarm clock. And that was when she discovered that it was thirty minutes past the time she usually got out of bed. That meant she'd slept through the whole night without waking once. Perhaps Mike had been right when he'd recommended delicious food, good wine, and sleep. Sleep was a great cure for anxiety . . . unless you woke up with a nightmare. Now that she'd assuaged her thirst, she felt much better. She also felt safe because Mike was sleeping on the couch in her living room. She'd slept so deeply, she hadn't even roused when her alarm had begun its irritating electronic beeping. Or had her alarm beeped at all? She might have been so tired, she'd forgotten to set it last night. Either that, or Michelle had come into her bedroom and turned it off to let her sleep longer.

There was a delicious scent in the air and Hannah began to smile. Michelle was up and she was baking. It took Hannah a moment to recognize the scent, and then she laughed.

"Apricot!" she said, leaning down to pet Moishe. "Michelle's baking something with apricots." And the moment she identified the scent, she remembered the strange dream she'd had. She must have smelled the scent in her sleep and spun the story of her dream.

"Let's get up, Moishe," she said, interrupting his morning stretch. "I'll take a quick shower and we'll go find out what Michelle has made for our breakfast."

"Apricot Coffee Cake," Michelle responded to Hannah's unspoken question. "I knew that baking something good would wake you up."

"It's smells wonderful, Michelle," Hannah said, heading straight for the kitchen coffeepot to get her first cup of eye-opening java. "How long have you been awake?"

"A couple of hours. I tested recipes and my Apricot Coffee Cake is just one of them. I've already packed up the others and we'll try them when we get to The Cookie Jar."

"I didn't see Lonnie in the living room," Hannah said, and then she wished she hadn't mentioned it. "Sorry. I didn't mean to pry into your personal life."

Michelle laughed. "You didn't. He got up when I did and headed for home to change clothes and take a shower. He told me that he'd be back before breakfast."

Hannah carried her full coffee mug to the kitchen table that, according to Delores, would be an antique in less than ten years. A moment later, Michelle joined her at the table with her own mug of fresh coffee. "Would you like me to take an Apricot Coffee Cake over to Marguerite and Clara? I baked four of them."

"That would be lovely, but you'd better check to see if they're up yet. They always open the curtains in their living room to let me know that they're awake for the day."

"And I'd better do it before Mike gets out of the shower," Michelle said with a smile. "Right?"

"Right!" Hannah watched as Michelle wrapped one of the coffee cakes on the cooling rack in aluminum foil and carried it to the living room to check on the status of their neighbors' curtains.

"They're up," Michelle reported. "I'll be right back, Hannah."

When Michelle left, Hannah took a deep swallow of her favorite wake-up beverage and smiled as she looked out of the kitchen window. One of the arc lights that bordered the condo complex was casting shadows on the snow, and she wondered whether Clara had completed her assignment for painting class by finishing her photos of shadows. She was still thinking about Clara's assignment and how much work it would be to take photos every two hours of the shadows falling in a particular spot, when she heard the door open and Michelle came back to her chair at the table.

"It's cold out there," Michelle said, picking up her mug of coffee and holding it in both hands. "Clara answered the door and she said to tell you that she had a few more photos to take of the pine tree."

"That's good." Hannah wondered again if Michelle had possibly read her mind. "I was just thinking about that."

"So was I, so I asked her. Remember how Great-grandma Elsa used to say, *Great minds think alike*?"

"I do. And she always used to follow it up with, *And fools seldom differ.*"

"That's right! I'd forgotten all about that part!" Michelle took a swallow of her coffee and stood up. "I'm going to make my bed before Mike comes in for his breakfast. Have another cup of coffee, Hannah. It'll only take me a minute or two and then, when Lonnie gets here, we'll all have breakfast."

"Do you want me to make some scrambled eggs and sausage?" Hannah asked her.

"Sure, if you don't mind. Otherwise, just wait until I come back and I'll do it."

Hannah had just put the sausage on to cook and was whipping up eggs with a little cream in a bowl on the counter when Mike came into the kitchen.

"How are you this morning?" he asked.

"I'm fine, Mike. I know I slept better because you were here."

Mike grinned his famous sexy grin. "That's good. It's probably because you felt safe."

"That's probably right," Hannah told him, not mentioning the fact that delicious food and good wine might have had a bit to do with it.

"The year before she died, my wife got me a bumper sticker. It said, *Feel safe at night. Sleep with a cop.*"

Hannah laughed. She couldn't help herself. It was funny. "Your wife had a sense of humor."

"Yes, she did. And so do you, Hannah."

Warning bells went off in Hannah's mind. Mike was comparing her to his wife. Should she be a bit worried about that?

"Something sure smells good," Mike commented, taking a deep breath of the Apricot Coffee Cake–scented air. "What is it?"

"Michelle baked a coffee cake with apricots."

"But that's not all. I smell sausage."

"Yes, you do. And pretty soon you'll smell scrambled eggs with cheese."

Just then the doorbell chimed and Mike turned to head for the living room. "That's probably Lonnie," he called back over his shoulder. "Go ahead and cook. I'll get it."

Hannah gave a fleeting thought to whether or not Mike would peer through the peephole before he opened the door, something he never failed to remind *her* to do. Then she concentrated on melting butter in her largest frying pan and grating some sharp cheddar to flavor her scrambled eggs.

"Hi, Hannah," Lonnie greeted her as he followed Mike back to the kitchen. "Where's Michelle?"

"Making her bed and getting dressed. She'll be out here in a minute, Lonnie."

"Something smells good!" Lonnie repeated Mike's earlier comment. "What is it?"

"Apricot Coffee Cake," Hannah told him. "Pour yourself some coffee and sit down, Lonnie. The eggs and sausage will be ready in less than five minutes and then we'll eat."

Apricot Coffee Cake

Preheat oven to 350 degrees F., rack in the middle position.

The Cake:

1 cup salted butter, softened ***(2 sticks, 8 ounces, 1/2 pound)***
1 and 3/4 cup white ***(granulated)*** sugar
1 teaspoon salt
2 teaspoons vanilla extract
1 and 1/2 teaspoons baking powder
6 large eggs
3 cups all-purpose flour ***(pack it down in the cup when you measure it)***

The Filling:

3 cups chopped apricots ***(I used canned apricot halves)***
1/3 cup white ***(granulated)*** sugar
1/2 teaspoon cinnamon
1/3 cup all-purpose flour ***(pack it down in the cup when you measure it)***

The Crumb Topping:

1/2 cup brown sugar ***(pack it down in the cup when you measure it)***
1/3 cup all-purpose flour ***(pack it down in the cup when you measure it)***
1/4 cup softened butter ***(1/2 stick, 2***

ounces, 1/8 pound)

Hannah's 1st Note: If you choose to use drained canned fruit, put it in a strainer and save the juice for the kids. Then pat the fruit dry with paper towels before you chop it in pieces.

Grease the inside of a 9-inch by 13-inch rectangular cake pan, or spray it with Pam or another nonstick cooking spray.

To Make the Cake:
Mix the cup of salted, softened butter with the white sugar until it's light and fluffy.

Mix in the salt, vanilla extract, and baking powder. Mix until everything is thoroughly combined.

Mix in the eggs one at a time, mixing thoroughly after each addition.

Mix in the flour in one-cup increments, mixing thoroughly after each addition.

Give the bowl a final stir by hand and then spoon HALF of the batter in the cake pan and spread it out with a rubber spatula. Leave the rest of the batter in the bowl.

You'll use it later.

To Make the Filling:
In another bowl, mix the chopped apricots with the white sugar.

Sprinkle in the half teaspoon of cinnamon and mix it in.

Sprinkle the flour on top of the fruit and mix it in thoroughly.

Spoon the fruit mixture on top of the batter in your cake pan. Distribute it as evenly as you can.

Drop spoonfuls of the remaining batter on top of the fruit. Spread them carefully with a rubber spatula, but it won't be enough to cover the apricots completely. That's okay. This coffee cake will look pretty with the apricots peeking up through the batter.

To Make the Crumb Topping:
Use a fork from your silverware drawer to mix the brown sugar and the flour together.

Mix in the softened salted butter with the fork. Continue to mix until everything is crumbly.

Hannah's 2nd Note: You can also make the Crumb Topping in a food processor if you use chilled butter. Process the ingredients in an on-and-off motion with the steel blade.

Hannah's 3rd Note: If you're using softened butter and the crumb topping becomes smooth and doesn't crumble, simply stick it in the refrigerator for 10 to 15 minutes. Then, when you add it to your coffee cake, it will crumble on top.

Use your impeccably clean fingers to crumble the topping over your coffee cake as evenly as you can.

Bake your Apricot Coffee Cake at 350 degrees F. for 45 to 60 minutes or until the top is golden brown. ***(Mine took 50 minutes.)***

Remove your Apricot Coffee Cake from the oven and set it on a cold stovetop burner or a wire rack. Let it cool until it is just barely warm.

Serve Apricot Coffee Cake by cutting it in

squares that are the size of sweet rolls, removing the squares with a metal spatula, and placing them on breakfast plates. Make sure that there is plenty of softened, salted butter for those who want to use it with their square of coffee cake, and a large pot of strong black coffee served with cream and sugar for those who want it. If there are children at the breakfast table, pour tall glasses of icy cold milk to go with their squares of Apricot Coffee Cake.

Hannah's 4th Note: Some people serve this Apricot Coffee Cake with powdered sugar icing drizzled on the top, but personally, I don't think it needs icing. Recipe follows just in case you'd like to try it.

POWDERED SUGAR ICING

1 cup powdered ***(confectioners)*** sugar
1/2 teaspoon vanilla extract
1/4 teaspoon salt
2 to 4 Tablespoons cream

Mix the powdered sugar with the vanilla extract and the salt. Make sure everything is thoroughly combined.

Mix in the cream gradually and whisk until the icing reaches the desired consistency to drizzle over your warm Apricot Coffee Cake.

Pour the icing into a cup or bowl with a spout and drizzle it over your Apricot Coffee Cake.

Let the icing cool and "set" before you cut squares and serve your coffee cake.

Chapter Thirteen

It was morning and Hannah had just finished taking the last pan of Molasses Walnut Drop Cookies out of the oven when Lisa hurried into the kitchen. "Doug just called you, Hannah. He'd like to see you and Mike down at the bank at nine."

Hannah was surprised at the request. Had Ross somehow managed to intimidate Doug into giving him the money? "Did Doug tell you why he wanted to see me?"

"No, he just asked me to pass on the message and said he'd explain everything when he saw you."

"I'll call Doug and tell him you'll be there," Mike offered, getting up from his stool at the work station. "And I'll ask him what this is about if you want me to."

"Yes, please do that. Doug's never asked me to come in before and I know my business account isn't overdrawn. Neither is my personal account, so I know it can't be anything like that. And since he wants to see you, too, it's got to be about Ross."

"I'll see what more I can find out," Mike promised, slipping into his parka and going out the back kitchen door to make the call.

"What did you bake, Hannah?" Lisa asked after Mike left.

"Molasses Walnut Drop Cookies. Mike tasted some from the first batch and told me that they were way too good to serve at The Cookie Jar."

Lisa laughed. "Because Mike wanted them all for himself?"

"That's probably right. He was on his second plateful when you came in from the coffee shop to tell me about Doug's call. Mike really gobbled those cookies before I could frost them with Brown Powdered Sugar Glaze."

"Did Michelle leave?" Lisa asked.

"Yes. She went to Jordan High. She had some papers to grade before class on Monday and she has tryouts for the play this afternoon."

"How does she like teaching?"

"She loves it, especially the drama classes. She told me a couple of days ago that she thought she wanted to go into teaching."

"If she does that, she can settle down right here in Lake Eden with the rest of the family and get married."

"Well . . . I'm not sure about the married part, but maybe. I don't think Michelle is ready for marriage yet."

"Does she still have dreams of making it on Broadway?"

Hannah shook her head. "I don't think so. Michelle's realistic. She's just trying out various things to see which ones she likes best. And it seems that teaching high school is at the top of her list right now."

"That's good," Lisa said, heading back to the swinging door that separated the kitchen from the coffee shop. "Let me know when those cookies are cool enough and we'll test them on our customers."

"I will." Hannah turned back to her cookie baking once Lisa had left. And that was when a dreadful possibility occurred to her concerning Doug's call. What if Ross had somehow managed to get into the bank and he was there right now with Doug, holding Doug hostage? And what if this was part of a trap that Ross had set for Mike and her?

"Please tell me I'm paranoid," Hannah said aloud, sinking down on a stool and holding her head in her hands.

"Paranoid about what?" Mike said, coming back into the kitchen just in time to hear

Hannah's comment.

"I was thinking about Doug's call and why he wants to see us at the bank. I know this will probably sound crazy, but I was worried that maybe Ross was there and he forced Doug into calling to lure both of us there."

Mike shook his head. "That doesn't sound crazy to me. It sounds careful, which is exactly what you should be. And I don't think you're paranoid, Hannah. I think you have good cause to be afraid of Ross. He's not the man either of us thought he was."

Hannah gave a long, heartfelt sigh. "I know. I realize that now. You're going to the bank with me, then?"

"You bet your . . ." Mike stopped speaking and Hannah waited, wondering what word he'd substitute for the one he'd been about to use. "You bet your *boots,*" Mike said.

Hannah smiled and accepted the substitution. "Did you ask Doug why he wants to see us?"

"Yes, but he wouldn't tell me anything. He just said it was a personal matter that he needed to discuss with you."

"Okay," Hannah said, even though she still had no idea why she'd been summoned to the bank. "I guess we'll find out when we get there."

Hannah settled back in the chair in front of Doug's desk as he made a cup of cappuccino for her. Mike had stayed in the lobby of the bank when Doug had asked to see her alone. Hannah knew that Mike was on the job, watching the entrance and the traffic on Main Street outside to make sure that Ross didn't pay a surprise visit to Lake Eden.

"I love the way you make this coffee," Hannah told Doug. This was the second time in as many days that she'd had a cup of cappuccino and she especially liked the way that Doug prepared it with frothy milk over the coffee and a sprinkling of sweet chocolate on the top.

"Here you go, Hannah," Doug said, carrying his own cup of espresso to his desk and sitting down in his leather chair. "Do you want one of these cookies you brought?"

"No, thanks. I sneaked several before they were completely cool. Go ahead, Doug. Try them and tell me what you think."

Doug took a big bite of Hannah's Molasses Walnut Drop Cookies and smiled. "They're great, Hannah. Do you want me to go out and ask Mike if he wants some coffee and cookies?"

"Don't bother, Doug. Mike already ate two platefuls of cookies and drank most of a pot of coffee at The Cookie Jar earlier this morning."

"Okay then. I suppose you're wondering why I wanted to see you privately."

"Yes, I am," Hannah replied.

"Let me ask you a question, Hannah. Did you know that KCOW-TV bought the rights to show *Crisis in Cherrywood* at their film festival?"

Hannah shook her head. "I didn't know that, but I guess it makes sense."

"Well, they did. And Ross signed a direct deposit slip when he started working at KCOW-TV."

Hannah wasn't sure where Doug was going with this conversation, but she nodded. "All right. I'm with you so far, Doug."

"The check from KCOW-TV for fifty thousand dollars just came into the bank and it was automatically deposited into Ross's business account."

"I understand. But what does that have to do with me?"

"You're a co-signer on all of Ross's accounts, including his business account. I thought you should know that several additional sums had been deposited since the last bank statement."

"Thanks for telling me, but I still don't know what that has to do with me."

"It means that you could withdraw any amount you want right now from that account or from any of his other accounts. They now have a combined total over a million dollars."

"Oh!" Hannah gulped. "That's . . . a *lot* of money!"

"Yes, it is. Would you like to make a withdrawal, Hannah?"

"I . . . no. No, I wouldn't."

A smile spread over Doug's face. "That's because you're an honest person, Hannah. But you'd probably get even more than that in damages if you sued Ross for bigamy."

It took Hannah another moment to frame what she wanted to say. "You're probably right, Doug. And I do appreciate the fact that you told me all this. But . . . no. That's not my money. I didn't earn it and . . . I don't want to feel beholden to Ross in any way. I just want to put this behind me and do my best to forget that he was ever a part of my life!"

MOLASSES WALNUT DROP COOKIES

DO NOT preheat the oven yet. This dough must chill before baking.

1 and 1/2 cups melted butter ***(3 sticks, 12 ounces, 3/4 pound)***
2 cups white ***(granulated)*** sugar
1/2 cup molasses ***(I used Grandma's Molasses)***
2 beaten eggs ***(just whip them up in a glass with a fork)***
2 teaspoons baking soda
1 teaspoon salt
2 teaspoons cinnamon
1/2 teaspoon nutmeg ***(freshly ground is best)***
1/4 teaspoon cardamom ***(if you don't have it, you can substitute more cinnamon for the cardamom)***
4 and 1/4 cups flour ***(don't sift it — pack it down in the cup when you measure it)***
1/2 cup finely chopped walnuts

Walnut halves to place on top of the cookies before baking if you DO NOT plan to glaze them with Brown Powdered Sugar Glaze. ***(Recipe follows.)*** If you DO plan to glaze your cookies, wait until you glaze them to place the walnut halves on top of your cookies.

Melt the butter in a large microwave-safe bowl. Heat it on HIGH for 1 minute. Leave the bowl in the microwave for another minute and then check the butter after to see it's melted. If it's not, give it more time, in 20-second increments, until it is.

Take the bowl out of the microwave and mix in the white sugar. Mix until it's all combined.

Add the molasses to the bowl and mix it in. Mix until it's thoroughly incorporated.

Let the butter, sugar, and molasses mixture sit on the counter while you get out the eggs.

When the mixture in the bowl is not so hot it'll cook the eggs, add them to the large bowl and stir them in thoroughly. Be sure to mix until they're well combined.

Hannah's 1st Note: This is a recipe that you can stir by hand if you wish, but it's a lot easier if you use an electric mixer.

Sprinkle in the baking soda, salt, cinnamon, nutmeg, and cardamom. Mix until all of the ingredients are well combined.

Add the flour in one-cup increments, mixing after each addition.

Hannah's 2nd Note: If you coat the inside of your measuring cup with Pam or another nonstick cooking spray before you measure the half-cup of molasses, it will slide right out of the measuring cup into your mixing bowl.

Hannah's 3rd Note: Once you add the flour, your cookie dough will be very stiff. Don't worry. This is exactly as it should be.

Mix in the chopped walnuts. If this is too difficult with a spoon, simply add the walnuts to the top of your mixing bowl and knead them in as you would if you were making bread.

Once the walnuts have been added and are incorporated into the cookie dough, cover the dough with plastic wrap and refrigerate it for at least 2 hours. ***(Overnight***

is even better.)

When you're ready to bake, take the cookie dough out of the refrigerator and let it sit, still covered with the plastic wrap, on your kitchen counter. It will need to warm just a bit so that you can work with it.

Preheat your oven to 350 degrees F., rack in the middle position.

While your oven is heating to the proper temperature, prepare your cookie sheets. You can either spray them with Pam or another nonstick cooking spray, or line them with parchment paper. ***(The parchment paper is more expensive, but easier in the long run. If you use it, you can simply pull the paper over to the wire cooling rack, cookies and all. It's also easier to glaze the cookies if they're still on the parchment paper.)***

Remove the plastic wrap from your cookie dough. Roll the dough into walnut-sized balls with your impeccably clean hands and place them on a prepared cookie sheet, 12 dough balls to a standard-size sheet.

Press a walnut half down into the top of

each dough ball.

Hannah's 4th Note: If you form the dough into smaller dough balls, the cookies will be crisper. If you choose to do this, you'll have to reduce the baking time. If I roll smaller balls, I start checking the Molasses Walnut Drop Cookies after 8 minutes in the oven.

Bake for 10 to 12 minutes or until they're nicely browned. The cookies will flatten out, all by themselves. Let them cool for 2 minutes on the cookie sheets and then move them to a wire rack to finish cooling.

Hannah's 5th Note: Molasses Walnut Drop Cookies freeze well. Roll them up in foil, the same way you'd roll coins in a wrapper, put them in a freezer bag, and they'll be fine for 3 months or so.

Yield: 6 to 10 dozen (depending on the size of your dough balls) tasty, molasses-infused, and delicious cookies.

Once your cookies have baked and cooled, move them all to parchment paper on your kitchen counter and glaze them with Brown Powdered Sugar Glaze ***(recipe follows).***

Brown Powdered Sugar Glaze

1/3 cup salted butter
1 Tablespoon molasses
1 teaspoon vanilla extract
2 cups powdered sugar
4 to 6 Tablespoons milk

Place the butter in a microwave-safe bowl. ***(I use a quart Pyrex measuring cup.)***

Pour the Tablespoon of molasses on top of the butter.

Heat the butter and molasses on HIGH for 15 seconds or until it has melted in the bottom of the bowl or cup.

Set the container with the melted butter on your kitchen counter.

Stir the butter and molasses together until they are well mixed.

Add the vanilla extract to the melted butter and stir it in.

Measure out two cups of powdered sugar. Pack the powdered sugar down in the cup when you measure it.

Hannah's 1st Note: There's no need to sift the powdered sugar unless it has big lumps in it. You are going to pack it down in the measuring cup anyway.

Fill a small cup with 6 Tablespoons of whole milk. You probably will NOT use all of this milk in this glaze, so don't add it to your bowl quite yet.

Hannah's 2nd Note: Sometimes, when I make these cookies for adults, I like to use rum instead of the milk. I don't do this when I make the cookies for children because the alcohol is not baked into the cookie and may not fully evaporate.

Add the milk ***(or rum)*** to your bowl, one Tablespoon at a time, stirring it in as you go. You will add only enough milk ***(or rum)*** to make this glaze liquid enough to brush on top of your cookies.

When your glaze reaches the proper brushing consistency, brush the tops of your Molasses Walnut Drop Cookies with the glaze with a pastry brush.

Hannah's 3rd Note: For years, I didn't

bother using a pastry brush. I took a small brush home from my father's hardware store, washed it thoroughly and dried it, and used that. It worked just fine and if it got sticky and I couldn't rinse it off well enough, I just stuck it on the top rack of the dishwasher and washed it that way.

Hannah's 4th Note: If you don't brush the glaze fast enough, your glaze may harden a bit. If this happens, simply stick the microwave-safe container back in the microwave for 15 to 20 seconds until the glaze is thin enough to brush again.

CHAPTER FOURTEEN

Her long day at The Cookie Jar was over and Hannah was sitting at the kitchen table at the condo, enjoying a tall glass of ginger ale with Norman. He was her guard for tonight, and Hannah and Michelle had promised to feed him dinner.

"I wish you'd brought Cuddles," Hannah told him. "I know Moishe would like some playtime."

"I can always go get her while you two relax a little," Norman offered, finishing his glass of ginger ale and standing up. "But are you sure you'll be all right here alone?"

"I'm not alone," Hannah said, gesturing toward Michelle. "And we won't let anyone in without checking the peephole. Go ahead, Norman. That'll give us time to shower and change before dinner."

Once Norman had left, Hannah turned to Michelle. "Do you think that Mike and Lonnie will show up for dinner?"

"Of course they will," Michelle answered. "They'll be here by the time we're finished setting the table."

Hannah laughed. "You're right, of course. It's a good thing we have plenty of Beery Good Beef Brisket."

Less than an hour later, after the two sisters had showered and changed into comfortable, at-home clothing, Hannah came back into the kitchen. She was just stirring the Crock-Pot containing their dinner when there was a knock at the door.

"I'll get it," Michelle said, heading for the door.

"Hi, Norman," Michelle greeted him as he came in with Cuddles in her carrier. "Just put her down right here and I'll go get . . ." Michelle stopped speaking as an orange-and-white striped cat came racing down the hallway. "Never mind. I think Moishe knows that you went to get Cuddles."

Hannah heard Moishe give the special yowl that was reserved for his favorite kitty friend. "Moishe's happy!" she called out from the kitchen. "Let her out, Norman. But please wait until I pour another ginger ale for you and get our wineglasses out of the refrigerator. We stuck them there right after you left because we wanted to wait until you got back. Then all three of us can do *feet up* while Cuddles and Moishe chase each other."

A few moments later, Hannah and Michelle were seated with Norman on the leather couch in Hannah's living room. "You were here much faster than I thought you'd be," Hannah commented, lifting her feet up and motioning to Norman and Michelle to do the same. "Feet up! Here come the cats!"

Pounding feline footfalls thundered down the hallway and Moishe skidded around the corner into the living room, followed a scant second later by Cuddles, who was in hot pursuit.

"Round one," Michelle said right after the cats had run past them and were making a circle around the perimeter of the kitchen. "We're safe for a couple of minutes."

"Don't get too comfortable," Hannah warned, as Michelle placed her wineglass back on the coffee table. "The second lap is about to begin and it'll be even faster than the first."

Feline footfalls sounded again, pounding closer and closer against the carpet in the hallway until the cats came thundering into the living room to streak past their upraised feet. The tandem racers disappeared around the back of the couch and sped into the kitchen, where their claws scrabbled against the floor. A second or two later, they zoomed back down the hallway for the second time in as many minutes.

"One more lap?" Michelle asked Norman.

"I think so. Cuddles didn't look all that tired yet."

"Neither did Moishe," Hannah added. "If he's tired, he always looks at me with his tongue out."

"That's a good sign," Norman agreed. "If Cuddles is in the lead this time around, they're almost ready to leave the feline speedway."

Michelle giggled. "I like that, Norman, and it's true. Hannah's condo gets turned into a feline speedway when Cuddles comes over to visit."

With feet up and clutching their glasses, the three of them waited for the thundering duo to come down the hallway. There were several seconds of silence and then they heard the staccato thudding of racing paws.

"Here they come!" Norman said, grinning at Michelle and Hannah. "If we're lucky, Cuddles will be in the lead this time and that'll mean it's the last lap."

The felines careened around the corner and headed down the straightaway past the couch. Cuddles was, indeed, in the lead, and Moishe was close behind her.

"Is it over?" Michelle asked when the cats had zipped past them.

"I think so," Norman answered, "but Cuddles' eyes didn't look quite wild enough."

"And Moishe still had plenty of speed," Hannah commented. "Let's keep a grip on our glasses just in case."

Slowly, cautiously, Hannah, Norman, and Michelle lowered their feet to the carpet. They sat there listening for what seemed like long minutes, but was probably only a few seconds. There was no sound from Hannah's bedroom, and all three of them began to relax.

"I think it's over," Michelle said, placing her wineglass back on the coffee table.

"Agreed." Norman nodded, and he put his soda glass next to Michelle's glass.

"I'm not so sure," Hannah said, keeping her wineglass and listening intently for any sound emanating from her bedroom. "Usually I can hear them purring by now. I'm going to give them another minute or two before I put down my glass."

And then it happened, the pounding of feline feet on the carpet in a mad rush back to the living room. Hannah barely had time to tuck her feet back up on the couch before the cats were rounding the corner again.

"Uh-oh!" Michelle grabbed her glass and executed a maneuver that any yoga instructor would have been proud to see, raising her legs and tucking them under her, hoping that she was in time to avoid a furry feline ankle crash.

"I got it, I think!" Norman grabbed his ginger ale, propped his feet on top of Hannah's lap, and gave her an apologetic grin. "Sorry, Hannah. I didn't have time to tuck."

"No problem," Hannah said, laughing. "Oh, no! Moishe's almost skidded into the corner!"

On this last and final lap, the cats screeched past them three times, rounding the back of the couch with claws digging in hard to make the corners and then flying past them. Their fur was ruffled, their ears were laid flat against their heads, and their tails were straight out behind them. It was a game and they knew it, but they were acting as if they were racing for their lives.

"Are they done?" Michelle asked as the cats headed back down the hallway to the bedroom.

"Listen," Hannah advised, holding her finger to her lips.

As all three of them listened, there was a thud and then a second, softer thud. A rustling ensued for several seconds and then all three of them heard the sound of loud purring.

"They're done," Hannah declared. "They're both on the bed, nestled in the feather pillows, purring because they caused so much havoc."

"But they think it's fun," Michelle added.

"Right," Norman said. "And they love to see us react."

They sat there for a moment, sipping their drinks and catching their collective breath. And then Hannah stood up.

"I have to stir the dinner in the Crock-Pot," she said.

"And I have to get everything else ready," Michelle stated, also rising to her feet.

"Can I do anything to help you?" Norman asked.

"I don't think so, unless . . ." Hannah stopped speaking and looked thoughtful. "Would you mind running next door to Marguerite and Clara's place? I'd like to ask Marguerite to join us for dinner if Clara doesn't mind. I know Clara can't join us because of her allergies, but we can always deliver her dinner. And if Marguerite comes here, she'll have a chance to see Cuddles again."

"Great idea!" Norman declared, heading for the door. "You girls go ahead and do what you have to do. I'll invite Marguerite and be right back to help you."

Hannah was stirring the contents of the Crock-Pot when there was another knock on the door.

"I'll get it," Michelle said, hurrying to answer the door. "It's probably Norman and he locked himself out."

Hannah listened, but she didn't hear Norman's voice. Instead, she heard Michelle greet Lonnie.

"Hi, Lonnie! Did Mike's food-dar kick into high gear because we were cooking dinner?"

"Not exactly. We were next door at Marguerite and Clara's condo when Norman came by."

"Were you visiting them?" Michelle asked.

"No, Marguerite called the sheriff's department and we came right out."

Hannah clamped the lid back on the slow cooker and hurried to intercept Lonnie and Michelle. "Is something wrong with Marguerite or Clara?"

Lonnie nodded. "Yes, Marguerite called us an hour ago to tell us about Clara's accident. Mike and I jumped in the cruiser and came out here right away. Mike's still over there trying to calm them down and Norman's helping him."

"What kind of accident did Clara have?" Hannah asked as she ushered Lonnie into the kitchen, gestured to a chair at the kitchen table, and gave him a cup of coffee. "Is Clara hurt?"

"No, just frightened. She was outside, taking photos of that big pine tree at the edge of the complex, when someone ran out of the woods, pushed her down in the snow, and stole her cell phone."

"Good heavens!" Hannah exchanged shocked glances with Michelle. "But why didn't Marguerite call us? Michelle and I would have helped them."

"She tried to, but you weren't home yet. Neither were Lorna or Phil or Sue Plotnik. So Marguerite called the sheriff's station, and Mike answered her call."

Hannah glanced at her apple-shaped kitchen clock to see what time it was. "Phil and Sue always take Kevin over to his sister's place on the weekends, and Lorna's probably working late. Poor Clara. She must be terribly upset."

"She's more angry than upset. She hadn't downloaded her shadow photos and now she doesn't have them for her painting class. And to make matters even worse, she had her house key in her pocket and it must have fallen out when she tumbled into the snow."

"Are they going to get their locks changed?" Michelle asked him.

"That's expensive and Mike didn't think it was necessary since the key was an extra one they had made and it wasn't marked in any way. Even if someone finds it, there's no way to tell which condo door it fits. Clara's more upset about the photos she lost than anything else."

"I'm sure her teacher will understand," Michelle said.

"That's what we told her. But she's still upset because she had some really good pictures of the shadows the pine tree cast on the snow."

"Did Clara call the phone company to turn off her service so the person who stole her phone can't use it?" Michelle asked him.

"Norman's doing that right now while Mike interviews Clara. He was asking her more about the man who pushed her down when I left."

"Did she recognize the man?" Hannah asked.

Lonnie shook his head. "Clara said she

didn't, that she was almost certain that she'd never seen him before."

"Then she didn't think he lived in this complex?" Michelle followed up on Hannah's question.

Lonnie shook his head. "No, and Marguerite told us that Clara's on the homeowner's board. She meets everyone who moves in because they deliver welcome packages to all the new arrivals."

"The train tracks aren't that far away," Michelle pointed out. "Do you think that Clara's attacker might have been a transient?"

"That's doubtful," Hannah vetoed that possibility. "The train doesn't make any stops here, and there's no reason for anyone to jump off here. It would make more sense for transients to ride into town and hop off there."

"You've got a point," Lonnie said. "It's cold at night out here, and there's a shelter in town at the Bible Church."

Michelle nodded agreement. "Reverend Strandberg provides three meals a day in the church kitchen for anyone who comes in hungry."

"And don't forget about the Helping Hands Thrift Store in town," Hannah reminded them. "They give all sorts of warm clothing and boots to everyone who can't afford them."

"Are you and Mike going out to look for the man in the woods?" Hannah asked Lonnie.

"Not tonight. Mike said it could wait until morning. It would be different if Clara had gotten hurt, but she's okay physically. The snow was deep and it cushioned her. She told us that her elbow's a little sore because she tried to catch herself, but Mike checked it out and it looked okay to him. He called Doc Knight to be sure, and Clara promised to go into the hospital for an X-ray in the morning."

"Stealing her phone is a crime, isn't it?" Michelle asked him.

"You bet! If it had happened in the middle of the day, we would have gone after him, but Mike decided that tracking him at night would be close to impossible. It's not supposed to snow tonight, so his tracks won't be covered with new snow."

"That makes sense," Hannah agreed. "Why don't you run back over there, Lonnie, and invite Mike here for dinner. And of course you're invited, too. I'd invite Marguerite, but I don't think she'll leave Clara."

"We can always dish it up and I can run over with their dinner," Michelle offered.

"Great idea!" Hannah complimented her.

"I'll go over there right now." Lonnie finished the last of his coffee, pushed back his chair, and headed for the door again. "I'll let them know that you'll deliver their dinner, and be back in a minute or two."

When the door had closed behind Lonnie, Michelle turned to Hannah. "Do we have anything to serve with your main dish?"

"The meat has carrots, onions, and red potatoes around it, but we may need something else."

"How about a cooked vegetable salad?" Michelle suggested. "You have a package of mixed vegetables in the freezer. I was going to make them during the blizzard, but we didn't need them."

"Vegetable salad would be good. There'll be a gravy with the brisket and we can always put that in a gravy boat. I think I'll try to make Savory Tortilla Cups to fill with the vegetable salad."

"Savory Tortilla Cups? What are those?"

"I've got a package of tortillas that I can dip in Italian dressing, coat with finely grated Parmesan cheese, and press into muffin cups. I'll bake them, cool them, and then we can fill them with the salad."

"Sounds great! I don't remember having

Savory Tortilla Cups before."

"That's because I've never baked them before. The recipe for Tortilla Snickerdoodle Cookies popped into my mind when I was baking them the last time. And I'll make Sweet Tortilla Cups dipped in cinnamon and sugar, too. There's ice cream in the freezer and we can have those for dessert."

Michelle looked slightly concerned. "I'm always a little nervous about trying out new recipes on company," she confessed.

"Normally, I'd agree with you. It's always risky without a trial run, but I've had more successes than failures. Besides, this time these recipes are foolproof."

"Foolproof? What do you mean?"

"I mean there's everything to gain and nothing to lose. If the Savory Tortilla Cups don't work, we'll just toss them in the trash, put the vegetable salad in a bowl, and let everyone serve themselves at the table. And if the Sweet Tortilla Cups don't work, we'll serve the ice cream in dessert dishes."

Michelle thought about that for a moment, and then she started to smile. "You're right. They are foolproof. I just wish . . ."

Michelle's voice trailed off and Hannah noticed that her sister looked thoughtful. "What do you wish, Michelle?"

"I was just wishing that love could be as

foolproof as trying your recipes for Savory Tortilla Cups and Sweet Tortilla Cups. Wouldn't that be wonderful?"

Hannah gave a little laugh. "It certainly would! If love were as easy as trying out new recipes, I'd be a lot happier today!"

"Because you never would have married Ross?"

"You got it! If I'd tried out love with Ross back in college, I wouldn't have even considered marrying him later. Instead, I would have taken him to the airport and let him fly off without getting engaged."

"Really?" Michelle looked surprised at her sister's admission.

"It could have happened that way. And right now, I *wish* it had happened that way. I would have saved myself a lot of grief."

Michelle nodded. "That's true. But maybe your heart would have won out and you would have married him anyway."

"I guess that's possible. Baking is a lot easier than love, isn't it!"

It was a statement rather than a question and Michelle laughed. "You said it!" she said, and then she hurried off to the freezer to get the package of mixed vegetables.

BEERY GOOD BEEF BRISKET

You will need a 4 to 5quart slow cooker for this recipe.

8 small red potatoes ***(not peeled, just wash them)***
12 fresh carrot nuggets ***(found in produce aisle already pared — I used Bunny brand)***
4 small onions, quartered
1 small can button mushrooms, drained
4-pound beef brisket, trimmed and cut in half
1 can (**14.5 ounces**) beef broth ***(I used Swanson)***
1/2 cup dark molasses ***(spray inside of measuring cup with Pam or another nonstick cooking spray for easy removal)***
1 cup beer ***(I used Guinness Stout)***
1 teaspoon marjoram
1 teaspoon thyme
1/4 teaspoon cardamom ***(if you don't have it, use cinnamon)***
1 Tablespoon minced jarred garlic
1/2 teaspoon coarsely ground black pepper
2 packages dry beef gravy mix, the kind that makes 1 cup ***(I used Schilling)***
salt and pepper to taste

Hannah's 1st Note: If you don't want to use beer in this recipe, you can substitute a cup of beef broth or a cup of tomato juice.

Spray the inside crock of your slow cooker with Pam or another nonstick cooking spray. ***(This will make it easier to wash later.)***

Place the red potatoes in the bottom of the crock.

Place the carrot nuggets on top of the potatoes.

Place the onion quarters on top of the carrot nuggets.

Place the drained, button mushrooms on top of the onion pieces.

If you haven't already done so, cut the beef brisket in half and trim off the layer of fat to make it as lean as possible.

Add both pieces of brisket to your crock.

Place the beef broth in a mixing bowl.

Add the dark molasses to the beef broth.

Add the cup of beer to the bowl.

Add the marjoram, thyme, and cardamom (or cinnamon) to your bowl.

Add the jarred garlic to the bowl.

Add the coarsely ground black pepper to the bowl.

Sprinkle the contents of **ONE** package of dry beef gravy mix over the pepper in the bowl.

Put the 2nd package of gravy mix on the counter next to the Crock-Pot in case you need it later. ***(You may, or you may not — it all depends on how juicy your onions and meat are.)***

Hannah's 2nd Note: I've used Lawry's Seasoned Pepper in place of the coarsely ground black pepper. It's good!

Mix the ingredients in the bowl together with a whisk or a wooden spoon. Continue to whisk or mix until everything is well blended.

Pour the contents of the bowl over the ingredients in the crock.

Put the cover on your slow cooker, plug it in, and turn it to LOW.

This dish needs to cook on LOW for 8 to 10 hours. You can also turn it up to HIGH for 2 hours and then turn it back down to LOW for an additional 4 to 5 hours.

You will be through cooking when you can easily pierce the brisket with a fork and the potatoes and carrots are also fork tender.

To serve, remove the pieces of brisket from the crock and place them on a cutting board. Cut the brisket into 8 to 12 pieces.

Remove the vegetables from the crock and place them in a serving bowl.

Cover the bowl and the meat platter with foil to keep them warm.

Check the gravy that has formed. If the gravy isn't thick enough, turn the Crock-Pot up to HIGH and sprinkle in the 2nd package of dry beef gravy mix.

Stir in the gravy mix and cook until the gravy is thick enough to pour over the warm brisket on the meat platter.

Yield: 8 to 10 servings of tender beef and tender vegetables.

SAVORY TORTILLA CUPS

Preheat oven to 350 degrees F., rack in the middle position.

1 bottle Italian dressing ***(I used Kraft)***
1 can finely grated Parmesan cheese ***(I used Kraft in the green foil can)***
12 ten-inch flour tortillas

Spray the inside of 12 regular-size muffin cups with Pam or another nonstick cooking spray.

Hannah's 1st Note: Usually muffin pans have 12 cups in them. You can also use 2 muffin pans with 6 cups in them.

Hannah's 2nd Note: I've filled these baked Tortilla Cups with mixed vegetables, rice, or beans. Just don't try to fill them with something that's too wet or the cups will get soggy.

Place the Italian dressing in a shallow bowl that's larger than the size of the tortillas.

Place the finely grated Parmesan cheese in another shallow bowl a bit larger than the size of your tortillas.

Using tongs, dip one tortilla in the bowl with the Italian dressing. Then flip it over so that both sides are coated with the dressing.

Again using tongs, remove the tortilla from the bowl with the dressing and lay it flat in the bowl with the finely grated Parmesan cheese.

Flip the tortilla over so that both sides are coated with the cheese.

With impeccably clean fingers, place the center of the coated tortilla in one of the muffin cups, pressing it down to the bottom.

Once the bottom is flat, press the tortilla cup against the sides of the muffin cup. Your object is to form a tortilla cup that lines the inside of the indentation.

Bake your Savory Tortilla Cups at 350 degrees F. for 8 to 10 minutes or until they are beginning to brown slightly.

Take the muffin tin out of the oven and set it on a cold stove burner for 10 to 15 minutes or until the muffin tin and its contents are cool to the touch.

Hannah's 3rd Note: Letting the Savory Tortilla Cups cool in the pan will firm them up so that they will maintain their cup shape when you remove them.

Flip the muffin tin over on a wire rack. The Tortilla Cups should tip right out. Since they're now upside down on the rack, flip them over, place them on a platter, and fill them with contents of your choice.

Michelle's Note: I'm going to use these Savory Tortilla Cups for potato salad, chicken salad, and tuna salad.

SWEET TORTILLA CUPS

Preheat oven to 350 degrees F., rack in the middle position.

5 teaspoons ground cinnamon
1 cup white ***(granulated)*** sugar
1/2 cup ***(1 stick, 4 ounces, 1/4 pound)*** salted butter
12 flour tortillas ***(I used Mission brand 8-inch size.)***

Hannah's 1st Note: I like to add a bit of cardamom to this recipe so I use 4 and 1/2 teaspoons of cinnamon and 1/2 teaspoon of cardamom.

Place the cinnamon in a shallow bowl on the counter that is an inch or so larger than the size of the tortillas.

Hannah's 2nd Note: I usually use a 10-inch pie pan for the spices and sugar and another one for the butter.

Add the white sugar to the bowl with the cinnamon ***(and cardamom if you used it)*** and mix them together with a fork.

Place the cup of salted butter in a second

shallow bowl that is microwave-safe.

Heat the butter on HIGH in the microwave for 30 seconds. Check to see if your butter is melted. If it is, take the bowl out of the microwave. If it isn't, heat it for another 15 seconds on HIGH.

When the butter is melted, take the bowl out of the microwave and set it on your kitchen counter next to the bowl with the cinnamon and sugar mixture. ***(Be careful. The bowl with the melted butter could be hot.)***

Move the prepared muffin pan next to the bowls for easy access.

Using your impeccably clean fingers or tongs, dip a flour tortilla into the bowl with the melted butter. Be sure to coat both sides of the tortilla.

Take the tortilla out of the butter bowl and dip it in the bowl with the cinnamon and sugar. Again, be sure to coat both sides with the cinnamon and sugar mixture.

With your impeccably clean fingers, press the center of your buttered and coated tortilla into one of the muffin cups. Then press the sides of the tortilla against the side of the muffin cup. (You may have to overlap the sides of the tortilla together to get a good fit.)

Repeat the above steps with the remaining 11 flour tortillas.

Hannah's 3rd Note: If you have quite a bit of melted butter and cinnamon and sugar mixture left, don't worry. You can always save it to make Tortilla Snickerdoodle Cookies. (The recipe is also in this book. You may have to re-melt the butter, but that's easy to do in the microwave.)

Bake your Sweet Tortilla Cups at 350 degrees F. for 13 to 15 minutes or until they are a nice golden brown.

Take the muffin tin out of the oven and set it on a cold stove burner for 10 to 15 minutes or until the muffin tin and its contents are cool to the touch.

Hannah's 4th Note: Letting the Sweet Tortilla Cups cool in the pan will firm them up so that they will maintain their

cup shape when you remove them.

Flip the muffin tin over on a wire rack. The Sweet Tortilla Cups should tip right out. Since they're now upside down on the rack, flip them over, place them on a platter, and fill them with a scoop of ice cream drizzled with syrup, or fruit pieces topped with sweetened, whipped cream.

Chapter Fifteen

Hannah glanced at the alarm clock on her dresser. It was three in the morning on Monday and she was wide awake. Her neck was stiff and she changed positions, but it didn't seem to help. She looked over at the cats sleeping beside her and realized that Cuddles was sleeping on Moishe's pillow, and Hannah's resident feline had appropriated her pillow in defense.

No wonder her neck felt stiff! Perhaps that was why she had opened her eyes an hour and a half before she had to get up.

She sat up and assessed her condition. Wide awake. Feeling reasonably well rested. Longing for a hot shower to erase the ache in her neck. Hannah knew that if she shooed Moishe off her pillow and tried to go back to sleep, she'd toss and turn for the entire hour and a half before her alarm went off.

You're not going to go back to sleep so you might as well get up, Hannah's rational mind told her. That made sense and Hannah folded back her quilt. As she always did when she looked at her quilt, Hannah smiled. It was printed with cute, frolicking cats, and Norman had given it to her the one time in her life that she'd been locked up in the Winnetka County Jail.

Once Hannah had made her way to the bathroom and taken her morning shower, she felt fully awake, her neck had loosened, and she craved coffee. She sniffed the air, half-hoping that Michelle had heard the master bedroom shower running and had decided to get up, too. But it was clear that Michelle was still asleep because all was silent outside her bedroom door.

It didn't take long for Hannah to dress since she'd chosen her morning outfit before she'd retired for the night. Jeans and a long-sleeved aqua-blue top would be perfect for winter weather, especially if she added the matching cardigan sweater. She could always take the sweater off when she got to work and tie on her signature apron with The Cookie Jar emblazoned on the bib in red.

Once she'd brushed her curly red hair, Hannah turned to look at the cats. They were still sleeping soundly and even though she half-wished for some company in the much-too-early morning, she didn't have the heart to wake them.

Hannah stopped in the hallway and listened, but there was still no sound from Michelle's room, so she resumed her trek down the carpeted hallway. When she entered the living room, she peered over at the couch where Norman was sleeping.

He looks like a little boy in his sleep, Hannah thought, smiling slightly. Everyone always said that people looked younger in their sleep, but she'd never really believed it before. Norman's chest was rising and falling evenly, and there was a slight smile on his face. He was obviously dreaming about something pleasant and Hannah found herself wishing that he was dreaming about her.

She stepped forward, moving silently across the living room carpet, and entered the kitchen, reaching out toward the light switch. And that was when she pulled her hand back. There was no way she was going to turn on the multiple banks of fluorescent fixtures that made the white walls of her kitchen resemble the inside of an operating theater. Norman was still sleeping and he had to go to work at his dental office today. The sudden change in illumination that would flood in from the kitchen could wake him and Hannah didn't want to do that.

Hannah reached for the light switch on the opposite side of the kitchen doorway. When she'd moved into the condo, she had installed soft lighting under the hanging cabinets that lined three walls of her kitchen. She switched that on and smiled as she realized that she now had plenty of light for her purposes.

As she always did when she couldn't sleep or she was upset about some situation in her life, Hannah needed clarity. She'd discovered, early on, that one method she could use to accomplish that clarity, to see things with fresh eyes, was to bake. There was something about performing the familiar steps involved in following a recipe that cleared her mind of distractions and gave her new ideas for dealing with problems.

Before coffee? Her rational mind asked her, and Hannah thought about that for a moment. Perhaps she'd wait to bake until she'd fortified herself with caffeine.

The recipe for Chocolate Cream Pie that Sally had given her was on the counter next to the toaster. Hannah paged through it, reading the ingredients and directions as she went. She had all the ingredients she needed to make Sally's pie. She didn't even have to turn on the oven because the chocolate pudding part of the pie was made on the stovetop.

She went to the cupboard that contained her baking things to get one of the prepared crusts she kept there. She had graham cracker, shortbread, and chocolate wafer crusts. Sally had used a chocolate wafer crust, but Hannah knew that any of the prepared crusts would do even though Sally made hers from scratch. Hannah didn't feel like being that much of a purist, and she didn't mind using a prepared crust if it saved her valuable time.

Once the crust was unwrapped and sitting on the counter, Hannah assembled the ingredients for the pudding that filled the chocolate pudding layer of the pie. In a very short period of time she had set out a package of mini chocolate chips, cocoa powder, white granulated sugar, a quarter of a stick of salted butter, a container of half-and-half, a carton of large eggs, and a box of cornstarch. She checked the recipe to make sure she hadn't forgotten anything, carried the recipe to the table to read, after she'd had her first cup of coffee, and hurried to the coffeemaker.

The first thing Hannah did was thank her lucky stars that Delores had given her a new coffeemaker for Christmas. The water in the reservoir heated very rapidly and she slipped in one of the large pods filled with coffee that made a whole pot. Once the carafe was in place, she pressed the button to brew the coffee and the coffeemaker gurgled and began to transfer hot water to the pod. A second or two later, brewed coffee dripped into the carafe. That was when Hannah did something the instructions did not recommend. With a coffee mug in one hand, she grabbed the carafe with the other, pulled it out quickly, and replaced it with her coffee mug. Once the machine had filled her mug, she quickly removed it with one hand and slid the carafe back in place with the other hand. All this had taken a bit of juggling, but once Hannah had taken her first sip of freshly brewed coffee, she was convinced it had been well worth it.

"Ahhhh!" She breathed, feeling euphoric as she carried the full mug to the kitchen table, pulled out a chair, and sat down. There was nothing like a bracing cup of strong coffee first thing in the morning!

"Can you sneak one out for me, too?" a male voice asked, and Hannah turned to see Norman standing in the doorway.

"I'm so sorry, Norman!" Hannah apologized. "I didn't mean to wake you!"

"You didn't. I woke up to my favorite

morning scent, freshly brewed coffee. Can you sneak out another mug, Hannah?"

"Of course I can," Hannah replied immediately, taking another coffee mug from the cupboard and beginning to execute a similar procedure for Norman. Once she'd successfully completed the maneuver, she carried his coffee to the table and sat down next to him.

"Watching you do that without spilling a drop makes me think I ought to teach you some of my magic tricks," Norman commented.

"Not unless you promise to be my assistant and you're willing to wear that awful purple gown."

"Never mind. I'm drawing the line at that!"

Hannah chuckled and so did Norman. They sat there, silent for a time, sipping their coffee and enjoying the feeling of being awake when everyone else was sleeping. Then Norman reached out to pat her shoulder. "Are you nervous about today, Hannah?"

Hannah knew exactly what he meant. It was Monday and Ross was scheduled to come back to Lake Eden to sign the withdrawal slip so that she could get his money from Doug at the bank. "I'm a little nervous," she admitted.

"A little? Or more than a little?"

Hannah thought about that for a moment. "Maybe a bit more nervous than I'd like to be. I wish I knew whether Ross was coming or not. And I wish I knew what he'll do when Doug says he couldn't get that much money on such short notice."

"Don't worry. After you went to bed last night, I called Mike and we talked about that. Mike and I are going to stay with you at The Cookie Jar, and Lonnie and Rick are going to back Doug up at the bank. You don't have to worry, Hannah. We won't leave your side until we get the word that Ross has left town."

"But . . . how about your dental appointments at the clinic?"

"No problem. I talked to Doc Bennett and he's happy to fill in for me and make a little extra cash. He's planning to go on another cruise with the widow he met on the last one."

Hannah gave a huge sigh of relief. She hadn't known she was that nervous about what Ross might do, but with Norman, Mike, Lonnie, and Rick looking out for her, she felt as if a tremendous weight had slid off her shoulders.

"Feel better?" Norman asked, smiling at her.

"A lot better. I guess I was more worried than I thought I was."

"What are you making?" Norman asked, gesturing toward the ingredients that were lined up on the counter.

"Sally's Chocolate Cream Pie. She gave me the recipe the last time I saw her and I wanted to try it this morning."

"Is there anything I can do to help you?"

Hannah thought about that for a moment and then she began to smile. "You can help me whisk the chocolate pudding when I make it. Sally's recipe calls for a lot of whisking."

"Then I'm your man. I can wield a whisk with the best of them," Norman promised. "Let's finish our coffee and try that pie."

It didn't take long to make the pie with both of them working. Once the pudding had cooled a bit, Hannah poured it into the prepared pie shell, covered the top of the pudding with plastic wrap, and stuck the pie in the refrigerator. "It has to chill before I can put on the whipped cream topping," she told Norman.

"Something smells like chocolate in here," Michelle said, coming into the kitchen. "What is it?"

"Sally's Chocolate Cream Pie," Norman told her. "Hannah and I just made the pudding part."

"Well, it smells delicious!" Michelle walked over to the coffee carafe and poured herself a full mug. "I'll make another pot of coffee. This one's almost gone. And then we can talk about breakfast."

"There's nothing to talk about," Norman told her. "I'm taking you and Hannah out to the Corner Tavern for breakfast. We're going to meet Mike and Lonnie there."

Michelle looked surprised. "Lonnie didn't say anything about that."

"He probably doesn't know yet. Mike and I arranged it. I'm going to be Hannah's guard detail at The Cookie Jar today, and Lonnie and Rick are going to support Doug at the bank."

"Then you think that Ross will show up at the bank?" Michelle asked Hannah.

"If he wants the money, he will! He's desperate to get his hands on that money, and the last time he called me, I told him that I couldn't withdraw it for him."

Michelle didn't look convinced. "Did Ross believe you?"

"I think so."

"Okay then." Michelle drained her coffee mug and stood up. "Is it okay if I use the guest bathroom shower first, Norman?"

"I'm sure it's fine," Hannah told her. "I've already showered, so Norman can use the one in the master bedroom. And then we can all go out for breakfast." Hannah said no more, but her suspicious mind added a final clause to the last sentence. It was, *before Ross comes to town and all hell breaks loose!*

SALLY'S CHOCOLATE CREAM PIE

This pie is a pudding pie with whipped cream and does not bake in the oven.

The Crust:

8-inch or 9-inch prepared crushed chocolate wafer or crushed Oreo pie crust.

Hannah's 1st Note: You can also use a prepared crushed cookie pie crust, a graham cracker pie crust, or a shortbread pie crust. You can even use a regular pie crust as long as you bake and cool it first.

The Chocolate Filling:

6 large egg yolks ***(save the whites to make your favorite meringue cookies)***

3/4 cup white ***(granulated)*** sugar

2 Tablespoons cornstarch

3 cups light cream ***(Half n' Half)***

1 cup mini semi-sweet chocolate chips, finely chopped ***(measure AFTER chopping)***

1/2 stick ***(4 Tablespoons, 1/4 cup, 1/8 pound)*** salted butter

The Whipped Cream Topping:
1 and 1/2 cups heavy cream
1/4 cup powdered ***(confectioners')*** sugar
1/2 teaspoon vanilla extract

Decorations: (Optional)
shaved chocolate
chocolate curls
maraschino cherry halves
butterscotch or caramel ice cream topping
to drizzle on top

Place the egg yolks in a medium-size saucepan, off the heat.

Whisk the egg yolks until they are well combined.

Add the white granulated sugar and the cornstarch. Whisk everything together, off the heat, until the ingredients are well incorporated.

Turn the stovetop burner on MEDIUM-HIGH heat and add the 3 cups of light cream ***(half and half)*** SLOWLY, whisking continuously while the mixture is heating.

Whisk and bring to a boil until the mixture is slightly thickened. ***(This will take from 3***

to 4 minutes.)

Stirring constantly, boil mixture for 3 minutes.

Hannah's 2nd Note: This is much easier to do if you have a hand mixer turned to LOW speed, but you'll have to make sure that all areas of the saucepan are being mixed. If you miss an area, your chocolate filling may scorch and you'll have to start over!

Whisk in the finely chopped mini chocolate chips and the half-stick of salted butter. Keep your whisk moving the entire time!

Lower the temperature of the burner to LOW and continue to whisk until the mixture is as thick as pudding. This should take about 5 to 6 minutes.

When the chocolate mixture has thickened, remove the saucepan to a cold stovetop burner and let it sit for 5 minutes.

Use a heat-resistant rubber spatula to transfer the contents of your saucepan to the pie crust of your choice and smooth the top with the heat-resistant spatula.

Cover the surface of the chocolate layer with plastic wrap and place your partially completed Chocolate Cream Pie in the refrigerator to chill for at least 2 hours. ***(Overnight is even better, too.)***

To Make the Whipped Cream Topping:

Hannah's 3rd Note: If you're tired or in a hurry and want a shortcut, simply thaw a small tub of Original Cool Whip and stir in butterscotch ice cream topping or caramel ice cream topping. It will hold its shape better than homemade whipped cream and you can put it on your chilled filling an hour or so before your guests arrive, rather than whipping the cream at the last minute!

Using an electric mixer, whip the heavy cream until stiff peaks form.

Turn the mixer off and sprinkle the powdered sugar on top of the whipped cream.

Mix on HIGH until the powdered sugar is mixed in.

With the mixer running on HIGH, sprinkle in the half-teaspoon of vanilla extract and mix it in.

When everything has been thoroughly incorporated, shut off the mixer and take out the bowl with the whipped cream topping. Give it a final stir with a rubber spatula and set it on the kitchen counter.

Get the pie crust with its chocolate filling out of the refrigerator and set it next to the mixer bowl with the whipped cream topping.

Peel the plastic wrap off the chocolate filling and use the rubber spatula to transfer mounds of whipped cream to the surface of the chocolate filling.

Work quickly to dot the entire surface of the chocolate filling with whipped cream. Continue transferring the whipped cream until the mixer bowl has been emptied.

Using the rubber spatula, spread the mounds of whipped cream together to cover the entire surface of your Chocolate Cream Pie. Make sure the whipped cream topping goes all the way out to the edge of the pie crust.

Using the flat edge of the rubber spatula, press it against the surface of the whipped cream topping and pull it up quickly. This should cause the whipped cream to form a point on top. Make "points" over the entire surface of your Chocolate Cream Pie.

Choose the decorating topping you wish to use on top of the whipped cream. You can use more than one topping to really make it look fancy.

If you choose shaved chocolate, use a sharp knife to "shave" the edge of a bar of sweet chocolate. Place the shaved pieces in a bowl and, using your impeccably clean fingers, sprinkle the shaved chocolate over the surface of your pie.

If you choose chocolate curls to decorate the top of your pie, simply run a sharp knife down the long edge of a bar of sweet chocolate. If you don't lift the knife blade, it will form a curl of chocolate. Use these chocolate curls to decorate the top of your Chocolate Cream Pie.

Maraschino cherries are always colorful

on top of a pie. Cut the maraschino cherries in half vertically and transfer the halves to the surface of the whipped cream topping, rounded side up. Make a large circle of cherry halves around the edge or a design of your own making using the cherry halves.

If you choose butterscotch or caramel ice cream topping, simply drizzle it all over the surface of your pie in a pretty design.

Refrigerate your Chocolate Cream Pie for at least 2 hours before serving.

To serve, cut your Chocolate Cream Pie into 8 pieces and remove the pieces with a triangle-shaped spatula. Place each piece on a dessert plate and serve with a carafe of strong, hot coffee or tall glasses of milk.

Yield: This pie will serve 8 people . . . or 7 if you invite Mother. She'll tell you she couldn't possibly eat more of something so rich, but you won't have to twist her arm to get her to agree to a second helping.

CHAPTER SIXTEEN

"What are those, Hannah?" Lisa pointed to the pan that Hannah had just moved to the bakers rack to cool.

"Tortilla Snickerdoodle Cookies. Except I'm not sure I should call them *cookies* when they're really sweet snacks."

"If they taste as good as they smell, you can call them anything you want to," Lisa said.

"They do!" Mike said from his stool at the work station. "Right, Norman?"

"Right!" Norman agreed.

Lisa hurried over to take one triangular-shaped piece from the bakers rack. She bit into it, started to smile, and popped the rest into her mouth. "Good?" she managed to say with her mouth full. "These are great, Hannah. We could sell bags of these to the kids from Jordan High who come in here after school."

Hannah smiled back. "That's one of the

best things about you, Lisa. You always see a way to promote things and you're almost always right. Jordan High students would love to munch these on their way home. Norman and I finished a whole bowl last night while we were watching an old movie on television."

"That's the sign of a good munchie," Lisa declared, grabbing another Tortilla Snickerdoodle Cookie from the rack. "Are these hard to make?"

Hannah shook her head. "They're really easy. All you have to do is cut flour tortillas into pieces, dip them in melted butter and then into cinnamon, sugar, and cardamom, and bake them for ten to twelve minutes in the oven. A kid could make them . . . Tracey!"

Lisa laughed, "You *just* thought of that?"

"Yes! And Bethie could help her mix the cinnamon, sugar, and cardamom. As long as Grandma McCann sets the oven temperature, they could do it all by themselves."

"That would be a great birthday present for Andrea," Lisa said. "You could teach the kids how to do it and they'd have Tortilla Snickerdoodle Cookies waiting for Andrea when she got home from work."

The phone on the wall rang and Hannah hurried over to answer it. A moment later, she was frowning. "Sure, Mother. I can come over in a few minutes. What's going on at Granny's Attic?"

There was a long pause and then Hannah sighed. "Okay. I'll do my best to calm Carrie down, but you have to tell me what she's worried about."

There was another pause while Hannah listened. "All right, Mother. You can tell me when I get there. I'll bring some cookies. That might help to . . ."

Hannah stopped speaking and looked shocked as she hung up the phone. "Mother hung up on me! She's *never* done *that* before!"

"Never?" Mike asked.

Hannah shook her head. "Never. Mother's too polite to hang up on anybody, even a telephone solicitor."

"Then we'd better go over there right now," Norman said, standing up and heading for the hooks by the back door, where he'd hung his parka.

"I'll stay here, just in case Ross shows up," Mike said. "Something must really be wrong over there. Just call if you need me and I'll come right over."

Hannah packed up a plateful of Tortilla Snickerdoodle Cookies, grabbed her parka, and headed across the parking lot with

Norman. Granny's Attic, Delores and Carrie's antique shop, was only one store away. They went in the back door, wound their way around the antiques that were stored in the back room, and came out by the cash register in the middle of the store.

"Hi, Hannah, Norman," Luanne Hanks, Delores and Carrie's bookkeeper and assistant, greeted them.

"Hi, Luanne." Norman gave her a smile.

"Hello, Luanne," Hannah responded. "Mother called me and asked me to come right over."

"They're upstairs in the break room." Luanne pointed to the staircase in the middle of the room. "Go right up."

"Do you know what's wrong? Mother sounded upset when she called me."

"No. I just know they're up there and they haven't come down. Delores must have made the call from her cell phone."

"I'll wait down here with Luanne," Norman told Hannah, and then he turned to Luanne. "Can I help you do anything while I'm waiting for Hannah?"

Luanne began to smile broadly. "You bet you can! I was about to reposition a couple of antiques that are awkward to move alone. Could you help me?"

"Of course," Norman answered. "I'll wait

for you here, Hannah."

"I'll be down in a bit," Hannah told him, turning and walking toward the central staircase.

The first six stairs went straight up and Hannah climbed them to the landing. A grandfather clock sat against the back wall on the landing and Hannah admired it as she walked across the floor. The remainder of the staircase was set at a ninety-degree angle to the lower stairs. Hannah made a sharp right and climbed the last few steps.

Once she'd reached the second story, Hannah hurried past the other antiques on display. There was a lovely cherrywood bedroom set with a tall chest of drawers and a vanity with an oval-shaped mirror. She admired it as she went past and decided to compliment her mother and Carrie on acquiring such beautiful items. They'd probably tell her that Luanne had found the bedroom set at an estate auction since Luanne now did most of the antique acquisitions. If that was the case, she'd compliment Luanne on her purchase when she went back downstairs.

"Hi, Mother. Hello, Carrie," Hannah greeted the two women who had been friends for years. "I brought you some Tortilla Snickerdoodle Cookies."

"I love these!" Delores told Carrie, and they both reached out for a cookie. Delores and Carrie had met at Lake Eden's Regency Romance Club more than twenty years ago and they had been best friends ever since.

"They're delicious, as usual," Delores told her, finishing her first cookie and reaching for a second.

"Yes, they are!" Carrie echoed her business partner's sentiment. "Thank you for bringing them, Hannah."

"There's coffee or tea if you want it, dear." Delores gestured toward the counter of the break room, where the coffeepot and electric teapot sat.

"I just bought a box of Florence's best peppermint tea," Carrie told Hannah. "I know you don't usually drink tea, but it's really delicious."

Even though Hannah preferred coffee to tea, she fixed herself a cup. It was a way of subtly connecting with Carrie. Then she sat down at the round oak table that sat in the center of the break room.

"Carrie has a problem, dear," Delores said, the moment Hannah had taken her first sip of tea and complimented Carrie on her choice.

"Tell me," Hannah said, giving Carrie an

encouraging smile. "I'd be happy to help, if I can."

"I think you can," Delores declared, and then she nodded to Carrie. "Go head, Carrie. Tell Hannah what's going on."

"Well . . . it's Earl," Carrie admitted in a voice that trembled slightly. "I'm afraid he's going to . . . to do something violent!"

"What makes you think he might?" Hannah asked.

"It's his background, Hannah. Most people don't know this, but Earl was sent overseas when he was in his twenties. I don't know where he went or what his job was because he never talks about anything that happened there. All he'll tell me is that it was very hard and he did some things that he'd never do again unless it was absolutely necessary."

"What do you think he did?" Hannah asked her.

"I don't know. I asked him if he was ever in the military and he told me he wasn't. When I mentioned it to your mother, she had an idea that might explain what he was talking about."

"Mother?" Hannah turned to her. "What do you think Earl did?"

Delores cleared her throat. "Of course I don't actually know, but Earl has a background in repairing and operating heavy machinery. He comes from around Lake Eden and I can remember my mother telling me that Earl went away to take construction courses somewhere in Florida. She was friends with Earl's mother and I didn't pay much attention at the time, but I'm sure it's true. After all, Earl works for the county and he keeps the snowplows and bulldozers running."

"And he told me that all the county equipment is as old as the hills," Carrie added.

"It all makes sense if you think about it," Delores continued. "I think that Earl could have been a civilian contractor who took a job overseas. If he found himself in a dangerous situation, Earl may have had to defend himself and his equipment. A job like that might place him in jeopardy without actually having been in the military."

Hannah thought about that for a moment. "You're right, Mother. That could explain everything. There's only one other explanation that occurs to me."

"What is it?" Carrie leaned forward expectantly.

"Perhaps Earl was in some kind of government organization like the CIA or something similar. Then perhaps he isn't allowed to talk about what happened."

"I didn't even think of that!" Delores said. "It's certainly possible, though." She turned to Carrie, "I think we've thought of all the reasonable explanations, Carrie."

Except, of course, that Earl is lying through his teeth about everything because he thinks it'll make him seem more important, Hannah's suspicious mind suggested, but she kept that thought to herself. Thinking it was one thing. Saying it was another. If she even suggested it to Carrie, it might make her worry even more. "What are you afraid Earl might do?" she asked Carrie instead.

It took Carrie a moment before she answered. Then she took a deep breath and blurted out, "I'm afraid that if Ross comes back to Lake Eden again, Earl will kill him! He was furious when he found out that Ross confronted you at The Cookie Jar."

"But do you really think that Earl might resort to something like that?" Hannah asked.

Carrie wouldn't meet Hannah's eyes. "Yes, I do. Earl carries a gun and a rifle on his snowplow. He told me it's just in case he runs into a bear or another dangerous animal and it attacks. And he told me that he killed a wildcat once when he got out to move a big tree branch from one of the isolated country roads at night."

"Where is Earl plowing today?" Hannah asked, hoping that Carrie wouldn't ask why she wanted to know.

"He's out on the roads around Eden Lake. Jessie Pillager called this morning and asked if Earl could plow the road that runs past his lake cabin. It's been snowed in since the blizzard and Jessie wants to go out to check the pipes."

Hannah drew a deep breath in relief. Earl was nowhere in town and if Ross did show up to try to get his cash from the bank, Earl wouldn't find out about it until after Ross had left.

"Jessie's got a problem on his hands if he didn't wrap those pipes," Delores commented. "It was really cold last week."

Carrie shrugged. "That's Jessie. Earl says he likes to roll the dice when it comes to going out to winterize his cabin. He had to replace all his pipes year before last because he waited too long to wrap them and they burst."

"What would you like me to do about this?" Hannah asked Carrie.

"Talk to Earl and tell him to be careful. The big problem is that Earl thinks the sun rises and sets on Norman. He adores my son. And he knows that Norman is in love with you. He also knows that Ross wronged you and he likes you a lot, Hannah. I wouldn't put it past Earl to want to get even with Ross for hurting you."

Hannah nodded even though she thought that Carrie was probably borrowing trouble. "I'll talk to Earl," she promised.

"Oh, good! He'll be coming in The Cookie Jar sometime in the late morning or early afternoon. I told him I wanted him to pick up some cookies for tonight's dessert. Will you tell Lisa to keep an eye out for Earl and tell you when he gets there?"

"Of course I will." Hannah finished her peppermint tea, even though she didn't really want it, and carried her cup to the sink. "I'd better get back to work now. Lisa probably needs more fresh cookies in the coffee shop."

"I'll walk you partway down," Delores said, rising from her chair. "I want to reset the grandfather clock on the landing. I heard it chime earlier this morning and it's five minutes slow."

Delores put her hand on Hannah's arm as they reached the landing. "Thank you for coming right over, dear," she said in a voice that couldn't be overheard from above. "I think Carrie is worried for no reason, but she knows Earl a lot better than I do."

"I'll take care of it, Mother," Hannah assured her. "Tell Carrie I'll talk to Earl the minute he comes in."

TORTILLA SNICKERDOODLE COOKIES

Preheat oven to 350 degrees F., rack in the middle position.

1 package containing 10 taco-sized ***(8-inch)*** flour tortillas ***(You will use 6 of these flour tortillas in this recipe.)***
3 teaspoons ground cinnamon
1/2 cup white ***(granulated)*** sugar
1/2 cup ***(1 stick, 4 ounces, 1/4 pound)*** salted butter

Prepare a baking sheet or a cookie sheet by lining it with parchment paper.

Cut each tortilla into 8 equal pieces.

Hannah's 1st Note: The easiest way to do this is to cut the circle in half, cut each half in half to make quarters, and cut each quarter in half to make 8 pieces.

Place the cinnamon in a shallow bowl on the counter.

Add the white granulated sugar to the bowl and mix them together with a fork.

Hannah's 2nd Note: We usually place the cinnamon and sugar in a sealable plastic bag and shake it to mix the two ingredients.

Place the half-cup of salted butter in a second shallow bowl that is microwave-safe.

Heat the butter on HIGH in the microwave for 30 seconds. Check to see if your butter is melted. If it is, leave the bowl in the microwave. If it isn't, heat it for another 15 seconds on HIGH.

Take the bowl out of the microwave and set it on your kitchen counter next to the bowl with the cinnamon and sugar mixture. ***(Be careful. The bowl with the melted butter could be hot.)***

Move the prepared cookie sheet next to the bowls for easy access.

Dip each flour tortilla piece into the bowl with the melted butter. Be sure to coat both sides of the piece.

Take the piece out of the butter bowl and dip it in the bowl with the cinnamon and sugar. Again, be sure to coat both sides with the cinnamon and sugar mixture.

Do this for all of your flour tortilla pieces.

Hannah's 3rd Note: If you have quite a bit of melted butter and cinnamon and sugar mixture left, don't worry. You can always save it to make more Tortilla Snickerdoodle Cookies after the first sheet comes out of the oven. You may have to re-melt the butter if your kitchen is cold, but that's easy to do in the microwave.

When all of your tortilla pieces have been coated with butter, the cinnamon and sugar mixture, and placed on the cookie sheet, you are ready to bake them.

Bake the Tortilla Snickerdoodle Cookies at 350 degrees F. for approximately 10 to 12 minutes or until they are a nice golden brown. ***(My cookies took the full 12 minutes.)***

Take the cookie sheet out of the oven, place it on a cold stovetop burner or a wire rack on the counter, and let your delicious snack cookies cool thoroughly. Then take them off the parchment paper and serve them.

If there are leftover Tortilla Snickerdoodle Cookies ***(and I'm willing to bet there won't be!)***, store them in a cool, dry place. ***(Your refrigerator is cool, but it is NOT dry!)***

Yield: 10 flour tortillas will make 6 dozen crunchy, sweet, and delightful little cookies. ***(Because I know that you will eat at least 8, before you serve them.)***

Chapter Seventeen

Hannah and Norman hurried back to the kitchen of The Cookie Jar and the first thing Hannah did was look at the clock. It was twenty minutes before ten in the morning and the Lake Eden First Mercantile Bank opened at ten. If Ross was coming to the bank this morning, he was probably here in town already.

"I'll be right back," she told Mike and Norman. "I have to tell Lisa something."

"And then you'll tell us what was wrong with Carrie?" Mike asked her.

Hannah took a split second to consider it and then she decided to keep Carrie's secret. "I would, but it's personal," she told them. "It's something to do with her marriage."

"But . . ." Norman looked worried. "It's not something serious, is it?"

"Not at all. Carrie just wanted my advice

about something and I gave it to her. That's all."

Norman began to smile and he turned to Mike. "Earl's birthday is next week," he told Mike. "Mother probably wanted advice on the surprise birthday party she's going to throw for Earl."

"Sorry. I can't tell you yes or no," Hannah hedged. "Just take my word for it. You really don't need to know. If I thought either one of you did, I'd tell you."

Once Hannah had rushed into the coffee shop to tell Lisa to notify her the moment Earl came in, she went back to the kitchen.

"He's not in the coffee shop, is he?" Mike asked her as she came back.

"No. I asked and Lisa said she hadn't seen him. Do you think he'll show up at the bank?"

"Six of one, half-dozen of another," Mike said with a shrug. "Do you think Ross believed Doug when Doug told him that you couldn't withdraw money without his approval?"

"I don't know. I thought I knew Ross really well, but I don't. Actually, I'm not sure I could ever accurately predict his intentions. And if I could, I certainly can't do it now!"

"I think he'll show up at the bank,"

Norman said, and Hannah noticed that he seemed very sure of that.

"What makes you say that?" she asked him.

"You said Ross sounded desperate to get his hands on that money. If you think about it, there's no reason for him *not* to show up."

"Other than the fact that I told him there were some people in town that wanted to punch him into oblivion," Mike said. "And I told him that I couldn't guarantee his safety if he came back to Lake Eden."

"True," Norman conceded. "But people like Ross always think they have an edge. He's a classic egomaniac. He's sure he's smart enough to talk his way out of anything. And he's convinced that he can make people like him again."

Hannah turned to stare at Norman in surprise. He'd described Ross's personality perfectly. Ross *was* an egomaniac.

"How do you know all that?" she asked Norman.

"From personal experience. My dad was like that. I discussed it with my mother after he died, and she said he was a master at blaming her for everything that went wrong in their lives and insisting that he never did anything wrong. My father was incapable of feeling guilt about anything."

Hannah thought about the photos that Norman's dad had taken of his patients and knew that Norman was right. Dr. Rhodes had probably felt no guilt for taking advantage of his patients.

Mike gave a little nod. "I've arrested criminals like that, even murderers, who believe that their victims deserved to die and by killing them, they were doing the right thing. People like that don't have any sense of right or wrong. And anyone who encounters them finds them very frightening."

Hannah gave a little shiver. She didn't want to think that Ross was like that, but she couldn't help having doubts. He must have known that he was already married when he'd proposed to her. And he hadn't even mentioned it to her. He hadn't said word one about it during the weeks leading up to their wedding when he'd told her things about his background and family. Were they all lies? Had Ross considered it perfectly all right to marry her when he was already married to someone else? Or was he hoping that he'd never get caught?

As she usually did when she needed to calm down, Hannah reached for the large loose-leaf recipe book at the work station.

"I need to bake, guys," she said to Mike and Norman. "I'm too nervous to just sit here and drink coffee, so I might as well be productive."

The first thing Hannah did was turn to the new recipe section in the back of the book. When someone gave her a recipe or she came up with one of her own that she wanted to try, she encased them in plastic three-hole folders and put them in her recipe book.

"Which would you rather eat?" Hannah asked them, paging through the recipes she'd collected but hadn't yet vetted. "I have one for Butterscotch and Chocolate Bar Cookies and another for Coconut Snow Cookies."

"I'd like the coconut one," Norman said.

And at the same time, Mike said, "I'd like to try the butterscotch and chocolate ones."

"Flip a coin," Hannah told them. "I can only bake one thing at a time."

Hannah watched as Norman pulled a coin from his pocket. "Better check that," she told Mike. "Norman's a magician, you know. He could have a coin that's the same on both sides."

"Right," Mike said, holding out his hand for the coin. He examined it, gave a little nod, and said, "You call it, I'll flip it."

"Tails," Norman said as Mike flipped the coin in the air. It went almost up to the kitchen ceiling and came tumbling back down again to land with a clatter on the stainless steel surface.

"It's heads," Norman announced, looking at the coin and giving Mike a sour look. "Did you cheat?"

"How could I cheat? I'm not *that* good at flipping coins. Best two out of three?"

"Deal," Norman agreed.

Mike picked up the coin and flipped it airborne again. "Call it, Norman!"

"Tails," Norman said as the coin began its downward descent.

All three friends watched as the coin landed and then Norman began to grin. "It's tails," he announced.

"I know." Mike picked it up and flipped it again.

"Tails," Norman chose for the third time.

Hannah found that she was holding her breath as the coin began to fall. She didn't really care which recipe she made, but she'd never had anyone flip a coin to choose a cookie before!

"Tails!" Mike said with a disgusted sigh. "Okay, Hannah. It's the coconut one. And I was all set for chocolate."

That gave Hannah an idea. "Then you

both win. You can have Coconut Snow Cookies plain, or I can make sandwich cookies out of them with Nutella in the middle."

"Sounds great!" Mike looked very pleased. "You're right, Hannah. Looks like we both won."

COCONUT SNOW COOKIES

DO NOT preheat oven — dough must chill before baking.

2 cups melted butter ***(4 sticks, 16 ounces, 1 pound)***
2 cups powdered ***(confectioners)*** sugar ***(don't sift unless it's got big lumps and then you shouldn't use it anyway)***
1 cup flaked coconut ***(pack it down in the cup when you measure it)***
1 cup white ***(granulated)*** sugar
2 large eggs
1 teaspoon vanilla extract
1 teaspoon coconut extract
1 teaspoon baking soda
1 teaspoon cream of tartar ***(critical!)***
1 teaspoon salt
4 and 1/4 cups flour ***(don't sift — pack it down in the cup when you measure it)***

1/2 cup powdered ***(confectioners')*** sugar ***(pack it down in the cup when you measure it)***
1/2 cup flaked coconut ***(pack it down in the cup when you measure it)***

Melt the butter in a microwave-safe bowl or in a saucepan over LOW heat on the stovetop. Set it aside off the heat to cool while you complete the next few steps.

Place the powdered sugar in the bowl of a food processor. ***(If you don't have a food processor, you can use a blender.)***

Measure out the flaked coconut and add that on top of the powdered sugar in the food processor or blender.

Process the powdered sugar and coconut in on/off motion with the steel blade. Continue until the coconut has been ground down into very small pieces.

Add the cup of white granulated sugar.

Crack open the eggs and place them in the bowl of an electric mixer.

Add the eggs and mix them together until everything is a uniform color.

Feel the sides of the container with the melted butter. If it's not so hot it might cook the eggs, you will be able to work with it now. If it feels too hot to you, sit down, have a cup of coffee, and wait until the butter is cool enough to add to the egg mixture.

With the mixer running on LOW, slowly pour the melted butter into the bowl of the mixer. Continue to mix until it is well combined.

Mix in the vanilla extract and the coconut extract.

Add the baking soda, cream of tartar, and salt. Mix until everything is thoroughly combined.

Remember the food processor with the powdered sugar and coconut mixture? Take the bowl out of the food processor and with the mixer running on LOW, add the powdered sugar and coconut mixture to the contents of your bowl. Mix until everything is thoroughly combined.

Hannah's 1st Note: Don't bother to wash the bowl of your food processor or blender. You will be using it again for the exact same ingredients.

Again, with the mixer running on LOW, add the flour in one-cup increments, mixing thoroughly after each addition.

Cover your Coconut Snow Cookie dough

with plastic wrap and put it in the refrigerator. Chill it for at least one hour. ***(Overnight is fine, too.)***

When you're ready to bake, take the bowl of dough out of the refrigerator and set it on the kitchen counter to warm a bit.

Preheat oven to 350 degrees F. with the rack in the middle position.

Hannah's 2nd Note: While the oven is preheating to the proper temperature, you will prepare your cookie sheets and make another powdered sugar and coconut mixture in that food processor or blender that you didn't wash.

Prepare your cookie sheets by spraying them with Pam or another cooking spray or, alternatively, lining them with parchment paper.

Hannah's 3rd Note: I prefer to use parchment paper to line my cookie sheets. That way, all I have to do when I take the cookies from the oven is to grab the edge of the parchment paper and pull it, cookies and all, over to a

wire rack to cool the cookies.

Place the powdered sugar in the bowl of your food processor or blender.

Measure out the flaked coconut and add that to the powdered sugar.

Process with the steel blade in an on-and-off motion until the coconut has been cut into very small pieces.

Place the powdered sugar and coconut mixture in a shallow bowl. You will use it to coat the cookie dough balls that you will roll.

Use your impeccably clean hands to roll the dough in walnut-sized balls.

Place the balls, one at a time, in the bowl with the powdered sugar and coconut mixture and roll them around until they are coated.

Place the balls on your prepared cookie sheets, 12 balls to a standard-size cookie sheet.

Flatten the dough balls with the back of a

metal spatula or the palm of your impeccably clean hand. The dough balls will spread out in nice circles that are approximately 3 inches in diameter.

Bake at 350 degrees F. for 10 to 13 minutes. ***(The cookies should have a tinge of gold on the top.)***

Cool your Coconut Snow Cookies on the cookie sheets by placing them on cold stovetop burners or wire racks. Cool this way for 2 to 3 minutes and then use a wide metal spatula to transfer the cookies themselves to the wire racks.

Hannah's 4th Note: If you used parchment paper, just grab the edge and pull it over to the wire racks.

Yield: approximately 10 dozen crunchy, buttery, sugary cookies, which will make 4 to 5 dozen Coconut Snow Sandwich Cookies.

Hannah's 5th Note: You can eat these cookies just the way they are and they're delicious. But you can also make them into fabulous sandwich cookies. Instructions follow on the next page.

COCONUT SNOW SANDWICH COOKIES

1 jar of Nutella ***(chocolate hazelnut spread)***

Open the jar of Nutella and spread the bottom of one cookie with the chocolate-hazelnut spread.

Place the other cookie, bottom down, on top of the Nutella filling.

Repeat above instructions for all of your cookies.

Store in a cookie jar or box in the pantry or cupboard. You can also refrigerate, but you'll take the chance of having your sandwich cookies get soggy.

Hannah's 1st Note: The following list suggests other spreads you can use in these Coconut Snow Sandwich Cookies

Any flavor of jam — use a thin layer or it will squeeze out between the cookie halves. To solve this problem, mix a little powdered ***(confectioners')*** sugar into the jam so that it is thicker and will maintain its shape.

Any flavor of jelly — use a thick layer or it will squeeze out between the cookie halves. To solve this problem, mix a little powdered ***(confectioners')*** sugar into the jelly so that it is thicker and will maintain its shape.

Cashew Butter

Peanut Butter

Almond Butter

Commercial frosting, the kind that you'll find on the baking aisle

Melted semi-sweet chocolate chips thickened with a little powdered ***(confectioners')*** sugar

Melted butterscotch chips thickened with a little powdered ***(confectioners')*** sugar

Melted milk chocolate chips thickened with

a little powdered ***(confectioners')*** sugar

Melted peanut butter chips thickened with a little powdered ***(confectioners')*** sugar

Melted white chocolate or vanilla chips thickened with a little powdered ***(confectioners')*** sugar

Hannah's 2nd Note: Believe it or not, Mike likes cheddar cheese spread between his cookies. Feel free to try it, but no one else I know seems to like Coconut Snow Sandwich Cookies that way!

CHAPTER EIGHTEEN

At a few minutes after eleven, Lonnie had called to report that there had been no action at the bank yet. Ross had not shown up. Mike had contacted Herb, who was keeping his eye on the entrance to town, and that was a negative, too.

"Do you think he'll show up?" Hannah asked Mike.

Mike shrugged. "Maybe. He's got plenty of time. The bank's open until three."

At eleven-fifteen, the swinging door from the coffee shop swung open and Earl Flensburg came into the kitchen. "You wanted to see me?" he asked Hannah.

"Yes," Hannah said, quickly dishing up a plate of Coconut Snow Cookies, even though they were barely cool enough to eat. "Try my new cookies, Earl. And I'll get you a cup of coffee."

"Hi, Norman," Earl greeted his son-in-law. "Mike? Good to see you."

"Good to see you, too," Mike responded. "Out with the plow again today?"

"Sure am. I'm plowing around the lake. Jessie Pillager wants to get out there to check his pipes."

Norman groaned. "Don't tell me he was late wrapping his pipes again this year!"

"He was. And, actually, he *is.* Jessie's going out there to do what he should have done last October."

"That's Jessie," Norman said. "He's a nice guy, but he's always a day late and a dollar short."

"In this case, it might be a thousand dollars short and four months late!" Earl predicted. "It got pretty cold during the blizzard and the wind that comes across the icy lake is freezing cold. I'll lay odds that Jessie's pipes have already burst."

"No way I'll bet on that," Mike told him.

Norman shook his head. "Me neither."

"These are really good, Hannah," Earl said when he'd tasted one of her Coconut Snow Cookie Sandwiches.

"Thank you. I'll let Carrie decide if she wants to serve them plain, or if she wants to make sandwich cookies out of them."

"We like Nutella," Earl told her. "What else could you use between the cookies?"

"Peanut, cashew, or almond butter. Or any

flavor of jam. Any flavor of frosting would be good, too. The possibilities are almost endless."

Earl smiled. "Knowing Carrie, she'll probably want to use crab apple jelly. She made some last year from the crab apple tree in our backyard. Or maybe rhubarb jam. She makes that, too."

"Mom's rhubarb jam is great!" Norman complimented his mother. "I miss it."

"Then you'd better take a trip to our basement," Earl told him. "Carrie filled a whole shelf with rhubarb jam."

When Earl got up to leave, his box of Coconut Snow Cookies in his hands, Hannah also rose from her stool. "Are you parked in back, Earl?"

"Yes, I didn't want to take up your parking spots in front."

"Then I'll walk you out," Hannah told him, motioning to Norman and Mike to stay seated. "I'll be right back, guys."

Hannah waited until the back kitchen door had closed behind them before she broached the subject of Carrie's concern. "Carrie's a little worried about you, Earl."

"She is?" Earl looked genuinely surprised. "Why?"

"Carrie's afraid that you might use one of those firearms you carry on the snowplow if you see Ross."

Earl looked absolutely shocked. "But she ought to know better! I carry those because I sometimes run into wild animals on the country roads when I'm plowing. I can't believe that Carrie actually thought that I'd do something like that!"

"Well, she didn't really think so, but she wanted me to talk to you about it," Hannah said quickly, doing her best to exonerate Carrie from what could be an argument between husband and wife.

"Why did she think I'd do something that drastic?" Earl asked her, and Hannah could see that he appeared completely puzzled.

"She knows how much you like Norman. And she said you know how much Norman loves me. And she thought . . ."

Earl began to smile. "That I'd defend your honor or something like that?"

"Yes, something like that."

"Well . . . she's right in a sense. I would, but not that way! Let's be honest here, Hannah. I don't like what Ross did to you one bit! I think it was . . ." Earl paused, and Hannah knew he was trying to think of the correct words to describe how he felt. "I think it was disgraceful and totally unforgivable! And I *do* believe that Ross should be held accountable for hurting you! A lot of people in town feel the way I do, but I don't think any of them would actually take any drastic action."

"You mean they wouldn't run him out of town on a rail?"

"I didn't say that. They might, if they knew what that meant. Or they might tar and feather him if they knew how to do it. Don't get me wrong. If they accused him and he sassed them back, or tried to say that everything that happened was all your fault and not his, they'd probably coldcock him. I know I would and I *do* know what that means."

Hannah drew a relieved breath. "I'm glad to hear you say that, Earl. I was afraid that Ross would come back here and some well-meaning, but misguided person would attack him and get into trouble by doing it."

"It could happen that way," Earl admitted. "I told Carrie that if I saw him back in Lake Eden, I'd scoop him off the road with my snowplow. That's probably why she was worried."

Hannah smiled at him. "Thanks for being so honest with me, Earl. I'll tell Carrie that she doesn't have to worry about you anymore."

When Hannah got back inside, she poured

herself a hot cup of coffee and joined Mike and Norman at the work station. She didn't really want the coffee, but it had been cold outside and she needed to warm up. She cupped her hands around the cup, lifted it to her mouth, and took a sip. The hot liquid helped, but she found herself wishing that it were chicken broth instead of coffee. Her stomach had been giving her a bit of trouble lately and she knew she'd been drinking too much coffee. Perhaps she should buy some bouillon cubes the next time she went to the Red Owl Grocery, and drink broth made in the kitchen microwave instead of the endless cups of black coffee she was in the habit of consuming every day.

There was a knock on the back kitchen door, and Mike got up quickly. "I'll get it," he said, heading to the door. There was a moment before he opened it, and Hannah knew he'd checked the peephole that he and Lonnie had installed right after she'd told them about Ross's early-morning visit to The Cookie Jar.

"Come in, guys!" Hannah heard Mike say, and she went to pour more cups of coffee. Lonnie and Rick were back from the bank and she could hardly wait to hear what had happened.

"Doug!" Hannah gasped when she turned

around with two cups of coffee in her hands. "I didn't expect you to come back here with Lonnie and Rick."

"I know, but I wanted to tell you what happened this morning myself," Doug said. "I'm not sure I handled the situation as well as I could have. And if I didn't, I want to personally apologize to you."

"As long as you did the best you could, that's good enough for me," Hannah assured him. "Just let me get another cup of coffee for you and then you can tell us what happened when Ross got there."

Hannah hurried to the coffeepot and poured another cup. She quickly put on another pot, carried Doug's coffee back to the work station, set it in front of him, and gave him an encouraging smile. "So what happened when Ross got to the bank?"

"That's just it. He didn't."

That caught Hannah completely by surprise and it took her a moment to respond. "Ross didn't show up?!"

"No. Lonnie and Rick and I waited in my office until almost eleven, but there was no sign of him. Then I went out and told Lydia that if Ross came into the bank, she should buzz me immediately and say that I was waiting for him in my office. That's where

Lonnie, Rick, and I sat until we came over here."

Hannah couldn't help the shocked expression that crossed her face. She'd been so sure that Ross would show up to sign the withdrawal slip. "So Ross didn't contact you at all?" she asked.

"Not physically. But about twenty minutes ago, Lydia buzzed me to say that I had a phone call. I asked who was calling and she didn't know, but she said the caller had told her that it was imperative for him to talk to me."

There was only one question to ask and Hannah asked it. "And it was Ross?"

"Yes."

"That makes sense," Mike said. "Ross only contacted Hannah once in person and that was before anyone else in town was awake."

"The other two times I talked to Ross, it was on my cell phone," Hannah explained. "What did you do when you realized that the phone call was from Ross?"

"As soon as I realized it was Ross, I wrote Ross's name in big, block letters on my notepad so Lonnie and Rick would know who it was. And then I put the call on speaker phone so they could listen in."

"Smart," Mike commented, giving Doug

an approving nod. "Go on, Doug."

Doug paused to take a sip of his coffee and then he went on with his account. "The first thing Ross did was identify himself. Then he asked me if I had his withdrawal slip ready to sign and I told him that I did. And then I said that the bank didn't normally keep that much cash on hand, but I'd managed to get it by armored truck early this morning. All I needed was the signed withdrawal slip before I could release it."

"What did he say to that?" Hannah asked.

Doug looked terribly embarrassed. "He accused me of playing games with him to try to get him into the bank. And he called me a name that I'd rather not repeat in polite company. I was shocked, Hannah. The first part of our conversation was friendly, almost like he was a regular bank customer. But then he turned ugly. He said I should listen to him and listen carefully, that he'd filled out a withdrawal slip that he had with him and taken a cell phone photo of it. He was faxing that photo to the bank and since he'd already signed the withdrawal slip, I should give the money to you and be quick about it."

"Did you explain that you couldn't accept a fax, that you had to personally witness his signature?" Mike asked.

"Of course I did. And then he called me another name, even worse than the first one, accused me of setting a trap for him, and said that if I didn't release the money to Hannah, there would be some very nasty consequences."

Rick nodded. "It was really frightening, Hannah. Ross sounded really unhinged. Both Lonnie and I think he's insane."

"That's right," Lonnie agreed. "It was almost like he had two personalities, the nice one and the nasty, vindictive one."

"I'm sorry, Hannah," Doug apologized, "but the change in his voice really rattled me."

"It rattled me, too," Hannah admitted. "What else did Ross say?"

"He accused me of lying to him. He said he knew that I'd given the money to you because we were friends. And he said the word *friends* in a very nasty way!"

"What came next?" Mike asked him.

"He repeated that there would be consequences for lying to him, that he knew the truth and I wouldn't get away with trying to trick him."

They sat there looking at each other for a moment. Ross truly *was* insane.

Doug shook his head. "That's really all I can tell you, Hannah."

Hannah picked up on Doug's phrasing. "I understand. But did Ross say anything else?"

"Yes, but I'd rather not say. It's . . . really bad."

"You have to tell us, Doug," Mike said, giving him a hard look. "It's important."

"I know." Doug sighed, and it was clear to everyone that he didn't want to go on.

"Go ahead," Hannah encouraged him. "We have to know what to expect from him, Doug."

"Okay." Doug swallowed again. "Ross gave that really nasty laugh again and said it wouldn't do any good, that he was going to get his money back from Hannah even if he had to . . ."

"If he had to . . . what?" Mike leaned forward.

Doug looked more troubled than Hannah had ever seen before. "Ross said he was going to get his money back from Hannah even if he had to kill her to get it!"

Chapter Nineteen

"Are you okay, Hannah?" Norman asked, when Hannah came back to her stool at the work station.

"I think so. I just got a little sick to my stomach when Doug told us about . . . what Ross said."

"I know. You looked as if you were about to faint."

"Maybe you're right. I did feel really dizzy and horribly sick to my stomach." Hannah took a sip of the orange juice she'd poured for herself. "Where did everybody go?"

"Mike assigned Rick and Lonnie to stay with Doug," Norman told her. "He thought that when Ross found out that you didn't have his money, he might blame Doug and try to hurt him."

"So Rick and Lonnie are at the bank with Doug again?"

"Not exactly. Lonnie is sticking with Doug at the bank, but Mike assigned Rick to guard Doug's family."

"Then Mike thinks that Doug and his family may be in danger from Ross?"

"That's what he said. And he also said that he didn't want to take any chances. He went back to the sheriff's station to assign some other deputies to various places, and then he's going to drive out to your condo to make sure that Ross isn't there. He left me here to protect you, but he doesn't think that you'll be in any danger as long as The Cookie Jar is open."

Hannah gave a little nod. "Because there are too many people around for Ross to risk doing anything to . . ." she paused, feeling a bit sick to her stomach again, "to hurt me?"

"That's right. Do you have much more work to do here, Hannah?"

Hannah thought about that for a moment. "Well . . . yes, I do. We have to mix up the cookie dough for tomorrow's baking and take care of the customers out in the coffee shop. Lisa and Aunt Nancy are out there now, but Aunt Nancy has to leave at four because she has a dinner date with Heiti."

Norman smiled. "How is their engagement going?"

"Really well. They're going to get married in June. It'll be a small wedding and I promised to cater it. Lisa's baking their wedding cake and it's going to be chocolate because Heiti loves chocolate."

"Sounds wonderful. Do you think I'll be invited?"

"I'm sure you will. And even though Aunt Nancy seems to think the wedding will be small, they're going to invite the whole sheriff's department since Heiti is working for them now."

Norman laughed. "Don't forget about Lisa's family. She has lots of aunts, and uncles, and cousins."

"True. Aunt Nancy and Heiti say they're going to keep the wedding small, but I have a feeling they won't be able to do it without risking some hurt feelings. Everyone here in Lake Eden is going to want to be invited."

"You're right. Weddings tend to grow larger every time you make out a revised guest list."

Hannah thought back to Norman's initial question. "Why did you want to know how much longer I have to be here, Norman?"

"Because I've got a few errands I want to run."

"Why don't you go and do what you need to do right now? I'm fine here by myself because I'm not really by myself. I'll lock the back kitchen door behind you, and I promise I won't let anyone in unless I know who it is."

"Okay, but don't open the door without checking the peephole," Norman reminded her. "I'll be back around four or so. Can we leave then?"

"I'm sure we can. I'll mix up tomorrow's cookie dough, and we can invite Mike and Lonnie to have dinner with us tonight. We'll pick up pizza at Bertanelli's on the way and I have the Chocolate Cream Pie for dessert."

"Sounds great! And we can get salad and garlic bread, too. Do you think you have enough pie?"

"I know I do. After you left, I made another pie. We'll have enough, Norman. And if there's any left over, we can take pieces to Clara and Marguerite."

"There may not be any leftovers if we invite Mike," Norman reminded her, heading for the hook where he'd hung his parka. "Come with me, Hannah. I want you to lock the door behind me and promise that you won't open it without checking the peephole."

"I promise," Hannah said, standing up and walking to the door with him. She waited until Norman had dressed in his parka and slipped into his boots.

"I'll see you then," Norman said, opening

the door and stepping out. "Remember, Hannah. Don't let anyone in unless you are sure you know who it is."

"I won't," Hannah promised, locking the door behind Norman. And then she turned and went to the pantry to gather the ingredients she needed for the next day's cookies.

Hannah was busy mixing up cookie dough when Michelle came into the kitchen from the coffee shop.

"Hi, Hannah," Michelle greeted her.

Hannah was surprised that her sister had come in from the street. "Didn't you park behind the building?"

"No, there was a perfect spot outside the front door and I took it. I stopped to talk to Lisa and Aunt Nancy, and then I came back here to help you. What are you baking for tomorrow?"

"Right now I'm mixing up Crunchy Chewy White Chocolate Cookies."

Michelle looked puzzled. "Is that a new recipe?"

"Yes. I thought I'd make a variation on one of our basic recipes using white chocolate and white Karo syrup."

"Are the cookies pink?"

"No. Why?"

"If you make them pink, you could use

them for Valentine's Day."

"You're right! I didn't even think of that! And there are a lot of people who really like crunchy, chewy cookies."

"How about nuts? Are you adding them to the recipe?"

Hannah shook her head. "I don't think so. These should be crunchy enough on their own."

"Just let me catch my breath for a moment and shake off the remains of my school day. Then I'll be happy to help you bake."

"It's a deal," Hannah told her as Michelle walked to the kitchen coffeepot, poured herself a cup, and came over to look at the ingredients lined up on the surface of the work station. Then she read through the recipe that Hannah had written, and nodded.

"Karo syrup and white chocolate," she said. "That's a great combination. Have you used those together before?"

"I don't think so. I've made a lot of cookies that are crunchy and other cookies that are chewy, but I don't think I've baked anything like these cookies before."

Michelle laughed so hard, she almost choked on her coffee. "But you're going to bake them tomorrow without testing them?"

"No, I thought I'd bake a test cookie now. Do you want to be my guinea pig?"

"It's a dirty job, but somebody's got to do it," Michelle said with a smile. "Of course I'll test them. I worked through lunch today at school and I'm starving. Make two test cookies. Or maybe three. I don't care how many you make. Whatever number it is, I'll eat them."

Once Hannah had baked test cookies, a whole sheet of them, the two sisters tasted them. They'd both declared them delicious when there was a knock at the back kitchen door.

"I'll get it," Michelle said, standing up from her stool.

"Be careful!" Hannah warned her. "Mike and Norman don't want that door opened unless we look through the peephole to see who it is. Mike was adamant about that."

"Mike's always adamant when it comes to safety," Michelle commented, heading for the door. "Don't worry, Hannah. I'll look first."

A moment later, Michelle opened the door and ushered their mother into the kitchen. "Mother's here to see you," she called out to Hannah.

"Hi, Mother," Hannah greeted Delores.

"Would you like one of our Crunchy Chewy White Chocolate Cookies?"

"No," Delores said, but Hannah noticed that there was a smile lurking at the corners of her mother's mouth.

"You wouldn't like one?" Michelle asked.

"No, I'd like two, or maybe three," Delores said, heading straight for a stool at the work station and taking a seat. "I don't suppose you have any coffee, do you?"

"That's one thing we always have around here," Michelle answered. "Just hold on and I'll pour you a cup."

Several moments later, Delores was sitting there with a cup of coffee and two cookies in front of her. "It's nice to be waited on by my daughters," she said as she took a sip of her coffee, smiled, picked up a cookie, and bit into it.

"Good!" she declared, taking another large bite. "I like these, Hannah. They'd make great dunkers if they were a slightly different shape."

"Dunkers?" Michelle questioned.

"Yes. Doc loves cookies that he can dunk in hot coffee and he calls them *dunkers.* I wonder if you could make these cookies oval-shaped. They might not be as chewy in the center, but the crunchy part would be really marvelous."

Hannah turned to look at Michelle. "Why not?" she asked her youngest sister.

"There's no reason we can't," Michelle responded. "Instead of rolling balls, we could roll cigar shapes. Then, when we flatten them out, the end will fit into a coffee mug."

"If you can wait until we bake another batch, you can take some home for Doc to try in his coffee tomorrow morning," Hannah suggested.

"For something like that, I'd wait an hour," Delores decided, taking another cookie. "But I think I'd better try them out first. I certainly wouldn't want to give just any dunker cookie to my husband that hadn't been thoroughly tested."

Michelle got up from her stool. "Sit with Mother, Hannah. I'll put in another batch of cookies and then we can all try them."

"Thank you, dear," Delores said to Michelle, and then she turned to Hannah. "I hate to bring this up, dear, but I have a bit of a problem concerning my next book launch party. That's part of the reason I came to see you this afternoon."

"What's the problem?" Hannah asked. Her mother's book launches had been very successful in Lake Eden. Almost everyone in town had come to purchase books and enjoy the refreshments. The town library had profited nicely from the sales because they'd gotten the books at a special library discount price from the publisher, and Lisa's mother-in-law, Marge, had made enough profit to stock the town library with a shelf of current best sellers. This, in itself, was good, but Delores's book launches were also fun. Everyone who came enjoyed the local social event.

"The launch is at the end of this month," Delores said, still looking concerned. "I was planning to hold it at the community center again, but they had some damage from the blizzard and they're re-carpeting the entire lower floor."

Hannah was surprised. "I didn't know that!"

"Normally, it wouldn't be a problem," Delores continued. "But the only time that the cleanup crew and carpet people could come was the week I scheduled my book launch."

"How about the Red Velvet Lounge?" Hannah suggested the restaurant on the ground floor of her mother's condo building. "Or the lobby of the Albion Hotel?"

"Both of them are already booked," Delores told her. "I just got a phone call this afternoon and that's why I came right over here. Do you think it might be possible to hold my book launch in the clubhouse of your condo complex?"

Hannah thought about that for a moment. "That could work," she told her mother. "There's plenty of guest parking, and our clubhouse has a full kitchen. Do you want me to check on availability?"

"That would be wonderful, dear!" Delores began to smile. "When you get home to-night, will you check to see how many tables there are and how many chairs are at each table? I'll need to know how many people we can seat."

"Of course," Hannah said immediately. "I think it'll work out just fine at the club-house, Mother. It'll be something a little bit different and people will like that. I can even post the event in our condo newsletter, and we could get some of the owners and rent-ers who live there to come."

"That sounds wonderful, dear!" Delores looked vastly relieved. "I knew I could count on you girls to help me find a suitable place to hold the event. And . . . I probably shouldn't ask this because I know you're so busy here for Valentine's Day, but do you think you could handle the catering for my book launch?"

Hannah exchanged glances with Michelle.

Their sisterly telepathy was operating well because Michelle gave a very slight nod and Hannah caught it immediately. "Of course we can, Mother. Don't worry about a thing. Michelle and I will make sure the refreshments are handled."

"Thank you!" Delores said, sounding very grateful for their help. "I must get back and tell Carrie. Do you think you could pack up some of those cookies for Carrie and Doc now?"

Michelle jumped to her feet. "I'll do it. Sit and finish your coffee, Mother. We can discuss what you want us to bake sometime in the week before the launch. Right now, we're all trying to come up with Valentine recipes."

"I can help you with that," Delores offered. "I think you should make things with chocolate. Everyone I know loves chocolate. Do you think you could make some bar cookies with chocolate and butterscotch?"

"I'm sure we could," Hannah told her.

"Then I know that Doc will order tons of them to give to his nurses at the hospital. They have a Valentine's party every year. And I'll tell everyone I know that you're making them. Most of my friends will come in to order some for their Valentine's Day parties. Everyone loves chocolate. And everyone loves butterscotch, too."

Hannah considered that for a moment. "Of course we can do that, Mother. We'll come up with a recipe and give you a sample to taste. If you like it, we'll make sure we have them available for your book launch, too."

"Wonderful!" Delores accepted the plastic-wrapped plate that Michelle had just filled for her. "Thank you, dears. Will you have fresh cookies ready for me to taste for breakfast tomorrow morning?"

"Yes, we will, we always have fresh cookies at The Cookie Jar," Hannah promised her.

"Oh, good! You girls have a wonderful evening and I'll check in with you again tomorrow to find out whether there's enough seating at the clubhouse."

Hannah made a mental note to herself. *Check clubhouse for seating.* Then she locked the door behind their mother and turned to Michelle. "Did we just agree to cater Mother's book launch party and provide the venue for her?"

Michelle laughed. "We certainly did! Now I know why everyone in town thinks Mother is such a dynamo when it comes to organizing things."

"Why do you think she's such a dynamo?"

"Because she's a genius at getting other people to do the work," Michelle responded. "She got you to check out the seating at the condo clubhouse, didn't she?"

"Yes, she certainly did."

"And she got both of us to agree to cater her event, didn't she?"

Hannah sighed and it was a resigned sigh. "Yes, she did that, too. And you're right, Michelle. Mother got us to do all the work and everyone there is going to think she organized the whole party all by herself."

"Ready, Hannah?" Norman asked, once Hannah had made a point of looking through the peephole and, only then, opening the back kitchen door. "I left the car running so it's nice and warm inside."

"I'm almost done here," Hannah told him, wrapping plastic wrap over the top of the last batch of cookies she'd mixed. "Just hold on a second and I'll put these in the cooler. Then all I have to do is say goodbye to Lisa and Aunt Nancy, and I'll be all ready to go."

There was a whole shelf lined with metal mixing bowls covered with plastic wrap, and Hannah felt proud as she surveyed the work she'd done since Norman had left The Cookie Jar.

"Ready," she said, stepping out of the

cooler and closing the door behind her. "I'll tell Lisa and Aunt Nancy I'm leaving."

"Not quite yet," Norman said, smiling at her. "I have one more thing I have to do while we're here."

Hannah recognized that smile. It was Norman's *I've-got-a-secret-and-you're-going-to-love-it* smile, the one he used when he was convinced he'd done something that would both surprise and please her. "What else do you have to do?" she asked him.

"I have to make a phone call to Clara Hollenbeck before we leave to make sure she's home."

Hannah was puzzled. "But Clara's okay, isn't she?"

"Clara's fine. And she's going to be even better when she gets my call. I stopped by the hardware store and talked to Cliff. And Cliff told me that Clara and Marguerite bought their phones from him and took out the insurance policy."

"Insurance policy?" Hannah questioned. "You mean Clara's phone was covered by insurance when it was stolen?"

"That's exactly what I mean. Cliff filed the insurance form for Clara and he found out that the insurance company will replace her phone free of charge."

"But . . . Marguerite told me that Clara

doesn't want another phone."

"I know, but she's entitled to one. And that's not the best part."

Hannah sat down on a stool. "Okay, Norman. Tell me. What's the best part?"

"All of Marguerite and Clara's information is on the cloud. They signed up for that kind of coverage when they bought their cell phone insurance."

Hannah blinked. "You mean . . . Clara's photos of the big pine tree and the shadows are on the cloud?"

"That's right. Her phone backed up to the cloud every time she saved a photo. And Marguerite told me that Clara always saved each photo after she took it. It's all there, Hannah. And Cliff is going to put them all on the new phone that Clara is getting from the insurance company."

"That's great news! Clara's going to be very happy that she doesn't have to take those photos all over again. When can she get her new phone, Norman?"

"Cliff took it out of the box while I was there and he hooked it up to download Clara's cloud backup. She'll have her photos and everything else on her new phone by the time Cliff opens the hardware store in the morning."

Crunchy Chewy White Chocolate Cookies

DO NOT preheat oven — dough must chill before baking.

1 and 1/2 cups melted butter ***(3 sticks, 12 ounces, 3/4 pound)***
2 cups white ***(granulated)*** sugar
2 large eggs beaten ***(just whip them up in a cup with a fork)***
1/2 cup white Karo syrup
1 teaspoon baking soda
1 teaspoon baking powder
1 teaspoon salt
1 teaspoon vanilla extract
1/2 cup finely chopped pecans ***(measure AFTER chopping)***
4 cups all-purpose flour ***(pack the flour down in the cup when you measure it)***
2 cups white chocolate ***(or vanilla baking)*** chips ***(an 11-ounce bag will be fine)***
1/2 cup white ***(granulated)*** sugar for coating the dough balls

Hannah's 1st Note: To measure Karo syrup, first spray the inside of a measuring cup with Pam so that the syrup won't stick to the sides of the cup.

Melt the butter in a microwave-safe bowl by heating it on HIGH for 90 seconds or until melted. ***(I use a 4-cup Pyrex measuring cup with a spout.)***

Hannah's 2nd Note: You can use a mixer from this point on if you wish.

Pour the melted butter in the bottom of a large mixing bowl and add the white sugar on top.

Mix until everything is well combined.

Feel the bowl. If it's not so hot that it will cook the eggs, add them now and mix them in.

Add the Karo syrup, baking soda, baking powder, salt, and vanilla extract. Mix thoroughly.

Mix in the finely chopped pecans and mix until thoroughly blended.

Hannah's 3rd Note: You can use finely chopped almonds or finely chopped walnuts if you prefer.

Add the flour in half-cup increments, mixing after each addition.

Remove the bowl from the mixer. Give it a final stir and set it on the counter.

Stir in the white chocolate (or vanilla baking) chips by hand.

Cover the dough in the mixing bowl with plastic wrap and stick it in the refrigerator.

Chill the dough for at least 1 hour. ***(Overnight is fine, too.)***

When you're ready to bake, take the cookie dough out of the refrigerator and set it on the counter.

Preheat the oven to 350 degrees F., rack in the middle position.

While your oven is preheating, prepare your cookie sheets by spraying them with Pam or another nonstick cooking spray, or lining them with parchment paper.

Once your cookie sheets have been prepared, measure out 1/2 cup white granulated sugar and place it in a shallow bowl.

You'll use this to coat your cookies.

With impeccably clean hands, shape the cookie dough into walnut-sized balls. ***(If your cookie dough is sticky, coat your fingers with sugar and then try to shape the balls.)***

Roll the dough balls in the bowl of white granulated sugar to coat them. Work with only one cookie dough ball at a time.

Place the coated cookie dough balls on your prepared cookie sheets, 12 balls to a standard-size sheet.

Press the dough balls down slightly so that they won't roll off on the way to the oven.

Bake Crunchy Chewy White Chocolate Cookies at 350 degrees F. for 12 to 14 minutes or until they are nicely browned. ***(Mine took 14 minutes.)***

Take the cookies out of the oven and place them on wire racks or cold stove burners.

Cool the cookies on the cookie sheets for 1 minute and then remove them to a wire rack to finish cooling. ***(If you used parch-***

ment paper to line your cookie sheets, you can simply pull it off the sheet and onto the wire rack, cookies and all.)

Yield: 5 to 7 dozen tasty cookies, depending on cookie size.

Chapter Twenty

"Please stop here, Norman," Hannah said as they approached the visitor parking lot in front of the condo clubhouse. "Mother wants to hold her book launch party here and I have to run in for a second to check out the seating."

"No problem." Norman pulled into the spot closest to the clubhouse and got out of the car. "I'll go with you, Hannah."

Hannah almost told him that she was perfectly capable of checking out the seating by herself, but before she could form the words, she thought better of it. Norman was protecting her and, if she admitted the truth, she was very grateful to have someone looking out for her. Her encounters with Ross, both in person and on the phone, had left her severely rattled. It made her feel much safer to have someone accompany her inside the large building that would probably be deserted at this hour.

"Thanks, Norman," she said as he walked around the car and opened the door for her. "I'm glad you're coming with me. It's dark this time of night and having you with me makes me feel safer."

The moment the words had left her mouth, Hannah was happy that she'd voiced them. Norman looked very pleased by her comment. They walked together to the front door of the building.

"It's locked," Norman said, trying the door.

"Yes, it's supposed to be. Our door keys fit this lock and it's kept locked. The only way visitors can use the clubhouse is if they're accompanied by a resident with a key."

The light switch was just inside the door on the right and Hannah flicked it on. The big, overhead banks of can lights came on and the central room was bathed in bright light.

"This is nice, Hannah," Norman said, gazing around at the octagonal tables that converted into card tables with holders for cards or poker chips on eight sides.

"Ten tables, eight chairs at each," Hannah said, doing a mental count. "This room, just the way it is, seats eighty people."

"Is that big enough for your mother's

book launch?" Norman asked her.

"I think so, but there should be extra stack chairs downstairs in the gym. Let's go down and check it out, Norman."

Hannah led the way to the wide staircase that led down to the gym. "Here's where they keep the exercise equipment," she told Norman as he followed her into the cavernous room. "There's a sauna down here that no one ever uses and all these machines."

Norman walked over to look at the exercise equipment. "This is like the one they advertise on television," he said, pointing to a machine that looked like a combination bicycle, treadmill, and weight-lifting apparatus. "It's supposed to give you a complete workout in eleven minutes."

"Really?" Hannah walked over to look at the machine. "Do you think it works?"

Norman shrugged. "I don't know. Maybe, if you follow the manufacturer's instructions." He picked up the manual that was hanging from a chain on the handle. "It sounds pretty complicated to me."

"I wonder how much extra that cost us in our homeowner's fees," Hannah mused, patting the leather seat. "Whatever it was, I don't think it was worth it. From the dust I can see on the seat, it looks like no one ever tried to use it."

"Perhaps they didn't want to get all sweaty and then have to walk home in the cold," Norman suggested.

"But they can shower right here," Hannah gestured toward two doors on the far wall, one marked *MEN* and the other marked *WOMEN*. "We have showers right down here."

"Does anyone ever use those?" Norman walked over and opened the door to the men's shower room. He stepped inside and a moment later, he came out carrying a large towel. "Someone used the shower today. This towel is still damp."

Hannah walked over to examine the towel. "This belongs to Gala Cruise Line," she told him. "It says so right on the bottom in big blue letters. And there's a picture of a cruise ship on it. Somebody went on a cruise on a ship called the *Expedition* and took one of their beach towels home with them."

"That happens all the time. People who stay in hotels take towels and washcloths home with them. I used to know someone who owned a motel and he said that it's one of the reasons room rates are so high. They have to continually replace the towels and sometimes, even the blankets."

"But that's stealing!" Hannah said with a

frown. "Those things belong to the hotel or, in this case, the cruise line. I'd never do something like that."

"Neither would I, but lots of people do. What do you want me to do with this beach towel?"

Hannah shrugged. "Leave it here, I guess. I wouldn't know how to return it. And even if I did, it's a little frayed on the edges and they probably wouldn't want it back."

Norman returned the towel to the shower room and when he came back, he walked over to look at the stack of extra chairs in the corner of the exercise room. He counted them and then he turned back to Hannah "There are another twenty-three chairs here, Hannah."

"Good. That means we'll have seating for over a hundred if Mother uses the extra chairs. That should be plenty for one of her book launch parties."

They walked across the tiled floor and Hannah led the way up the staircase. "I'll tell Mother about this tomorrow. And then I'll call the president of the homeowner's committee to see if I can rent the clubhouse for the date Mother wants."

Norman opened the outer door and held it for Hannah as she turned off the bright overhead lights. They were about to leave when Hannah grabbed his arm.

"Wait a second, Norman. There's something on one of the card tables that doesn't belong there." She walked over to see what it was and began to frown. "It's a pair of binoculars! I wonder why someone needed those."

Norman shrugged. "Birdwatching?" he suggested.

"Maybe. We do have a birdwatchers' club that meets here. I'd better leave these here, too. They look expensive and I'm sure they'll be missed."

Hannah used her key to lock the clubhouse door behind them. Once that was accomplished, they headed back toward Norman's car.

"It's going to be cold tonight," Norman said. "That breeze is icy. Do you want me to drive to the garage and park there? Then we won't have as far to walk."

"No, I'm okay," Hannah told him. "It's only one building away and we can go across the planter to get there. Mike's probably parked his cruiser in my spot anyway, and I'll leave the extra space open for Michelle."

It was only a short walk and Hannah was about to start up her open staircase when she heard a plaintive yowl. "That sounds like Moishe!" she said.

"And it came from down here." Norman bent over to look under the staircase. "It *is* Moishe! What are you doing under there, Moishe?"

Moishe gave another yowl and crawled out on his belly. His fur was matted down, his ears were flat against his head, and he looked terribly frightened.

"Come here, Moishe," Hannah said, holding out her arms. No more than a millisecond later, Moishe was in her arms, trying to tunnel inside her parka.

"He's scared to death!" Hannah said, turning to Norman with wide eyes. "What's wrong? And how did he get out?"

"I don't know," Norman said, standing back so that he could see the upstairs door to Hannah's condo. "The door's closed."

"Thank God you found him!" a familiar voice said, and Hannah turned to see her mother rushing up the garage steps. "I've been looking all over for him!"

"He was here, under the staircase," Norman told her, and then he turned to Hannah. "We'd better take him upstairs where he feels more comfortable."

Hannah began to approach the outside staircase, but Moishe yowled again. "He's shaking even harder," she said, staring down at her pet in surprise. "He's afraid to go up there, Norman!"

"Bring him to my car," Delores said. "I'll take him home with me. He loves to hunt in my penthouse garden and it'll calm him down."

Just then, Michelle came out of the garage. "What's happening?" she asked them. "And why are you parked in my spot, Mother?"

Hannah turned to stare at her mother. "All I know is that Moishe was hiding under the open staircase and he's scared to death to go upstairs. Something's wrong and I think Mother knows what it is. What is it, Mother?"

"I . . . I can't tell you. They told me not to."

"Who told you not to?" There was an edge in Hannah's voice that brooked no argument. "Tell me, Mother!"

"Mike. And Doc. They wanted me to find Moishe and catch you when you got home. They said that under no circumstances was I supposed to let you go upstairs."

"Here," Hannah said, handing Moishe to Michelle. "Go with Mother and take Moishe with you. She can drive and you can hold Moishe. I'm going up there to see what's happened."

"But you can't!" Delores said, trying to

get in front of Hannah to block her way.

"The hell I can't!" Hannah told her, pushing her mother out of the way. "Take Moishe to your place and keep him safe. I'm going upstairs and there's nothing you can do to stop me!"

And with that said, Hannah muscled her way past her mother, Michelle, and Norman, and ran up the stairs to her home. Her heart was beating a rapid tattoo in her chest and she hoped she wasn't about to have a heart attack. At this point, she didn't give it more than a passing thought as she reached her door, unlocked it, and barreled inside. There was something terribly wrong and she needed to know what it was.

"Try to stop me and I'll flatten you," she said as Lonnie attempted to grab her arm. "Get out of my way!"

"You can't come in here, Hannah!" Mike came racing down the hallway to intercept her.

"Oh yes, I can!" Hannah said, and there was pure steel in her voice. "It's my house and you're the intruder. Get out of my way or I'll mow you down!"

With a strength borne of pure determination, Hannah muscled her way past Mike and opened her bedroom door. And that was when she saw it, the blood splattered on the wall and the carpet. She reeled on her feet, almost stumbling over the plate of Chocolate Cream Pie that had fallen on the floor. Her mind was filled with a kaleidoscope of images she could not immediately process. The overturned chair that had been sitting in the corner. The suitcase that was propped open on the bed table. The open closet with clothes and boxes strewn on the floor. And then the final, hideous image of the bed that had once been their bed, and the unspeakable violence that had been inflicted on the man she'd once thought was her husband. And then Hannah Louise Swensen did something she'd sworn she'd never do again in her lifetime. Her world closed in with dizzying speed and she fainted dead away.

CHAPTER TWENTY-ONE

There was a horrid, pungent stench in the air and she had to get away from it. She turned her head this way and that, attempting to get away from it, but it seemed to follow her. It was sharp and astringent, taking her breath away. She coughed once. Twice. And a deep voice said, "She's coming out of it now."

Coming out of what? her rational mind asked, but she couldn't seem to form the words out loud. It was as if the smell had taken away her voice and her body had ceased to function normally. Even the simple action of blinking her eyes seemed to be in slow motion.

"Huh," she managed to force the sound from her throat, but it was more of a moan than a word. *You need a question mark at the end,* her rational mind told her. Hannah took another breath and tried to concentrate. And then, somehow, she managed to force out the sound again.

"Huh?" she heard herself say, and this time it sounded like a question. *Atta girl! You did it!* her rational mind praised her, and Hannah felt inordinately proud of herself.

"Huh?" she uttered the word again, doing her best to put some emotion in the very short word. "Huh?"

"You fainted, Hannah," the same voice answered her, and this time she recognized it. The deep, comforting voice belonged to her stepfather, Doc Knight.

"Doc!" she forced out another word, and she drew a relieved breath. She still felt a little dizzy and muddle-headed, but being able to recognize Doc's voice was encouraging.

"Sick?" she asked, struggling to sit up. And that's when she realized that she was on her own sofa in her own living room, surrounded by Doc and several other people.

She turned her head slightly. Norman. And Mike. And there was Lonnie. "Wha . . . happened?" she asked them.

"You fainted from the shock," Doc told her. "Norman and Lonnie carried you in here."

"Moishe!" The word came out clearly and

full of fear for her pet.

"Delores and Michelle took him to the penthouse," Mike answered. "They called a couple of minutes ago to tell us that he was in the garden and he'd even eaten a couple of cat treats."

Dimly, Hannah remembered hearing bells. Perhaps that had been the telephone and the reason she'd regained consciousness. But there had been some horrible smell and . . . Hannah began to smile. She'd only smelled that particular odor once before and now she knew what it was. "Smelling salts," she said out loud.

"Yes, it's terribly old-fashioned, but I always carry them in my bag," Doc confessed. "Open your eyes wide, Hannah. I want to make sure you didn't hurt yourself when you fell."

Hannah opened her eyes all the way and let Doc shine his little flashlight in them. "I fell?"

"Yes," Mike told her. "We caught you halfway down, but you hit your head on the side of the bed."

"Oh!" Hannah could feel herself getting slightly dizzy again as she remembered why she'd been in the bedroom and what she'd seen. She didn't want to ask the next question that occurred to her, but she had to know. "Is he . . . dead?"

"Yes. Norman's going to take you back to your mother's place now, Hannah. Doc says you need to rest tonight, but I'll be there in the morning to ask you some questions." All this was delivered in a neutral tone, a cop's tone that held no emotion.

"All right," Hannah said, agreeing quickly. Now that she'd remembered what she'd seen, she wanted to leave the condo as fast as she could. "Can I . . . go now?"

Mike moved closer and put his arm around her shoulders. He gave her a little hug and said, "Yes, Hannah. Go now and get some rest. And if you need anything at all, I'm only a phone call away."

Somehow, Hannah managed to maintain her composure on the ride back to Lake Eden. Norman pulled up in front of the Albion Hotel, parked in one of the reserved spots, and came around to open the passenger door for Hannah.

"Come on, Hannah," he said, taking her hand and helping her out of the car. "I'll take you up to the penthouse."

Hannah wanted to thank him, but she seemed to have lost her voice again. All she could do was nod and give his arm a little pat to show that she'd understood what he'd said. They walked through the lobby, past the rolls of new carpeting that would be installed, and headed straight for the elevator on the back wall.

"Come on, Hannah." Norman took her arm and ushered her inside the elevator. "It's going to be okay. Just hang on for a few minutes longer and you'll be with your mother and Michelle."

There's a choice? Hannah's mind prodded her, but of course she didn't say that. Actually, there *was* a choice. If she collapsed right now, Norman would have to lift her off the floor of the elevator and carry her into her mother's penthouse. She had no doubt that Norman could do that if he had to, but she knew she could manage to maintain on her own.

"I'm okay," she said, even though *okay* was not an accurate description of the way she felt. *Shaky* would have described the way her legs felt as they began to ascend to the penthouse floor. And *faint* would have been the word to explain the buzzing that was filling her head with noise. *Light-headed* would have explained why she felt like gripping Norman's arm to keep her balance, and *frightening* would have explained the phenomenon that made the elevator walls seem to close in and then recede.

"Are you with me?" Norman asked her.

Of course I'm with you. I'm right here in an elevator with you, Hannah's rational mind replied. But Hannah said, "I'm just hunky-dory," hoping he would appreciate her attempt at humor.

"Don't, Hannah," Norman said sympathetically, putting his arm around her shoulders and giving her a comforting squeeze. "I know it's hard, but we're almost here and then your family will help."

Hannah thought about that for a moment and then she nodded. "Yes. They will."

"I'll stay with you, too," Norman offered, "if you want me to."

Is this a trap? her suspicious mind asked her. *Will Norman expect more than you're able to give him if you tell him you want him to stay?*

Don't be ridiculous, the rational part of her mind countered. *Norman just wants to help and he's not quite sure what to do.*

As the elevator doors opened on the penthouse floor, Hannah reached a decision. She'd tell the truth. It was always the best way. And she turned to Norman and said, "Yes, please. I want you to stay with me, Norman."

He took Hannah's arm and shepherded her down the hallway to the penthouse door. Then he half-supported her as he rang the doorbell.

"Hannah!" Delores said, opening the door almost immediately. "Oh, honey! Come in. Let me help you."

"Mom!" Hannah said, swallowing hard and trying to maintain her composure. But trying to be calm and act as if her heart wasn't breaking was impossible. Tears welled up in her eyes and rolled down her cheeks. And she sobbed as she felt her mother's arms close around her. "Oh, Mommy! He's dead!"

"I know, honey." Delores held her tightly. "Thank you, sweetheart."

It took Hannah a moment to realize what her mother had said. "Why are you thanking me?"

"Because you haven't called me *mommy* since you were three years old. Oh, honey. You have no idea how much that means to me."

And then Delores and Norman half-carried her through the living room and out into the penthouse garden, where they helped to seat her on a chaise longue.

"Here's Moishe," Delores said as Moishe spotted Hannah and ran toward her.

"Rrroow!" Moishe yowled a greeting as he jumped up into her lap. He crawled up her body to lick her face, and she laughed through her tears and reached down to pet him. "It's okay, Moishe," she told him. And surprisingly, it *was* okay. Here they were, nestled in the bosom of her family, surrounded by the people that loved her. Hannah felt the weight of shock and grief lighten and she drew a relieved breath. The weight was still there but wasn't as heavy as it had been.

Moishe purred as she stroked his soft fur and Hannah knew that he was putting the trauma of hiding outside in the dark behind him. He was safe here in her lap, surrounded by Delores, and Michelle, and Andrea, and Norman. And that was when Hannah realized that she was safe too, and she managed a shaky smile.

"Thank you," she said to all of them. "I'm so glad I'm here with you."

Chapter Twenty-Two

When Hannah woke up in the morning, the sun was in the wrong place. For one brief moment she thought she'd slept all morning and it was late afternoon. But then she realized that the sun wasn't the only thing out of place. The dresser wasn't against the right wall next to the door. The closet wasn't on her right, and the mirrors had been replaced with wooden doors. And the bed was king-size rather than queen-size. And that was when she finally realized that she was not at home in her own condo.

Reality swam in, doing a rapid Australian crawl, and even though she fought to stop its advance before it got to the bad part, the memories of the previous night rushed back. Ross on the bed, covered in blood and almost unrecognizable. Splatters of his lifeblood on the wall and the carpet that Andrea had chosen for their condo. She was in her mother and Doc's penthouse, and the guest bedroom began to spin around her in dizzying circles.

You're stronger than that. Get over it, her rational mind told her. And when she opened her eyes, the bedroom was stationary once again.

Oh, how she wanted to stay right where she was now, safe in her mother's guest room, not thinking and not feeling! *You can't do that,* her rational mind reminded her. *You have work to do and only you can do it.*

Hannah sat up and shoved her feet into her slippers. Her mission, her obligation, was clear. It was her duty to discover the identity of Ross's killer, learn why he'd been murdered in the condo they'd shared for such a brief time, and make sure that the killer was punished for the awful crime that had been committed. She had to make sure that justice was done.

Even though her tired body clamored for more rest, Hannah rose to her feet. She turned to look at the pillow next to hers and felt grateful as she saw that Moishe was sleeping there. He was a comfort and he loved her unconditionally. If only Ross could have been that way!

Don't think, just do, her rational mind told her, and Hannah shrugged into her chenille robe, the one her mother hated because it was so old and so worn. How had her robe gotten here? She pondered that question as she walked to the adjoining bathroom to take her morning shower.

Her question was answered when she came out of the shower. There was a note propped up on her dresser and it was in Michelle's handwriting. *Sleep in this morning, Hannah. You don't have to go to work. Aunt Nancy, Lisa, and I have everything covered at The Cookie Jar.*

Hannah's lips curved up in a small smile. And then she noticed the open suitcase on the bench at the foot of the bed. Clean clothes, but how had they gotten to her mother's penthouse?

These were in the dryer, another note read. It was propped up on top of a pair of Hannah's clean jeans and Hannah didn't need a signature to know that this was more of her thoughtful youngest sister's work. Michelle must have gone back to the condo last night to collect clean clothes for her. And since the master bedroom was probably taped off as a crime scene, Michelle had been resourceful enough to check the dryer in the laundry room and discover the clothes Hannah hadn't taken out before they'd left for work.

Several minutes later, Hannah was dressed in clean clothes. She opened the bedroom door, stepped out into the carpeted hallway, and realized that there was a delicious smell in the air.

Pineapple, she thought, beginning to smile. And then she led the way to the kitchen with Moishe following at her heels. Michelle was baking something with pineapple.

When woman and cat entered the kitchen, they parted ways. Moishe's feeder, the one Norman had given him that never ran out of dry kitty crunchies, sat against the far wall. Moishe made a beeline for the rug Michelle had placed under the feeder. He took a bite, crunched loudly, and moved to his water bowl to drink.

"Good morning, Hannah," Michelle greeted her. "Sit down and I'll get you a cup of coffee."

Smart sister, Hannah thought as she slid into the cushioned booth her mother and Doc had installed in a corner of their kitchen, and accepted the mug of coffee that Michelle handed to her. *I'm really glad Michelle didn't ask how I was feeling. The word I might have chosen is not the right word to utter before one's first sip of coffee.*

"Thanks, Michelle," Hannah said, taking

a big sip of coffee and swallowing. "This should help. I don't know why, but I'm a little groggy this morning."

"I know why," Michelle said, pouring a cup of coffee for herself and setting it down across from Hannah. "Doc said he gave you something to help you sleep last night."

"He did?" Hannah thought back to the previous evening, but she didn't remember taking any pills except a couple of aspirins for the headache she'd felt coming on.

"He put it in the paper cup with your aspirin," Michelle explained. "He told us that it was a very light tranquilizer that would keep you sleeping without nightmares."

Just then the stove timer sounded and Michelle grabbed oven mitts, opened the oven door, and took out two muffin tins. She hurried to the wire cooling racks sitting on the counter and set the pans on them.

"Remind me to get Mother new oven mitts," she said to Hannah. "Hers are wearing out and they're thin."

Hannah began to smile. "That's okay. Mother doesn't bake anyway."

"True," Michelle agreed, coming over to sit in the booth.

"Are those pineapple cupcakes?" Hannah guessed.

"Close, but no cigar. They're Pineapple and Walnut Muffins. Mother had crushed pineapple in the pantry and I found a package of walnuts. I made up the recipe as I went along. I hope they're good enough to eat for breakfast."

"I'll be happy to make that decision," Hannah offered. "I'm as hungry as a bear this morning."

"That's probably because you didn't eat any dinner last night."

"No wonder my stomach's growling."

Michelle took a sip of her coffee and then she looked up at Hannah. "What are you going to do, Hannah?"

"I'm going to work. Thanks for the notes and the clothes, Michelle, but I can't just sit here in Mother's penthouse and think about things."

"Okay. But does that mean that you're planning to . . ." Michelle's voice trailed off. "Never mind. I'll ask you when you really wake up. You still look like you could drop off to sleep any second."

"You're right," Hannah admitted. The cobwebs in her head were beginning to dissipate, and she wasn't sure if that was a good or a bad thing. "Is Norman still here?"

Michelle shook her head. "He went home after you went to bed last night, but he should be back any minute with Cuddles. Mother thought Moishe would like to have a play date with Cuddles in the penthouse garden and she invited Norman for breakfast."

The doorbell rang and Hannah began to slide out of the booth, but Michelle held up a hand to stop her. "Stay here, Hannah. You still look a little unfocused. I'll go let Norman and Cuddles in. And don't try to get those muffins out of the pan while I'm gone. They're too hot to eat."

When Michelle left to open the door for Norman and Cuddles, Hannah was sorely tempted to see if she could extricate one muffin from its cup. Somehow she managed to control herself despite the mouth watering scent, and she waited impatiently for Michelle to come back.

"Rrooww!"

There was a plaintive cry from the living room and Hannah heard a soft thud as Norman set the cat carrier down on the living room rug.

"Rrrooooooow!" Moishe gave the yowl he usually used to greet Cuddles and abandoned Hannah without a backward glance, streaking out of the kitchen door to greet his favorite friend.

A moment later, Norman walked into the

kitchen and poured himself a cup of coffee. "Michelle took them out to the garden," Norman told her. "How are you, Hannah?"

Since she'd already almost finished her coffee, Hannah felt calm enough to answer his question. "I'm okay, Norman . . . or as okay as I can be under the circumstances."

Michelle came back into the kitchen, smiling broadly. "I seeded the plants with the ladybugs that I picked up from CostMart's garden center last night. The cats are having a great time trying to catch them."

Norman looked slightly worried. "Do they ever succeed?"

"No," Hannah reassured him. "They just paw at the plants and the ladybugs fly to another plant. Don't worry, Norman. I think it's a game with the cats and also with the ladybugs. Neither Moishe nor Cuddles has ever caught one."

"Good." Norman gave her a smile. "So how did you sleep, Hannah?"

"Deeply and soundly. Doc gave me something to help me sleep and I didn't even know that I was taking it. It knocked me out for a solid eight hours and that's the most sleep I've had in weeks."

"Hello, Norman." Doc came into the kitchen and poured himself a cup of coffee. "How are you doing, Hannah?"

"Better," Hannah settled for a short reply. "Thanks for whatever pill you gave me last night, Doc. I slept all night and didn't wake up once."

"She was a little groggy this morning, but now that she's had a cup of coffee, she's fine," Michelle reported.

"Good. I thought it would work that way. What's that great aroma? It's making me hungry and it smells like I actually have a wife."

Delores came in the kitchen door just in time to hear her husband's comment. "You *do* have a wife. But your wife doesn't bake like Hannah and Michelle do. What do we have this morning, girls?"

"Oops! You weren't supposed to hear that," Doc told Delores, going over to give her a hug. "I love you just the way you are, Lori."

"You'd better." Delores sat down at Doc's place at the table and commandeered his coffee cup. "Just for that, I get your coffee. Go pour another cup for yourself."

Doc laughed and went off to the coffeepot, and Delores reached over to give Hannah a hug. "Are you okay, Hannah?"

"I will be," Hannah answered. "I decided that the best way to deal with all this was to pretend that it was a normal workday."

"You're going to work?" Norman asked, sounding shocked.

"Yes. Work calms me down. If I stay here all day, I'm just going to think about . . ." Hannah stopped speaking and took a deep breath. "You know what I mean."

Norman nodded. "I do. Work is the best cure for a lot of things. If you're going through your normal, everyday routine, you don't have time to feel angry, or depressed, or sorry for yourself. Work is one of those all-consuming things that don't allow for any other emotions."

Hannah turned to look at Norman in surprise. She'd never thought of work in quite that way before, but he was right.

"That's exactly the way I feel," Hannah told him. "I do my best thinking when I'm baking. There's something about gathering ingredients and mixing them together that's very satisfying. And when you're doing something like rolling cookie dough balls, or dipping them in sugar, or anything else that you have to do by rote, you don't have to think."

At that point, Cuddles raced into the kitchen and jumped up on Norman's lap. Moishe was right behind her and he jumped up on Hannah's lap. The two cats looked at each other and began to purr.

"I think they approve," Norman commented.

"And I think you're right," Michelle said, tipping her Pineapple and Walnut Muffins out of the muffin pans, setting them on a serving platter, and carrying them to the booth. "Let's all have one and then I'll start the bacon and cheese scramble."

"If these smell as good as they look, we could serve them at The Cookie Jar," Hannah commented. "But we wouldn't want to serve anything that didn't have a seal of approval. I think we should all have two muffins, and then we'll decide."

"Great idea!" Doc said, taking two muffins and putting them on his plate.

Delores laughed. "Agreed," she said, snatching his muffins and making him reach for two more.

For the next several moments there was no conversation, only smiles, sips of coffee, and big bites of Michelle's delicious creation. Then Norman turned to Hannah. "You're not going to . . ." he stopped, obviously unsure of exactly how to voice his question.

"Yes, I am," Hannah told him. "It may not be easy, but I need to know who killed Ross and why."

Doc nodded. "I knew you'd want to do

that. As a matter of fact, that's what I told Mike last night."

"Last night?" Hannah was confused. "I don't remember seeing Mike here last night."

"You were already in bed when Mike came by," Delores explained. "He just wanted to check on you to make sure you were all right."

"That's nice," Hannah said, feeling glad that he'd cared enough to be concerned about her when he was in the middle of a murder investigation. "I suppose he'll be here for . . ." she stopped speaking abruptly when the doorbell rang. "I should have known," she said, turning to Michelle. "Mike and Lonnie probably smelled your incredibly delicious muffins all the way out at the sheriff's station."

Pineapple and Walnut Muffins

Preheat oven to 375 degrees F., rack in the middle position.

The Batter:

1 cup crushed pineapple, drained ***(measure AFTER draining and patting dry)***
1 Tablespoon all-purpose flour
1 cup white ***(granulated)*** sugar
3/4 cup salted butter ***(1 and 1/2 sticks, 6 ounces)***
2 beaten eggs ***(just whip them up in a glass with a fork)***
2 teaspoons baking powder
1/2 teaspoon salt
1/2 teaspoon cinnamon
2 cups all-purpose flour ***(pack it down in the cup when you measure it)***
1/2 cup whole milk
1/2 cup finely chopped walnuts ***(measure AFTER chopping)***

Crumb Topping:

1/2 cup white ***(granulated)*** sugar
1/3 cup all-purpose flour
1/4 cup salted butter ***(1/2 stick, 2 ounces)*** softened to room temperature

Grease the **bottoms only** of a 12-cup

muffin pan ***(or line the cups with double cupcake papers — that's what I do at The Cookie Jar).***

If you haven't done so already, put the crushed pineapple in a strainer with a small bowl underneath it. Press it down with the back of a mixing spoon, trying to get out as much juice as you can.

Pour the drained juice in a refrigerator container and save it for someone who likes to drink pineapple juice.

Once you've completely drained your pineapple, measure out 1 cup of pineapple and place it in a small bowl.

Sprinkle the crushed, drained pineapple with 1 Tablespoon of the all-purpose flour. Then mix the flour with the pineapple. ***(The flour will help to soak up any moisture left in your crushed pineapple.)***

Get out a medium-size mixing bowl and a wooden spoon if you intend to make this recipe by hand, but you can use an electric stand mixer or a hand-held mixer from this point on if you wish.

Place the white ***(granulated)*** sugar in the bottom of the mixing bowl.

Add the softened, salted butter and mix it with the sugar. Mix until the ingredients are light and fluffy.

Add the eggs, one at a time, mixing them in thoroughly after each addition.

Sprinkle in the baking powder, salt, and cinnamon. Mix them in thoroughly.

Add HALF of the all-purpose flour to a mixing bowl and mix it in with HALF of the whole milk.

Add the remaining flour and the remaining milk. Mix until everything is thoroughly blended.

Mix in the crushed pineapple and the finely chopped walnuts by hand.

Fill the muffin cups three-quarters full and set them aside. If you have batter left over, grease the bottom of a small tea bread loaf pan and fill it with your remaining batter.

Crumb Topping:
Mix the sugar and the flour in a small bowl. Add the butter and cut it in until it's crumbly. ***(You can also do this in a food processor with chilled butter and the steel blade by processing in an on-and-off motion.)***

Hannah's Note: If your topping isn't crumbly enough, just put it in a plastic bag and stick it in the freezer of your refrigerator for 5 minutes or so. That should be enough to make it crumble in your fingers.

Fill the remaining space in the muffin cups with the crumb topping. Then bake the muffins in a 375 degree F. oven for 25 to 30 minutes. ***(The tea bread should bake about 10 minutes longer than the muffins.)***

When your muffins are baked, set the muffin pan on a wire rack to cool for at least 30 minutes. ***(The muffins need to cool in the pan for easy removal.)*** Then just tip them out of the cups and enjoy.

These are wonderful when they're slightly warm, but they're also good cold.

Yield: 12 muffins and perhaps a tea bread.

CHAPTER TWENTY-THREE

Once they got to The Cookie Jar, Michelle went up front to the coffee shop to help Lisa, and Hannah stayed in the kitchen. She knew what would be happening today, and she dreaded it. Everyone would come in to hear about Ross. They'd want to hear about Moishe and how Norman had found him, and they'd want to know how she had reacted after she'd discovered that the man she'd thought was her husband had been murdered.

Hannah didn't want to relive the events of the previous evening, but her customers would expect Lisa to tell the story of the murder. And since Lisa hadn't been there, it was up to Hannah to set the scene for her.

Even though it was the last thing in the world that she wanted to do, Hannah walked to the swinging door that led to the coffee shop, and pushed it open far enough to see that Lisa was behind the counter, arranging the large glass jars they used to display the day's cookie offerings.

"Michelle?" Hannah addressed her youngest sister over her shoulder. "Will you take over out here for a few minutes? I need to speak to Lisa."

"No problem," Michelle answered. "I don't have to leave for school for another hour."

"Thanks! Lisa? I need to see you in the kitchen for a couple of minutes."

"I'll be right there," Lisa promised, picking up one of the empty jars. "Do you want to sell the Molasses Crackles this morning? Or would you prefer to substitute something else?"

"The Molasses Crackles will do just fine," Hannah told her, and then she retreated to the kitchen.

Since she knew exactly what she wanted to bake, it only took Hannah a couple of minutes to gather ingredients and put them next to the industrial-size stand mixer on the counter. By the time she'd arranged them in the order she'd need them, Lisa came in from the coffee shop.

Hannah gestured toward the work station. "Sit down and I'll get you a cup of coffee."

"I'm so sorry about what happened last

night, Hannah," Lisa said when Hannah delivered coffee for both of them and sat down on a stool. "If you don't feel like staying and working today, just leave. Aunt Nancy and I can handle anything that comes up. And if we get really busy, all I have to do is call Marge and she'll come right over."

"Thanks, Lisa, but I think I'll be all right if I stay in the kitchen and bake. We're going to be very busy today. And I certainly won't listen to the story you're going to tell about the murder."

"But, Hannah!" Lisa looked shocked. "You don't want me to tell *this* story, do you?"

"Yes, I think you should. I wasn't there when Mike and Lonnie found the body so you can't tell that part, but you can begin when Norman and I got to the condo complex."

"But how can I tell our customers about that if I don't know what happened?"

"I'm going to tell you what happened right now."

"But do you really want to talk about it?"

"Of course I don't, but I've always told you exactly what happened when I found a murder victim. This time I didn't find Ross first, but I was there later and I can describe the murder scene for you."

"You mean you actually *saw* him?"

"Oh, yes. Everyone tried to keep me back, but I barged past them."

Lisa shivered. "It must have been awful!"

"It was."

"Are you absolutely sure you want to tell me about it?" Lisa asked, and when Hannah nodded, she asked another question. "Do you think it might help you to talk about it?"

"Maybe," Hannah said, even though she really didn't believe that describing what she'd found in her master bedroom would help her in the slightest.

"Okay then." Lisa gave a little sigh. "What happened when you got home to the condo, Hannah?"

With Lisa listening attentively, Hannah described how Norman had found Moishe under the stairs and how frightened he'd been, how Delores had tried to keep her from going up the stairs, and what she'd found when she'd pushed past everyone who wanted to stop her. That was when a completely unexpected event happened.

"What is it?" Lisa asked, noticing the startled expression on Hannah's face.

"I didn't think describing things to you would help, but . . . it did! I always thought that was psychological nonsense, but talking to you about what I saw is . . ." Hannah stopped speaking, not sure how to describe what she was feeling.

"Is it defusing it for you?" Lisa suggested.

"Yes. Everyone kept trying to get me to talk about it last night, but I didn't want to."

"Of course you didn't."

Hannah decided to change the subject by asking the question that was uppermost in her mind. "When are you going to start telling the story?"

"I usually start about ten in the morning. Do you want me to give you a heads-up so you can put in ear plugs or something?"

Hannah laughed. "No, I'll be all right. I'll be busy baking so we can keep up with everyone who comes in to hear you."

"Are you really sure that you want me to do this, Hannah?"

"Yes."

"Okay. Is there anything else I can do . . . ?"

"I don't think there's . . . wait! There *is* one thing you can do."

"What's that?"

"When Grandma Knudson comes in, let her listen to your story once and then ask her if she'll come back to the kitchen. There's something I want to ask her."

Hannah had just finished filling the bakers rack with freshly-baked Butterscotch Chocolate Bar Cookies when she heard an authoritative knock on the back kitchen door. She rolled the bakers rack back into place by the wall, went to the door, and stopped with her hand on the knob to open it. She'd recognized the knock and she was sure it was Mike, but she looked through the peephole anyway. She was right. Mike was standing there outside the back door.

"Come in, Mike," she said loudly enough so that he could hear it, and only then did she unlock the door and open it.

"Good girl!" Mike said, entering the kitchen and stomping the snow off his boots on the shag rug that Hannah kept there for that purpose. "I'm really glad you're using the peephole."

Hannah had all she could do not to laugh. When Mike had said, *Good girl!* it had been in the same tone of voice he would use to train a young puppy to sit or heel. "I think looking through the peephole is becoming a habit with me," she told him.

"That's excellent," he said and this time it wasn't in his puppy training voice. "Just keep doing it every time and it'll become second nature to you."

"I'm surprised to see you, Mike," Hannah said, heading to the kitchen coffeepot to pour him a cup. She set it down in front of him and took her own seat at the work station. "Since I wasn't the one who discovered Ross's body and you and Lonnie were, you don't really need my statement, do you?"

"No, and that's not why I'm here."

Hannah waited while Mike took a sip of his coffee. "You don't have any cookies to go with this, do you, Hannah?"

Hannah's sense of humor kicked in and she began to laugh. "Of course I do. This is a bakery, remember?"

"I know that, but you only got here twenty-five minutes ago. You didn't have time to bake yet, did you?"

Hannah glanced at the clock on the wall. Mike was right. She'd walked in the door with Michelle exactly twenty-five minutes ago. "How do you know when I got here?"

"I was parked at the other end of the alley."

"You're surveilling *me*?"

Mike shook his head. "No, of course not. I just wanted to give you time to get settled before I came in."

Hannah noticed that Mike still looked

uncomfortable. "Why did you want me settled in?" she asked him. "Is there something you want to tell me about the murder case?"

"No, I just need to assure you that I'll do everything in my power to catch whoever did this to Ross."

Hannah was surprised that Mike thought she needed reassurance on that point. "I know you will, Mike. You're a very good detective."

"Thanks, but this is a little different. This time we won't be comparing notes like we usually do."

You mean you won't be pumping me for information? Hannah's suspicious mind prompted her, but Hannah bit back the urge to ask that question.

"I mean that this time, of course, you won't be . . . uh . . . actively involved."

"I won't?"

Mike began to frown. "No, you won't. You're too close to this situation, Hannah. You can't be objective."

"No, but I've *never* been objective," Hannah retorted, feeling her ire begin to rise. "I wouldn't get involved at all if I didn't care about the victim."

"But Ross hurt you. He betrayed you, Hannah. The guy was a liar and louse!"

Hannah began to smile. "And you're claiming that *you're* objective after saying something like that?"

"Well . . . no. Not entirely. But I know how to curb my emotions and conduct myself in a rational manner."

"Really?"

"Yes. You're not trained to do anything like that. Besides . . ." Mike looked as if he wished he hadn't started this conversation, but he continued it anyway. "You don't owe Ross anything, Hannah. Ross treated you like dirt. I wouldn't have blamed you if *you'd* killed him yourself!"

"Does that mean that I'm a suspect?" Hannah asked, even though she knew she wasn't.

"No! Not at all! You were with Norman and he's corroborated that. It's just that you don't have to help to catch Ross's killer. There's no reason for you to do that for him."

"Well, I'm going to investigate anyway and I'm not doing it for Ross. I'm doing it for me!"

Mike stared at her for a moment and then he gave a resigned sigh. "I knew nothing I could say would do any good," he said in such a sorrowful tone that Hannah came close to feeling a bit sorry for him. "I wish you wouldn't get involved, Hannah. I just wish you'd . . . go on vacation or something. Go somewhere else and try to forget you ever met the guy."

Hannah knew that Mike was only trying to help her, but she held firm. "Thanks, Mike, but I have to stay here. I can't go off to Aruba, or somewhere when I don't know who killed Ross and why he was murdered. I have to help you find out and I have to do it for myself."

Mike thought about that for a moment and then he sighed again. "All right. I guess there's nothing I can say to change your mind."

"That's right. So are we going to work together? Or will I be forced to leave you in the dust?"

The silence between them was much longer this time, but finally Mike nodded. "My dad used to say that if you can't beat 'em, you might as well join 'em."

"Your father was a wise man," Hannah said, getting up from her stool to freshen Mike's coffee and fill a plate with cookies. "Here you go," she said, setting the plate in front of him. "I don't suppose you have the autopsy report in yet."

Mike took a cookie and bit into it. Then he sipped his coffee. "I have it," he said at last. "What do you want to know?"

"The time of death," Hannah said, hoping that her voice was as strong as she wanted it to be.

"Doc says between noon and five p.m."

"What time did you get to my condo?"

"A little after three. The door was standing open so I knew right away that something was wrong."

"And you noticed that Moishe was missing?"

Mike nodded. "At first I figured that he was under the bed, but when I looked, he wasn't there. And since the closet was open, I could see that he wasn't hiding in there either."

Hannah shivered slightly, imagining the scene when Mike had arrived at her condo. "Did you look for Moishe?"

"Not right then. I couldn't. I called Lonnie and when he got there, I sent him out to search for Moishe."

"You didn't go with him?"

"I couldn't. I had to stay with . . ." Mike hesitated, and Hannah knew he was searching for words that would have less emotional impact than using Ross's name. "I positioned myself at your bedroom doorway," he continued, "and I called Doc from there. He got there in less than twenty minutes and your mother came, too."

"But you didn't let Mother come upstairs, did you?"

"No. Doc told her to stay outside and help Lonnie search for Moishe."

Hannah thought about Mike standing guard at her bedroom doorway, waiting there for Lonnie and Doc to arrive. She had been in his position before, staying at the scene of a murder and waiting for Mike to arrive. She knew exactly how difficult it was to stay there, not touching anything that might turn out to be evidence, and doing nothing but thinking about what had happened to the victim.

"Don't you ever wish you did something else like working at a desk job instead of what you do now?" she asked him.

"Sometimes. Murder scenes are always bad and some are worse than others. But after the coroner and the crime scene guys get there, I can start my real work."

"Catching the murderer?"

"Yes. There's real satisfaction when I solve a case and catch a killer."

Hannah thought about that and she gave a little nod of agreement. "I understand perfectly. And I really hope we're successful this time."

"We will be. I won't stop working until I

get him. Or her."

"Do you think the killer could be a woman?"

"Maybe. I never rule anything out." Mike took another cookie and devoured it. "What else do you want to know from me, Hannah?"

"I'd like to know why my closet doors were open. I distinctly remember closing them before I left for work."

"Are you sure?"

"I'm positive. One door was stuck and it wouldn't close until I pulled out one of Moishe's mouse toys that had gotten stuck in the track. I tossed it to him and he ran out to the living room to hide it there."

"You don't suppose Moishe could have . . ." Mike stopped speaking in mid-thought. "No, of course he couldn't have pulled all those clothes and boxes out into the bedroom."

"I knew what you were thinking and you're right. Moishe couldn't have done it, not if there were boxes pulled out on the floor. I had things that were packed in boxes, but the boxes were all on the top closet shelf."

"Okay. If you're sure you closed the closet doors, then either the victim or his killer was looking for something hidden in your closet. You didn't leave any boxes of clothes on the bedroom floor, did you?"

"No. I always put things away when I leave the bedroom in the morning."

"Then whoever it was assumed that something was hidden in your closet or in one of your dresser drawers. And whoever it was didn't take the time to put anything back." Mike frowned slightly. "You didn't notice the mess on the carpet, Hannah?"

"I don't remember if I did or not. The only thing I remember clearly was the bed. And . . . him. That's all."

"You're sure?"

Even though she didn't want to relive those painful moments, Hannah thought back to her first sight of the bedroom. "If I saw the things on the floor, my mind didn't process it."

"All right. Is there anything that you normally keep in your bedroom that either Ross or the killer might have wanted?"

"The money!" Hannah gasped, the answer hitting her squarely in her solar plexus. "I think someone was searching for the money! Remember when Doug told us he didn't think Ross believed him when he claimed that he never kept the large amount of money that Ross wanted in the bank safe? That's when Ross accused Doug of giving the money to me."

"Exactly." Mike reached out to give her a little pat on the back. "That was the first thing that occurred to me. It could have been the money, but it also could have been something else."

"Like what?"

"Like something Ross left behind in your bedroom, something he needed to take with him when he left."

"That makes sense," Hannah said. "It could even be something he hid in my bedroom on purpose and he planned to come back for it later."

"That's possible, too. Did you clean out your closet, or reorganize it, or anything like that after Ross left?"

"No. I didn't have the heart or the time to do that. And don't forget that, at least at first, I expected him to come back any day. I just closed his side of the closet and didn't even open it while he was gone, and then, when I realized that he probably wasn't coming back, I felt so betrayed, I didn't want to see anything that reminded me of him."

"That's understandable, Hannah. It was a very painful time for you. I felt that way on a smaller scale when my wife was killed. I didn't want to look at her clothes and remember. It was over six months before I was able to pack them up and give them to charity."

Mike looked so sad that Hannah knew she had to change the subject. "Do you think that I should go back to the condo and look to see if I notice anything that's missing?"

"Eventually, yes. Right now your condo is still off-limits to everyone. The crime scene team is lifting fingerprints and it's going to take them a while."

Hannah gave a little groan. Her condo would be an absolute mess when the crime scene people got through. She'd gone through this once before when Connie Mac was killed in her walk-in cooler and she'd needed to run countless loads of baking pans, cookie sheets, and mixing bowls through her industrial dishwasher to make sure they were free of fingerprint powder.

"I know they leave a mess," Mike said, accurately reading her thoughts. "I'm sorry, but there's nothing I can do about that. They have to be thorough, and they may find something that'll help to catch the killer."

"I know. It's okay, Mike. Do you have a crime scene photo of my closet, one that doesn't show . . ." Hannah stopped speaking and took a deep, calming breath. ". . .

that doesn't show . . . him?"

"Yes, I've got one," Mike said. He opened his briefcase, pulled out a photo, and handed it to her. "Here. It doesn't show anything else, Hannah. I won't give you those."

"You don't have to. I remember." Hannah took the photo from Mike and studied it. "The boxes on the floor were on the top shelf when I left for work in the morning. Whoever did this pulled them down, took off the lids, and dumped them out. Then they pawed through the contents and just left them on the floor. Ross must have done it. It couldn't have been the killer."

"Why not?"

"Because Ross was . . . shot, wasn't he?" Hannah paused to take another deep breath. "And then the killer would have wanted to get out of my condo right after he shot him. He wouldn't have taken the time to take down those boxes and dump them out. He'd be much more concerned about getting away before anyone realized that the noise they'd heard was a gunshot and they called the police."

"Yes, Hannah, he was shot. You make a good point about the noise, but everything changes if the killer used a silencer."

"Did he?"

Mike shrugged. "I don't know. There's no way to tell by just looking."

"Do you know the caliber of the bullet? The ballistics report hasn't come in yet?"

"Not yet. I'll tell you when it does."

"So we really don't know anything except that Ross was murdered and Ross needed a hundred thousand dollars in cash for some reason."

"That's about it. This is going to be a challenge, Hannah."

Both of them were silent then, sipping their coffee and thinking. When the plate of cookies was as empty as their coffee cups, Mike said goodbye and left. Hannah locked the back kitchen door behind him, walked directly to the drawer where she kept her blank shorthand notebooks, and took one out. Then she sat down at the work station and began to write down the suspects she already had in Ross's murder case.

"Hannah." Grandma Knudson came into the kitchen. "How are you?"

"Still a little shaky, but I'm all right. Have you told anyone about your new hearing aids yet?"

"Not yet. I will eventually though. You want to know if I've heard anything, don't you, Hannah?"

"Yes. Someone killed Ross and I have to find out who did it and why."

"Of course you do. It's that insatiable curiosity of yours. That drives you as much as your thirst for justice." Grandma Knudson smiled. "You're a good person, Hannah. And before you ask me, I didn't do it."

Hannah was shocked. "I never thought that you did!"

"What a pity. I'd like to think that I might be capable of a bold action like that. But no, Hannah, I haven't heard anyone in town mention anything about it. Everyone's speculating just like you and Mike are."

"Carrie was worried about Earl because he carried a rifle and a handgun on his snowplow."

"Do you suspect Earl?"

"Not really. I talked to him and I don't think he'd be that violent. But there's always the possibility that I'm wrong."

"What time was Ross shot, Hannah?"

"Doc says between noon and five p.m., but since Mike arrived at my condo at a little past three, we know that the time of death was between noon and three."

"Then Earl didn't do it."

"How do you know? Earl said he wished that Ross would come back to Lake Eden so that he could teach Ross a permanent lesson."

Grandma Knudson laughed. "Earl talks a good game, but he wouldn't hurt a fly. Have you heard the story about the bobcat he shot?"

"Yes. Carrie mentioned it when she told me about the firearms that Earl carried on his snowplow."

"Earl loves that story, but he told me the truth about the whole incident."

Hannah was surprised. "Earl didn't shoot the bobcat?"

"Earl shot *over* the bobcat."

"You mean . . . he didn't actually kill the bobcat."

"I mean Earl didn't hit the bobcat at all. He just fired over the bobcat's head to scare it away from the snowplow. There's no way Earl killed Ross. The worst he'd do if he ran into Ross would be to hit Ross's car with his snowplow and run him off the road."

Hannah breathed a sigh of relief. "That's good to know! But still . . . sometimes people do terrible things in the heat of the moment and regret it later."

"True, but Earl was nowhere near your condo complex when Ross was murdered."

"How do you know that?"

"Because he was up on our street at a

quarter to one, plowing out the church parking lot, and there's no way he could have killed Ross at noon and gotten back to town in the snowplow that fast. I looked out the window at twelve forty-five and saw him working on the church parking lot. And he'd already cleared the street that runs past the church. After that, Earl cleared our circular driveway at the parsonage and he didn't finish until one-thirty."

"But he still could have driven out to my condo and killed Ross before three."

"There's nothing wrong with your math, Hannah. You just don't know the whole story. After Earl cleared our parsonage driveway, I went out and invited him in for coffee. Earl was really cold. There's a heater on the snowplow, but the wind was blowing and it's an open cab. His feet stay warm, but the snow blows in when he's plowing."

"Did Earl tell you that?" Hannah asked, wondering if that was accurate.

"No, Carrie did. She tapes cardboard over the inside of the cab when she rides with Earl."

That was good enough for Hannah and she quickly revised her timetable. "How long did Earl stay at the parsonage?" she asked.

Grandma Knudson smiled. It was what

Delores would have termed *the smile on the cat that got into the cream pot* in one of her Regency romance novels.

"I gave Earl coffee and since he'd been out there in the cold since morning, I convinced him to have a tot of my homemade rhubarb wine with it. I make my own, you know."

"I didn't know."

"There's no reason you should. I don't advertise it, or I'd have a lot more visitors at the parsonage. Rhubarb wine used to be my husband's favorite treat. Every time he ate ice cream, he wanted my rhubarb wine poured over the top as syrup."

Hannah started to grin. "You're a woman of many talents, Grandma Knudson."

"That's exactly what he used to say! And Earl said it yesterday afternoon, right after his third glass. When he left me, he told me that he was going to Granny's Attic to pick up Carrie because he'd given her a ride to town on his snowplow. And since Carrie had always wanted to drive his snowplow, he thought he might let her drive him home."

"So Carrie was with Earl after he left you?"

Grandma Knudson nodded. "Lisa said they came in for coffee before they left for home and Earl ordered two coffees to go.

That was past three, so Earl couldn't have killed Ross."

"You're right," Hannah admitted, reaching for her murder book and flipping to Earl's page. She crossed out that page with a big x-mark and flipped to the next page.

"How about Bud Hauge?" she asked. "You told me you heard him say something about teaching Ross a lesson after my talk at church on Sunday."

"He did, but Bud is all bark and no bite. Besides, he's hobbling around on crutches. There's no way he could have made it up your outside staircase."

"What happened to Bud?"

"I'm not sure. All I heard was that it had something to do with a revival of the limbo at the Golden Eagle and Bud came in third."

Two down, one to go, Hannah said to herself. She almost hated to ask and nullify her whole suspect list, but she had to know.

"How about Hal McDermott? You told me that he was pretty hot under the collar about Ross at the social hour after Sunday's church services. Do you think it's possible that he's involved?"

"Hal's got a temper on him, but I don't think he has anything to do with it. You'd better check with Rose. I think Hal's weekly poker game was yesterday afternoon and he wouldn't miss one of those. Rose told me that Hal lost last week to Al Percy and he vowed to win it all back this week."

Hannah was surprised. "I knew they played poker, but I thought it was just for chips or something like that. I never realized that real money was at stake."

"Well, it is, but it's only penny ante. Rose said Hal lost four dollars and seventy cents, but money's not the issue."

"Then what's the issue?" Hannah asked her.

"It's ego. Hal wants to hang on to his title as the best poker player in Lake Eden. Hal wouldn't miss that poker game, Hannah. And I'd bet real money on that, not just pennies!"

"I understand," Hannah said. "It's not the money at stake in Hal's poker games, it's the honor."

"Honor's not the only thing. The weekly winner gets a free dessert every day from Rose. And that reminds me . . ." Grandma Knudson stopped talking and reached down to pull a box out of the tapestry tote bag she always carried. "These are for you," she said, handing the box to Hannah. "It's a little like carrying coals to Newcastle, but I thought you'd like them."

Hannah lifted the lid on the box and

began to laugh. "Cookies!" she exclaimed.

"Yes. It was my mother's recipe and I just found it in one of her recipe boxes. They're called Forgotten Cookies."

"That's a great name," Hannah commented. "Is the name because you forgot that your mother made them?"

"Not exactly. Have one now and tell me if you like them. And if you do, I wrote out the recipe and it's in that little envelope on top."

Hannah took a cookie and bit into it. It was made of meringue and it melted in her mouth. "Wonderful!" she said, popping the rest of the cookie into her mouth.

"Read the recipe," Grandma Knudson suggested. "I don't know if it'll work in your industrial oven, but it can't hurt to try it. And if you can't make them here, you can make them at home."

Hannah read through the recipe and then she laughed. "I think I understand why they're called Forgotten Cookies now."

"That's right. The name's appropriate because if you use your oven for supper, you just mix up these cookies, put them on a sheet, and stick them in the oven. Then you turn off the oven, forget about them, and they'll be baked and ready to eat in the morning."

FORGOTTEN COOKIES

Preheat oven to 400 F., rack in the middle position.

(Make these cookies right before bedtime and they'll be ready to eat in the morning. They must be in the oven at least 4 hours and overnight is fine, too.)

Hannah's 1st Note: This recipe is from Aunt Nancy's friend, Judy Baer.

2 egg whites ***(save the yolks in a covered container in the refrigerator and add them to scrambled eggs in the morning)***
3/4 cup white ***(granulated)*** sugar
pinch of salt ***(a pinch is the amount of salt you can pick up from a salt cellar and hold between your thumb and your forefinger)***
6-ounce ***(by weight)*** package ***(about 1 cup)*** mini chocolate chips
1 cup finely chopped pecans

Prepare your cookie sheet by lining it with parchment paper.

Place the egg whites in the bowl of an electric mixer and beat them until they are foamy.

Continue to beat while adding the white sugar by Tablespoons, sprinkling in the sugar over the very foamy egg whites.

Add the pinch of salt and beat until the egg whites are very stiff. ***(You are making a meringue.)***

Once the egg whites are stiff enough to hold a peak when you shut off the mixer and test them, shut off the mixer and take out the bowl.

Hannah's 2nd Note: Test for stiff peaks by shutting off the mixer, dipping the rounded back of a spoon into the beaten egg whites and pulling it up. If the peak that forms is stiff, you are done beating.

Sprinkle in the chocolate chips and gently fold them in with a rubber spatula, being careful not to lose any air.

Hannah's 3rd Note: "Folding" is done by inserting the blade of the rubber spatula into the center of the bowl, turning it to the flat side and "shoveling" the stiff egg whites up to cover part

of the chips. Turn the bowl and repeat this action until you have pulled up all the egg whites from the bottom and have covered all of the chips.

Add the finely chopped pecans to the top of the bowl and fold them in by the same method you used with the chocolate chips.

Give the mixing bowl one more very gentle stir with the spatula.

Place your prepared cookie sheet next to your cookie bowl and transfer the dough by heaping teaspoons to the parchment paper.

Hannah's 4th Note: One standard-size cookie sheet will hold all the Forgotten Cookies if you place them about an inch apart.

If your oven has reached the proper temperature, quickly open the door, slip in the cookies, and close it again.

TURN OFF THE OVEN and DO NOT OPEN the oven door again until you get up in the morning.

Yield: 1 to 2 dozen melt-in-your-mouth cookies, depending on cookie size.

CHAPTER TWENTY-FOUR

Hannah was just cutting her newest creation, Butterscotch Chocolate Bar Cookies, and placing them on a platter when Lisa came through the swinging door from the coffee shop. "Lynne Larchmont's on the phone for you, Hannah."

"Thanks, Lisa. Take a pan of these out to the coffee shop and ask our customers to taste-test them for us."

"They smell great!" Lisa said, coming over to grab a pan of bar cookies from the bakers rack. "What are they called?"

"Butterscotch Chocolate Bar Cookies."

"I don't think you need to worry about anyone not liking them," Lisa said with a laugh. "Our customers adore bar cookies, the stickier and gooier, the better."

"Then they're going to love these. That butterscotch is sticky."

Hannah licked her fingers and went to the sink to wash her hands before she reached for the phone. "Hi, Lynne," she greeted her friend. "What's new?"

"A lot, but I'll wait to tell you when I see you. I called to ask you if you could have dinner with Tom and me tomorrow night."

"Tom's back?"

"Not yet, but he called me this morning to say that he'll be back tonight or early tomorrow morning."

Hannah thought about that for a moment. She really didn't want to socialize right now. "I'm not sure I'd be very good company right now, Lynne."

"I understand, but it might do you some good to get out. I'm going to stay out here for another week, Hannah."

"I know. You're going to be interviewed at the film festival, aren't you?"

"Yes, but KCOW is going to postpone the festival until the first week in June."

Hannah was surprised, but it did make sense. "Because of what happened to Ross?" she managed to say.

"I'm sure that's part of it. They didn't come right out and say that, but it's got to be a factor, especially since *Crisis in Cherrywood* won the award for the most popular Minnesota film, and Ross won't be here to be interviewed, or to accept his award."

"That *is* a problem," Hannah admitted.

"Do you think they'll ask Dean Lawrence to accept the award for Ross?" Hannah named the director of the film.

"That would be a logical choice, but Dean moved to England and he's working full-time there. I doubt that he'd fly back to the States for a small, regional film festival."

"How about Dom?" Hannah named the assistant director.

"I don't know. It all depends on whether or not they can find him and if he's free to come. Everyone on the cast and crew split up after we wrapped the film. I've stayed in touch with some of the actors, but everyone on the crew has scattered all over the place."

"Then it'll be a real problem?"

"Not necessarily. Since the award show will be covered on television, almost everyone in the cast will come. It's like a paid advertisement for how good they are at their jobs."

"I can understand that. How about you?" Hannah asked her. "You're coming to the film festival, aren't you, Lynne?"

"Yes. It's the first time I've been invited to an award show and I wouldn't miss it for the world. Not only that, I love Lake Eden. I'll jump at any excuse I get to come back here."

"Did you tell the PR person at KCOW

that you'll come back?"

"Yes, I did."

"Then maybe they'll ask *you* to accept the award for Ross."

Lynne was silent for a moment and when she answered, she sounded hopeful. "It's possible they'll ask me. People accept awards for other people all the time."

"I know." Hannah thought back to the last award show she'd watched and how Mayor Bascomb had accepted his sister's STAG statuette.

"If they didn't mention Ross when they called you, what reason did they give you for postponing the festival?"

"They blamed it on weather. They told me that since more severe winter storms were predicted and it could be difficult for people to travel to Lake Eden."

"That's possible. KCOW's counting on good ratings and they won't get them if most of the big names bow out. And Mayor Bascomb was counting on a lot of people coming into Lake Eden and spending money." Hannah stopped talking for a moment and began to frown. "I wonder if the mayor knows that they decided to postpone the festival."

"I'm not sure. They said they called me first because I won the leading actress award and they knew I'd arrived two weeks early. Do you want to call the mayor and let him know, Hannah? I called you right after I got the call from the PR guy at KCOW."

Hannah gave a short laugh. "There's no way I'm going to break the news to the mayor!"

"Then do you think I should call him?"

"Absolutely not! There's no way you should give the mayor bad news. Mayor Bascomb's the type of person who'd shoot the messenger!"

"Thanks for the warning, Hannah. I know exactly what you mean and I won't even consider calling him."

After she'd accepted the dinner invitation with Lynne and Tom, Hannah said her goodbyes and hung up. Then she went to the freezer to check the status of the peanut butter balls she'd formed. She'd decided to make candy for Valentine's Day. They'd never done that before, but there was always a first time.

Hannah slipped on a pair of food service gloves and picked up one of the candy balls to see if they were hard enough to dip in chocolate. They weren't so she returned them to the freezer and turned to look at the clock. Another hour should be enough, especially if she kept the temperature of the melted chocolate that she'd use for dipping as low as possible.

Hannah was just gathering the ingredients for more cookies when there was a knock on the back kitchen door. It was a distinctive knock and even though she didn't really have to look through the peephole to know who was there, Hannah looked before she opened the door. "Hi, Norman," she said, ushering him in. "I was wondering when you'd get here."

"I'm sorry it took so long. I thought I'd be back earlier, but Cliff had a problem downloading the photos from Clara's phone."

"You mean he couldn't do it?"

"No, he got them, but it took longer than he thought it would. I got everything, Hannah. And I printed out several photos I'd like you to see."

"I'll get coffee for us and then you can show me," Hannah said, setting a platter of bar cookies on the surface of the work station. "Will you try my newest bar cookie?"

"You betcha!" Norman reached out for one, took a big bite, and gave her a thumbs-up signal. Then he swallowed and smiled. "They're great, Hannah! Is that butterscotch with the chocolate?"

"Yes, Mother thought that combination

would be good."

"She was right," Norman said as he reached for another bar cookie.

Hannah carried two mugs of coffee to the work station and took a stool across from Norman. "Do you have Clara's phone with you?"

"I have it, but after Cliff gave me her new phone, I went home and put all her photos on my computer. And then I printed out the ones that I thought were important."

Hannah watched as Norman opened the folder he'd carried in with him. "I enhanced them a bit because they were taken at night in moonlight. The first is one of the pine tree Clara used as the constant in her shadow photos."

"I've always thought that pine was the most beautiful one," Hannah said. And then her slight smile faltered a bit as she remembered stopping beneath that very tree on one of the walks she'd taken with Ross and how he'd pulled her into his arms and kissed her.

"Here's the second photo Clara took." Norman handed it to Hannah. "I worked on the color, but since it's taken after dark and the moon was out, it's difficult to judge colors."

Hannah glanced down at the photo and

gasped. "There's a man standing under the pine!"

"Yes. I think that he saw Clara taking the photo and that's why he pushed her down and stole her phone."

"That makes sense if he knew that Clara had taken a picture of him and he didn't want anyone to know he was there."

"Yes, and since Clara said she hadn't even seen the man, she probably didn't realize that she'd caught his image in her photo. But she would have noticed him when she printed out her photos. And she would have wondered why he was crouching there."

"That's true," Hannah agreed. "What's around the man's neck, Norman?"

"I think it's a pair of binoculars. One of the lenses is catching the moonlight."

Hannah studied the photo again. "Yes, I think you're right. I wish we could see his face."

"So do I, but I've enhanced the image to the maximum. Any more and it'll break down. I did manage to catch the color of his cap, though. It could be blue, but moonlight adds blue to most colors. I used a meter to measure the strength of the blue hue in the shadow and when I subtracted that from the man's hat, it looked more green than blue."

"So it's a Buffalo Plaid hat with squares of black and green?"

"Yes, if that's what you call that big checkerboard design. Where did they get a name like Buffalo Plaid anyway? I've never seen a buffalo wearing plaid."

Hannah laughed. "And I doubt you will unless one of the park employees in Little Falls decides to put a Buffalo Plaid blanket on one of their bison."

"If they did, it would be Bison Plaid," Norman said. "They're not the same animal, you know."

"I *do* know, but in North America the names are used interchangeably. It's not entirely correct, but it's so common, it's acceptable. If we lived in South America or Africa, we'd have Cape Buffalo or Water Buffalo and they're entirely different. Our North American buffalo or bison roamed the plains and our bison is a bovid."

"Like cows?"

"Yes. I also know how they got the name Buffalo Plaid if you're interested."

"I am. Tell me."

"A company called Woolrich Woolen Mills made shirts in the eighteen-fifties with a large checkerboard design. Legend has it that their designer owned a herd of buffalo and that's why they called the design Buffalo Plaid."

Norman picked up the phone he'd put down on the work station. "I wonder if I should run out to your complex and give this phone to Clara now."

"Yes, I think you should. And I also think you should run out to the sheriff's station on your way and show Mike your enhanced photo. I'd go with you, but . . . I don't really want to go back to the condo complex, at least not yet."

"Of course you don't. I can stop at the sheriff's station, take Clara her new phone, and be back here in an hour. Then I can take you back to the penthouse."

"Good. I've got one more thing I want to do before I leave anyway. And that's about as long as it'll take me."

Butterscotch Chocolate Bar Cookies

Preheat oven to 325 degrees F., rack in the middle position.

The Crust and Topping:

2 cups ***(4 sticks, 16 ounces, 1 pound)*** salted butter softened to room temperature

1 cup white ***(granulated)*** sugar

1 and 1/2 cups powdered ***(confectioners)*** sugar

2 Tablespoons vanilla extract

4 cups all-purpose flour ***(pack it down in the cup when you measure it)***

The Butterscotch Chocolate Filling:

12.25-ounce jar butterscotch ice cream topping ***(I used Smucker's)***

12-ounce bag (approximately 2 cups) semi-sweet chocolate chips ***(I used Nestlé)***

1 Tablespoon sea or Kosher salt ***(the coarse-ground kind)***

Before you begin to make the crust and filling, spray a 9-inch by 13-inch cake pan with Pam or another nonstick baking spray.

Hannah's 1st Note: This crust and filling is a lot easier to make with an

electric mixer. You can do it by hand, but it will take some muscle.

Combine the butter, white sugar, and powdered sugar in a large bowl or in the bowl of an electric mixer. Beat at MEDIUM speed until the mixture is light and creamy.

Add the vanilla extract. Mix it in until it is thoroughly combined.

Add the flour in half-cup increments, beating at LOW speed after each addition. Beat until everything is combined.

Hannah's 2nd Note: When you've mixed in the flour, the resulting sweet dough will be soft. Don't worry. That's the way it's supposed to be.

Measure out a heaping cup of sweet dough and place it in a sealable plastic bag. Seal the bag and put it in the refrigerator.

With impeccably clean hands, press the rest of the sweet dough into the bottom of your prepared cake pan. This will form a bottom crust. Press it all the way out to the edges of the pan and a half-inch up the sides, as evenly as you can. Don't worry if your sweet dough is a bit uneven. It won't matter to any of your guests.

Bake your bottom crust at 325 degrees F., for approximately 20 minutes or until the edges are beginning to turn a pale golden brown color.

When the crust has turned pale golden brown, remove the pan from the oven, but DON'T SHUT OFF THE OVEN! Set the pan with your baked crust on a cold stovetop burner or a wire rack to cool. It should cool approximately 15 minutes.

After your crust has cooled approximately 15 minutes, take the lid off the jar of butterscotch ice cream topping and put it in the microwave.

Heat the butterscotch topping for 15 to 20 seconds on HIGH.

Let the jar cool in the microwave for 1 minute. Then use potholders to take the jar out of the microwave.

Pour the butterscotch ice cream topping over the baked bottom crust in the pan as evenly as you can.

Smooth it out to the edges of your crust with a heat-resistant spatula.

Open the bag of semi-sweet chocolate chips and sprinkle them over the butterscotch ice cream topping as evenly as you can.

Here comes the salt! Sprinkle the Tablespoon of sea salt or Kosher salt over the butterscotch layer in the pan.

Take the remaining sweet dough out of the refrigerator and unwrap it. It has been refrigerated for 35 minutes or more and it should be thoroughly chilled.

With your impeccably clean fingers, crumble the dough over the butterscotch and chocolate chip layer as evenly as you can. Leave a little space between the crumbles, so the butterscotch sauce can bubble up through the crumbles.

Hannah's 3rd Note: If the butterscotch topping bubbles up through the top of your bar cookies, it will look very pretty.

Return the pan to the oven and bake your bar cookies for 25 to 30 additional minutes, or until the crumbles on top are a light golden brown.

Hannah's 4th Note: Your pan of Butterscotch Chocolate Bar Cookies will smell so delicious, you'll be tempted to cut it into squares and eat one immediately. Resist that urge! The bubbly hot butterscotch topping will burn your mouth.

After 5 minutes of cooling time, use potholders to carry the pan to a wire rack to cool completely.

Hannah's 5th Note: When I bake these bar cookies at home in the winter, I place a wire rack out on the little table on my condo balcony and carry the pan out there. The Butterscotch Chocolate Bar Cookies cool quite fast when exposed to a Minnesota winter.

When your Butterscotch Chocolate Bar Cookies are completely cool, cut them into brownie-size pieces, place them on a pretty plate, and serve them to your guests.

Yield: A cake pan full of yummy brownie-sized treats that everyone will love. Serve with icy-cold glasses of milk, mugs of hot chocolate, or cups of strong, hot coffee.

Hannah's 6th Note: These are Doc Knight's favorite bar cookies.

CHAPTER TWENTY-FIVE

Hannah was melting semi-sweet chocolate chips in a saucepan on the stove when Aunt Nancy came in from the coffee shop. "What are you making, Hannah?" she asked.

"Chocolate-Covered Peanut Butter Candy. I thought we could offer it for sale on Valentine's Day."

"Good idea! If it's okay with you, Hannah, Lisa and I are going to leave soon. We already locked the front door and we're almost done with the cleanup in the coffee shop."

Hannah glanced up at the clock and was surprised to see that it was after five-thirty. "Go ahead. I'm just waiting for Norman to come back and then I'll leave, too."

After Aunt Nancy went back in the coffee shop, Hannah realized that the chocolate she'd been stirring was bubbling. She pulled it off the heat, set it on a pot holder on the stainless-steel work station, and waited for it to cool a bit. If she dipped the refrigerated peanut butter balls in the hot melted chocolate now, they could slide off the food picks before she could take them out of the chocolate and transfer them to the cookie sheet she'd covered with wax paper.

Hannah went to the coffeepot, poured herself one last cup, and sat down on a stool at the work station. She took one sip of coffee, realized that she didn't really want it and her stomach was upset again, and got up to empty her cup at the sink. She was just wondering if she should eat a soda cracker to try to settle her stomach when Lisa and Aunt Nancy came into the kitchen.

"Unless you have something else you want us to do, we're leaving now," Lisa told her. "Would you like to leave a note for Norman on the door and come with us? I can drop you off at your mother's condo."

"No, Norman will be here in fifteen minutes or so and . . ." Hannah stopped speaking and listened. "Is that someone at the front door?"

"I'll go see," Lisa said, heading back into the coffee shop. Hannah heard her say something to whoever was out there and a moment later, Lisa came back into the kitchen. "Tom Larchmont is out there. He says the heater went out on his rental car and he's freezing. He wants to know if we still have the coffee on."

Hannah glanced over at the kitchen coffeepot. "Let him in and bring him back here, Lisa. I've got half a pot left."

A moment later, Tom came through the swinging door with Lisa. "Hi, Hannah," he greeted her. "Did Lisa tell you that I'm freezing?"

"She did." Hannah gestured toward one of the stools at the work station. "Sit down, Tom. I'll get you a cup of hot coffee from the kitchen pot. I'm glad you came in before I left."

"Oh?" Tom looked curious. "Why's that?"

"Because I want you to take some candy out to the Lake Eden Inn for Lynne and now I can give it to you."

"I should get my coat and hat. I left them on the rack by the front door."

"That's okay. You can get them right before you leave. If you're parked in front, I'll let you out that way."

"That's where I'm parked. Thanks, Hannah." Tom cupped his hands around the hot mug of coffee that she'd set in front of him. "I'm chilled to the bone."

"Do you want us to help you with the candy?" Aunt Nancy asked Hannah.

Hannah shook her head. "You two go

ahead. I can do it once Tom warms up and is ready to leave. Go home and I'll see you both in the morning."

"How about the front door?" Lisa asked Hannah. "Do you want me to lock it?"

Hannah shook her head. "You can leave it open. I'll lock it when Tom leaves."

Once Lisa and Aunt Nancy had left, Hannah sat down across from Tom. "Lynne called to tell me that you were coming back late tonight or early tomorrow."

"Yes, and I decided I'd come back tonight. I've been away too much lately. And I feel really guilty because I promised Lynne that we'd come to Lake Eden early and it would be like a mini-vacation. And then I had to leave on the second day we were here."

"I know she missed you," Hannah said truthfully. "She said you two hadn't been able to spend much time together lately."

"It's true. And that's why I didn't take the time to switch to a rental car with a better heater. I wanted to get back here to Lynne."

Hannah smiled. This boded well for their marriage. "I hope everything works out, Tom."

"So do I. I know we should spend more time together. It's just that Lynne's been busy doing commercials for a cosmetic company and I've been swamped with work.

It seems like we're never home at the same time anymore. And that's why I called this morning and booked a twenty-day cruise. I know Lynne doesn't have any assignments until the middle of next month, and I've told all my clients that I won't be available by phone or e-mail during that time."

"That's wonderful, Tom," Hannah said. "Does Lynne enjoy being on the ocean?"

"She loves it. And I booked the owner's suite on her favorite cruise line."

"Which one is that?"

"Gala. Lynne really enjoys their specialty restaurants and the Jacuzzi on the top deck. She likes to sit in the Jacuzzi with me and watch the sun set over the water."

"That sounds lovely," Hannah commented, but her mind was racing. The beach towel that Norman had found in the clubhouse had been taken from a ship in the Gala fleet. "Does Lynne have a favorite ship?"

"Yes, the *Expedition.* We were on it for our honeymoon."

Find out more, Hannah's suspicious mind prodded her. But before she could open her mouth, her rational mind reminded her, *Lots of people go on cruises. This may not mean anything at all.*

But it could mean something, her suspicious mind argued. *Think of a way to find out more.*

Okay. Think of a way, but be very careful, her rational mind cautioned. *If Tom is the person who pushed Clara down and stole her phone, you don't want to ask anything that'll let him know that you suspect him.*

Hannah thought fast, remembering what she'd noticed in her condo clubhouse. *Ask Tom if he lost a pair of binoculars,* her suspicious mind prodded.

No, don't do that! her rational mind argued. *That question is way out of left field.*

What do you mean? Hannah's suspicious mind asked.

It's simple. If Tom is the person who pushed Clara down in the snow, stole her phone, took her door key, and gained access to the clubhouse, you'll tip him off that you know. Besides, why would he go in the condo clubhouse and use his binoculars? It just doesn't make sense.

Oh, yes it does! I thought you were the rational one here! Just let me explain it to you. Clara took a photo of Tom and Tom knew it. He didn't want to be seen right outside the condo complex so he pushed Clara down, stole her phone and her door key, got in the clubhouse, and probably stayed there for several nights.

That tells us what you think he might have done, but why would Tom stay in the clubhouse instead of going to Minneapolis? And why did he need those binoculars?

Hannah thought about the table where she'd found the binoculars. It faced her building and it would enable Tom to watch for anyone entering her condo.

Very good! both sides of her mind exclaimed at once. And then her suspicious mind carried it even further. *Tom was watching to see if Ross would come out to her condo.*

But how will you discover if that's true? the rational part of her mind asked.

The Buffalo Plaid hat! the suspicious part of Hannah's mind answered the question. *Tom left his coat and hat on the rack by the front door in the coffee shop. All I have to do is figure out some way to look at that coatrack.*

"Let me put on another pot of coffee," Hannah said, smiling at Tom. "You're still shaking from the cold and you're going to need more than one cup. I'm going up front to grab your coat from the rack. You have to get warm for the drive out to the Lake Eden Inn."

"Thanks, Hannah," Tom said, still cupping his hands around his coffee mug and lifting it to take a sip. "But am I keeping you here when you want to lock up and leave?"

"Not at all," Hannah said quickly, gesturing toward the chocolate cooling on the work station. "I still have to dip some peanut butter candy balls in this chocolate and put them in the cooler for the night. Don't worry, Tom. I was going to work for another half hour or so anyway. Just let me put on that pot of coffee and I'll get your coat."

Hannah refilled Tom's mug, put on another pot, and then she made her escape to the coffee shop. She hurried to the coatrack by the front door, lifted Tom's parka from the hook, and gave a little gasp as she spotted his hat. It was black-and-green Buffalo Plaid exactly like the one in the photo that Norman had enhanced! She had to tell Mike right away!

If you call him on the phone, Tom will hear you, her rational mind cautioned.

That was true and Hannah knew it. Instead of using the wall phone, she drew her cell phone from the pocket of her apron and took a photo of the cap. Then she typed in a short message that read, TOM LARCHMONT'S HAT. COME TO FRONT DOOR QUICK! HERE AT TCJ!

Leaving the hat on the hook, Hannah hurried back to the kitchen, clutching Tom's coat. "Here," she said, slipping the parka over Tom's shoulders. "This should help."

"Thanks, Hannah." Tom slipped his arms in the sleeves and pulled the parka closely around him. "It's helping. I'm feeling warmer already."

"Good. Just let me get the peanut butter balls and start dipping them in chocolate. Then, as soon as they cool, you can have one."

Hannah made a quick trip to the freezer to retrieve her frozen peanut butter balls and brought them back to the work station. Then she picked up one of the frozen balls by the end of the food pick and dipped it into the melted chocolate. After she'd coated it, she set it on the cookie sheet that was lined with wax paper. "I'm thinking about buying a pair of binoculars," she said in a way she hoped would sound casual. "Have you ever used binoculars, Tom?"

"Yes, when I go out to a job site, I sometimes use them to survey the work in progress before I actually talk to the contractor."

"You survey construction sites?" Hannah was puzzled. "But I thought you were an investment counselor for large, corporations."

"That's right and I sometimes recommend investing in real-estate projects like sports arenas, shopping malls, and apartment and condo complexes. I always check out past projects and those in progress to make sure the work being done matches the blueprints the builders provide."

"Oh. That sounds like interesting work. Do you have a background in construction?"

"Yes, my father owned a construction company."

"So you know what to look for then." Hannah knew she had to get the conversation back to binoculars. "I can see where binoculars would come in handy for you. What type of binoculars would you recommend for someone like me?"

"That all depends on how you want to use them. If you're talking about birdwatching, I'd recommend binoculars with high magnification, true color, and an excellent focal range. Tell me why you need binoculars."

Hannah thought fast. "I'm planning a river boat cruise and I want to get a cabin with a balcony. I'd like to be able to watch the shoreline for scenic places to visit, and I want to watch for indigenous wildlife along the shores."

"Then you should look into Bausch and

Lomb." Tom gave a little smile. "For a moment there, I thought you wanted to spy on your neighbors."

Hannah shook her head. "My neighbors aren't that interesting, but I might use binoculars on my landing. There's a pine grove behind us and I might be able to spot a porcupine or a deer."

"You could probably see things like that with the naked eye. You must have a good view from the second floor."

He knows where you live, the suspicious part of Hannah's mind pointed out.

Don't freak! You may have mentioned it to Lynne, and Lynne may have mentioned it to Tom, the rational part of Hannah's mind made that connection. *You don't keep where you live a secret. Everyone in Lake Eden knows, and Tom was here for the filming of the movie*.

"Are you warmer now?" Hannah asked as she refilled Tom's coffee cup again.

"Yes. I'm finally warming up," Tom told her. "The coffee and the parka really helped."

"I can always run back in the coffee shop and get your hat," Hannah offered. "Mother always says that most of your body heat escapes from the extremities and if your feet and your head are warm in the winter, you'll stay warm all over."

"It's okay, Hannah. I don't need my hat. It's warm here in the kitchen."

"I noticed your hat and it's really nice," Hannah opened the subject of Tom's hat. "I haven't seen Buffalo Plaid on a hat before."

Careful! the rational part of Hannah's mind warned. *He's beginning to look suspicious.*

Go ahead, Hannah, the suspicious part of her mind egged her on. *You have to find out if Tom pushed Clara down in the snow because he didn't want anyone to know that he was hiding out in the clubhouse and watching our staircase for Ross.*

But where's the motive? the rational part of her mind asked. *If Tom killed Ross, he had to have a reason.*

Hannah ignored the ongoing debate in her mind and asked another question. "Do you know anyone who lives in my condo complex, Tom?"

Tom looked puzzled by her question. "I don't think so. Why do you ask?"

"Because I was in the clubhouse yesterday and there was a towel from the Gala *Expedition* hanging in the men's shower room. I thought that it might be yours."

Now you've stepped in it! the suspicious

part of Hannah's mind chided her. *Just look at his face. He's on to you!*

You're right, the rational part of Hannah's mind agreed. *The fat's in the fire now. But if Tom watched for Ross and killed him, what's the motive?*

Hannah dipped another frozen peanut butter ball in the chocolate. She had to work quickly because it wasn't quite cool enough.

"I should never have stopped here," Tom said, reaching inside his pocket and pulling out a gun. "I should have known you'd figure it out. Sorry, Hannah. I liked you. And I liked Ross, too, until he double-crossed me with the movie."

Hannah froze with her hand on the handle of the pan with the chocolate. *Do something!* both sides of her mind shouted. *Keep him talking!*

It was good advice and Hannah took it. She had to keep Tom talking until Mike arrived! "I don't understand. Ross double-crossed me, but how did he double-cross you?"

The pistol pointed at Hannah's head didn't waver, but a slight smile crossed Tom's face. "It won't do you any good, you know. I have to kill you whether I tell you or not."

"I understand that. What I don't understand is how Ross double-crossed you."

"It was an investment. I invested other people's money in Ross's movie."

"Are you talking about *Crisis in Cherrywood*?"

"Yes, and I convinced several of my biggest investment clients to join me. We completely financed the movie."

"But *Crisis in Cherrywood* made money, didn't it?"

Tom gave a humorless laugh. "Yes, it did. And that's the problem."

Hannah could tell that Tom was watching her face and not paying much attention to her hands. Her right hand was on the handle of the chocolate pan and her left hand was holding the food pick that contained the peanut butter candy ball. Slowly, Hannah released her hold on the food pick and let the peanut butter ball slip down into the melted chocolate. This meant she had both hands free. She wasn't quite sure how much good this did, but she told herself to concentrate on asking questions. Somehow, she had to keep Tom talking until Mike got here.

"I knew that *Crisis in Cherrywood* made money. A few weeks before we got married . . ." Hannah stopped speaking and sighed. "I guess I should rephrase that. A few weeks before *I thought* we got married, Ross sold his independent films to WCCO-TV and he told me he made a lot of money. Didn't he pay you and your clients back for your investment?"

"That wasn't the problem, Hannah. You see . . . we'd invested in Ross's films before and all of them had *lost* money. My clients and I thought that *Crisis in Cherrywood* would lose money, too."

"You wanted it to lose money?"

"That's right. You can buy insurance against bad investments. Backers of Broadway plays do it all the time. The insurance pays off if the play fails to make money in a certain time frame. I found an insurance company that did this for indie films, and my clients and I bought the insurance."

Hannah knew exactly what Tom was talking about, but she decided to play dumb. If he had to explain it to her, it would buy her a few more minutes.

"That seems . . . wrong somehow. You and your clients paid to finance *Crisis in Cherrywood,* but you wanted it to fail?"

"That's right. It all has to do with the insurance, Hannah. We were all ready to collect on the insurance when Ross sold *Crisis in Cherrywood* as a television movie. If he'd waited a month, we would have collected on the insurance company."

"But . . . how was that double-crossing you?"

"Ross knew about the insurance and he agreed to hold off on the sale. But what they offered him was a lot more than we'd invested, and he decided to go for the bigger bucks."

"And he didn't pay back your original investment?"

"Oh, he paid that back. But we weren't looking for our money back. We were looking for the insurance payoff. And that was a lot more money."

"And Ross knew that?"

"He knew, but he didn't care. Fame was more important to Ross than fortune. He loved going to film festivals and being touted as the new *auteur* in the indie circuit. And remember . . . we also lost money because we couldn't write off the losing investment on this year's taxes. Instead, every one of my clients simply broke even and they were counting on taking advantage of the loss."

"I think I'm beginning to understand," Hannah said, sending up a silent prayer for Mike to hurry.

"And now, Hannah . . . hand me one of those candies you just made and I'll tell you if I like them right before I pull the trigger."

Hannah reached for a piece of candy with her left hand and carefully lifted the melted chocolate with her right hand. "Here you go," she said, holding out the candy so that Tom would have to reach out with his hand to pull the candy off the food pick.

Things happened very fast from that point on, although Hannah saw them in slow motion.

Tom reached out for the candy. Hannah lifted the pan with the hot, melted chocolate. Tom grasped the candy, preparing to pull it off the food pick. Hannah threw the chocolate. Tom screamed as the heated chocolate drenched his face. A shot rang out. There was another scream and Hannah knew that it came from her as Tom crumpled to the floor.

It took long moments for the realization to hit her. She was still alive. Tom was stretched out on the floor, but she was still alive.

Hannah sat down hard as her legs gave out beneath her. She was still alive. She could feel her toes and her legs, and her arms, and there was chocolate everywhere. Then strong arms wrapped around her and Hannah burrowed into them.

"Easy, Hannah. It's over now," Mike said.

"And if you ever do this again, I'm going to take away your license to heat chocolate."

Hannah couldn't help it. She started to laugh. And as she laughed, the room stopped whirling around her and she drew a deep breath of air.

"Thank you, Mike," she said. "But next time, please get here faster."

CHOCOLATE-COVERED PEANUT BUTTER CANDY

No need to preheat oven — this is a NO-BAKE recipe.

1/2 cup peanut butter ***(I used Jif)***
1/4 cup salted butter ***(1/2 stick, 2 ounces),*** softened
1/4 cup finely chopped salted peanuts ***(measure AFTER chopping)***
1/2 teaspoon vanilla extract
2 cups powdered ***(confectioners)*** sugar ***(do not sift)***
1 small box food picks or long toothpicks
2 cups ***(12-ounce by weight package)*** semi-sweet chocolate chips ***(I used Nestlé)***
1 rounded Tablespoon salted butter, softened

Hannah's 1st Note: If you can't find food picks in your grocery store, you can buy them at a party store or a restaurant supply store. Most food picks look like toothpicks, but they have a colored cellophane decoration on one end and you've probably seen them used on cheese platters or on platters of

little appetizers.

Prepare your pan by lining a cookie sheet with wax paper.

Use a wooden spoon or fork to mix the peanut butter with the 1/4 cup softened butter in a medium-sized bowl.

Sprinkle the 1/4 cup finely chopped salted peanuts on top and mix them in thoroughly.

Add the vanilla extract and mix that in.

Add the powdered sugar in half-cup increments, mixing well after each addition.

Cover the bowl with plastic wrap and place it in the refrigerator for at least one hour so that the mixture will firm up. ***(Longer than one hour is fine, too.)***

Using impeccably clean hands, roll pop-in-your-mouth-size balls from the peanut butter mixture.

Stick a food pick into each ball and place the completed balls on your prepared cookie sheet lined with wax paper.

Hannah's 2nd Note: The food picks will make it easier for you to dip the balls in melted chocolate chips once they've firmed up in the refrigerator again.

Place the cookie sheet with your Chocolate-Covered Peanut Butter Candy in the freezer for at least 1 hour. ***(Overnight is even better.)***

When your candy balls are frozen, prepare to melt your chocolate coating. ***Leave your candy balls in the freezer until your chocolate coating has melted and you are ready to dip them.***

Place your 2 cups of chocolate chips in a microwave-safe bowl. Add the rounded Tablespoon of butter on top. ***(I used a 1-quart Pyrex measuring cup to do this.)***

Heat the chocolate chips and butter on HIGH for 1 minute. Let them sit in the microwave for an additional minute and then stir to see if the chocolate chips are melted. If they're not, continue to heat in 30-second increments followed by 30 seconds of standing time until you can stir them smooth.

Take the cookie sheet with the candy balls out of the freezer and set it on the counter. Using the food picks as handles, dip the balls, one by one, in the melted chocolate and then return them to the cookie sheet. Work quickly so that the balls do not soften.

Place the cookie sheet with the Chocolate-Covered Peanut Butter Candy in the refrigerator for at least 2 hours before serving.

When you're ready to serve, remove the candy from the refrigerator, arrange the balls on a pretty plate or platter, and leave the food picks in place so that your guests can use them as a handle when they eat the candy.

Hannah's 3rd Note: If you plan to serve these at a party, you can either leave the food picks in place or pull them out and use cake decorator frosting with a star tip to cover the hole with a pretty frosting rosette. Then, if you like, you can place the candy, rosette up, in fluted paper candy cups.

Yield: Approximately 3 dozen Chocolate-

Covered Peanut Butter Candies. The quantity depends on the size of the candy balls.

Chapter Twenty-Six

One week later, Hannah rolled down the window in her cookie truck as she drove out of town. She breathed deeply of the fresh, cold air and turned on the road that led around Eden Lake. She had an appointment in twenty minutes, and she both welcomed and dreaded it.

Unanswered questions rolled through her mind like a bowling ball on its way toward the pocket. She had facts, plenty of them, but they didn't answer her questions.

They knew who'd killed Ross. It had been Tom Larchmont and he'd told Hannah exactly why he'd committed the crime. That much was known, but there were still irritating, niggling, frustrating questions to be answered.

Ross had been desperate for the money. Hannah would testify to that fact. But exactly why had Ross needed a hundred thousand dollars? It wasn't to pay Tom and his investors back. Ross had already done that. There had to be another reason, a reason that Hannah had not yet discovered.

Then there was the matter of the locker key. She had looked. Michelle and Norman had looked. Mike had looked, and Mike's team of detectives had looked, but no one had been able to find the storage locker that could be opened by the key that Hannah and Mike had found in Ross's safe deposit box. Where was it? What was in it? Did it have anything to do with the reason Ross had so desperately needed the money?

Had Ross told the truth when he said that his wife needed the money to file for a divorce? Hannah needed to know. And did Ross's wife have anything to do with her husband's murder?

Hannah turned at the sign with an arrow that pointed toward Lake Eden Hospital. She drove down the snowy road, turned into the parking lot, and got out of her cookie truck. Her legs were shaking slightly as she got out of the truck and walked toward the hospital. She was early, but that was better than being late.

"Hi, Hannah," Vonnie Blair, Doc Knight's secretary, greeted her as she came in the door. "Doc sent me down to bring you to his office."

"Thanks, Vonnie. Mother's not here, is she?"

"Not today. Did you want to see any of the other Rainbow Ladies?"

"No, that's all right. I couldn't remember if this was her day to volunteer."

Hannah breathed a sigh of relief as she followed Vonnie down the hallway. She'd deliberately chosen to see Doc on a day that her mother wasn't scheduled to work.

"Hannah." Doc stood up and came around his desk to give her a hug. "What can I do for you?"

"I need to ask you a couple of questions," Hannah said, glancing at Vonnie.

"Of course. You can go on your break now, Vonnie. I'll catch the phone while you're gone."

Once Vonnie had left and shut the office door behind her, Hannah gave Doc a thumbs-up. "Thanks, Doc. I was hoping you'd realize that I wanted a private conversation with you."

"No problem. Or maybe it is. What's wrong, honey?"

He'd called her honey. The unexpected endearment took Hannah by surprise and tears began to roll down her cheeks. She cleared her throat, took a deep breath, and blurted out the secret she'd been living with for weeks on end. “I’ve got to know the truth, Doc. I think that I may be pregnant.”

CHOCOLATE CREAM PIE MURDER INDEX OF RECIPES

BAKING CONVERSION CHART

These conversions are approximate, but they'll work just fine for Hannah Swensen's recipes.

VOLUME

U.S.	Metric
1/2 teaspoon	2 milliliters
1 teaspoon	5 milliliters
1 Tablespoon	15 milliliters
1/4 cup	50 milliliters
1/3 cup	75 milliliters
1/2 cup	125 milliliters
3/4 cup	175 milliliters
1 cup	1/4 liter

WEIGHT

U.S.	Metric
1 ounce	28 grams
1 pound	454 grams

OVEN TEMPERATURE

Degrees Fahrenheit	Degrees Centigrade	British (Regulo) Gas Mark
325 degrees F.	165 degrees C.	3
350 degrees F.	175 degrees C.	4
375 degrees F.	190 degrees C.	5

Note: Hannah's rectangular sheet cake pan, 9 inches by 13 inches, is approximately 23 centimeters by 32.5 centimeters.

ABOUT THE AUTHOR

Joanne Fluke is the *New York Times* bestselling author of the Hannah Swensen mysteries, which include *Double Fudge Brownie Murder, Blackberry Pie Murder, Cinnamon Roll Murder,* and the book that started it all, *Chocolate Chip Cookie Murder.* That first installment in the series premiered as *Murder, She Baked: A Chocolate Chip Cookie Mystery* on the Hallmark Movies & Mysteries Channel. Like Hannah Swensen, Joanne Fluke was born and raised in a small town in rural Minnesota, but now lives in Southern California. Please visit her online at www.JoanneFluke.com.

The employees of Thorndike Press hope you have enjoyed this Large Print book. All our Thorndike, Wheeler, and Kennebec Large Print titles are designed for easy reading, and all our books are made to last. Other Thorndike Press Large Print books are available at your library, through selected bookstores, or directly from us.

For information about titles, please call:
(800) 223-1244

or visit our website at:
gale.com/thorndike

To share your comments, please write:

Publisher
Thorndike Press
10 Water St., Suite 310
Waterville, ME 04901